TOMORROW STARTS TODAY

ESCAPE TO THE LAKES BOOK 5

JESSICA REDLAND

Boldwood

First published in Great Britain in 2026 by Boldwood Books Ltd.

Copyright © Jessica Redland, 2026

Cover Design by Lizzie Gardiner

Cover Images: Shutterstock and Adobe Stock

Chapter Image: Shutterstock

The moral right of Jessica Redland to be identified as the author of this work has been asserted in accordance with the Copyright, Designs and Patents Act 1988.

A CIP catalogue record for this book is available from the British Library.

Paperback ISBN 978-1-80162-514-2

Large Print ISBN 978-1-80162-515-9

Hardback ISBN 978-1-80162-513-5

Trade Paperback ISBN 978-1-80625-626-6

Ebook ISBN 978-1-80162-517-3

Kindle ISBN 978-1-80162-516-6

Audio CD ISBN 978-1-80162-508-1

MP3 CD ISBN 978-1-80162-509-8

Digital audio download ISBN 978-1-80162-510-4

This book is printed on certified sustainable paper. Boldwood Books is dedicated to putting sustainability at the heart of our business. For more information please visit https://www.boldwoodbooks.com/about-us/sustainability/

Boldwood Books Ltd, 23 Bowerdean Street, London, SW6 3TN

www.boldwoodbooks.com

*To Mrs Waters, my childhood piano teacher who took
me through grades one to four and inspired me to pass with
merits and distinctions. And to my wonderful mum who took
her playing to grade five, kept it going for decades, and was a million
times better than I ever could be xx*

AUTHOR'S NOTE

The Willowdale series is set around Derwent Water in the Lake District National Park – an area I know and love from many wonderful holidays. When I started writing the series, I had a burning question. Is it Derwent Water or Derwentwater? As it happens, there's no definitive agreement, with the versions being used interchangeably. I have chosen to consistently use the two-word spelling of Derwent Water because both Ordnance Survey and the National Trust use this. Neither version is incorrect.

There are also variations in spellings of fells and other places (e.g. Cat Bells and Friar's Crag), in which case I have gone with Ordnance Survey's spelling.

Please further note that, while I've used Keswick as an anchor for the fictional setting of Willowdale and do mention several real places in this series such as Carlisle and Ambleside, any businesses, farms and schools mentioned are fictional.

CAST OF RECURRING CHARACTERS

There are several recurring characters across the Escape to the Lakes series. While I can include backstory reminders as to who they are and their connections to other characters, I prefer to only do this when the information is relevant to the new story being told. I therefore thought readers might find this cast of recurring characters helpful. Please note that it only lists characters who have appeared in previous books.

Rosie Jacobs
Owner of Willowdale Hall Riding Stables & Equestrian Centre at Willowdale Hall. Partner of Oliver

Oliver Cranleigh
Owner of Willowdale Hall. GP at a practice in Keswick. Partner of Rosie

Alice Jacobs
Rosie's mam. Lives in Horseshoe Cottage at Willowdale Hall with dogs Toffee and Chester and partner Xander

Xander Cranleigh
Rosie's dad. Hubert's cousin. Divorced with two grown-up children, Angelica and Evan. Lives with partner Alice

Christian Wynterson
Oliver and Emma's dad. Retired science teacher. Lives in Pippinthwaite

Kathryn Cranleigh
Oliver's mum who died when he was twelve. Willowdale Hall has been in her family for generations

Hubert Cranleigh aka his Lordship
Former custodian of Willowdale Hall. Kathryn's husband and the man Oliver believed was his dad

Emma Wynterson
Christian's daughter. Oliver's half-sister. Partner of Killian. Owns and runs My Alpaca Adventure – an alpaca-walking business at Willowdale Hall

Killian Buchanan
Groundsman at Willowdale Hall. Partner of Emma. Adoptive dad to his brother's children, Lyla and Elsa. Lives near Willowdale with his sister Aoife

Autumn Laine
Rosie's best friend. Illustrator and aspiring author. Lives with fiancé Dane in Cotton-tail's Cottage in Willowdale

Dane Featherstone
Author. Member of Mountain Rescue. Father to grown-up son, Ellis. Lives with fiancée Autumn

Kelly and Aled Reeves
Dane's aunt and uncle who own The White Willow. Parents to Felix and Maya

Felix Reeves
Dane's cousin, Kelly and Aled's son. Chef at The White Willow

Trudy Eccles
Retired teacher. Chair of the village halls committee. Lives in Pippinthwaite. Former owner of Cotton-tail's Cottage where Autumn and Dane live (belonged to her mum, Beatrice Eccles)

THE CAKE & CRAFT
CLUB MAIN MEMBERS

I wouldn't normally include any characters appearing for the first time in this book as doing so can give spoilers for the story about to unfold. However, much of this story focuses around a group of five friends at the Cake & Craft Club and many of them have children and grandchildren so I've included a brief guide to them too. This is a summary of their ages and relationship status at the very start of the book in the August. Some ages and timescales will therefore change as the story unfolds and time passes.

Yvonne Kellerman
Age fifty-nine. Was married to Cliff but widowed nearly five years ago. No children

Veronica Hayward
Age sixty-two. Was married to Carson but widowed over seven years ago. Eldest daughter Rebecca lives in Germany with her husband and twin boys. Youngest daughter Felicity lives in St Andrews, Scotland, with husband and three children

Paulette Duxbury
Age seventy-five. Was married to Hector Maddens but widowed
over forty years ago. They had three children – Martha who has
no children, David who has a boy and girl and Julia who has two
girls. Married Stephen Duxbury but widowed two and a half
years ago. Through Stephen, she has a stepdaughter Nicola (who
has two boys) and a stepson Andrew who has one girl, Saffy

Milly Tidwell
Age fifty-three. Married to Harry for twenty-four years. They have
one daughter, Coral, who's approaching twenty-one and about to
start her final year at university

Laughlin Byrne
Age seventy-one. Was married to Noreen but widowed four
months ago. Met later in life so have no children. Has a four-year-
old dachshund called Lancelot

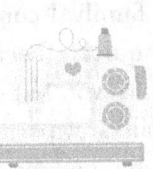

'Visitor!' Trevor announced. 'Visitor!'

I eased my foot off the sewing machine pedal and looked towards the lounge window, but I couldn't see anyone outside.

'Are you sure, Trevor?' I wasn't expecting any deliveries and I never had visitors.

'Visitor!' he repeated. 'Come in!'

I abandoned the patchwork quilt I was making on the dining table and headed to the window, spotting a branded car parked outside my next-door neighbour's house.

'It's Betsy's estate agent, Trevor. She must have another viewing.'

Betsy and I had been neighbours for twelve years but had only become friends after my husband, Cliff, died unexpectedly nearly five years ago. Betsy and her husband, Eric, were such a support and comfort and I'm not sure how I'd have got through it without them. Eighteen months later, Eric passed away too and I supported Betsy through her bereavement. Aged seventy-five, Betsy was sixteen years older than me and had been struggling with her balance for a while. After falling down the stairs at the start of the year, it didn't surprise me when she announced she'd be leaving Pippinthwaite – a village a few miles outside Keswick in the Lake District National Park – to live closer to her children and grandchildren in Derbyshire. Her house went on the market in the spring and she'd had an offer reasonably quickly but the sale had fallen through. While I wanted my friend to be happy, settled and safe with her family, I couldn't help hoping another offer wouldn't follow too quickly because, without Betsy, I had nobody to talk to. Except Trevor, but my conversations with my thirty-eight-year-old African Grey parrot were a little one-sided.

Betsy was staying with her daughter, Caroline, at the moment, while she viewed some retirement flats. She'd told me the estate agent would continue with viewings while she was away so I expected him to head towards the house but, instead, he retrieved something from the boot.

'Visitor!' Trevor repeated.

'I know, Trevor, but he's not coming here. He's... oh no!' My stomach sank as the estate agent stopped beside Betsy's 'for sale' board and attached a red 'sold' sign to it.

'Betsy's leaving,' I murmured, the words catching in my throat.

Trevor dipped his head several times and I liked to think he understood. He shuffled along his perch and I released the catch on his cage door so he could hop out onto the towel beside it. I picked up the plant mister filled with rainwater and sprayed the air above him. Trevor loved being misted – something I did several times daily to more closely emulate the humidity of an African rainforest climate – and the little wiggle of delight he gave as the mist landed on his feathers never failed to lift me.

A car door slamming returned my attention to the window. The estate agent was back in the driver's seat and, moments later, the car was gone. While Trevor admired himself in the mirror propped up beside his cage, awarding himself a wolf whistle, I did a swift calculation in my head. It was the last week of August now so Betsy would likely be gone before Christmas, which meant we wouldn't be together for our usual pre-Christmas activities – a festive afternoon tea where we laughed like naughty schoolchildren when our shared love of cake meant eating our desserts before the savoury selection, and making Christmas wreaths for our doors, sitting at my dining table while listening to Betsy's favourite Christmas songs from the likes of Andy Williams, Nat King Cole and Bing Crosby.

Tears slipped down my cheeks and I tutted as I wiped them with the back of my hand. 'You'd think I'd be used to being on my own by now,' I said to Trevor. 'And, before you say anything, I know I've got you, but it is nice to have a human conversation sometimes.'

'Pretty bird!' he squawked.

'Yes, you are. Very pretty bird. What would I do without you?'

Movement in the street drew my gaze towards the window once more.

'That's Christian back on his bike. It'll have been a lovely day for a ride.'

Christian Wynterson, a retired teacher, lived opposite me. He was in his late sixties but looked younger and, with all the cycling and hiking he'd embraced since his retirement, was probably fitter than a lot of men half his age. As he dismounted at the end of his drive, he looked towards Betsy's house.

'I think he's just spotted the sold sign, Trevor.'

I considered going outside to say 'hello' but I didn't want to get a reputation as the woman who lurked by her window ready to pounce on the neighbours the moment they arrived home. Christian removed his cycling helmet and wheeled his bike round the back of his house and I sighed. Today would be yet another day without any human interaction.

There were only seven houses in Mallard Close – a 1970s-built cul-de-sac of three- and four-bedroom detached properties on the edge of the village – so it should have been possible to know all my neighbours, but I didn't. Not anymore. Betsy and Christian were the only ones I knew by name now although, in fairness, they were the only residents in my age bracket. All the other houses were occupied by young families and I was increasingly feeling as though I didn't belong here. Betsy had felt the same, making the decision to move away a little easier. She'd lamented the *good old days* when everyone knew their neighbours and there'd been a stronger sense of community and, although I'd enjoyed hearing her talk about her childhood and early mother-hood, I'd never experienced anything like that myself. I'd been raised in a remote hamlet consisting of a farm and four former farmworkers' cottages and I'd only known the Kellermans in the house attached to ours. We'd had nothing to do with the owner of Hayscroft Farm, Eli Farrow, despite Dad working on the farm for many years before buying a piece of land from him and running it as a smallholding. The people in the other pair of cottages kept themselves to themselves so I'd concluded that some people deliberately chose to live in tiny communities because they didn't want to be around other people. Or didn't know how to be.

Leaving Trevor pecking at a slice of apple, I returned to my quilt. I never used to sew at the dining table. With having a three-bedroom house but no children, the smallest bedroom was a dedicated craft room. A couple of months after Cliff died, it struck me that I spent more time than ever in there and Trevor must be lonely downstairs, so I brought my sewing machine down to the dining table to give him some company. It was meant to be temporary while we both came to terms with the loss of a wonderful man, but the dining room had great light and the table was much bigger than my sewing desk upstairs so it had become my permanent creative space. It wasn't like I used the dining table for eating anymore – so much easier to eat off a folding table or a lap tray in front of the television.

Betsy rang a couple of hours later.

'I've accepted an offer on the house this morning,' she said after we'd exchanged pleasantries. 'The estate agent will probably be round in the next few days to put the sold sign up so I wanted you to hear it from me first.'

I didn't have the heart to tell her she was too late and the sign was already up. 'Congratulations! I'm really pleased for you.'

'Thank you. I might have found somewhere to live down here too. I've got a second viewing on Friday.'

I lightly stroked Trevor's plumage as Betsy told me about the retirement apartment. It sounded as though she loved it and Friday's viewing was more of a formality.

'The couple buying my house are moving out of a rental so there's no chain. She's expecting a baby in November so they're keen to be in before the baby arrives.'

'It's all going to go through quickly then?'

'That's the plan.'

There was a pause and I had an uneasy feeling in my stomach about what was coming.

'Caroline's worried about me having another fall so she's suggested I stay with her in the meantime. When we have a moving-in date, we'll all come back and do some sorting and packing, but that means...'

'We won't see much of each other,' I finished for her when she tailed off, forcing the words over the lump in my throat. 'I'll really miss you, Betsy, but Caroline's right. You're better staying with her. When you come back, perhaps we can find time for tea and cake between packing.'

'I'll make sure we do. And I'll miss you too, Yvonne. You've been a good friend to me and such a comfort after losing Eric. I'll never forget your kindness.'

'I'll never forget yours either. Take care of yourself and let me know when you're coming back. I'll keep watering your plants in the meantime.'

We discussed some practicalities around me forwarding her mail before saying our goodbyes. When the call disconnected, I sank back in the armchair and released a heavy sigh. Anything could happen to derail a house sale but a chain-free couple with a baby on the way didn't sound like the riskiest of purchasers. So Mallard Close would be welcoming another family and Christian and I would be the only ones of advancing years. I wasn't looking forward to becoming even more isolated, to life without Betsy next door, to being all alone.

2

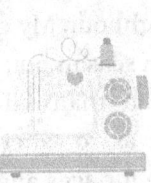

Late the following morning, Trevor announced, 'Visitor!' once more. 'Come in!'

'Just some kids delivering leaflets,' I said, spotting a couple of teenaged girls making their way round Mallard Close. Moments later, my letterbox rattled. I expected to find a takeaway menu lying on the mat in the hall but it was a newsletter from Willowdale and Pippinthwaite Village Halls outlining the events until the end of the year and the clubs starting next month.

My initial instinct was to dispose of it in the recycling bin but an article on the front page about a new wood-turning club caught my eye so I placed the newsletter on the radiator cover as a reminder to flag it up to Christian next time I saw him. As a joiner, Cliff had spent his lifetime working with wood and, even though he'd been ready to retire five years ago, he hadn't wanted to stop working with his hands. He'd been steadily acquiring the tools and equipment needed for wood turning and other wood-related crafts as well as building up a supply of suitable wood and logs, intending to learn some new skills as a hobby. But just a couple of months later, he was gone and I had a garage packed full of tools, equipment and wood which I was never going to use.

I managed to ignore it for a long time but in the spring a couple of years after Cliff died, I'd had enough. I didn't use my car very often as I had nowhere to go but, when I did, I was sick of it being covered in blossom from the large tree in the front garden of my other next-door neighbour. My car needed to be housed in the garage during blossom season but, when I opened the garage door, it was more packed than I'd remembered and I felt completely overwhelmed as to where to start. Christian had spotted me standing there for ages and, thinking the door might be stuck, had come over to see if I needed any help. I explained my problem and that I didn't know what to do with all the tools and equipment, most of which were brand new. Christian had been retired for a year and had found himself floundering, unsure what to do with all his spare time. He was a DIY enthusiast who loved working with his hands and this could be the perfect hobby for him. He'd ended up taking most of it and had kindly helped me dispose of the rest. He wanted to pay me but I wouldn't hear of it. All I cared about was that everything went to someone who'd make good use of it and Christian had certainly done that, finding a passion for creating chainsaw carvings. He'd asked me what my favourite animal was and I'd told him I adored red squirrels so he'd presented me with the most stunning pair of squirrel carvings as a thank you. The smaller one had pride of place on my doorstep and the larger squirrel was on the patio out the back.

I'd seen some of his other carvings including an impressive alpaca he'd made for his daughter, Emma, who ran an alpaca-walking business in the grounds of Willowdale Hall. Emma was lovely. She'd moved in with her dad about a year ago after a relationship break-up, and she always stopped to say hello and have a quick chat if our paths crossed. I hadn't seen her around much lately and wondered whether she might have moved in with the groundskeeper at Willowdale Hall who she'd been dating. I'd never met him but I'd spotted him picking her up and dropping her off and they looked really happy together so I wished them well.

Trevor called out, 'Visitor!' again and, moments later, the letterbox rattled and a few envelopes landed by my feet. I riffled through them but nothing shouted out as urgent so I left them on the radiator cover with the newsletter and returned to the dining table with a heavy sigh.

Most of the time, I could lose myself in my sewing, but there were days like today when I struggled to concentrate, feeling restless and fidgety. I hated those days and they'd been far too frequent lately. I managed thirty minutes at the table before pausing to make a mug of tea, sipping on it while watching birds on the feeder in the back garden.

When I took my mug into the kitchen, I cleaned the sink and taps, even though they really didn't need it. I looked around the kitchen for something else to do but it was immaculate. In the lounge, I plumped the scatter cushions and tweaked the position of the patchwork quilt draped over the back of the sofa.

'I'm so bored,' I told Trevor.

'Bored!' he repeated. 'Sing!'

I usually indulged his request, loving the way he whistled alongside me, but my unsettled brain couldn't even muster a song. Desperate for something to do, I retrieved the post from the radiator cover, slit open the envelopes and tutted – all unsolicited circulars. As I returned the letter opener to its home in a drawer in the lounge, my eyes rested on the slimline calendar hanging on the wall. The only entry for August was the date Betsy had gone to Caroline's. With only three more days of the month left after today, each of them blank, I turned the page over to September. There were no entries at all for the forthcoming month and I didn't need to turn further pages to know that October, November and December were just as blank. Why did I even bother buying a calendar anymore? I went nowhere and did nothing.

I scrunched my hands, a feeling of anxiety welling inside me. Was this it? At the age of fifty-nine, was I already living a sorry template for how the rest of my life was going to pan out? No people to see and nothing to do except cook, clean, sew, watch television and talk to a parrot. It couldn't be! My heart pounded and I swayed, feeling lightheaded. I grabbed for the nearby chair arm and closed my eyes, taking several deep, shaky breaths as I attempted to quash the rising panic.

'Pretty bird!' Trevor squawked, followed by a wolf whistle. 'Pretty Vonnie.'

My eyes snapped open. The only person who'd ever called me Vonnie had been Cliff and I'd never heard Trevor saying it.

'What did you say?' I asked, feeling steady enough on my feet to cross the room towards his cage.

'Pretty bird!'

'I heard that, but you said something after. Did you say *pretty Vonnie*?'

'Pretty bird!'

'Pretty Vonnie?' I could hear the desperation in my tone.

'Pretty bird!'

My shoulders slumped. I must have imagined it. 'Yes, you are. Pretty bird. Pretty Trevor.'

I misted him and watched him for a while as my heart rate returned to normal and the feelings of panic subsided. I was still holding the post and needed to take it to the recycling crate. As I passed the mantelpiece, I paused to look at the two matching silver frames on it – one containing a photo of Cliff and me on our wedding day and the other of us in Madeira during our last holiday in the spring before he died.

'They say it's meant to get easier,' I said, shaking my head as I lifted up the holiday photo. 'It feels like it's getting worse instead. Betsy's leaving and I'm already feeling lost. What if the only real person I speak to all week is the cashier at the supermarket? What am I going to do?'

I stared at Cliff's smiling face and repeated the question over and over in my head, hoping something would come to mind, but I had nothing.

'I'm so sorry, Cliff,' I muttered, returning the frame to the mantelpiece. 'I've let you down. You were all about living life to the full and I'm not doing that. Far from it. All my strength and optimism came from you and, without you, I'm floundering.' I sighed heavily. 'Lost, lonely, sad... pathetic, eh? And now I'm talking to a photo and expecting a response. Honestly!'

I took the post into the kitchen and ripped it into quarters but, as the pieces fluttered down into the recycling crate, my stomach sank. I'd planned to keep the newsletter for Christian in case he'd binned his without spotting the article about the wood-turning class. It might be the only conversation I had all week. I needed it! I rummaged in the crate, retrieved the pieces, and spread them out on the worktop before shaking my head. This was ridiculous behaviour. Who in their right mind toddled across the road and presented their neighbour with a taped-together newsletter which he'd already had through his own letterbox? It would look like I was nagging him to put the wood-turning equipment to use and we could end up having an awkward conversation where he tried to pay me again, which certainly wasn't the point.

I pushed the pieces back into a pile, intending to drop them

into the recycling crate, but my eyes were drawn to some words in
a box.

DO YOU LOVE CRAFTS?
DO YOU LOVE CAKE?
THEN YOU'LL LOVE CAKE & CRAFT CLUB!
WILLOWDALE VILLAGE HALL AT 2–4 P.M. EVERY WEDNESDAY
ALL CRAFTS AND ALL ABILITIES WELCOME
NEW TERM STARTS 3 SEPTEMBER

'Yes to both questions,' I whispered, excitement bubbling
inside me. I rushed through to the lounge, lifted my calendar
from the hook, my hands shaking as I added the first entry for
September:

2–4 p.m. – Cake & Craft Club at Willowdale Village Hall

I glanced over to the photos on the mantelpiece. 'Was that a
sign from you?'

'Pretty bird!' Trevor squawked. 'Pretty Vonnie!'

Hanging the calendar back on the hook, I smiled. September
was no longer blank. And if that first meeting went well, there'd
be several more entries I could make. Two hours a week wasn't
much of a social life but it was two hours more than I had at the
moment. It was a chance to get out of the house and talk to real
people. It was a ray of hope and, my goodness, did I need one of
those right now?

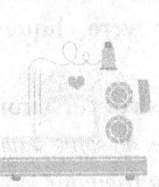

3

A week later, I parked on the approach road to Willowdale Village Hall ready for my very first Cake & Craft Club. I was a bit early so I decided to leave the engine ticking over, the radio on low, and give it a few minutes.

The Hardy Herdwick – one of two pubs in the village – was on the corner on the right. Ahead of me was the village hall after which the road curved round into Daffodil Mews – a small development of modern whitewashed dormer bungalows with slate roofs and tidy front gardens. Cliff and I had come very close to putting in an offer on one of them – the second one along from the village hall – but the single garage hadn't been big enough for his workshop. We'd both been bitterly disappointed as Willowdale had been our preferred location and the house by far our favourite. We'd have loved to be the first owners, picking out the perfect kitchen and bathroom from the outset, but we had to be practical and the house in Pippinthwaite ticked that box. Was Daffodil Mews a vibrant, friendly community or were they all strangers like in Mallard Close?

A few minutes waiting in the car turned into ten during

which time several women and a couple of men passed through the village hall's doors carrying a mixture of crafting bags, sewing boxes and sewing machines. With each passing minute, I became steadily more nervous and, by the time the dashboard clock turned to 14.00, my stomach was in knots. I wanted this – needed it – but I was terrified too. What if I was the only newcomer? What if they were cliquey? What if nobody spoke to me?

I imagined having this conversation with Cliff and what he'd say: *Then you eat some cake, do some sewing, and never go back again. But what if they're all really friendly? What if they welcome you with open arms? What if walking through those doors turns out to be the best thing you've ever done?* I missed his optimism so much. I missed him.

As the clock changed to 14.02, my stomach lurched.

'It's now or never,' I murmured, switching off the ignition and trying to ignore the voice inside me that suggested *never* might be the best strategy. I could do this. I was a grown adult joining a craft club – not a young girl moving school in the middle of term. If it was awful, it was only for two hours and I need never return.

But as I walked up the front steps with my sewing machine in one hand and a crafting bag slung over my shoulder, my resolve weakened and I couldn't seem to make myself reach out for the door handle.

'Are you okay there?'

I turned at the question and came face to face with a tall woman maybe in her early seventies with voluminous grey hair. She was wearing a long orange, cream and turquoise jacket over a red top and jeans, with a chunky bead necklace, several bangles and huge earrings. Her smile was as bright as her attire.

'I was, erm…' My throat had gone very dry.

'Walking into a room of strangers is daunting, isn't it? And I personally think it gets harder rather than easier with age. I'm Paulette.'

'Yvonne. And you're right. I've been trying to psyche myself up for about twenty minutes.' I wasn't sure why I'd shared that, but there was something immediately engaging about Paulette.

'We're a friendly bunch, I promise. Although I will get a ribbing for being late as usual and I deserve it considering I live the closest.'

'You live in Willowdale?'

'I live there!' She pointed to the second bungalow. 'Two doors down and I'm still late!'

'You're not going to believe this, but my husband and I nearly bought that exact house.'

'Really? What stopped you?'

'He was a joiner and needed the garage to be a workshop but a single one wasn't big enough.'

'I'm glad for me that you didn't buy it as I love it here, but I hope you found somewhere suitable.'

'We did in Pippinthwaite, but if ever you want to sell...' It just slipped out as a joke but the words rang true in my head. I'd trade my home on Mallard Close for Paulette's house on Daffodil Mews in a heartbeat, even if there was no community. I liked Pippinthwaite but there was something about Willowdale that had always drawn me. Cliff and I had often walked alongside Derwent Water but I hadn't done that since he died. I'd stopped doing so many of the things we used to do.

'I'll bear that in mind,' Paulette said, smiling widely. 'Come on in.'

There were about a dozen people inside the hall, setting up their crafts on folding tables which had been laid out in a U-shape. A few more emerged from another door at the back of the hall, drinks in their hands.

'You can sit next to me,' Paulette said, striding towards a couple of empty tables. 'Pop your stuff down here and let's get you a cuppa and introduce you to a few people, starting with Veronica.'

Paulette steered me towards the kitchen, telling me that Veronica had established Cake & Craft Club ten years ago. The aim had been to bring likeminded individuals together and, as the members had different areas of expertise, they'd all learned from each other. They also intermittently scheduled in sessions from non-member experts who taught the group new skills.

Paulette paused by the door. 'Veronica's extremely stylish, very proper and a bit posh,' she said, her voice low, 'and she's one of the kindest people I've ever met.'

There were three women in the kitchen and, given Paulette's brief description, I picked out Veronica immediately. She looked expensively attired in a cream satin blouse, dark tailored trousers over heeled boots, diamond stud earrings and a small gold and diamond cross on a delicate chain. Her salt and pepper hair – cut into her neck and shaped over her ears with volume layers on the top – was styled to perfection, as though she'd just stepped out of a salon, and her make-up was immaculate. I speculated she was a similar age as me and felt extremely self-conscious about my own contrasting dishevelled appearance – long greying hair way overdue a cut and colour, no make-up and wearing a homemade forest-green tunic top over black leggings and trainers.

As we walked towards Veronica, the little spark of confidence instilled by Paulette's warm welcome ran for the nearest exit. Why hadn't I made more of an effort with my appearance? But I knew the answer to that. Because I'd given up. On me, on life, on everything. That had to change.

'We have a newbie,' Paulette said to Veronica. 'This is Yvonne.'

'Yvonne! Welcome to our little club. So lovely to have you

here.' As Paulette had said, Veronica was well-spoken and, in her warm smile and the sparkle of her grey eyes, I could see the kindness she'd mentioned. As Veronica shook my hand with enthusiasm my confidence returned, apologising for its hasty retreat. These people were friendly and, if nothing else, we had crafting in common. This was going to be all right.

'Are you an experienced crafter, a dabbler or completely new to it?' Veronica asked.

'I sew a lot. My mum taught me when I was little. I make most of my own clothes.' I automatically tugged at my tunic.

'You made this?' Veronica asked. 'Oh, I love it! I tried to make a pair of trousers once. Absolute disaster. One leg was longer and thinner than the other and, to this day, I have no idea how I managed it. Is dressmaking your speciality?'

'My big passion's making patchwork quilts.'

'How wonderful! I've only ever dabbled with quilting and have always meant to do more. I look forward to getting some inspiration from your work. Great to have you here, Yvonne.'

A younger woman whose name went straight in and out of my head took my drink order – a strong tea with a splash of milk and no sugar – and, moments later, handed me a cup and saucer.

Paulette must have spotted my expression of surprise. 'Veronica likes to do things properly,' she said in a hushed voice as we left the kitchen. 'But, never fear, you can come back for as many top-ups as you want. Do you like cake?'

'Love it!'

'Then come with me before it's all gone.'

There was another table set up away from the crafts which held a chocolate cake, a carrot cake, a small stack of side plates, some forks and floral paper serviettes. Paulette explained that there was a rota for two members a week to bring in cakes and, while homemade was encouraged, everyone understood when a shop-bought one appeared due to lack of time or ability.

'I love baking,' I told Paulette. 'I used to make a cake every week for my husband and me but, since losing him, I haven't baked much.'

'I'm so sorry. How long ago was that?'

'Coming up five years in January.'

'You're in sympathetic company here. Since the group started, Veronica, Laughlin and I have all lost our partners, and Milly might as well be widowed for all she sees of her workaholic husband. Cake & Craft Club has been quite the lifeline for us all.'

A lifeline? Just what I needed!

She placed her hand on my forearm. 'We're here for you if ever you want to talk about your husband or here for you if you want to keep it all about the crafts.' She gave my arm a gentle squeeze and smiled as she released her hand. 'So, what's your poison? Carrot or chocolate?'

'Chocolate every time.'

'Me too. I'll be honest with you, Yvonne, carrots in a cake? What possesses someone to make a cake out of vegetables? If you're going to indulge, do it properly.' She cut two generous slices of chocolate cake and added them to plates, passing me one. 'But don't tell Veronica I said that. She's a carrot cake fiend. Makes cake out of beetroot too. I know! Don't even get me started on that one.'

Paulette passed me a fork and serviette and we returned to our tables but, before we could eat, she said she wanted to make a few more introductions. The next ten minutes passed in a whirl of names and faces and, when we finally sat down, I was fairly certain I wouldn't retain a single name except Paulette's and Veronica's. The introductions had thankfully wiped away the nerves and I was glad I'd come. I already adored Paulette and everyone she'd introduced me to had been warm and friendly. What she'd said about several of them losing their partners was interesting. I'd come here hoping to find some friends with whom I'd have crafting in common, but I'd never thought about finding people with bereavement in common. After Eric from next door died, that shared understanding of loss had deepened my friendship with Betsy. Perhaps I'd find the same here.

Looking round the room, seeing the smiles, hearing the chatter and laughter, I felt as though a little colour had returned to my world. Cliff would be proud of me. *I* was proud of me. Coming along today had been a huge thing, although I did realise it was a small step in a long journey to establishing a life for myself without Cliff. But didn't they say from little acorns mighty oaks grew? This was my acorn moment and hopefully it would grow into something bigger.

4

THREE AND A HALF MONTHS LATER

'Oh, my goodness, Yvonne!' Veronica placed the cake box lid on the table. 'This is a masterpiece.'

I wouldn't go as far as calling it a masterpiece but it was by far the most ambitious design I'd attempted and I was very pleased with the result. As soon as I'd seen my name on the cake rota for the final meeting of Cake & Craft Club before we paused for Christmas, I'd planned something extra special as my thank you to the people who'd given me such a warm welcome over the past few months.

'It's simply wonderful,' Veronica continued, moving round the table to see the cake from different angles. 'Everywhere I look, I notice something new.'

The centrepiece had taken me the longest – a sewing machine made from small pieces of sponge cake wrapped in cream-coloured fondant. Under the presser foot and draped across one side of the cake was a patchwork quilt and I'd crafted a pair of scissors, some cotton reels and a thimble for the other side. The sides of the cake were covered in pastel-coloured buttons of assorted sizes and the base was trimmed with a tape measure. As many of the club members knitted or crocheted, I'd added a couple of balls of yarn to the cake board, one with knitting needles sticking out of it and the other accompanied by some crochet hooks.

Paulette, Milly and Laughlin edged closer and my cheeks glowed with their generous compliments. *I didn't realise you could decorate cakes. Is there no end to your talents? That's incredible, Yvonne. You could go into business doing this.*

Although I was flattered that my new friends thought my work was good enough to sell, I had no intention of turning cake decorating into a business. Experimenting with fondant icing had merely been the new skill I'd chosen to learn this year – something I always did to both challenge myself and to help fill the empty days.

'It's so beautiful,' Paulette said, whipping out her phone and taking a couple of photos. 'It's almost a shame to cut into it.' She gave me a cheeky smile. 'Note the use of the word *almost*.'

A few weeks after joining Cake & Craft Club, I'd discovered that Paulette was a retired funeral director, which had been a huge surprise. She was loud, chatty and always wore vibrant colours and bold patterns accompanied by statement pieces of costume jewellery so really didn't fit with the image I had of a sombre funeral director dressed in black. At seventy-five – slightly older than I'd guessed – she was the eldest member of the group but arguably the most childish. With a hearty laugh and eyes that twinkled with mischief, she frequently declared, *the day I stop laughing at fart jokes is the day you need to ask my previous employer to order my coffin.*

If there was a spectrum for immaturity, our sixty-two-year-old founder Veronica would be at the opposite end to Paulette. Her husband had been a senior officer in the British Army, retiring as a brigadier after a long and distinguished career. Veronica had fully embraced the role of a military wife, organising a host of events, running various clubs and always doing things 'properly', hence the cups and saucers. To be fair to her, Veronica did have a good sense of humour but she drew the line at toilet jokes.

'The only reason I still come here is for the cake,' Laughlin quipped. 'So I don't care how stunning it is, I'm ready to dive in.'

We all laughed at his comment, knowing that the cake was the least important part of the meeting for him. For all of us. But it helped. I'd never forget Paulette describing Cake & Craft Club as a 'lifeline' during my first meeting in September and I'd absolutely felt that. I'd been so lost when I joined but the two-hour meeting every week gave me something to look forward to and helped break up the monotony. Although everyone was friendly, there were specific friendship groups within the club – inevitable in any large collection of people – and I'd found myself adopted by what appeared to be the core group of Veronica, Paulette, Laughlin and Milly.

Milly, a curvy brunette with flawless skin and dimples, was the youngest member at fifty-three and the only one of our immediate group who was still working. Formerly an English teacher in Manchester, she'd retrained as a proofreader and copy editor when she moved back to her roots in the Lake District.

As for seventy-one-year-old Laughlin, he'd told me he'd started accompanying his wife Noreen several years ago to assist her after the arthritis in her hands meant she struggled with anything fiddly. When Noreen passed away in April this year, he'd asked the others if they'd mind him still attending as he valued their company. They'd assured him he was as welcome as Noreen had always been and they couldn't imagine him not being there. That spurred him into finding his own craft instead of favouring crocheting like his late wife. Pyrography – decorating wood with burn marks – had become his thing and, my goodness, did he have a talent for it? Paulette had told me that the discovery of pyrography had also coincided with the discovery of his own personal style, ditching smart trousers for jeans and ties for a tweed waistcoat over an open-necked shirt. He also had a tweed cap to keep his balding head warm while he walked to his Willowdale home.

Laughlin was a quiet, thoughtful individual but, when he did speak, he always had something interesting to say and would soon have the group captivated, his rich and deep voice so easy to listen to. He could have read me an old telephone directory and I'd have been hanging onto every word. And I was completely in love with Lancelot – Laughlin's adorable four-year-old dapple Dachshund who came to class accompanied by his soft toy red panda, Spud. Lancelot was as good as gold, curling up on his favourite orange blanket in a sunny patch and dozing all session. When the sun moved, he dragged his blanket and red panda across the floor to find it again, which was so sweet to watch. My camera roll was full of photos and videos of Lancelot and Spud.

As Milly and Laughlin headed into the kitchen to help Veronica get the cups and saucers out, a few more members arrived and my cheeks deepened in colour with further compliments about the cake. Before long, we were seated around tables with our drinks and slices of Victoria sponge. Laughlin, who had an exceptionally sweet tooth, had asked me if it was okay to take one of the fondant bobbins and it warmed my heart to see him biting into it and closing his eyes as he savoured the sweetness. Cliff used to do the same thing.

Cake eaten, we dug out our crafting projects. I'd recently started a new patchwork quilt and it was a bit of an experiment for me. I'd made loads of quilts over the years and usually followed a symmetrical pattern but this time I was recreating a photo I'd taken years ago of one of my favourite places around

Derwent Water – a wooden jetty into the lake just south of the Willowdale Hall estate. It was still a patchwork design; just not a symmetrical one.

While I enjoyed making clothes, I could get lost in patchwork quilting for hours. There was something so soothing and rewarding about the patchwork part – taking hundreds of small pieces of fabric which weren't anything special on their own and joining them together to create something incredibly beautiful. I equally loved the quilting aspect – the process of stitching together the three layers of patchwork, wadding (or batting in the USA – the cosy layer in the middle) and the backing fabric. It required concentration and precision, keeping my mind focused on the task instead of drifting off into the past where there were too many difficult memories.

With Christmas Day being a week tomorrow, the conversation inevitably turned to Christmas plans. Veronica's eldest daughter, Rebecca, was flying over from Germany with her family, Germany being where Veronica's husband had previously been stationed.

'They're arriving on Tuesday and flying back the day after Boxing Day,' Veronica said. 'Not quite as long as I'd hoped for but any time with family is precious.'

'Will you see Felicity too?' I asked. Veronica's youngest daughter had met a Scot not long after she'd returned to the UK with her parents and had settled in St Andrews with him.

'Not this time, but I'll see her for my birthday in February.'

Both girls had children – twin twelve-year-old boys for Rebecca and two girls and a boy under ten for Felicity. Veronica had joked that being so far away from her daughters meant escaping five more rounds of dirty nappies and toilet training but I couldn't help thinking the humour was a cover and she was really sad about the limited time with them. When Carson died,

Rebecca and Felicity had both offered for Veronica to move in with them. She told me she'd stayed with each of her girls for a while but accepting either of their offers was out of the question. Choosing one over the other would cause friction between the girls and the move wasn't right for her anyway. She'd made Willowdale her home and had a large circle of friends and an active social life. She'd started over several times when moving to different bases with the army and, in her mid-fifties at the time of Carson's passing, the last thing she'd wanted to do was start over again somewhere new.

'What about you, Milly?' Veronica asked. 'Did you say Coral's working over Christmas?'

Milly nodded. 'Yes – another season in Finnish Lapland. She flew out as soon as term ended.'

Milly's daughter, Coral, had recently turned twenty-one and was in her final year at university studying performing arts. This would be her third season taking on the part of a singing and dancing elf in a show at a Christmas village near the Arctic Circle. Milly had shown me some videos from her stint there last year and Coral was exceptionally talented.

'You won't be alone, though?' I asked.

'If you're asking whether Harry will be home for Christmas...' She sighed and rolled her eyes. 'It's probably a good thing because he hates Christmas and always manages to put a damp-ener on it. I'm spending a few days with my parents in Winder-mere. It's been years since I spent Christmas with them so we're all really looking forward to it. I'll come home for a few days and return to theirs for New Year.'

'Do you know when Harry'll be back?' Paulette asked.

'No idea. I'm only his wife. I'm not privy to that kind of information.'

Milly hadn't said a lot about her husband but the little she'd shared made me wonder why she stayed married to him. But then I told myself that all marriages had their complexities and I had no right to judge what went on in someone else's, especially when my own hadn't exactly been conventional.

'The usual big family get-together for you, Paulette?' Milly asked. 'Did you say Northumberland?'

'That's right. We've booked a place between Alnwick and Bamburgh and I can't wait. I've already started packing.'

On my first day, Paulette had shared that she'd lost her husband but I'd since learned that she was twice widowed, her first husband passing away when their children were young. She had a large family – three children and four grandchildren from her first marriage and two stepchildren and three step-grandchildren from her second. The two families had blended easily and loved spending time together but they were spread out over the north and the Midlands which made meeting up a challenge so they rented an enormous holiday property every Christmas, allowing the whole family to be together. Paulette was the only grandparent left and had attention lavished on her, although she joked that her ears were still ringing weeks later and she needed a holiday to get over her holiday.

What must it be like spending Christmas with so many people? I was pretty sure there were two or three dogs in the mix too so the noise levels had to be through the roof. I couldn't decide whether being away with a large group sounded like heaven or hell, but it would have been nice to have the opportunity to find out. My grandparents had died before I was born, my parents were gone, and I didn't have any aunts, uncles or cousins. It was just my sister Marianne and me and, as we were both childless, it was strange thinking that our branch of the family tree had ended with us.

'First Christmas without Noreen,' Paulette said, turning to

Laughlin. 'Did you make a decision about going to your brother's?'

Laughlin's younger brother and sister-in-law had invited him to stay at their farm in the Yorkshire Dales but they, like Paulette, always had a big family get-together with children, grandchildren and even a couple of great-grandchildren. Over the past couple of months, Laughlin had gone back and forth as to whether to accept his brother's invitation, wondering whether he'd feel Noreen's absence more strongly in a crowd than he would on his own.

'I've decided to accept,' he said. 'I'm going a little earlier than the others so I can have some quality time with my brother and his wife before everyone else descends on them, and I'm leaving sooner.'

'That sounds like a great compromise,' Veronica said.

The others shared their plans, after which I felt all eyes on me. I'd hoped nobody would notice that I hadn't spoken yet.

'Yvonne?' Veronica prompted. 'Any plans for Christmas?'

'I'm, er... I'm spending the day with my sister.'

I kept my eyes down, concentrating on pinning the two pieces of fabric I was about to sew together, but that didn't stop me hearing the intakes of breath.

'You've got a sister?' Paulette didn't even attempt to hide the surprise in her voice.

My heart pounded as I put my work-in-progress down and raised my head, taking in the confused expressions.

'I haven't seen her in years.' I shrugged, not sure I was able to offer them any more than that.

A barrage of questions hit me – *Is she local? Older or younger? When did you last see her?* – and I wasn't ready to answer any of them. I glugged back the last of my tea. 'I've got a thirst on today. Anyone want a glass of water?'

As I paced across the hall to the kitchen, I bit my lip so hard that I actually drew blood. I shouldn't have said I was seeing Marianne. I should have lied and said I was having a quiet Christmas on my own as usual. They wouldn't have flinched at that. Now what must they think of me? They were all so close to their families and, if I'd told them before that I had a sister, they'd have wanted to know why I didn't see her and I couldn't explain that without telling them about my complicated childhood. And if I went there, I'd have to tell them about Cliff and me because it was all intrinsically linked. How would I begin to explain that to anyone else when I wasn't sure I'd ever truly understood it myself?

5

Nobody followed me into the kitchen, which was a relief, although I wasn't sure what that indicated. Had they collectively acknowledged that I needed some time to myself or had they not realised how much the mention of my sister had affected me? I drank half a glass of tap water and refilled it, breathing deeply. I couldn't hide in the kitchen all session. When I returned to the group, the conversation had turned to New Year and a couple of our more recent members were talking about a black-tie charity ball they attended every year.

'It'll be a quiet one for me after the big family Christmas,' Paulette said.

'Same here,' Veronica added.

Milly repeated that she was going back to her parents' house and Laughlin shared that he had no plans. I couldn't fail to pick up on the tinge of sadness in their voices or see it in their wistful expressions as they presumably recalled happier times when they'd welcomed in the New Year with the partners they loved.

I was expected at Marianne's after lunch on Christmas Day and imagined I'd stay until late afternoon or early evening, which meant I'd be on my own for most of the festive period. I'd grown used to it. Thinking of Christmas Day and New Year as being 'normal' days helped and, since Cliff died, I'd stopped putting in any effort to stay up past midnight on New Year's Eve, making it easier to imagine it wasn't a special evening.

Looking round at my friends, I couldn't bear the thought of them all being alone, especially Laughlin for his first New Year without Noreen. The firsts were always the hardest. A few weeks back when Laughlin had mentioned his uncertainty about Christmas Day, we'd shared our experiences of the dreaded firsts without our spouses – first birthday, first anniversary, first Christmas – and how there was no clear way to navigate any of it. The only advice we could give him was not to let anyone pressure him into doing something he didn't want to do because they thought it was time or that it would be good for him. The only person who knew what was best for Laughlin was Laughlin himself. Yes, firsts were the hardest, although I wasn't convinced the seconds were much easier. Or the thirds...

I glanced at Milly as she stabbed a barbed needle into the needle felted penguin she was making. Her mouth was downcast, no sign of those dimples of hers, and I wondered whether she was taking out her frustration on the penguin for her useless husband who never seemed to put her first. I wanted to ease her pain, but how? *Why don't you all come round to mine?* The sentence was clear in my head but I couldn't get the words out and I knew why. It was too much, too soon. I'd only known them since September – sixteen two-hour meetings including this one. We'd never met outside of Cake & Craft Club so why would any of them want to see in the New Year with me? Besides, the most people I'd ever entertained at my house had been two – Betsy and Eric – and I wasn't sure I'd know where to start with a group.

'What are you working on, Yvonne?' Laughlin asked a little later. 'It looks a bit different to your last quilt.'

I loved how observant Laughlin was and how eager he was to learn. Paulette had told me that, before he got into pyrography, he hadn't been the quickest at picking up new skills but he listened and watched carefully then persevered until he'd grasped it.

'I've designed it myself rather than working from a template.' I removed the photo of the jetty from a clear plastic wallet. 'Recognise this?'

'Is it the jetty near Willowdale Hall?'

'That's right.' I pulled out the rough pattern I'd drawn and talked him through what I was trying to recreate with the fabrics. 'I've no idea if it'll work, but I want to give it a try.'

The others looked up and expressed admiration for my creativity as well as confidence that it would turn out beautifully. Paulette was unusually quiet as she studied the photo and pattern and I was sure there were tears glistening in her eyes, but I didn't say anything in case she didn't want attention drawing to her. I'd have a quiet word later if I had the chance.

* * *

At the end of the session, the five of us remained behind to tidy up, having wished the others a happy Christmas. Paulette went into the kitchen to start on the washing up, Veronica and Laughlin cleared the tables and chairs away and Milly helped me pack away what was left of my cake.

'It didn't just look incredible,' Milly said as she held my bag open. 'It tasted divine too.'

'Thank you.'

'You never mentioned what you're doing at New Year.'

My stomach lurched. 'Nothing much. I'm not really a New Year person.'

'Me neither. I get a bit melancholy when I'm by myself. I was dreading spending it on my own again so it was a relief when my parents suggested I go back to theirs. I like to think I'm a positive person most of the time...'

Milly paused as though seeking my confirmation and I nodded vigorously, scarcely able to believe that somebody so bubbly and optimistic could doubt herself. 'You definitely are.'

She shrugged. 'I don't know what it is about the New Year but, if I'm on my own, it's like all the positivity is sucked out of me and I focus on all the things I didn't achieve in the past year, kicking myself about them, instead of reflecting on the good stuff. Do you ever feel like that?'

'Sometimes.' I gave her a gentle smile to show I understood, while wondering why I hadn't given the honest answer – *all of the time.*

While Milly stacked the chairs, I placed my bag near the door with the rest of my belongings then joined Paulette in the kitchen.

'Would you mind me asking you a personal question?' I said as I picked up a tea towel. 'You seemed to be affected by the photo I'm using for my quilt. Does that jetty mean something special to you?'

She smiled at me. 'Well spotted. It's where I met Hector – my first husband – when we were fourteen. I was sitting on the side of the jetty with a friend when these three lads ran past us, shouting. Next thing, the two bigger ones pushed the younger one into the lake and ran off laughing. He surfaced but it was obvious to me he was in trouble so I kicked off my shoes and jumped in to get him.'

'You saved his life?'

She nodded. 'It's lucky I was there. His brothers should never have pushed him in when they knew he couldn't swim.'

'It was his brothers? What were they thinking?'

'They'd decided that a survival instinct would kick in and Hector would learn to swim pretty fast when placed in danger. It beggars belief, doesn't it? Anyway, that show of stupidity got them grounded for the rest of the summer but it brought Hector and me together. We often visited that jetty – our special place. He asked me to marry him there, it's where I told him I was pregnant with Martha, David and Julia, and it's where I scattered his ashes.'

'Gosh, it really *is* special to you.'

Paulette nodded. 'So many memories, Yvonne, and if there's anyone who can do justice to that beautiful place in quilt form, it's you. I can't wait to see how it turns out.'

I didn't want to make any promises in case I couldn't pull off my vision but, if it did work, I'd be gifting the quilt to Paulette. I'd never made one as a gift before and the thought of it gave me a buzz of excitement. I'd try to hang onto that instead of thinking about the difficult festive period ahead.

We left the village hall shortly after, wishing each other all the best for the Christmas break. I loaded my belongings into the car and turned back to face the village hall. Being part of Cake & Craft Club over the past few months had given me such a lift and my life didn't seem nearly so grey, but I still had a long way to go before I fully emerged from the shell I'd been hiding in. One day I'd have the confidence to suggest doing something together outside of the club. And one day I'd be brave enough to talk about my past. One day...

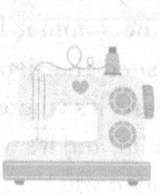

6

On Christmas Day, I woke up with a feeling of dread in my stomach. I hadn't seen Marianne for five years – not since I visited her a few days after Cliff died. Being my only surviving relative, it had felt right to give her the news in person rather than over the phone. She'd told me she was sorry for my loss and asked me what happened, but there'd been no emotion in her voice, no words of comfort, no hugs. I don't know why I'd ever thought there would be.

Marianne and I had never been close. I think the fifteen-year age gap was partly to blame – so big that we had nothing in common. It hadn't been what our parents had planned. Mum had told me that she and Dad had wanted a big family but, after three miscarriages, had given up on that ever happening. Then I arrived and, as Mum put it, their prayers were finally answered. I suspected I hadn't been the answer to any prayers my sister had uttered and was convinced she'd resented me for stealing our parents' attention after she'd been the centre of it for so long.

All my childhood memories of Marianne involved absolute uninterest in me – not wanting to play, read stories, or even talk to me. Mum would often encourage her to make an effort – *she's your sister, Marianne, and she deserves your attention* – but Marianne would simply stare at Mum, her expression unreadable, before storming up to her bedroom where she spent increasingly more time alone.

It didn't really bother me that Marianne and I weren't close because I had a wonderful mum. She played with me when I was really young and, when I was a bit older, we cooked and baked together and she taught me how to sew and knit. She loved nature so we spent a lot of time outside together, going for walks in the beautiful Cumbrian countryside where she taught me the names of trees, wildflowers, birds and insects. An invitation was always extended to Marianne to join us, but she rarely accepted. The few times she did join us, she complained that we were walking too far, that it was too muddy, that the songs of the birds were too loud and mocking. I'd never forget the last time she came out with us. It was the summer between finishing primary school and starting at senior school so I was eleven and Marianne was twenty-six. Large clouds floated across a cerulean sky and Mum and I were lying on our backs, our heads touching, our feet pointing in opposite directions.

'Look!' I cried. 'There's a hippopotamus in that one.'

'Oh, yes!' Mum said. 'I see it! Well done, Yvonne.'

A shadow covered my face as Marianne stood beside me, looking up. 'That's ridiculous. It looks nothing like a hippo.'

'With a little imagination, it does,' Mum insisted.

'It doesn't. It looks like a cloud because it *is* a cloud.'

'It's a hippo.' I pointed to another cloud. 'And that one's a rabbit.'

'A cloud,' Marianne snapped. 'Just another cloud.'

Mum sat upright. 'Oh, come on, Marianne! It's just a little fantasy.'

My sister planted her hands on her hips. 'A fantasy? And it's all right to live in a world of fantasies, is it? Because that's really healthy. You should be teaching her about reality. Cold, harsh reality because, let's face it, life sucks.'

I turned my head, bewildered by her outburst. Mum's eyes were following Marianne as she ran across the field in the direction of home. I wanted to ask Mum what Marianne had meant but a couple of tears slipped down her cheeks and she wiped them away before turning to me, her voice overly bright as she asked if there was anything else I could see in the clouds. Something told me not to ask Mum about Marianne and not to let on that I'd seen her tears.

After that, Marianne barely left the cottage at all and the distance between us widened. Throughout primary school, Mum had asked me to knock on my sister's bedroom door every Friday after school to show her any artwork or crafts I'd completed and to tell her how my week had been. Sometimes Marianne granted me a few minutes but most of the time she told me to clear off. I hated it. Mum wanted me to continue the routine once I started senior school but I was finding the rejection harder and harder to brush off. After a couple of terms of far more misses than hits, I told Mum I wasn't going to knock on Marianne's door anymore.

'She doesn't like me,' I said.

'That's not true! She loves you. She just struggles with her emotions. It would mean the world to me if you'd keep trying.'

'I can't. I hate Fridays, Mum. I feel sick all day.'

Mum drew me into a tight hug. 'I'm so sorry, my love. I didn't realise you felt that way. It's okay. You don't have to do it anymore and I promise I won't keep on asking you.'

She was true to her word and I was so relieved my unwelcome visits were over. I wished my sister did have time for me but barely catching sight of her was infinitely preferable to the painfully uncomfortable Friday afternoon ritual of forced bonding.

Marianne wasn't the only one who'd shown little interest in me. My dad barely acknowledged my existence, although I wasn't alone there. He worked incredibly long hours, leaving the cottage at 5 a.m. and taking his lunch with him. He'd return for tea but often head out again, only communicating through a series of grunts. Mum idolised him and I honestly couldn't see why. I told myself that he must act differently towards her when I wasn't around as I couldn't bear the thought of her being ignored by him and Marianne while I was out at school all day.

The remoteness of our hamlet in the northern tip of the Lake District National Park meant it was difficult to form and maintain friendships. Mum didn't drive and it was too far to walk to the closest village. The only bus that passed was the school one so I couldn't play with any of my classmates outside of school, get to parties or attend after-school clubs. I could have been lonely but Mum was always there for me – my friend, my champion, the only person who made me feel loved. I could cope with Dad's and Marianne's uninterest in me as long as I had my lovely mum. Except I didn't have her for nearly long enough. She suddenly passed away when I was twelve and it was as though the brightness was sucked from my world, leaving me in darkness and misery. If it hadn't been for Cliff, that's the way it might have stayed.

* * *

It was shortly after 2 p.m. when I pulled off the B-road and onto Hayscroft Lane, carefully navigating my car around the potholes on the farm track. The first three cottages had Christmas trees displayed in the lounge windows and fairy lights draped round trees or across hedges outside but number four – my childhood home – was in darkness. It saddened but didn't surprise me. Mum had loved Christmas but, after she died, it was barely acknowledged.

I pulled onto the drive, switched off the engine and sat in the car, my heart heavy as I took in the overgrown tangle of weeds where there'd once been a pristine front lawn with pretty floral borders. It hadn't been in the greatest condition last time I'd been here, gardening not being one of my sister's interests, but she'd clearly stopped doing anything to care for it which annoyed me. The cottage was, after all, half mine. I wouldn't have dreamed of making her sell up and leave so I could have my share, but I didn't think it was unreasonable to expect her to make a little effort to keep the garden under control.

Exiting the car, I looked up at the whitewashed cottage and tutted. The garden evidently wasn't the only thing my sister had neglected. The cottage desperately needed painting, there were weeds growing in the guttering which could be causing damp problems inside and, even from a distance, I could see that there were rotten patches in the wooden window frames. She should never have let it get into this state, especially when I'd emphasised on several occasions that I was happy to contribute to – or even fully cover – any maintenance needed.

Marianne had instructed me that I wasn't to bring any gifts but there was no way I could turn up empty-handed on Christmas Day so I retrieved a gift bag containing a large box of locally made chocolates from the passenger footwell. Making my way along the drive, I forced my frustrations aside. Interrogating Marianne about the state of the cottage the moment she opened the door was not the ideal way to start the visit. Instead, I needed to focus on the positive of my sister wanting to spend some time with me. She'd never invited me to visit before and it was especially touching that she wanted to see me on Christmas Day. Marianne wasn't the greatest conversationalist and was usually curt so I wasn't expecting the easiest of afternoons in her company, but a few hours of small talk beat being all alone. I wondered whether she ever felt lonely. It had, after all, been twenty years since Dad died. I'd struggled through five years without Cliff. What must it feel like to have four times that long without anyone to talk to?

The front door opened when I was a couple of feet away and there she was, clinging onto the doorframe with one hand and the door with the other, as though she'd collapse without their support. And indeed she might. Marianne had always been slim but she'd lost weight since I last saw her and my stomach lurched. Was she all right? A dark grey knitted jumper hung limply from her tiny frame, her collarbone was protruding and her cheeks were hollow beneath haunted eyes. She appeared to have aged considerably. If I hadn't known she was seventy-five, I'd probably have put her in her late eighties and guilt nudged at me. Should I have made more of an effort to visit her? Should I have phoned more often?

'Happy Christmas!' I declared, the words coming out overly bright.

Marianne held my gaze for a moment but didn't return the greeting.

'I've brought you some chocolates.' I thrust the gift bag towards her.

'We said no presents.'

'They're a *thank you for having me* gift.'

She still didn't take the bag and I wished I'd listened to her and not bothered. A gust of wind made me shiver. It was a bitterly cold day and I hadn't put a coat on, not expecting to be outside for long.

'Can I come in?' I asked when she didn't show any sign of moving. 'If it's still okay to visit, that is.' Part of me wanted her to say it wasn't.

'Erm, yes. Come in. It's a bit messy. I, erm...'

I followed her into the entrance hall and the first thing that hit me was the smell – that rotten food aroma you get when you're stuck behind a bin lorry on a hot day, so strong you can actually taste it. The next thing that hit me was the mess. Everywhere. Plastic carrier bags, bags for life and bin bags containing goodness knows what were piled on top of each other along the hall and up the stairs, leaving only a small passageway beside the handrail. *It's a bit messy.* That was the understatement of the century. I stared around me in shock. How had she let it get like this?

'You still there?' Marianne called from the lounge.

I took a deep breath, immediately regretting it as the stench made me gag. Marianne didn't want the chocolates and there was nowhere to put them so I hung the bag on the door handle and stepped into the lounge, my stomach lurching. It was even worse than the hall! There were piles of books and newspapers so high that they'd have toppled over if it wasn't for the towers of bags supporting them.

'I warned you it was a bit messy.' Marianne's tone was defensive but, as I turned to her, there was nothing hostile about her body language. She was tugging at the end of her sleeves, her shoulders drooping, her eyes lowered, and my heart broke for her. How could she live this way?

'How long has it been like this?' I asked gently.

She shrugged.

'You do realise this is more than *a bit messy*?'

'I bet your house is immaculate.' That defensive tone was still there.

'This isn't about me or my house. How long, Marianne?'

She shrugged again.

I looked around the lounge, my stomach churning. There was nowhere for me to sit. The sofa and one of the armchairs were covered in books, bags and clothes leaving only one armchair free which was presumably where my sister sat.

'Are any of the rooms clear?' I asked.

'Yours is. It's like it was before.'

'Okay. Let's go upstairs.'

I expected her to protest but she followed me as I carefully navigated my way up the stairs and along the landing. The bathroom door was closed but the doors to Marianne's bedroom and what had been our parents' room were open and they were both just as packed with stuff as the lounge. The door to my old bedroom at the front of the cottage was closed and I paused with my hand on the knob. My mouth felt dry, my body shaky from a combination of fear as to what I might find inside and memories of the last time I'd been in that room. The last time I spoke to my dad. The last time I ever saw him.

7

THIRTY-EIGHT AND A HALF YEARS AGO

'I've already said no to him so why the hell would you think I'd say yes to you?'

Dad's voice was low and controlled but the rest of his demeanour conveyed his anger. His face was red and a vein pulsed on his forehead as he narrowed his dark eyes at me.

'Because I don't understand why you'd say no.' It was hard to keep my voice steady when I was fuming with him. He'd pretty much ignored me my whole life and now he wanted to control me?

'He's too old for you,' Dad snapped.

'We're both in our twenties.'

'You're barely out your teens—'

'Twenty-one.'

'And he's nearly thirty.'

'Twenty-nine.' I released an exasperated sigh. 'So we don't need your blessing.'

'Then why ask for it?'

'Because Cliff's a decent man and it's the right thing to do.'

'You're not...' He glanced down at my stomach and I instinctively pulled my cardigan around me.

'No!'

'Then why are you throwing your life away?'

'I'm not!'

'You are! I know what he is.'

My stomach lurched. Did he really know? No! How could he? I was the only one Cliff had ever told.

'Bloody freak!' Dad said, his lip curled up.

Mustering some strength from goodness knows where, I pushed back my shoulders and stared at Dad defiantly. *Freak?* What a disgusting word to use. How dare he?

'You know *nothing* about him. You've lived next door to him all his life and you've barely exchanged two words. I *am* marrying Cliff, whether we have your blessing or not.'

'Then you can pack your bags and get out of my house.'

'Now?'

'Yes!'

My own dad was kicking me out? What had I ever done to him to make him hate me so much? Tears burned behind my eyes but I refused to let him see how hurt I was so I turned my pain into strength.

'With pleasure.'

That seemed to inflame him further. 'You've got ten minutes,' he yelled.

I slammed the lounge door behind me and ran up the stairs, pausing at the top as Marianne's bedroom door opened.

'You're marrying Cliff?' she asked.

'Yes, and if you think I'm making a mistake, you can save your words.'

'Escaping from this godforsaken place could never be a mistake. My advice is to get away and stay away.'

She held my gaze, tears clouding her eyes, before she closed her door. I wanted to ask why she hadn't taken her own advice but there was no time. Dad's mood was foul and I could guarantee he wouldn't let me have a second longer than ten minutes. I dashed into my bedroom and pulled out a battered old brown suitcase from under the bed. Mum had given me it for extra storage and I'd kept my childhood belongings in there – books, games, dolls and soft toys.

'Sorry,' I muttered as I tipped the contents onto my bedspread. 'No room to take you all.'

I grabbed my jewellery box and a dressing table set – hairbrush, comb and mirror – which had belonged to Mum and wrapped them in one of my jumpers to protect them. I added my favourite childhood teddy – a gift from Mum – and the book I was currently reading as well as a couple of other favourites in which Mum had written me messages, before moving on to my wardrobe. I didn't have many clothes and I could have packed them all if I'd been given my full ten minutes but I heard Dad thundering up the stairs.

'Time's up!' he bellowed.

'I've only had five minutes.'

'My house. My rules.' He appeared in the doorway. 'Last chance to change your mind.'

I didn't want it to end this way but there was no way I could stay here.

'I'm marrying Cliff.'

'Then you're on your own.'

'Can I just have...'

The flash of Dad's eyes told me it wasn't worth finishing the sentence. If I asked for that extra five minutes, I was likely to leave with nothing at all. Clothes were easily replaced, especially when I made most of my own, but my cherished items from my mum couldn't be and it was essential I left with them. I snapped the suitcase clasps shut, grabbed the handle and left my bedroom without a backwards glance. Dad was so close behind me as I descended the stairs that I could feel his breath on my neck.

Mum's sewing machine was set up on the dining table, but Dad grabbed my arm as I reached for the lounge doorknob.

'Where do you think you're going?'

'To get my sewing machine.'

'Oh, no, you don't.' He shifted round me to block the doorway. 'Time's up.'

'Please! Mum gave it to me.'

'Then you have a choice to make. It's him and no sewing machine or us and the machine.'

What sort of choice was that? I didn't need to imagine what the future looked like if I stayed because I'd already seen my sister living it. I couldn't turn into Marianne, trapped between these four walls, friendless and alone, fearful of the outside world. I needed to get out and live and Cliff had offered me the chance to do that. I wasn't naïve enough to think a better offer would come along.

Pushing down the lump in my throat at the thought of abandoning Mum's sewing machine, I met Dad's glare and held my head high. 'I choose Cliff.'

'Then you're dafter than you look. Don't come crying to me when it all goes wrong.'

'I won't need to because it won't go wrong.'

'It will. Mark my words.'

Tightening my grip on the suitcase, I walked out of the only home I'd ever known. Not that it had felt like a home for many years. Since Mum died, it had felt more like a prison and I couldn't be more grateful to Cliff for giving me the key to escape. I wasn't daft like Dad said. I was very clear about what I was getting into and it was a hundred times better than the alternative of staying and festering, feeling the life steadily sucked out of me.

I strode along the lane, my head held high, my eyes focused on Cliff's car parked at the end. There was no need to look back. Dad and Marianne were my past and Cliff was my future and I'd made the right decision, choosing him over them. But I couldn't help myself. I turned for one more look at the cottage that Mum had loved so much and pictured her trimming the hedge, dead-heading her beloved roses, chasing me around the garden, and it all felt too much. Tears rained down my cheeks as I sank onto my knees.

Next moment, Cliff was crouched beside me, his arms around me.

'He threw me out,' I cried.

'I'm so sorry, but it'll be all right. I'm here for you. I always will be.'

And I knew he would. Cliff was kind, supportive and reliable, just like my mum had been. When the tears subsided, Cliff helped me to my feet and put my suitcase in the boot.

'It's not very heavy,' he said.

'He didn't give me time to fill it.' I shuddered as I relived that horrible moment. 'He wouldn't even let me take Mum's sewing machine.'

My voice cracked and Cliff held me once more. I loved that he didn't say *I'll buy you a new one*, knowing how much Mum's machine meant to me.

'Mum's things...' I said. 'All those memories... I had to leave them behind.'

'The things, perhaps,' Cliff said, 'but not the memories. You'll always carry them with you. All you need to do is close your eyes and you'll see your mum.'

And with that one statement, I knew without a shadow of a

doubt that I'd made the right decision. Cliff knew me and understood me. Dad and Marianne didn't and, frankly, it was vice versa. Cliff was my family now and I knew he'd do everything in his power to make me happy.

'Ready to go home?' he asked.

'Ready.' New home, new life, new me.

8

PRESENT DAY

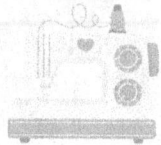

I pushed open my bedroom door and it was like I'd stepped back in time. The childhood belongings I'd hastily tipped out of my suitcase were exactly where I'd left them. The bedspread was still rumpled from where I'd dragged my part-filled case off it. My dressing table drawers were ajar and my wardrobe doors were open with several items of clothing in a dusty heap at the bottom where I must have knocked them off their hangers in my haste. I pressed my hand over my mouth, shocked to see nothing had changed.

'I told you your room was like it was before,' Marianne said.

I picked up an item of clothing – a navy pencil skirt with a split up the back which I remembered making after I was offered my first ever job in the typing pool at the council – and shook it out, spluttering as I covered myself in dust. I tossed the skirt back into the bottom of the wardrobe and turned to Marianne.

'I thought you meant you hadn't stored anything in here, not that you'd never been inside since I left.'

'Dad told me not to.'

I opened my mouth to tell her that he'd been dead for over

two decades and she could do what she liked now, but that haunted look in her eyes kept me quiet. It wasn't my place to interfere in her life, not that she'd listen to me if I tried.

My gaze passed round the room. The awful memory of that final day swirled round my mind alongside several happy memories of being here with Mum, making me feel quite emotional.

'You can use my room if you want somewhere tidy to sleep,' I said.

Marianne glanced at the dolls and games on the bed. 'I'm not sure. It's a bit messy in here.'

I bit my lip to stop myself from laughing out loud at the irony of that. 'I can soon clear this lot away.'

She shook her head and left. I wasn't sure if she expected me to follow her, but I couldn't draw myself away. I sank down onto the bedspread, taking it all in. Back then, I'd been infatuated with Tom Cruise and the film posters from *Top Gun* and *The Color of Money* were pinned to the walls at the head and foot of my single bed. Cliff had taken me to see both films, proposing to me after the latter.

My fingers brushed against something on the bed and I glanced down. 'Scarlett Skye,' I whispered, picking up the reversible rag doll Mum had made for me when I was little. 'I thought I'd lost you.'

I was certain I'd packed her the day I left but I'd been unable to find her when I emptied my case at Cliff's house. He'd offered to drive back and get both her and my sewing machine but I hadn't wanted to risk subjecting him to Dad's wrath. It was good to see Scarlett Skye now. The side showing was Skye – a blonde girl with brown eyes wearing a pretty blue-and-white summer's dress. I flipped the dress over her head revealing Scarlett – a brunette with blue eyes, red lips and a beautiful long-sleeved scarlet dress, perfect for a Christmas ball. I'd take her home with me today.

'I've made you a tea,' Marianne called up the stairs. I placed the doll on my pillow and gingerly made my way down the stairs and into the kitchen, wrinkling my nose at the intensity of the smell, like sour milk blended with rotten chicken. There was barely an inch of clear space on the worktops. Empty ready-meal cartons and yoghurt pots were stacked high and there were dozens more bin bags precariously piled on top of each other.

'Has the bin lorry stopped coming?' I asked, wondering if that was the reason behind the rubbish building up.

'No. They come every Wednesday.'

'Is there a reason for you keeping the rubbish in here instead of putting it out?'

Marianne shrugged, picked up a mug of tea from beside the kettle and left the kitchen. I reached for the remaining mug but something on the worktop caught my eye and my stomach churned. I peered a little closer, hoping it would be black pepper or some sort of spice but it was definitely mouse droppings. Shuddering, I poured my tea down the sink.

'Did I make it too strong for you?' Marianne asked, looking at my empty hands when I joined her in the lounge.

'I had a drink just before I left home so I wasn't ready for another. Sorry.'

'My fault. I didn't ask if you were thirsty.'

As she sipped on her tea, I looked around for somewhere to sit but drew a blank. Everything looked so carefully balanced that I feared the removal of one bag would be like withdrawing a key stick from a game of KerPlunk, bringing everything toppling down. I couldn't make sense of the mess. Marianne hadn't liked me going into her bedroom when I was a kid but, the few times I did, I'd been struck by how tidy everything was. How had she gone from that to this? There had to be something wrong – physically, mentally or both – but was Christmas Day the right time to try to address it?

'Why don't we go back up to my bedroom?' I suggested. 'There's space for us both to sit there.'

I thought she'd protest but she followed me up the stairs and we sat side by side on my bed in uncomfortable silence. Why was I here?

'Would you like me to help you tidy up?' I asked eventually, wondering if the mess could be the reason she'd invited me – a call for help, perhaps – although why make it Christmas Day?

'You want to spend Christmas Day tidying?' she asked.

'No, but I wondered if that's why...' I tailed off as her eyebrows raised.

'You think that's why I invited you here?'

'No, but...' I shrugged, unsure how that sentence ended.

'I wanted to see you,' she said. 'Make sure you're coping without Cliff.'

'Erm...' I stared at her in disbelief. She was actually asking how I was? 'I'm okay. One day at a time.' It was such a non-answer but her question had stunned me.

'Five years, isn't it?'

I nodded, thrown even more that she knew how long it had been.

'You must miss him.'

'Every single day.'

Desperate not to cry in front of Marianne, I focused on the *Top Gun* poster. I used to lie on my bed staring at it and wishing I could jump on the back of Tom Cruise's motorbike, ride off into the sunset with him and start over somewhere new. Cliff Kellerman in his russet-coloured Ford Cortina hadn't exactly been my Maverick but he had given me the fresh start I so badly needed.

'Were you happy with him?' Marianne asked.

'Of course I was. We were married for thirty-three years, you know.'

'There isn't always a correlation between the length of a marriage and how happy a couple are. Look at Mum and Dad. Married twenty-nine years and miserable for at least half of them.'

I frowned at her. 'They weren't miserable. They loved each other.'

'You can love someone and still be completely and utterly miserable. Did you not wonder why...' She sighed. 'It doesn't matter. So back to my original question, were you happy with Cliff?'

'A repeat of my original answer – of course I was. He was a wonderful husband and my best friend and, as I said, I miss him every day.'

'Good. Not good that you miss him every day. I mean the rest of it. I'm glad you were happy.'

Silence settled on us once more, only broken by Marianne's intermittent slurping on her tea.

'Why the questions about Cliff?' I asked, bewildered by her sudden interest in my marriage.

'Just wondering.'

'But why?'

She shrugged and that was the conversation over – no more questions from her and nothing I wanted to share with her. How could I admit that every day was a struggle for me when she lived like this? I searched around for a topic of conversation. It was pointless asking if she'd been anywhere because she never left the cottage.

'Are you keeping okay?' I asked.

'I'm tired.' She sighed. 'Very tired recently.'

'Is there anything I can—'

She stood up suddenly, cutting me off. 'I need to show you something.'

Intrigued, I followed her into Mum and Dad's bedroom. There were boxes piled up in there but no bin bags so she evidently didn't use their room to dump her rubbish. She placed her mug on the bedside cabinet, slowly sank to her knees beside the bed, peeled back the rug and lifted up a couple of the wooden floorboards.

'Everything you need is in here,' she said.

'Need for what?'

'If anything happens to me.'

Her words sent a chill through me. She replaced the floorboards and flicked the rug into place before sitting back on her ankles, breathing heavily.

'Are you okay?'

'The boards are heavy. I just need a moment.'

'Not now. I mean in general. Are you ill?'

'I'm tired. I've already told you that.'

I offered her my hand as she rose but she didn't accept it, grabbing for the bed instead then sitting down on it and retrieving her drink. 'I might finish this in here.'

'Okay. We can stay in here.'

I stared at the rug. *If anything happens to me.* Something was definitely going on.

'Marianne, please tell me the truth. Are you sick?'

'Do you mind seeing yourself out?'

'Marianne! Talk to me!'

'I'm tired.'

'Then have a nap and talk to me afterwards.'

She raised her eyebrows at me. 'Why would you want to stay? We've got nothing to say to each other. Go home, Yvonne.'

'But I've only been here for ten minutes.'

'And you were probably ready to leave after two.'

'I never said that.' Even though it was the truth.

'You didn't have to. We both know we've never enjoyed each other's company so let's not start pretending now. I needed to show you where the documents are and I've done that.'

I couldn't believe this. What a waste of time. 'That was all you wanted me for?' I said, unable to hide my frustration.

'Yes.'

'Nothing you want to tell me?'

'No. Absolutely nothing.'

'Then why drag me out here on Christmas Day? You could have asked me to come by any other time.'

'Did you have better plans for today?'

No, but anything was better than this. I wasn't cruel enough to voice that, even though I knew she'd have no qualms about saying it to me.

'You're sure you're not ill?'

She rolled her eyes. 'You sound like a stuck record. Take those chocolates with you. I won't eat them.'

'Fine. Happy Christmas, Marianne.'

Shaking my head, I left the room and went downstairs as fast as I could. I unhooked the gift bag from the handle and slammed the door behind me, grinding my teeth in frustration. I stormed along the drive, yanked the car door open and tossed my handbag and the chocolates onto the passenger seat before getting in the other side. Sitting rigidly in my seat, I closed my eyes for a moment, trying to quell the urge to scream. What a pointless waste of time. The round trip here was over an hour and for what? As I'd pointed out to her, Marianne could have shown me where the hidey hole was any time. In fact, she could have told me the location over the phone instead of dragging me away from my home on Christmas Day. Yes, I had had better plans! They might not have involved human interaction but I could have had an enjoyable enough day watching some television and cracking on with my jetty quilt instead of wasting the morning feeling anxious about seeing my sister and wasting the afternoon on this pointless visit.

A knock on the car window made me jump and I opened my eyes, expecting to see Marianne there, but I didn't recognise the woman smiling at me. I started the engine so I could wind down the window. She was wearing a purple paper hat from a cracker over shoulder-length blonde hair and, at a guess, was in her early thirties.

'Sorry for startling you,' she said, smiling at me. 'I'm Amelia. I live at number three. You must be Marianne's sister. She's told me so much about you.'

'She has?'

'Absolutely! Anyway, I won't keep you. I just wanted to say hello and that you've got a lovely sister. Of course, you already know that.' She laughed and I laughed with her, wondering who she'd met because *lovely* was not a word I'd apply to Marianne. Grumpy, disagreeable, awkward, bitter... I could go on. But lovely? I'd never seen it myself.

'Have you lived here long?' I asked.

'We moved here in September two years ago.'

'And you see a lot of Marianne?'

'Not as often as when we first moved in. I was on maternity leave with my second back then and desperate for adult company so your sister had no choice but to become my friend. I don't manage to see as much of her now I'm back at work but she usually stops by for a cuppa and a chinwag at some point over the weekend and, of course, she joined us earlier for Christmas dinner.'

She'd had Christmas dinner with her next-door neighbour? How was I supposed to respond to that when I'd been sent packing after ten minutes? My sister clearly favoured her young neighbour over her own flesh and blood.

'I thought you'd be staying longer.' She clapped her hand over her mouth. 'That sounded like a criticism. I didn't mean it that way.'

She looked mortified at her faux pas. 'It's fine. I thought I'd be here longer too but Marianne's tired.'

'Aw, bless her. We all thought she looked tired earlier. She hasn't been sleeping well lately.'

'Hasn't she? Did she say why?'

'Just that she has a lot on her mind.' A gust of wind ruffled Amelia's hair and she grabbed for her paper hat. 'It's freezing out here so I'd better get back inside. Happy Christmas! Nice to finally meet you.'

'Same to you.'

Amelia waved as I reversed off the drive. In my rear-view mirror, I watched her go into her cottage – Mrs Kellerman's and Cliff's former home. This day was becoming increasingly bewildering.

When I reached the end of the track, there was no traffic in sight but I didn't pull out. What had Amelia said? *She hasn't been sleeping well lately... she has a lot on her mind.* I'd asked Marianne several times if she was ill and she hadn't given a direct answer; just claimed she was tired. I wasn't convinced. What if being tired was a symptom of something else? What if the mess in the cottage was also symptomatic? Lifting the floorboards seemed to tire her so it would stand to reason that lugging a heavy bin bag out to the wheelie bin then dragging it down the long drive for collection would be exhausting too. It didn't sound as though she'd confided in Amelia but Amelia was clearly much closer to my sister than I was so she might be the person Marianne opened up to about any health challenges.

I opened my handbag, pulled out a notepad and pen and scribbled down my name and phone number before reversing the car back down the track and stopping outside number three.

'Hello again,' Amelia said, smiling widely as she answered the door.

'Sorry for interrupting your family time but I wanted to give you this.' I handed her the piece of paper. 'Just in case.'

She glanced down at my number and nodded. 'I'll keep it safe.'

'Thank you.' I turned to leave, but stopped and pointed to the adjoining cottage. 'Have you ever been inside?'

'Can't say I have.'

'Has she ever given you a reason why?'

Amelia scrunched up her forehead. 'It's never cropped up. It's easier for her to come here because I've got the kids. Why do you ask?'

'Just wondering.' There was a burst of laughter from the lounge and I felt bad for encroaching. 'I've taken enough of your time. Enjoy the rest of your Christmas and do make sure you call me if anything seems...' I hunted around for a suitable word, '... amiss.'

'You look worried.'

I shrugged. 'I am. She wasn't herself but, whatever it is, she didn't want to talk about it.'

'I'll keep an eye on her.'

'Thank you. I appreciate that.'

Before getting in the car, I paused to look back at my child-hood home, sadness engulfing me. I wished Marianne had escaped like I had. Things might have been different between us if she'd had friends, a partner, a life. We might have been close. She might have opened up to me about whatever was going on with her. But if things had been different for her, there probably wouldn't have been anything to open up about. I shook my head and sighed. So many what ifs and maybes.

As I drove away and the cottage disappeared from view, I pictured my sister's pale face against the backdrop of mess, and guilt joined the sadness. Should I have insisted on staying? Should I have demanded she talk to me? Should I go back now? Nervous butterflies swirled round my stomach at the mere thought of it. I couldn't do it. I couldn't face being pushed away again. Marianne's repeated rejections of me on Fridays after school and Dad throwing me out and refusing to ever speak to me again were painful memories which still affected me decades later. Why keep putting myself through that?

I was roughly halfway home when I realised with a sinking heart that I'd left Scarlett Skye behind. I chewed on my lip, toying with turning round, but I could imagine Marianne's annoyance if I turned up on the doorstep for a second time and couldn't face it. It hurt too much.

9

Shortly after lunch on New Year's Eve, I finished Paulette's patchwork quilt. I draped it over the top of the sofa cushions and spread it out before standing back to get the full effect, pride flowing through me. Definitely not a disaster. The scene was from an early spring morning with the sun rising over Derwent Water in a blue and peach sky, and ducks floating beside the wooden jetty. I opened my mouth to call for Cliff and closed it, my stomach sinking as my brain reminded me he wasn't around anymore.

'What do you think, Trevor?' I asked, but Trevor was busy working on a piece of celery and not paying me the slightest bit of attention.

I folded up the quilt and went upstairs to my craft room to get a clear plastic pouch in which to store it. I hadn't anticipated finishing it quite so soon but the strange visit to Marianne on Christmas Day had stirred up all sorts of difficult memories and confused questions. Desperate to quieten my mind, I'd thrown myself into my crafting and it had soon become a personal challenge to see if I could finish Paulette's quilt by the end of the year. Mission accomplished. The problem I had now was what to do with the rest of my day. After each completed quilt, I always took some time off to think about my next project rather than diving straight into something new.

I could kill a bit of time by dropping the quilt off at Paulette's house in Willowdale and perhaps pick up a sweet treat from The White Willow if they were still open. They carried a great range of cakes and tray bakes which I'd discovered could be purchased to take out as well as eat in, which was perfect for me when I couldn't face sitting at a table on my own.

* * *

The White Willow was busier than I'd expected with at least half the tables occupied. The log burner at one end and the large Christmas tree at the opposite end of the room created a warm, cosy and festive atmosphere. Cliff was a huge fan of a Sunday morning walk followed by a full English breakfast and he'd have loved it in here but The White Willow only opened the year after he died. In some ways it was nice to visit somewhere with no connection to my husband but in other ways it made me sad because he should have still been here. Sixty-three was no age to go.

Unable to decide between the tempting selection, I purchased a slice of lemon drizzle cake, a chocolate brownie and a flapjack, figuring I could stretch out the enjoyment over a few days.

Next stop was Paulette's house. I'd planned to park outside the village hall but there were cars everywhere so presumably there was a party on – probably a children's one given the after-noon timing. Although there was only a single garage at

Paulette's, there was a double drive so I pulled in beside her car. As I opened my back door to retrieve the quilt, doubts set in. Was it rude to turn up at someone's house unannounced on New Year's Eve? I couldn't imagine Veronica ever doing this. Although I couldn't imagine Veronica having six days in a row during which the only conversation she had with a human was the supermarket cashier asking if she wanted a bag. To be fair, the woman who'd served me in The White Willow had been lovely but a two-minute conversation about cake had done little to stave off the intense feeling of loneliness which had cloaked me since seeing Marianne.

Deciding that being armed with a gift would make my intrusion forgiven, I grabbed the quilt and made my way to Paulette's front door. It wasn't like I was expecting an invitation inside – I'd just drop and go.

It took a while for anyone to answer but when the door finally opened, it wasn't Paulette standing there. A young woman, probably in her late teens, was smiling at me. Naturally pretty with long tousled light brown hair, a wide smile and sparkly dark eyes, she looked familiar from photographs Paulette had shown me of her family so presumably she was a granddaughter, although I couldn't say which one.

'Hi,' I said. 'I'm guessing you're one of Paulette's granddaughters.'

'Yes. I'm Saffy.'

'Hi, Saffy. I'm one of your grandma's crafting friends. Can you give her this and say it's from Yvonne?'

I raised the bag towards Saffy but she didn't take it, opening the door wider instead. 'You can come in and give it to her yourself.'

'I couldn't impose when she has family here.'

'It's only me and it's no problem. Grandma would have words if I sent you away.'

I wasn't convinced but I stepped inside anyway and followed Saffy into the lounge. With Paulette's vibrant dress sense and larger-than-life personality, I'd expected her home to be full of statement furniture and bright colours but it was surprisingly modern, neutral and calming in a white, grey and blue palette.

'Grandma's upstairs on the phone but she should be down in a minute. I was just making us a tea. Would you like one?'

'I wasn't planning on staying.'

She smiled at me. 'Big plans for tonight?'

'Gosh, no. Just me and the TV.'

'So you must have time for a cuppa.'

'Go on, then,' I said, feeling quite thirsty.

I wasn't sure what to do with myself while I waited. Saffy hadn't said I should sit down but I could hardly wander around the room when I was here uninvited, so I stood awkwardly just inside the lounge door. The house had still been a building site when we'd viewed it and the lounge seemed bigger than I remembered.

When Saffy returned with a tray of mugs a few minutes later, she laughed. 'You are allowed to sit down, you know.'

I took my drink and had just sat down when I heard footsteps on the stairs. 'Sorry about that, Saffy,' Paulette called. 'Who was at the door?'

Paulette entered the room at that point, smiling widely when she saw me. 'Yvonne! What a lovely surprise!'

'I'm sorry for dropping in unannounced but I wanted to bring you a gift.' There was a table beside me with a coaster on it so I placed my drink down and picked up the package. 'I got it finished sooner than expected.'

Paulette removed the quilt and opened it out with a gasp.

'Oh, my! Saffy, can you hold this up so I can see it properly?'

Saffy took the quilt from Paulette, spreading her arms wide and high. Paulette's eyes filled with tears and she shook her head.

'This is spectacular, Yvonne!' she said after running her fingers along the jetty then stepping back to get a full view. 'But I can't possibly accept it. The work that's gone into this... It's too much.'

'I designed it as a challenge and because I liked the photo but it's a place that's important to you so, if you like it, I really want you to have it.'

'Like it? I *love* it!'

She switched places with Saffy to give her granddaughter a look.

'It's lush,' Saffy said. 'You're super talented, Yvonne.'

Their reactions gave me a warm, fuzzy feeling inside and exactly the boost I needed after such a tough week. I was so glad I hadn't talked myself out of visiting.

'Thank you. I love making quilts. I've lost count of how many I've made over the years but I've enjoyed every single one.'

'Where do you sell them?' Saffy asked.

'Nowhere.'

'So you have a pile of quilts at home doing nothing?'

'Yes.'

'How many?'

'Not sure. Thirty or so? Which is why I really need your grandma to accept this one.'

'Consider it accepted.' Paulette draped it over the back of the sofa, smiling at it. 'It's so beautiful. I can't thank you enough, Yvonne.'

I was still on my feet and Paulette surprised me by grabbing me in a hug. I stiffened for a moment, then relaxed into it. I'd almost forgotten how good it felt to be hugged – that comfort and warmth from another person's body – and felt momentarily tearful. Cliff had been a great hugger, as had my mum, but nobody else in my life had been tactile. At Cliff's funeral, a few mourners had given me half-hugs – holding my arms as they gave me a kiss on the cheek or an air kiss – but that hadn't felt particularly personal. Not like this. I longed to tighten my hold on Paulette but I was conscious that might be a bit weird for two women who'd only known each other for a few months and had never been tactile before, so I gave her a quick squeeze then released her.

'You must let me pay you,' Paulette said.

'Absolutely not. It's a gift. Your expression when you saw it was payment enough.'

'Then let me take you out for a meal to say thank you.'

'She's not doing anything tonight,' Saffy said. 'She could stay for tea.'

Paulette clapped her hands together. 'That's perfect! We're ordering a Chinese banquet tonight and intending to stuff our faces so there's more than enough for three. In fact, if you want to nip home and pack an overnight bag, you'd be welcome to stay and see the New Year in with us. We've got a couple of bottles of bubbly in the fridge.'

It was so kind of them but panic welled inside me because there was no way I could accept. Not tonight of all nights.

'Party!' Saffy cried. 'And small ones are the best. You will stay, won't you?'

She looked and sounded genuinely excited at the prospect and I felt tearful once more. A week ago, Marianne had made me feel so unwanted and now Paulette and a teenager I'd only just met were eager to see in the New Year with me. I wished I could accept but it really was out of the question.

Paulette evidently spotted my discomfort. 'No offence if you'd rather do your own thing. We can take a raincheck if you like.'

'Yes, please. I, erm...'

A series of beeps saved me from finding an excuse.

'Urgh!' Saffy muttered. 'My phone's about to die. I need to find my charger.'

She left the room and, moments later, I heard her running up the stairs. Paulette closed the lounge door behind her and indicated that we should both sit down.

'There's some family tension at home,' she said, her voice hushed. 'Saffy's Andrew's daughter – my stepson from my second marriage – and she started university in Birmingham in September but, while we were away, she broke the news that she's decided not to go back. Not the Christmas gift any of us expected.'

'Oh! That must have been awkward.'

'It was one of the most memorable family Christmases but for all the wrong reasons. You could have cut the tension with a knife. After I caught Saffy in tears on our final night, dreading going home, I suggested to Andrew and Joanne that she came back with me for a few days to give everyone some space. Joanne had a go at me for interfering but, thankfully, Andrew could see the benefit and managed to calm her down, so I've got some company while Andrew and Joanne have some time to digest things.'

'Do you think some time apart will make a difference?'

'I hope so. They're convinced she wants to drop out because she's split up with her boyfriend. Saffy and Kyle were childhood sweethearts and we all thought they'd get married one day so it's understandable they'd think her decision is because of the break-up, but there's a lot more to it than that and they weren't listening to her. If me being in Joanne's bad books helps restore peace between Saffy and her parents, so be it.' She rolled her eyes at me and I could feel the exhaustion of the family drama emanating from her. 'Anyway, how was Christmas Day with your sister?'

'I don't know if you can really call it Christmas *Day* when I was only there for ten minutes.'

'Ten minutes? Why? What happened?'

'Beats me! She wanted to show me something, she showed me it, then she said I could go, so I did. It was all a bit peculiar.' I was conscious of being vague. If we'd been having this conversation on any other day, I'd likely have opened up to Paulette but this was New Year and my emotions were all over the place.

'Sounds it,' Paulette said. 'How come none of us knew you had a sister?'

'We're not close.'

'I gathered that, but why?'

'There's a fifteen-year age gap between Marianne and me and I'm pretty sure she resented me coming along. She never showed any interest in me. I tried to just get on with it while Mum was around but she died when I was twelve. After that, being at home with Marianne and our dad was...'

I paused, trying to find the best way to describe it. Difficult? Challenging? They didn't seem strong enough to describe my hellish teen years. Paulette evidently sensed my struggle and stepped in.

'You must have stayed in contact, though?'

'I was twenty-one when I left home to marry Cliff and there was no point inviting them to the wedding because they wouldn't have come. Dad was against the marriage and Marianne rarely left the cottage. I phoned her maybe once a year, but it was always hard work. The one and only time she called me was to tell me Dad had died.'

'When was that?'

'A long time ago – twenty-one years this February. I saw her at his funeral and I felt really sorry for her. She'd never left home, didn't have any friends and I was the only family left. I couldn't imagine what it must be like having no one so I kept in touch more regularly after that.'

'That was good of you.'

I scrunched up my nose. 'You think? To be honest, Paulette, it came from a place of obligation rather than desire and I know how awful that sounds.'

'I still say it was good of you to reach out. Families can be complicated and contact works both ways.'

'That's true. Anyway, since then, I've only seen her a handful of times, the last one being when I told her Cliff had died. I was stunned when she invited me over for Christmas Day and bewildered when she so obviously didn't want me there.'

'Perhaps she thought that Christmas Day would be a good time to reconnect but, when the moment came, she found it too hard to be around anyone for long.'

'Perhaps, but she'd already spent an hour or two having Christmas dinner with her neighbours, so being around *people* clearly wasn't the issue and being around *me* was. I just feel...' I shuddered as I pictured her gaunt appearance and all the mess. 'I don't really know what I feel. I wish I could say it was good to see her but it wasn't. Being back in that cottage stirred up lots of memories I'd rather have left dormant and now I'm worried about her. She didn't look well but she deflected all my questions about it, and the place was in a right state but...' I shrugged. 'She was adamant she wanted me to leave so I did, but I don't know if that was the right thing to do.'

'Sounds like it was the right thing for you and, if your sister was adamant you go, sounds like it was right for her too.' Paulette sipped on her drink. 'You never talk about your family. If you ever want to, I'm a good listener.'

'No, it's fine. It's not a big...' Who was I kidding? It *was* a big deal and it still affected me nearly four decades after leaving home. I sighed and nodded. 'Maybe one day. Thanks for the offer.'

Paulette reached across and gently placed her hand on my forearm. 'Whenever you're ready. I won't pressure you but I might remind you every so often that the offer's there.'

Tears rushed to my eyes once more. Since Cliff died, nobody had shown this level of interest in me. Betsy had never asked me about the past and it struck me that our friendship had been fairly superficial – companionship as opposed to anything deep – but there was scope for so much more with Paulette if I was brave enough to fully let her in.

'Same here if you ever want to talk about anything,' I said.

Paulette squeezed my arm and smiled at me. 'I might just take you up on that. You know, I miss—'

'Found it!' Saffy burst into the room, holding a charger high in her hand. 'It was at the bottom of the laundry basket. No idea how it got in there.' She plugged her phone into a spare socket.

'Is your bedroom trashed?' Paulette asked.

'No! Well, maybe a little bit.'

'Then how about you go back upstairs and sort that out?'

'Okay.' Saffy pulled the plug out of the wall.

'Has your phone suddenly sprouted hands?' Paulette asked. 'No? Then I think it can stay where it is, don't you, because it's going to be no help tidying?'

Saffy plugged it back in and I wondered for a moment if she was going to sulk but she smiled when she looked up. 'You know me too well, Grandma.'

'Teenagers,' Paulette muttered after Saffy left the room again.

I smiled politely but didn't say anything. With no children and no nephews or nieces in my life, my only insight into teenagers came from television programmes and films.

We chatted for a little longer, Paulette sharing some tension-free moments from her Christmas away and I complimented her on how beautifully decorated her home was. By the time Saffy reappeared, I'd finished my drink and was ready to head off.

'It's been lovely seeing you,' Paulette said as we reached her front door, 'and thank you again for the beautiful quilt. I'm going to cherish that.'

'You're welcome. Couldn't think of a better home for it. Hope you and Saffy enjoy your Chinese tonight.'

'Oh, we will! You enjoy your evening too.'

As she reached for the door handle, I felt bad that I hadn't offered any sort of explanation for turning her invitation down.

'About tonight. It would have been lovely, but—'

She raised her hands, stopping me. 'You don't need to explain anything. I could tell from your expression that it wasn't right for you. New Year can be a strange and emotional time when the person you used to spend it with is no longer around.'

'It's more than that. It's when Cliff died.'

'Oh, Yvonne! I didn't realise.'

'You weren't to know. I've spent a lot of time over the years longing for company, but New Year is the one time when I need to be by myself.'

'Will you be all right?'

'I'll be fine. I've got my TV viewing planned and some nice food. I would like to take a raincheck on a Chinese, though.'

'Good. At the first meeting back, we'll put a date in the diary.'

She gave me another hug and we wished each other all the best for the forthcoming year before waving goodbye.

Driving back to Pippinthwaite, I wondered whether I should

have stepped outside my comfort zone and accepted Paulette's invitation to stay – for the Chinese rather than overnight – but it was too late now. Should I go back? My gut said no. I wasn't quite ready yet but I felt close. This would be the last New Year's Eve I spent on my own, mourning not just the loss of Cliff but also the life I could have had if I'd been brave enough to go for it. A life with another man. Will.

10

Another year dawned and I lay in bed for several minutes listening to the wind outside, hurling bits of broken twig and leaves at the window. Today was officially five years since Cliff's death, although it was possible it had been late on New Year's Eve when he left us.

During our thirty-three-year marriage, we'd never ventured out on New Year's Eve. We'd booked a table in a restaurant for our first New Year's Eve as a married couple but I'd come down with a horrendous cold and couldn't face it. Cliff had made me a mulled wine *for medicinal purposes* and had challenged me to a game of chess. Our chess skills (or perhaps lack of them) were evenly matched so it was always enjoyable playing together. The game took my mind off how ill I felt and I'd admitted afterwards that it had been the best New Year I'd ever had, despite feeling lousy. We'd concluded we preferred spending quality time together at home rather than going out so chess and wine became our New Year's Eve tradition.

We usually played the best of three games. By 11 p.m. five years ago, we were at one win each but my eyes were heavy and there was no way I could focus on another game or stay up until midnight. I'd been struck down with flu over Christmas and, while I was on the mend, the fatigue lingered. Cliff hadn't long since topped up his glass so he said he'd clear the board away then see in midnight with the rest of his drink. I'd been playing white and he picked up the white queen he'd toppled and held her up.

'I'll keep you with me for company. Sleep well and see you next year.'

But he didn't see me again.

'Good morning, sleepyhead,' I called, crossing the room the next morning to draw back the curtains. 'I can't believe you've slept at the table. You'll have such a crick in your neck.'

No answer.

'Cliff?'

Heart thudding, I rushed over to him and gave him a gentle shake. Something fell from his hand onto the wooden floor – the white queen – and my stomach lurched. My fingers grappled for his wrist, desperately searching for a pulse, but I already knew I was too late. The room was eerily quiet, he was too still, too cold.

They told me later that the massive cardiac arrest which took him away from me would have been instant and he wouldn't have felt anything. It was a tiny sliver of comfort as I couldn't bear the thought that he could have been alone and scared, unable to call out for help as his life slowly ebbed away.

The wind hurling another twig at the window made me jump and I pulled the duvet tighter around me, wishing I could stay in bed all day. But the longer I lay there, the more thoughts circled round my head about the two major crossroads I'd encountered in my life and whether I'd made the right decision. The first one – accepting Cliff's proposal and leaving home – still felt right, but the decision I'd made at the second crossroads when I turned forty remained shrouded with doubt. If I'd taken the other route, would it have worked? Would I be in a different house with Will by my side right now? Would Cliff and I have been able to stay friends or would me leaving have destroyed him? A million what ifs and maybes clawed at me and I threw back the duvet, gasping for air. Why did I start off every New Year torturing myself in this way? It wasn't as though Cliff and I hadn't been happy together. It was just that things could have been so very different.

I stood in the shower for several minutes with my eyes closed as the hot water cascaded over me, seeking comfort from the warmth. A strong tea and a chat with Trevor helped me feel more like myself but it didn't take long before the restlessness set in. Maybe I should start a new crafting project? Or decide on the new skill I'd learn this year as I hadn't yet done that. I went back upstairs into my craft room to seek inspiration but found myself staring blankly at the shelves.

The rain had stopped and, although it was still windy, the sun had put in an appearance. I checked the weather app on my phone to see whether it was temporary, but it indicated sun and cloud for the rest of the day. I'd go for a walk instead, blowing off the proverbial cobwebs.

* * *

Pippinthwaite wasn't quite as picturesque as Willowdale with its enviable position between Derwent Water and the fells, but it was still a pretty village. It was bigger than Willowdale thanks to the two housing estates stretching the borders to the east and west, but it had fewer amenities – one pub compared to Willowdale's two and a small café which wasn't a patch on The White Willow in terms of space or food range. The butcher was excellent and Betsy had said the hairdresser was superb, but I hadn't tried her.

Going to the hairdresser wasn't my thing. I'd only ever coloured my hair from a box dye and Cliff had always cut it for me – something I attempted myself these days although a cut was now long overdue.

I set off from our estate in the east. It was late morning and there were a fair few folk about. Young children in colourful wellington boots splashed through the puddles and couples linked arms or held hands, love and contentment radiating from them as they faced a fresh year together. Watching two dogs chasing each other on the village green, I wondered for the umpteenth time whether a dog might take the edge off the long days by myself, but I couldn't have one because of Trevor. Dogs and parrots didn't mix.

As I approached The Fox and Rabbit which overlooked the village green, the door opened and a young man emerged holding an A-board which he secured to the wall with some chains. *Happy New Year to our wonderful customers!* We used to be customers. Cliff and I had enjoyed Sunday lunch in there every few weeks followed by a walk around the village to burn off the pudding. I'd booked the function room for his wake but had never stepped inside since. Cliff would be disappointed in me for not supporting our local business. Not that I supported a chain instead – I just didn't go out at all.

I continued past the pub. The houses all around the green were the oldest and, in my opinion, the prettiest in the village. Milly had said she lived in an old cottage near the pub, but I wasn't sure which one. I imagined she'd have a beautifully presented home but, as they all looked good, that didn't help me narrow it down. I glanced back towards The Fox and Rabbit. When Cake & Craft Club resumed, could I be bold and ask Milly if she fancied meeting me in the pub for lunch one day or for an evening drink? Perhaps we could extend the invitation to the others? I shook my head and tutted to myself. I was getting carried away. One step at a time. I'd see if Paulette held me to that raincheck for a Chinese and take it from there.

I'd reached the far end of the village. Wandering aimlessly around the other estate didn't appeal so I headed for a tree-flanked track which skirted the top of Pippinthwaite and emerged near the village green. It was a lovely walk with rays of sunlight dancing between the branches, making the puddles shine.

'Will!' a woman called and I stopped dead, my breath held, my heart pounding.

A Lakeland terrier ran past me and a woman appeared round the bend, a dog lead in her hand, gasping for breath. She grimaced at me before calling, 'Will!' once more and resuming her chase.

Every. Single. Time. Will was a common name and every time I heard it, I had the exact same reaction. How was it that I still thought about him after twenty years? Still dreamed. Still hoped.

When I got back home, my cheeks red from the cold and my hair in knots from where the wind had whipped it, I made a mug of tea before removing the old slimline calendar from the wall and turning over my new one to January. I didn't want every month to be blank like it had been for most of last year and I didn't want the only entries to be my weekly Cake & Craft Club either. Cliff and I had always gone out together for coffee, meals, walks, trips to the cinema or theatre and on holiday. I wasn't sure I'd ever feel comfortable enough in my own skin to go out for a meal or on holiday on my own, but what was stopping me going for walks or to the cinema or theatre? I'd done that on my own loads of times before I lost Cliff.

And what was stopping me asking any of my new Cake & Craft Club friends if they wanted to join me for any of those things? Me! I was stopping me. It was that little voice in my head that told me that when you started spending time with people, you had to talk to them about more than the weather and everyday life. You needed to exchange stories about the past and that was where things became tricky. Would they understand? Would they judge? Would they walk away? I couldn't bear the thought of that, but fear of rejection had controlled my life for far too long and I didn't want it to anymore. I'd had enough of keeping my distance from people so they didn't get a chance to push me away. I had a milestone birthday coming up on the 18th of the month and I was damned if I was going to let fear control my sixties. I was in charge. I was going to make this year special and the first step had to be letting my new friends in.

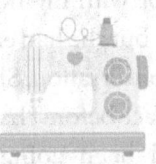

11

The following day the wind had blown over, leaving a clear blue sky. Standing on the back doorstep with a mug of tea cradled between my hands and looking towards the distant fells, I breathed in the freshness of a new day. It was so quiet and peaceful and I closed my eyes, feeling determination running through my veins along with hope for better days ahead. Could I really do it this year? Could I finally step out of the shadows of widowhood and create a life for myself without Cliff in it?

A loud wail punctuated the silence and I opened my eyes, my stomach clenching as next door's baby continued to cry. I didn't know whether they'd had a boy or a girl. I didn't even know their names and it wasn't like I hadn't tried. I'd seen them move into Betsy's home back in November and, after giving them a couple of days to settle in, I'd decided to say hello because it seemed the right thing to do. With the age gap placing us at such different stages of our lives, I hadn't expected to become great friends but I had expected to be on speaking terms, building a polite neighbourly relationship of taking in parcels or putting out the bins for each other.

I'd decided to give them some flowers and had even purchased them from a florist's in Keswick rather than the supermarket so I could ask for advice on the most suitable blooms for pregnant women. The florist told me that flowers with strong fragrances and high pollen counts like lilies should be avoided and she'd created me a beautiful bouquet of white blooms and foliage. I'd swallowed my nerves and went next door with my flowers and a big smile. The woman answered the door but she had earbuds in and was clearly in the midst of a telephone conversation. She took the flowers from me and closed the door in my face before I had a chance to give my name.

A few days later, I'd been going out in my car and she happened to be leaving her house at the same time. Our drives ran alongside each other so I smiled and said, 'Hi, I'm Yvonne. I'm not sure if you realised the flowers were—'

'I'm in a rush,' she said, getting into her car, starting the engine and reversing off her drive with a screech.

'From me,' I muttered, staring after her. 'Welcome to the street.'

Since then, I'd seen them on several occasions including returning from hospital with their newborn, but they'd never acknowledged me and I couldn't have felt more invisible. More rejection. But as I closed the back door to mute the baby's cries now, I realised I didn't care about my neighbours rejecting me. Why would I want such a rude couple to be part of my life? I had far more respect for myself than that.

As I finished my drink, I looked around the kitchen, wondering what to do next. Nothing needed cleaning. The whole house was spotless but I knew somewhere that was far from that. No matter what I did, I couldn't shake Marianne out of my mind. Something wasn't right with her and I was going to have to try again.

* * *

It was stupidly impulsive and not like me at all but, as I drove across to Hayscroft Lane, I managed to convince myself that Marianne would be pleased to see me. She'd apologise for her behaviour on Christmas Day and share that her New Year's resolution was for us to get to know each other – something which we could achieve as we cleared the cottage together. I refused to listen to the voice in my head which told me that living on my own for too long had evidently sent me a bit doolally for thinking my sister would not only be delighted to see me but she'd be happy for me to start cleaning her cottage.

The doubts set in as I pulled onto the drive. For now, it might be better to leave the bags full of gloves, cloths, cleaning products and bin bags in the boot, along with my vacuum cleaner, mop and bucket.

It took a while for Marianne to answer the door and she looked surprised to see me there.

'Happy New Year!' I said. 'How was it?'

'Like every other day. Why are you here?'

The defensive tone – accompanied by defensive body language this time – burst my bubble. Why did I always expect more from my sister when I always received so much less? But I had to keep trying.

'We didn't spend much time together on Christmas Day so I thought we could rectify that.'

Marianne shook her head. 'It's not a good time. I'm busy.'

'Busy tidying?' It was a feeble attempt at a joke, and admittedly an inappropriate one.

She glared at me.

'Sorry. I shouldn't have said that but even you admitted the cottage was messy. I thought I could help. I've got some stuff in the car.'

'Did I ask for your help?'

'No, but I just thought...'

'It's fine as it is.'

'There's barely anywhere for you to sit or cook or—'

Marianne's eyes widened. 'Are you judging me?'

'No! It's just that—'

But she cut me off once more. 'You don't know anything about me.'

'So tell me. Let me in. Please, Marianne. We've only got each other.'

'Then I suggest you find yourself some friends.'

I winced. That was harsh when my visit today had been with the best intentions.

'I'm worried about you,' I said.

She stared at me for a moment and I wondered if my words had touched her, but then her expression darkened. 'I'm not your responsibility.'

'But you're my sister.'

She sighed heavily. 'Go away, Yvonne. I mean it. Leave me alone.'

Before I could say anything else, she slammed the door shut and locked it. I knocked again and called her name through the letterbox but it was fruitless. My sister had never wanted anything to do with me and it was time I stopped clinging on to the idea that we were family so we should be in each other's lives. Why bother when it caused discomfort on both sides? And she was right about me. I *had* judged the mess and had assumed that a dozen bottles of anti-bacterial spray could sort out something that was clearly a mental health issue. I knew that people didn't live the way my sister did because they were too lazy or incapable of tidying up.

I drove back to Pippinthwaite, cursing myself for being so impulsive and, if I was honest, a bit selfish too. My visit hadn't purely been about good intentions so I had no right to feel upset by yet another rejection. After seeing the state of the cottage on Christmas Day, Marianne had been in my thoughts way more than she'd ever been before and I hadn't liked it. I'd figured that I wouldn't think about her or worry so much if I knew her home was hygienic. But she'd made it clear from childhood that I wasn't an important part of her life and the enforced Friday afternoon recaps of my week had been excruciating. I didn't need to continue that into adulthood. Marianne was right that she wasn't my responsibility and I needed to accept that. Or try to.

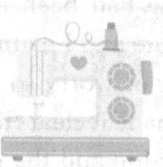

12

With Christmas Eve and New Year's Eve both falling on Wednesdays, Cake & Craft Club had taken a three-week break which had been far too long for me. The last week in particular had dragged and I was so looking forward to being back with my friends today. Every so often, Cake & Craft Club welcomed guest crafters who taught us a new skill over a week or two. In late October, we'd had a stained-glass expert in and, as it was close to Halloween, we'd all made a pumpkin. I'd loved learning about the process and had been really pleased with my creation. Today we were expecting a willow-weaving expert, showing us how to make bird feeders.

Arriving at Willowdale Village Hall, I was surprised to see Paulette and Saffy at the far end of the room setting up on what was usually the guest's table. I'd have assumed they were helping out but the items they were unloading from crates and bags definitely weren't willow rods.

'Happy New Year, Yvonne!' Veronica called, joining me by the door.

'Same to you. I'm guessing we're not willow weaving today.'

'No. I had a phone call first thing from our expert. Her father's had a fall and she's taken him to hospital so we were a bit stuck, but Paulette's granddaughter offered to step in and show us her favoured craft. Cup of tea?'

I followed Veronica into the kitchen, exchanging greetings with various members along the way. Milly was in there with Laughlin and it was so good to see them all again.

Tea in hand, I returned to the hall and sat down at my usual table as Veronica called for the group to hush.

'Happy New Year, everyone! I hope you had a wonderful break. Three weeks without Cake & Craft Club felt very long to me so it's lovely to be back with you all again.'

She paused for murmurs of agreement and I loved that I wasn't the only one who'd struggled with so long apart.

'We're going to do things slightly differently today,' Veronica said. 'You'll notice there's no cake out but, don't panic, cake *is* coming. We wanted to launch straight into our guest slot as the craft we're exploring today requires some thinking time and you might like to do that over cake. I'll hand over to Paulette who'll explain a bit more but, firstly, can you bring your chairs closer so you can see better?'

When we were all settled, Paulette – looking resplendent in a bold cerise pink-and-orange dress – stood up and smiled round the group. 'We're not willow weaving today as originally planned. Our expert has had a family emergency but my fabulous grand-daughter, Saffy, has offered to help out with something she's passionate about. She's a bit nervous as she's never run a training session before but I've assured her that you're all lovely and, if we hold the cake hostage, you'll listen intently.'

Everyone laughed as Paulette handed over to Saffy.

'Hi, as Grandma said, I'm Saffy and I'm nineteen. Grandma told me you love trying new crafts so I hope you'll enjoy today's session – journalling. It's something I used to do a lot a few years back and I could lose myself in it for hours. Because of that, I had to take a break to focus on my GCSEs and A levels. I've returned to it recently and been reminded not only about how much I love journalling but also how helpful it is. Grandma and I thought it might be helpful to some of you, especially with it being the New Year.'

She paused and glanced at Paulette who gave her a reassuring smile and a thumbs up.

'I wanted to start by telling you what's been going on with me lately because it's relevant to the focus of my new journal. I told my parents over Christmas that I don't want to go back to university. My mum thinks I've dropped out because I split up with my boyfriend, but Kyle's only a small part of the problem. The university wasn't right for me and neither was my course so why put myself through a whole year of it only to drop out at the end? I had a few issues when I was younger and it was suggested I keep a diary to make sense of them. Writing everything down wasn't for me but a few words, some doodles and a handful of stickers was my vibe. As I said, I haven't done any journalling for years but it helped sort my head out back then so I thought I'd give it another go now to help figure out what I want from my life.'

She picked up a spiralbound book – about the height of A4 but wider.

'When better to sort your life out than the start of a new year? I've asked myself four questions.' She opened up the journal to reveal the first one:

What 3 things will you STOP doing this year?

'I picked three because it's a manageable number and it helps me focus on the most important things to me. More than that can feel overwhelming.'

She turned over several pages to reveal her other questions:

What 3 things will you START doing this year?

Which 3 places will you SEE this year?

Which 3 emotions do you mostly want to FEEL this year?

'They're all excellent questions,' Veronica said. 'I particularly like that last one.'

'Me too,' Milly agreed. 'I've made loads of New Year resolutions but they're always things like lose weight or get fit. I've never thought about how I want to feel.'

'I like the one about places to see,' Laughlin said. 'I like the wording – which places *will* you see rather than which ones do you *want* to see? It makes it more definite.'

'That's the point,' Saffy said, nodding. 'The first three are all positive statements because I see them as things I can control, but the final one about feelings isn't something I can control quite so easily so I've worded it as an aim although, when I achieve the others, those feelings should fall into place.'

She flicked back the pages to the first question. 'I'll show you how I've tackled this one. What do you think is the first thing I want to stop doing?'

A washi-tape border showed compasses and maps and the stickers and pictures on the page were a mixture of signposts, stop signs, groups of people and flocks of sheep.

'You're going to stop following directions?' Laughlin muttered. 'Ignore me. That doesn't make sense.'

'You're closer than you think,' Saffy said.

'Why the sheep?' Milly muttered. 'Oh! I've got it! You're going to stop following what other people do.'

'Absolutely that! I ignored my gut and followed Kyle to Birmingham but, even before that, I followed him and all my friends into doing the university thing without questioning whether I even wanted it. This year, I'm going to stop doing things just because my friends are doing them or because it's what's expected of me.'

She showed us another one – a colourful page covered in cosmetics and pictures of hands indicating an intention to stop biting her fingernails – before closing the book. 'I haven't done the page for my third *stop* entry yet so I can't show you it, but I hope you get the gist.'

She talked us through the various items she favoured for her journalling – washi tape, stickers and ribbon – and where she sourced them.

'Some people use pictures cut out of magazines, photos, postcards, greetings cards. Some like to put lots of writing in their journals and others don't use any words. The type of journal, the pens and the materials you use are all completely up to you. Who's kept a diary before?'

I hadn't, but the show of hands revealed that I was in the minority.

'You're basically doing a diary with added bling. Have fun with it. You don't have to use my four questions. The pink sheets on the table list other New Year-style questions you could use but, if the New Year/new me thing doesn't appeal, the yellow sheets have other questions and ideas on it. You could create a journal for your favourite recipes, your gardening plans, your grandchildren, your craft projects. No rules. Anything goes.' She took a deep breath. 'Any questions?'

After Saffy answered a few questions from the group, Veronica joined her at the front and led us in a round of applause.

'Some of you will want to dive straight in,' Veronica said, 'but others will prefer that thinking time I mentioned. There's notepads here if you want to scribble down your thoughts first and a pile of journals if you want to dive straight in.'

Saffy nodded. 'Writing it down first is a great idea, but I'd say don't spend too long thinking. Scribble down the first thing your gut tells you. You can always perfect the wording later.'

Feeling in awe of how wise and confident Saffy came across, especially for her age, I looked at the information on the two coloured sheets of paper. I was mostly drawn towards the same four questions Saffy was using so I grabbed a notepad and wrote each one down at the top of a fresh page, adding the numbers one to three down the sides.

What did I want to stop doing this year? I stared at the page for several minutes, thoughts swirling around my head, and even scribbled down a couple of ideas, inspired by Saffy's entry to stop biting her nails:

What 3 things will you STOP doing this year?

   1. *Ironing everything*
   2. *Displaying the tins label out*

Tutting to myself, I scribbled out both entries.

Milly was on the table next to me. 'Changed your mind?' she asked.

'I've gone with the questions Saffy suggested, starting with the things I want to stop but what I've written down is rubbish – things I'm really not bothered about stopping.'

'I like Saffy's questions too,' Milly said, 'but I need a lot more thinking time and I need quiet so I'm not going to push it this afternoon. I'm going to write the questions in my journal and decorate them. You could do the same if you're struggling. Ooh! The cakes are out.'

Milly's suggestion worked for me. Feeling the self-imposed pressure lifted, I collected a plain white spiralbound journal from the table before helping myself to a slice of coffee and walnut cake and a top-up of my cup of tea.

The rest of the afternoon was spent carefully writing out the questions and decorating each with washi tape and stickers. I could easily see how Saffy lost herself in journalling for hours. The attention to detail needed – deciding on the right items, colours and where to position them in an aesthetically pleasing way – reminded me a little of the approach to my patchwork quilts and it gave me a similar buzz. But preparing the questions was the easy part. Actually answering them truthfully and mean-ingfully was so much harder and also a little scary. If I was going to do this properly, I needed to go deep. Was I ready for that?

At home later that afternoon, I placed my journal on the dining table before releasing Trevor from his cage.

'It was a good meeting,' I told him. 'I've got some homework to do and it involves a lot of soul searching. It could be painful, but I think it might help me get my act together.'

'Pretty Vonnie!' Trevor called, making my heart leap. The one and only other time I'd heard him call me that was the day I'd seen the advert for Cake & Craft Club – a sign from Cliff when I'd been struggling. I picked up the holiday photo and gazed at his smiling face.

'I think doing this journal could help me, but only if I'm really honest with what I write in it. Can you send me the strength to do that?'

* * *

That night I tossed and turned, thinking about Saffy's four questions but, as I pulled on my dressing gown the following morning, I felt incredibly calm. I knew exactly what I wanted this year and I had an overwhelming sense that writing it all down would be the first step in achieving it. And I wasn't afraid.

I went downstairs, let Trevor out of his cage, sat down in the armchair beside him with my notepad and pen and the words flowed. When I reached the final point, I scanned through what I'd written and could honestly say that it was the truth, straight from my heart. I was fed up of the old Yvonne and ready to make room for the new, improved one.

The first section had been the easiest – I needed to stop doing all the things that dragged me down.

What 3 things will you STOP doing this year?

1. *Feeling sorry for myself*
2. *Blaming the past and hiding myself away*
3. *Chasing a relationship with Marianne*

The second section was harder.

What 3 things will you START doing this year?

1. *Living*
2. *Loving*

I stared at the blank third entry but I couldn't think of anything to add. There was no point scribbling down an entry to which I wasn't fully committed. Something might present itself later.

For the third section, I surprised myself by how quickly the answers came.

Which 3 places will you SEE this year?

1. *A new home for me*
2. *More of the local area with my new friends*
3. *Venice*

Seeing *a new home for me* written down, moving seemed so obvious. I'd felt out of place in Mallard Close for a long time but I'd stayed because it was the easy option and, of course, having Betsy next door had helped. The house itself had never captured my heart so why was I staying somewhere I didn't love, didn't feel welcome, didn't want to be anymore?

The second entry about seeing more of the local area was about getting back the active life I used to have with Cliff, but with my friends from Cake & Craft Club instead. They were all on their own too. Surely they'd appreciate the occasional day trip or meal out.

As for Venice... I sighed longingly. That one took me back to Will. I'd told him how I imagined Venice to be the most romantic place in the world and how much I longed to go there. He'd visited with some friends and confirmed that it was as romantic as I believed and had vowed to himself that he'd return one day with someone he loved deeply. Had he found that person? Had he taken her there? And had he thought about me?

Feeling overwhelmed by the memory of my brief but beautiful time with Will, I fixed my gaze on the final section.

Which 3 emotions do you mostly want to FEEL this year?

1. *Love*
2. *Happiness*
3. *A sense of belonging*

Picking up a red biro, I drew a love heart by the *love* entry and the *loving* one on the second section and coloured them in before turning my gaze back to Cliff's photo.

'What do you think?' I asked. 'Is this my year? Am I brave enough to try?'

I flicked through my responses once more, tears welling in my eyes. I had to do this. I had to make it happen otherwise I'd have escaped from one prison thanks to Cliff only to trap myself in another. These were my heart's desires but I wasn't going to be able to achieve them all on my own. I was going to need support and encouragement from my four new friends, which meant letting them in. My gut told me that they wouldn't reject me when they knew the truth about Cliff and me, but it was still a huge leap of faith. A leap I had to take.

13

'Visitor!' Trevor called on Sunday morning.

The blinds were only tilted a little and I could see the shape of someone approaching the door but couldn't see who it was. Seconds later, the doorbell rang. I secured Trevor back in his cage and opened the door tentatively, relaxing when I saw it was Milly.

'I'd have rung first but I realised we haven't swapped numbers. I knew roughly where you lived so I've been wandering round the streets hoping to spot your car and...' Her voice cracked and I was alarmed to see tears escaping.

'What's happened? Come in.'

She followed me inside and, knowing that Trevor would keep calling, 'Visitor!' if we went into the lounge, I led her straight to the kitchen and flicked the kettle on.

'Sorry,' she said, wiping her cheeks. 'I wasn't expecting to start crying. I came to ask whether you'd like to join me for a carvery at the pub but...'

'But the thought of having lunch with me was too much to bear and you burst into tears?'

The joke worked its magic and Milly started laughing. 'Not at all. It would be a pleasure.'

'So why the tears?'

'I drove Coral back to university yesterday – my eighth start of term drop-off and they don't get any easier. This one was especially hard because she'd spent most of the Christmas break in Lapland. It felt like I got her back and moments later she was gone again.' She clicked her fingers to emphasise her point.

'Goodbyes are never easy,' I said, thinking about how tearful I'd been the day Betsy left. 'Do you want a cuppa or would you rather head to the pub now? It'll have just opened and tables fill quickly on a Sunday.'

'Heading straight to the pub sounds like a plan. You're sure I haven't interrupted anything?'

'A ready meal in front of the telly.'

'Story of my life,' she said, smiling at me.

After checking she didn't have a fear of birds or allergy to feathers, I took Milly through to the lounge and introduced her to Trevor so they could chat while I smartened myself up. Shortly after, we set off on foot to The Fox and Rabbit.

'I'm completely in love with Trevor,' Milly said. 'And how amazing is his name? There's something about animals with human names that tickles me.'

An image of a Lakeland terrier called Will running past me on New Year's Day sprang to mind and I pushed it aside. I needed to focus on Milly – not get lost in thoughts of Will.

'Me too,' I agreed. 'Cliff chose it. We'd made a list of exotic-sounding parrot names but he looked at him and said, "He looks more like a Trevor to me." I laughed, thinking he was taking the mickey but it did seem to suit him so Trevor it was. Do you have any pets?'

'No. I've always wanted a dog but I can't because Harry hates them.'

'That's a bit unfair when he's hardly ever home.'

We walked in silence for a little way and I wondered if I might have put my foot in it by criticising her husband. I was about to apologise but Milly changed the subject, asking whether I liked living in Mallard Close.

'Not really.' I told her about Betsy moving out, the couple moving in next door and the incident with the flowers. 'I've been feeling out of place there for a while and I've decided that I'm going to do something about it this year. I've been doing my journal and I followed Saffy's questions and went with my gut like she said. Under places to see this year, I wrote down *a new home* and it was one of those light bulb moments. So I've decided to move this year, assuming I can find somewhere I like.'

'Still in the area?' Milly asked.

'Definitely. When we moved out of town, Cliff and I originally wanted to settle in Willowdale but it didn't work out. I like Pippinthwaite but Willowdale has my heart.'

We chatted about what we liked about both villages until we reached the pub. Outside, I felt a twinge of apprehension. Would it feel uncomfortable being in The Fox and Rabbit without Cliff, picturing him leaning against the bar chatting to the landlord and giving a good-natured tut if somebody had beaten us to his favourite table? I swallowed down my nerves and followed Milly inside, but I barely recognised the place.

'The bar's moved!' I exclaimed.

'You haven't been in recently?' Milly asked. 'It changed hands maybe four years back and the new owners did a major refurb. Nice, isn't it?'

'It's lovely.' Not that it hadn't been nice before but, with such major changes, it was like being somewhere completely new and my concerns disappeared.

'I've been working on my journal too,' Milly said when we sat down at a table with our drinks. 'It might not be an action point for this year but I *am* going to get a dog at some point because right at the top of my *what am I going to stop doing?* list is *stop being married to Harry*. When he comes home in a couple of weeks, I'll be telling him I want a divorce.'

'Oh my gosh, Milly! That's a big decision. Are you okay?'

'Better than I've been for a long time. I'm tired, Yvonne. I'm tired of making excuses for why he's never here, tired of being married to someone who I never see, tired of trying to make it work when it hasn't for more years than I care to remember.'

That sounded awful. No wonder she wanted out. I felt proud of her for making that decision. It seemed journalling could do wonders for both of us.

'How do you think he'll react?' I asked.

'He'll probably be relieved. He never wanted to get married or have a family.'

I raised my eyebrows, shocked. 'He told you that?'

She sighed as she nodded. 'He made it clear from the start and it was fine with me because I was feeling pretty cynical about the happy families thing at the time and...' She shook her head. 'I'd better start at the beginning, if that's okay with you. I don't want to bore you with my woes.'

My first reaction was to panic. This had the hallmark of something really personal and, if Milly opened up to me, then I'd surely need to open up to her. But wasn't that exactly what I'd concluded I needed to do – that leap of faith in my friends in order to move forward with my life? My biggest fear had been rejection but if Milly wanted to share her story with me, that had to mean she felt comfortable around me which in turn meant she saw me as someone to confide in. A friend. And that last sentence about boring me showed a vulnerability too. Perhaps Milly also feared judgement. The nerves settled and I gave her a reassuring smile, feeling as though something had just shifted in our friendship.

'Nothing you say could bore me, Milly. Take your time.'

There was no mistaking the relief in her smile. She needed to talk and I was here to listen and, soon, I knew she'd do the same for me.

'Do you remember me saying how I get melancholy at New Year and I wasn't sure why?' she asked. 'Well, I *do* know why. Before I met Harry, I was in a long-term relationship with Rob. We got engaged and bought a house after about eighteen months together but, three years down the line, we hadn't got round to setting a wedding date. I didn't think anything of it because the house needed a lot of work and we'd decided to prioritise that. Rob took me out for a meal on New Year's Eve and said we needed to talk about our future. His expression was really dark and idiot here thought he was winding me up so I adopted this serious tone and told him I wholeheartedly agreed and the first point on the agenda should be setting a date for our wedding and we weren't leaving the restaurant until we had. I'd expected him to laugh but he didn't and...'

As Milly paused and took a deep breath, my heart went out to her. It was clear that whatever had happened next still hurt many years down the line.

'...and I knew at that moment that he didn't want to talk about *our* future. He wanted to talk about a future without me.'

'Aw, Milly, that must have been horrendous.'

'It was the most painful moment of my life. He said he was moving out and I remember staring at him, mouth open but no words coming out. You hear people talking about long-term relationships ending and them having no inkling anything was wrong and I always thought that was ridiculous. How could you possibly not know that your partner had fallen out of love with you and was about to leave? But it happened to me and, if there were signs, I missed every single one of them. I genuinely thought we were happy and would be together forever but Rob had wanted out for months.'

'Did he say why?'

'He'd met someone else. A colleague. He swore that nothing had happened between them and, to this day, I believe that was the truth. But she'd made it clear she was interested and would only do something about it if he was single.'

'So she gave him an ultimatum – you or her?'

'Effectively, and he chose her. I've often wondered whether it would have been easier if he *had* cheated on me with her because he'd at least have made an informed decision to be with her. For him to choose her over me when they hadn't even kissed made me feel so worthless.'

Her eyes filled with tears and she blinked them back. 'Why am I still crying over it? It was twenty-three years ago, for goodness' sake.'

'Because he hurt you badly and time doesn't heal all wounds – not completely.' I was living proof of that. Time certainly hadn't eased any of my pain.

While Milly sipped on her drink, I asked her how long after Rob she'd met Harry.

'It was about five months later at parents' evening. Harry was the uncle of one of my students and had stepped in when the parents couldn't make it. He was the last appointment of the night and I was shattered and completely peopled out but he made me laugh. I'd just turned thirty and he was thirty-six, divorced with no kids and, corny as it sounds, he swept me off my feet. He trav-

elled a lot with his job and, at first, I loved the distance relationship thing – just what I needed after Rob. He sent me gifts and
wrote me long emails and was so attentive when he was home. It
all seemed so romantic and, even though I used to believe there
was only one true love for everyone and mine had been Rob, I
realised that was rubbish because I was hopelessly in love with
Harry and desperate for us to be a family. Not ideal when he'd
made it clear he didn't want to get married again or ever have
kids.'

'Obviously you have Coral, so what changed for him?'

Milly grimaced. 'Nothing. Coral was an accident – although,
for me, a very happy one. When I told him I was pregnant, I was
sure it would be the end of us and I'd be raising her on my own,
but Harry surprised me by proposing. We got married quickly –
before Coral came along – and Harry was around for the first
couple of months but then he went abroad for three months and I
had a hard dose of reality. The distance relationship thing
suddenly wasn't quite so romantic anymore, especially when the
trips abroad became more frequent and for longer.'

'So you effectively raised her on your own anyway?'

'Exactly!' Milly took another sip of her drink. 'I decided not to
go back to teaching after my maternity leave ended. I spent most
of my time at Mum and Dad's in Windermere so they could help
with Coral while I retrained for the job I do now. I decided I
wanted to move to the Lakes before Coral started school and I
expected Harry to refuse but he went with it. We rented out our
flat in Manchester, bought the house in Pippinthwaite and I
focused on raising my daughter and building my business while
burying my head in the sand about my marriage being a disaster.'

'Milly, I'm so sorry. It can't have been easy to make the decision to end things.' I knew that from personal experience.

'It wasn't. I've known for a long time that we don't have a

proper marriage and, in dark moments, I've wondered about calling time on it but I never quite got to the point where I felt it was something I had to do.'

'But you've hit that point now?'

She nodded. 'While Coral was at home, she was my life and it didn't bother me that I had no romance in it. Even when she went away to university, I could kid myself that she hadn't properly left home, but it all changes this year. The Easter break will be the last time she's home for any significant time. She'll be graduating in the summer and moving down to London with her boyfriend and I'll be properly on my own.'

'You wouldn't consider following her to London?' I asked.

'God, no! I wouldn't want to cramp their style and London's not for me. I love this area and I'm close to my parents, but I feel as though I've spent long enough on my own. I want to meet someone who loves me more than their job and actually wants to spend time here with me rather than on the other side of the world. That's not too much to ask, is it?'

I shook my head. 'Of course not! You absolutely deserve that.'

'I think so! Not that I have any clue how I'd find that person. The thought of using a dating app makes my blood run cold and I don't meet anyone in person through my work, so finding the man of my dreams is going to be one heck of a challenge but I'm open to it happening somehow. It's scary but it's time to take the plunge again and hope for third time lucky.'

Milly held up crossed fingers and I did the same, feeling so sorry for her that she'd trusted two men with her heart only for them both to break it.

'I'm sure it *will* happen, probably when you least expect it.'

'I love the idea of an unexpected romantic meet-cute.' She smiled at me and I loved how her eyes sparkled with the possibilities that lay ahead.

'You sound really positive.'

'I feel it. Finally making the decision that it's over has lifted such a weight from me and it's all thanks to Saffy's journal questions. They forced me to do some serious soul searching.'

'They were good questions.'

'How have you got on with the rest of yours? You mentioned the house move, but was there anything else big?'

So many things but our lunch would arrive at any moment and my life story was not something I could casually share between mouthfuls of roast potato and Yorkshire pudding. When I let Milly in – which I absolutely would – I wanted to be able to take my time. It also felt fairer to keep today about Milly and the momentous decision she'd made about her future. I was beyond flattered that she'd sought me out to share such a major life decision with me, demonstrating trust and friendship.

'A few biggies, but I'll tell you about them when they're set in stone. I do have another confirmed entry in my *things to see* section. Cliff and I used to go out a lot and I've become a bit reclusive since he died so I'm determined to get out and about more. We used to be regulars at the cinema and theatre and I haven't been since, so if you ever fancy going to either...?'

'Ooh, I'd love to! I haven't been to the cinema in ages and I can't remember the last time I went to the theatre. Count me in.'

Our meals did arrive at that point and, as we tucked in, we talked about films, plays and musicals we'd seen and loved. I discovered that Milly had also had a Tom Cruise crush with film posters from *Cocktail* and *Rain Man* on her bedroom walls. We had so much in common and Milly was beginning to feel like a kindred spirit.

'I wish I could stay here chatting to you all afternoon,' she said a little later, 'but I have to get back to do some work. Why don't we make Sunday lunch a regular thing – maybe the first Sunday of each month?'

'That would be great.'

'Excellent.' She checked her diary on her phone. 'The first Sunday in February is the first of the month. Typing it in now. Lunch... with... Yvonne.' She looked up with a wide smile. 'Done.'

We left the pub and paused outside.

'Thank you for today,' she said. 'I really needed a friend and you've perked me up no end.'

She hugged me and my heart soared as I hugged her back. First Paulette and now Milly making me feel needed and important. Joining Cake & Craft Club had already changed my life and I couldn't help thinking this was just the tip of the iceberg with so much more to come.

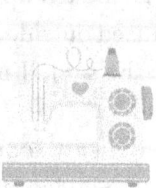

14

Back at home after my Sunday roast with Milly, I couldn't stop smiling as I wrote our February lunch date on the calendar – my first entry that wasn't a Cake & Craft Club meeting! Was this the start of *living* for me? I added in the first Sunday for the next few months and felt hopeful about adding further events, although I realised that meant me stepping forward and taking the lead rather than waiting for the others to suggest them. Milly had shown a clear interest in the cinema and theatre and we'd exchanged phone numbers so I'd definitely get in touch when I spotted something that would appeal to us both.

Inspired by the way in which Milly's journal had instigated such a major change in her life, I looked back over what I'd written. I still couldn't think of a third *start* entry but the others definitely reflected how I wanted my year to pan out. My priority was *living* and I felt as though I'd made great progress with that and would continue to do so as long as I kept the momentum going. As for *start loving* and *feel love*, it could relate to friendship and it could also mean self-love – something I *definitely* needed to work on – but my real intention was romantic love. Like Milly, I wanted to find someone special who loved me with all their heart in every way possible for the rest of my days. I closed my eyes, hoping to manifest it, but all I could conjure up was Will's face.

'Stop it!' I murmured to myself. 'You had your chance and you blew it.'

* * *

That evening, I went online and ordered some washi tape and stickers in designs which reflected my plans. The following morning, I nipped into Keswick to check out the shops stocking stationery and craft supplies and bought up a few more items, which meant I could crack on with my journal rather than waiting for my online order to arrive. Committing most of the entries to paper gave me a fizz of excitement around taking control of my life at last and pulling myself out of my reclusive slump. But the entry around stopping *chasing a relationship with Marianne* made me sad. I knew it was the right thing for me – and for my sister too, considering how she reacted around me – but I hated how cutting out my only remaining family member was essential to truly move on with my life.

Between journalling, I spent time online checking out the sale prices of houses like mine in Pippinthwaite and searching for a potential new home. There were six houses currently for sale in Willowdale. Four were too big or financially out of my reach but there were two possibilities so, on Wednesday afternoon, I set off for Cake & Craft Club half an hour early to walk around the village and check them out.

The first was an old semi-detached cottage which I ruled out immediately – too similar to my childhood home. The second was a 1950s-built semi on the edge of the village and I shook my head. What had I been thinking? It was significantly larger than my current house and Trevor and I didn't need all the space we had now. When I moved, I needed to downsize rather than go bigger.

I returned to my car and removed my bag from the boot. As I hadn't decided on my next quilting project, I'd brought my journal with me, intending to finish decorating the last couple of entries. Paulette and Saffy were walking towards the village hall and Saffy was pulling a pink crate on wheels behind her.

'Lovely to see you again,' I said to Saffy, 'but I thought you were going back to your mum and dad's.'

'I was. I did. And it was an epic fail so I'm back with Grandma for a while.'

'My bag's heavy,' Paulette said to Saffy. 'Would you be a sweetheart and take everything inside?'

Saffy took Paulette's bag and disappeared into the village hall.

'Did I put my foot in it?' I asked, grimacing.

'Not at all, but I wanted to give you an update. Saffy caught the train home last Thursday and told Andrew and Joanne that her mind was made up and she wasn't returning to Birmingham. Joanne hit the roof and said they were meant to be talking about it before any big decisions were made. Saffy, quite rightly, said that they'd already talked a lot and Joanne clearly wasn't going to change her mind but Saffy wasn't either and, as she was an adult now and this was about her future, she had the ultimate say. She asked if they could take her to Birmingham to clear her room in the halls and Joanne refused. She said that if Saffy was determined to be an independent adult then she could behave like one, starting with working out for herself how to get her belongings back.'

I winced. 'That's harsh.'

Paulette nodded. 'I don't understand why she's digging her heels in so hard. Saffy caught the train across to Birmingham on

Saturday, I drove down to meet her and we cleared her room together. Now Andrew and Joanne aren't speaking to me.'

'Oh, Paulette, I'm so sorry. But what did they expect you to do? Abandon Saffy when she needed you?'

She shrugged. 'It's been a difficult start to the year to say the least but it'll all come out in the wash eventually.'

'If there's anything I can do…'

Paulette smiled. 'I appreciate that. What I need right now is cake but it's Veronica's turn and it had better not be carrot, beetroot or parsnip.'

'She's made parsnip cake before?'

'No, but I wouldn't put it past her.'

As it turned out, Veronica had baked the most divine red velvet cake with a mouthwatering cream cheese frosting which had Paulette and I salivating and longing for seconds.

Milly usually favoured needle felting but had brought a cross-stitch kit with her today – a beautiful sunset view of Castlerigg Stone Circle – and Paulette was knitting a cardigan for Saffy, but I wasn't the only one working on my journal. Veronica, Laughlin and a few of the other members had brought theirs with them and I was impressed by the way Saffy passed round us all, checking we had enough materials and giving design ideas. All the while, she had a smile on her face which was amazing considering the turmoil she must be feeling right now.

'Did you go with Saffy's questions?' I asked Veronica when she returned from the kitchen with a fresh cup of tea for me halfway through the meeting.

'I rather liked her suggestion of making a journal full of favourite recipes so I decided to make one each for Rebecca and Felicity.'

I pulled my chair closer to hers and she showed me what she'd created so far.

'We did a lot of baking together when they were little and I always made them a special birthday cake so I've got quite a few photos of them baking and blowing out candles and I thought it would be a nice touch to include them all.'

'That's such a lovely idea,' I said, smiling at a photo of them as young girls licking cake mixture from wooden spoons. 'I used to bake a lot with my mum too and I seem to remember her taking a photo of me doing that.'

I flicked through the rest of the journal. 'I'm sure your daughters will love it.'

'I hope so but, if they don't, I've loved the process although it won't be quite as enjoyable making an exact duplicate.'

'You're not making them different?'

'I wouldn't dare! They might live in different countries but I guarantee they'll compare them and if Rebecca likes something in Felicity's journal more than in hers, or vice versa, I'll never hear the end of it.'

Veronica sounded fed up, which wasn't like her. 'They're really that bad?'

She nodded. 'Everything's about one-upmanship. They claim it's just a bit of fun and I should lighten up, but how does one *lighten up* when one's eldest daughter questions why one's youngest heard the news of their father's death first?'

I pressed my hand to my mouth, shocked that Veronica's daughter would make a comment like that at such a terrible time. And it had clearly had a lasting impact on Veronica, given her strained voice and pained expression.

'They were six and nine in this photo,' Veronica said, lightly tapping the image with her index finger. 'They were so close but it all changed around the time Felicity hit her teen years. Now, if there's a family gathering, they're all smiles and politeness but I see an undercurrent. Something happened to drive a wedge between them but, any time I raise it, they tell me I'm imagining it. I'm not. My girls despise each other and I don't know why.'

The pain in her voice and the hurt and confusion in her eyes made me think of Mum's disappointment that Marianne and I weren't close. I wished I could offer Veronica some advice or a solution but nothing Mum or I had tried had ever yielded positive results.

'I'm so sorry,' I said. 'I hope you know it's not your fault.'

Veronica looked up at me. 'How did you know I was blaming myself?'

'Because my mum blamed herself for my sister Marianne and me not getting on, but it wasn't her. She did everything she possibly could have to make us friends and, for whatever reason, Marianne didn't want to know. Sometimes siblings just don't get on and there's nothing anyone can do about it so please, please *don't* blame yourself. This is between them and maybe one day something will happen to make them address it and maybe it won't, but the most important thing is your relationship with them.'

She gave me a weak smile. 'This might sound foolish but I fear for what will happen to them when I'm gone. Hopefully that's a long way into the future but I don't want my legacy to be a broken family. I don't want my girls to lose contact, especially when it isn't just them – it's their children too. Family was always so important to Carson and me. No matter where we lived, we always stayed in touch with our extended family and I have this fear of it ending.'

'Have you ever shared this with them?'

'Goodness, no.'

'Maybe you should. It won't be easy but it might make a difference.'

A new member appeared at that moment and asked if she could have a private word with Veronica.

'Of course!' Veronica rose from her chair and patted my shoulder. 'Thanks for listening, Yvonne. I'll think about what you said.'

As she led the new member away, I watched her visibly switch from vulnerable to professional mode. It struck me that we were only a fortnight into January but, already this year, Paulette, Milly and Veronica had shared something incredibly personal with me and had seemed to appreciate and value my support. To think I'd once been concerned about being the outsider in an established friendship group. Now I felt like I was a key member who they all felt comfortable talking to about real things, real feelings, real life. They were all kind and friendly and I knew without a shadow of a doubt that I could trust them with my truth. I just needed to find the right moment and Cake & Craft Club wasn't it – far too many people around – but the right time would present itself and, when it did, I was ready to share.

I resumed working on my journal, focusing on the *places to see* section which wasn't quite as personal as some of the others. While I'd been in Keswick on Monday, I'd picked up a couple of travel brochures for European city breaks so I flicked to the pages covering Venice and started cutting round the images.

'Planning a trip to Venice?' Laughlin slipped into the chair Veronica had vacated.

I really liked Laughlin – found his quiet presence soothing – but I didn't feel as though I knew him as well as the others. This was an ideal opportunity to change that.

'It's on my *places to see* list for this year,' I said. 'Have you been?'

'Yes. When I retired, Noreen and I spent a couple of years

exploring Europe. We'd travel for a month or two, come home for a bit, travel again.'

'I bet that was incredible.'

'It really was. We visited some places two or three times to capture the changing seasons or to experience festivals. Venice was beautiful in May but we also went in October and caught the *acqua alta*.'

'What's that?' I asked, unfamiliar with the phrase.

'It translates as "high water". It's the exceptionally high tides in the Adriatic – a natural phenomenon which causes parts of Venice to flood. We thought it'd be interesting to see it like that too.'

'Do you have any photos?'

'Stacks of them.' He took his phone out of his waistcoat pocket and scrolled for a moment before passing it to me and talking me through the various locations. It was fascinating seeing the popular tourist spots with people wading through the water or crossing raised plinths.

'This is my favourite photo,' he said.

I smiled at the image of Laughlin wearing wellington boots and standing in a flooded St Mark's Square in front of the Basilica, carrying Noreen in a piggyback. Her feet were clad in bright yellow wellies and the pair of them looked as though they were laughing so much that Laughlin might drop her in the water at any moment.

'I can see why. It's a fantastic shot. Gosh, Laughlin, I bet you have some wonderful memories of your travels.'

He sat back in his chair, his smile speaking volumes. 'So many. Exploring Europe like we did was the best experience I've ever had. We were worried about all that time away from home, not to mention the expense, but we decided to throw caution to the wind and I'm so glad we did because, the year after we got back, Noreen's health started deteriorating and we'd never have been able to do all the things we did. Valuable life lesson in not putting off till tomorrow what can be done today.'

'You obviously loved Venice,' I said, 'but where else did you love?'

I didn't get much journalling done for the rest of the session, but I did have the most incredible virtual tour of Europe through Laughlin's photos and holiday stories and I could happily have listened for hours more. I'd been to some of the places he mentioned so I shared my own happy memories and had such a lovely afternoon. Although Laughlin hadn't confided in me about anything that might be bothering him, I felt a much closer connection to him through the memories he'd shared. For the briefest moment, I wondered about Laughlin as potential for a future romance but I dismissed the idea quickly. There wasn't a spark there. I was getting older brother vibes from him and I was happy to keep it that way.

Back at home a little later, I opened up my journal to my Venice page, reflecting on Laughlin's words – *not putting off till tomorrow what can be done today.* I'd added Venice as an unfulfilled bucket list entry with no real conviction around making it happen. I was the woman who hadn't even known that The Fox and Rabbit was under new ownership because I could never have entertained the idea of going in and dining alone. I was the woman who'd only ventured into The White Willow because I'd heard they offered a takeaway service. I was the woman who'd taken five years to walk around the village on my own. I ran my fingers over a sticker with the words 'Adventure starts here' sitting on top of a suitcase. Could I? A turn around the village was hardly on the same scale as boarding a plane and holidaying alone but did being single mean I could never travel again? I flicked back a few pages to the three things I was going to start doing this year.

'*Living*,' I muttered. 'I'm not doing that now, am I?' I flicked onto the next page – *loving*. 'If I met someone, I wouldn't have to travel alone.'

But that took me back to the conversation in the pub with Milly when she'd talked about having no idea how to meet someone new. The same applied to me. Where would I even begin to meet a new man? And the voice in my head said, *But you don't want to meet a* new *man. You want Will. You always have.* I ran my hands through my hair with a sigh. I'd already tried searching for Will and it was like looking for a needle in a haystack and, even if I had managed to find him, the likelihood of him being willing to even speak to me after what I did was miniscule. As for being single and still interested... I needed to forget about Will and focus on new love. There was somebody out there for me. There had to be.

15

Seeing Milly with her Castlerigg Stone Circle cross-stitch kit had inspired me. I used to love cross stitching and hadn't done any for years but, riffling through my crate of kits, nothing called to me. They were all beautiful designs but, having derived so much pleasure from creating a patchwork quilt that meant something to Paulette, I wondered if I could create a special cross stitch for one of the others. What about Laughlin? There were websites where customers could upload a photograph and have it converted into a pattern for a cross stitch and I could do that with the photo of him and Noreen during the *acqua alta*. I hadn't wanted to spoil the surprise by asking Laughlin for the photo but we were friends on Facebook and it didn't take much scrolling to find it there so I'd ordered the pattern.

I was busy working on it on Friday morning when Trevor announced, 'Visitor! Come in!'

'Have you got a minute?' Paulette asked when I answered the door.

'I've got all day. Would you like a cuppa?'

'I'd love a strong coffee.'

I led Paulette into the lounge and introduced her to Trevor, leaving them to get acquainted while I made the drinks.

'I have a huge favour to ask,' Paulette said the moment I handed over her coffee. 'I've been trying all week to smooth things over with Andrew, Joanne and Saffy but we're going round in circles and getting nowhere. I need to speak to them in person rather than over the phone so I've decided to drive down to theirs in the morning and have it out with them.'

'Just you or you and Saffy?'

'Just me. I need to come down pretty hard on Joanne with some home truths about what her tunnel vision is doing to her daughter and there's no need to subject Saffy to that. She's such a positive sweetheart but it's taking its toll on her. I've heard her crying in the night and it breaks my heart. So my favour is to ask whether there's any chance of Saffy spending the day with you tomorrow. I know she doesn't need a babysitter at her age but it's about having some company. She's really sociable and gets her energy from being around others. If she's left on her own for too long, she retreats into herself and starts overthinking things. What do you say?'

'It would be a delight to spend the day with her.' It really would, but my insecurities set in. 'You don't think she'd be bored spending a full day with me?'

'No chance. She'll bring her journalling with her and I guarantee she'll want to spend some time with Trevor. She had a cockatiel when she was younger and misses having a feathered friend.'

'In that case, she's more than welcome.' Saffy was lovely and I was honoured that Paulette had asked for my help. It backed up what I'd been thinking on Wednesday about how they all seemed to value my friendship.

Paulette sank back into the chair, clearly relieved at having sorted that out.

'What sort of things does she eat?' I asked.

'Pretty much anything, but there's no need to go to any trouble. I thought the pair of you could go to The Fox and Rabbit for lunch or tea, my treat to say thank you.'

The determined expression on Paulette's face told me not to argue about paying so I thanked her and reassured her that we'd have a great day because I genuinely believed we would. I wished Paulette hadn't been put in this position as I could imagine it would be an incredibly uncomfortable visit, but I was looking forward to spending the day with Saffy and doing what I could to help my friend in a time of need.

* * *

The following morning, Paulette dropped Saffy off at 7.15 a.m. She hadn't warned Andrew and Joanne of her plans, anticipating that she'd either be told to stay away or that Joanne would demand that Saffy accompany her. The early start lessened the possibility of them going out for the day before Paulette arrived and, as I was usually up and dressed early anyway, it was no problem for me.

'Good luck,' I said, hugging Paulette while Saffy wheeled her pink crate of journalling materials through to the dining room. 'You're doing the right thing.'

Saffy reappeared and hugged and thanked her grandma and, when I closed the door, she thanked me too.

'I'm looking forward to it,' I said. 'And there's somebody else who's looking forward to meeting you.'

Saffy grinned. 'Grandma said you have a parrot. What sort is he?'

'An African Grey called Trevor. Come and say hello.'

Saffy and Trevor bonded instantly. He climbed up her arm and sat on her shoulder as she fed him a slice of banana. She was eager to hear all his sounds and words and seeing them together reminded me of how much pleasure I'd always derived from watching Cliff and Trevor interacting.

After an hour or so, Saffy asked if there was any chance of looking round my craft room, telling me how much she loved spending time in Paulette's.

'Wow! That's a lot of quilts,' she said, her eyes scanning down the shelves. 'There has to be more than thirty there.'

'After you asked me how many I had, I counted them. Slight underestimate. There's fifty-seven and all those crates contain completed projects too.'

Saffy's eyes widened. 'You should deffo think about selling them. People go insane for homemade stuff like this.'

'Do they? Where would I find those people?'

'There's websites set up especially for creatives.' She rattled off a few names. 'I can help you get set up on one of them if you're interested. If you don't fancy going online, you could try craft fairs or even set up a pop-up shop.'

'A what?' I'd never heard that term before.

'It's where someone sets up a shop – usually in an empty retail unit – but only temporarily. You often get pop-up shops appearing in empty units at Christmas. It's better for a landlord to get some rent in from a two- or three-month lease than leave it standing empty all year.'

'I've seen Christmas shops like that but I didn't realise they had a name.'

'Do any of those suggestions appeal?'

I shrugged. 'Definitely not craft fairs. I did one maybe fifteen years ago and it was awful. One of my husband's customers had organised it and, when somebody dropped out at the eleventh hour, she begged me to step in. I'd never tried to sell my stuff before – I craft because I love it – so I wasn't keen, but she went on and on and I finally relented. What she hadn't told me was that the stallholders knew each other well, often attended fairs together, and they had an agreement not to undercut each other on the pricing of similar crafts. My quilts were selling well and nobody else's seemed to be and I naively assumed that it was because the customers liked my designs better. Turned out it was my prices that were the pull. Mine were significantly cheaper and several of the stallholders came over to have a right go at me. You'd think I'd deliberately set out to destroy their trade from the way they went on about it. I couldn't stay after that – packed up early and never attempted it since.'

'That sounds awful,' Saffy said. 'I can see why it'd put you off for life. What about selling online instead?'

'Depends on how intuitive the site is. I get by with tech, but I don't like anything complicated. The pop-up shop probably appeals more but I'm not sure I have enough crafts to make it work.' When Saffy pointed at the shelves, laughing, I clarified, 'Enough *different* crafts. Patchwork quilts are an expensive purchase – one thing I did at least learn from my craft fair nightmare. The fabric and materials are already pricey before you add in anything for labour so I don't imagine they're an item that'd sell every day and they're not to everyone's taste.'

Saffy scanned her eyes down the quilts, her brow furrowed. 'So you're saying that, for a pop-up shop to work, it'd need a big range of crafts.'

'Yes, and different price points too. Impulse buys, I think they call it.'

She nodded slowly before turning to face me. 'Here's an idea. You have fifty-seven quilts and, I dunno, ten crates full of crafts but you don't think there's enough variety. Grandma has a room full of homeless crafts too and I bet Milly, Veronica, Laughlin and your other friends from Cake & Craft Club do too. What if you did a collab? You'd have everything you need – massive range of stock, big-money items and impulse buys – and you'd be able to split the rent and share the workload.'

My initial instinct was to laugh and declare, *We couldn't do that!* But then I thought about the *living* entry on my *start* list. I hadn't really thought about what that meant – I just knew that I wasn't doing it. Joining Cake & Craft Club had been a great start and this could build on that. It would be a chance to do something different – something for me – and it'd also be an opportunity to meet some new people. And it wasn't as though I had any doubts about my crafts being of a high standard. It was one of the few things I didn't have any insecurities about, having learned how to sew from the best.

'It's actually a brilliant idea,' I said, smiling at Saffy. 'I don't know if the others would go for it but do you fancy sounding one of them out? I could ring Milly and see if she wants to join us for lunch at the pub. If she's a yes, we could take the idea to the others.'

'Perfect! You ring Milly and I'll google units in Keswick – see if there's any who'd consider a pop-up shop.'

As I waited for the call to Milly to connect, butterflies soared in my stomach and my heart raced with excitement. Imagine the five of us running our very own pop-up shop. What an adventure that could be!

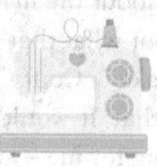

16

'I love it!' Milly declared, eyes shining when Saffy finished outlining her idea for the pop-up shop after we'd settled at a table in The Fox and Rabbit. 'My only problem is I wouldn't be able to fit in many shifts around my job but I'd do what I could. Do you have an empty shop in mind?'

'Saffy did some research earlier,' I said. 'There are a few in Keswick at the moment but we're not sure if they'll be options.'

Saffy nodded. 'One specified no pop-ups but I spoke to the other estate agents who said they'd look into it. One was fairly convinced it would be a no but the other sounded upbeat.'

We hadn't long finished our meal when that estate agent rang Saffy back with the news that the landlord would only consider a pop-up lease if we could provide proof of previous success which was absurd when the whole point of many pop-up businesses was trying something new.

'The best bet is to have a word with Veronica,' Milly said. 'She knows *every*one so, even if she doesn't have a direct contact, she'll know someone who does. Would Keswick be the best place for it? Maybe it's just me but it feels like a village thing. I know there wouldn't be the same footfall as in a town but if you pick the right village – a pretty, popular one – and get the advertising right...'

'Are there any shops in this village?' Saffy asked.

I shook my head. 'A few, but no empty ones and I don't think Pippinthwaite's right anyway. Not enough visitors. Willowdale would be better.'

'Oh, my gosh!' Milly grabbed my arm. 'There *is* an empty unit in Willowdale. It's opposite Lakeside Inn, next to the village store. Used to be a gift shop but it closed down a few years back and has been empty ever since.'

'Oh, yes! I know where you mean.'

Saffy looked up from her phone. 'There's no lease details online for it.'

'Veronica!' Milly and I said together.

I didn't have Veronica's phone number but Milly did. The phone signal was patchy in the corner where we were sitting so she nipped outside.

'Ooh, it's cold out!' She rubbed her hands together when she returned. 'She'll be with us in five minutes with Laughlin and Lancelot. They're on their way back from the vet's.'

'Is Lancelot okay?' I asked, feeling concerned.

'I don't know any details but I'm assuming so. I don't think they'd be joining us if there'd been a disaster.'

Veronica and Laughlin appeared five minutes later. Lancelot had a bandaged front leg and was wearing a plastic recovery cone round his neck and looking very sorry for himself, although he hadn't let the cone stop him from carrying Spud the red panda in his mouth. Laughlin shared that Lancelot had cut his leg on a piece of broken glass during their morning walk but some idiot had parked across the bottom of Laughlin's drive, blocking him in. Veronica, who lived nearby, had thankfully been free to give him a lift. They hadn't eaten so they placed a lunch order and, while we waited for it, Saffy outlined the idea which was met with enthusiasm from both of them.

'I'm not sure my creations are good enough to sell...' Laughlin started and we all shouted him down.

'Admittedly your early attempts at crocheting were a little... shall we say wobbly?' Veronica said, her choice of word making us laugh. 'You've perfected it now and those keyrings are adorable.'

'And your pyrography is fantastic,' Milly said, to which I added my wholehearted agreement.

'Do you still have Noreen's crafts?' Veronica asked.

'The garage is full of them. Noreen told me to clear them out but I didn't know what to do with them. I didn't think charity shops would be interested and there was no way I was going to throw them out after all the hours and care she'd put into them.'

'Do you think you'd be up for selling them in our pop-up shop?' Saffy asked him.

He nodded. 'I think Noreen would have liked that.'

I didn't miss the catch in his voice and the glisten of tears in his eyes. If we got to that point, I'd offer to help him sort through everything as he might appreciate the support. Clearing out a dead spouse's belongings for whatever reason wasn't easy. I'd managed the garage but all Cliff's clothes were still hanging in the wardrobe.

The conversation turned to the empty gift shop in Willowdale and Veronica was indeed in the know.

'It's a sad story, actually. A pair of sisters, Ava and Jocelyn, ran it for years but Jocelyn had an affair with Ava's husband and they ran off together. Ava closed the shop at Christmas three years ago, expecting to open again at Easter, but that became impossible after she discovered that Jocelyn had emptied the shop bank account and also kept the money that should have been paid to their suppliers for months previously. The business owed thousands. Ava needed to remortgage her house to pay the debts and find another job to pay the mortgage.'

'That's awful,' I said. 'Poor woman.'

Veronica nodded. 'Fortunately, there was a light in the darkness. The solicitor who dealt with it all was an old school friend of hers and they fell in love. I don't personally know either of them but a good friend of mine does and she says they're incredibly happy together – far happier than Ava had ever been with her husband.'

'What happened to Jocelyn and the husband?' Saffy asked.

'They split up and he returned, begging Ava to take him back. Can you believe that? How he had the front to do that after he'd had an affair with her sister, of all people, and destroyed their business and—' Veronica stopped abruptly and pressed her fingers to her lips. 'I'm so sorry. I can't believe I got on my high horse like that about people I don't personally know. Please forgive me for sounding like a terrible gossip, spilling out their private business.'

'You're not a gossip,' Milly assured her. 'We specifically asked and you shared what you know.'

'It wasn't very charitable of me to do so.'

Laughlin lightly touched her arm. 'I echo what Milly says. You are *not* a gossip. Gossips often share unconfirmed information and typically do it with unkind intentions or disapprovingly and that's simply not you.'

As Veronica smiled at him with evident gratitude, I marvelled at how Laughlin didn't say a lot but the things he said were so helpful and considered.

'I know a bit about it too,' Laughlin said, addressing the group. 'Noreen was friends with Ava. The premises situation is complicated. Ava and Jocelyn both had daughters who were really close. There's a flat above the shop and the intention was for the girls to move into it together when they were ready to leave home – a rent-free starter home for them both. When everything went wrong, the girls fell out and have been at loggerheads ever since. They won't live together but each refuses to let the other live in the flat. Jocelyn and her daughter want Ava to buy them out and, although Ava and her daughter would be willing to do that, they can't agree on a price. Jocelyn wants a 50:50 split and Ava wants more in compensation for the debts she had to settle so it's been stalemate for quite some time.'

'So we're going to have no chance of a pop-up shop there,' Milly said.

'Not necessarily,' Veronica said, looking thoughtful. 'If you'd been battling with your sister over an empty premises for three years and you had the chance to make some quick money for a few months, wouldn't you lay down your arms? Leave it with me and I'll put some feelers out next week.'

* * *

Laughlin wanted to get Lancelot home for some rest after his ordeal so Veronica drove them back to Willowdale and Milly joined Saffy and me at my house for a coffee. The three of us started a new journal for our potential pop-up shop. Saffy found the Facebook page for Willowdale Gifts and scrolled through dozens of photos of the inside, which gave us a good feel for the space and how the sisters had used it. None of us knew whether the pop-up shop would happen, but it was exciting imagining what it could be.

Milly had a light bite with us for tea before heading home, and Saffy and I had just settled down to watch some television when a text came through.

FROM PAULETTE

It's been a tough day. Setting off home now.
Hope you and Saffy are OK

TO PAULETTE

We're both great. Sorry it's been hard. Are you
OK to drive? Saffy's welcome to stay if you're
tired and want to book into a hotel overnight

Half an hour later, my phone rang and Paulette's name flashed up. Given the content of her message and the fact she'd phoned me rather than Saffy, I slipped into the kitchen to answer it.

'Can I take you up on your offer to have Saffy overnight?' Paulette asked.

'Of course. How did it go?'

'It was bad.' She sighed heavily. 'I'm drained so I've taken your advice and pulled into some services. The hotel here has a room free but I wanted to check about Saffy before I book it.'

'If she's happy to stay here, she's very welcome, but if she'd rather go home, I can drop her off – whatever she prefers. Do you want to speak to her yourself?'

'I'll check in and get settled first, then I'll ring her.'

'Okay. I'm here for you if you want to talk.'

'Thanks. I'll definitely take you up on that. It's just a bit raw at the moment.'

'Completely understand. You try to get some rest.'

Paulette rang Saffy shortly after and Saffy said she'd rather have the company overnight.

'Grandma said she was too tired to talk about it,' Saffy said as we drove to Willowdale so she could pack an overnight bag, 'but I'm guessing it was bad. Did she say anything else to you?'

'No, but I'm sure she'll explain everything when she's back tomorrow.'

'I feel so guilty that she's fallen out with Mum and Dad because of me.'

Her voice had a wobble and I hated how much pain this situation was causing Saffy and Paulette.

'You do know that none of this is your fault, Saffy? I know your grandma would say the same if she was here.'

'It's one thing Mum having a strop with me, but why does she have to take it out on Grandma too? It's not fair.'

'No, it's not, but your grandma was never going to stand back and let you take all the flack. She's a strong, caring woman who loves her family and wants to keep everyone happy and at peace, which means stepping in as a mediator if things get heated. That's a tough role and comes with some backlash, but your grandma's made of sturdy stuff and she'll bounce back from whatever happened today. She just needs some sleep first.'

Saffy didn't speak but, out of my peripheral vision, I saw her nodding. When we arrived at Paulette's house, I stayed in the car with the heater on while Saffy dashed inside. Five minutes later, she returned with a backpack.

'Can we drive round to see the shop?' she asked, brightness back in her voice. 'I can't picture where it is.'

I drove into the centre of the village and parked outside The White Willow. We walked back on ourselves past the village green and across the road. Several terraced properties – whitewashed with slate roofs and slate stonework round the windows – curved round the corner from the main road into a side street. The small general store was on the corner, then Willowdale Gifts and the bakery.

'Ooh! Pretty!' Saffy declared. 'Weird that they left that sign up.'

A sign was taped to the inside of a glass panel in the door.

Thank you for your custom. Taking our winter break. Open
again at Easter.

'Yeah, you'd think they'd have removed it by now,' I agreed.

Saffy stood back and looked up at the building. 'It's bigger than I thought. It's giving me all the vibes.'

I wasn't sure what *all the vibes* were but I certainly had a good feeling about the shop and could see it being perfect for us. There was a large bay window and I could picture a range of our crafts beautifully displayed in it. Shutters across the back of the window prevented us from seeing into the shop itself and, even though Saffy activated the torch on her phone and shone it through the glass on the door, we still couldn't see inside.

'Best to come back in daylight,' I said, 'but at least you know where it is now.'

'Yeah, that was really helpful, thanks. And thanks for what you said about Grandma earlier. I sometimes worry about her living on her own away from all the family but I get it now. Why would she want to move when she's got good friends like you here?'

What a lovely thing to say! It was icy cold but Saffy's comments gave me a warm glow as we walked back to the car. This time last year, I could never have imagined I'd have a group of friends with whom I might be going into business, who confided in me, came to me for help and to whom I was going to open up about my past. Thank goodness I'd seen that Cake & Craft Club advert.

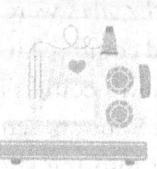

17

When I entered the lounge the following morning holding a tray of tea and toast, Saffy was standing in front of the mantelpiece.

'Is that your husband?' she asked.

'Yes. That's Cliff.'

'He has a kind face.'

I smiled. 'He had a kind heart too. He'd do anything for anyone, especially me.'

'How did you meet?'

I placed the tray on the coffee table and we settled on either end of the sofa with a plate of buttered toast each.

'He was quite literally the boy next door. His mum, Mrs Kellerman, was a brilliant pianist and I'd sit in the garden listening to the most beautiful music drifting through her open windows. I was desperate to learn the piano and be able to play like her so Mum asked her if she'd teach me. She said no because she played for pleasure and had no aspirations to teach but, after four years of us pestering, she eventually gave in. I had my first lesson on my tenth birthday. Mrs Kellerman was adamant it was a one-month trial and, if I didn't listen to her properly or didn't practise, it would end. But it didn't end because I fell in love with the piano and practising for hours every day was a pleasure – never a chore.'

Saffy looked around the room, frowning. 'I can't see a piano.'

'That's because I don't have one.' I knew Saffy would ask me why. The real explanation was far too complicated so I threw in something plausible, even though I didn't feel comfortable lying. 'After I got married, life got in the way and I never found the time to practise. Anyway, Cliff was Mrs Kellerman's only child. He'd always been polite, smiling and saying hello if we saw him around, but he was eight years older than me – eighteen when I started my lessons – so I never imagined we'd become friends. There wasn't much time for chit chat before lessons – Mrs Kellerman was a stickler for starting promptly – but I had a difficult relationship with my dad and sister so it was nice to know that somebody other than my mum was interested in my life. My mum died when I was twelve and, as Cliff had lost his dad at a similar age, he was a great support and we became friends. When I was twenty, Mrs Kellerman sadly passed away. Cliff didn't have any other family so it was a lot to deal with and I helped him. We became closer and got married a year later.'

'Aw, that's so sweet. I'm sorry he isn't here anymore.'

I glanced towards his photos and nodded. 'Me too. He was one of a kind.'

A notification on Saffy's phone drew her attention away from me and I sipped on my tea, my heart pounding. I wasn't used to questions about Cliff and me and I'd needed to pick my words so carefully to make it the truth... but not the whole truth.

Saffy only ate one piece of toast and admitted her stomach was in knots, worried about what her parents had said to Paulette. I suggested more journalling to distract her. We couldn't add anything else to the pop-up shop journal until we'd heard back from Veronica so we sat at the dining table together focusing on our personal journals. I was careful with the pages I worked on in front of Saffy, conscious of being unwilling and unable to answer the questions that might arise from some of the entries. The Venice one was complete, as was the one about a new home for me, and I didn't mind if Saffy saw my *stop* entries of *feeling sorry for myself* and *chasing a relationship with Marianne*. The former could easily be tied into losing Cliff and she already knew I didn't get on with my sister.

Trevor had joined us at the table and kept strutting up and down, nodding at our work, as though he was the supervisor. Every so often, he flapped his wings and sent a few stickers flying in all directions but it was otherwise a productive session in which I didn't reveal anything I didn't want to. Until I turned to a fresh page in my journal where I'd slotted the original scribbled list of entries. At the same moment, Trevor flapped his wings and the list drifted over to Saffy. She laughed as she picked it up and handed it back to me, but not before she'd glanced at it.

'I didn't mean to look,' she said, her cheeks reddening. 'Sorry.'

'It's okay. Trevor obviously wanted you to.' My heart pounded. 'What did you see?'

'You want to start loving and you want to feel love. I couldn't help it. There were—'

'Red hearts,' I said at the same time as her. I wished she hadn't seen the entries but it could have been worse. I could have written more and given myself away or she could have seen some of the other entries.

'Have you dated since your husband died?' she asked.

'No.'

'But you want to? Or were those entries about something different? Tell me to shut up if you don't want to talk about it. I know I ask a lot of questions. Grandma keeps telling me to switch my filter on, but it's only because I'm interested in people.'

I gave her a reassuring smile. 'It's all right and, yes, it *is* about finding a loving relationship but I'm not sure it'll ever happen.'

'Why not?'

So many reasons! 'Because I'm too old.'

'Too old? You're younger than Grandma and, if she wanted to find someone else, I wouldn't think she was too old so you're certainly not. How old are you anyway?'

'Sixty today.'

Her eyes widened and the smile slipped from her face and I wished I hadn't added the *today* part.

'You *are* joking.'

I shook my head.

'It's your sixtieth birthday today?'

'Yes.'

She glanced towards the mantelpiece and I knew what was coming next.

'Where are your cards?'

'I haven't got any.'

Saffy raised her eyebrows at me and then she smiled. 'Oh! Because your birthday's on a Sunday?'

'I won't get any in the post tomorrow either.'

The shocked expression returned. 'What about presents?'

I shook my head.

'But...'

'The only family I have left is my sister and she's never sent me a card or bought me a gift in her whole life, even when we were kids, and...' I sighed. It was embarrassing to admit it, but I might as well throw it on the table. 'I don't have any friends. Well, not long-term friends. I only joined the Cake & Craft Club in

September so everyone connected to that is a new friend and none of them know it's my birthday today.'

Saffy's eyes glistened and I feared she was going to start crying.

'I'm not bothered. Age is just a number and today's just another date on the calendar.' I sounded positive but, as I heard the words out loud, I felt far from it. Birthdays should be special, especially milestone ones like sixty, but I'd grown used to my birthday not being celebrated since Cliff's passing that it had never entered my head to mention it to my friends. I could have said something in the pub yesterday. I could have mentioned it at Cake & Craft Club last week when Veronica was handing out invitations for her birthday party in February. Feeling my throat tighten, I returned to Saffy's original question.

'Going back to finding love, I wouldn't know where to start.'

'Apps?'

I rolled my eyes at her and she laughed.

'Maybe your dream hottie will walk into the shop, your eyes will lock over one of your patchwork quilts and you'll both fall hopelessly in love.'

I thought about Milly's recent comment about wanting to meet someone naturally and smiled at Saffy. 'That would be lovely. You never know!' And you really didn't. It *could* happen, especially in this exciting new world I was creating for myself.

'I don't know whether I want another boyfriend,' Saffy said. 'I don't mean ever – just not right now. I need to decide whether university's my thing but a different course somewhere else. I'm fairly sure it's not, but what do I do instead? I think I'd better get my own life sorted before I think about boyfriends.'

'That sounds sensible. There's definitely no chance of you and Kyle getting back together?'

'None. He changed when we got to uni. He was out partying

every night and skipping lectures and that's not me. Six months ago, I'd have sworn it wasn't him either but his parents were really strict and I think the freedom went to his head. I thought he'd calm down when the novelty wore off but it didn't. He kept turning up at my flat drunk, causing beef with my flatmates. This one time, he threw up on the kitchen floor. My flatmates got really aggy about that. Like it was my fault!'

'Oh, Saffy, that sounds horrendous.'

'It was, but it was the trigger I needed to go *this isn't for me*. I hated the uni and my course, I hadn't made friends, and I didn't recognise my boyfriend anymore.'

'You told your parents this?'

'No. Mum's besties with Kyle's mum and, because his parents are so strict with him, he's fed them a pack of lies about why we split up. He told them *he* was the one who'd ended it and it was because *I* was seeing someone else. Who does that? I get that he's only trying to protect himself but why throw me under the bus?'

I didn't like the sound of this Kyle at all and felt strangely protective towards Saffy, glad that she'd sent him packing.

'I've got evidence,' she said. 'I could prove to my mum that Kyle was the problem but I want her to believe me without me having to show her it. I don't get why she was so quick to assume the worst of me.'

'What sort of evidence?'

'Photos of him passed out on the sofa in the kitchen with sick down his T-shirt. I only took them cos I wanted to show him the state he'd got into, hoping it'd make him want to sort his life out. I've got videos too. One of my flatmates was especially aggy and she filmed him every time he turned up plastered. She sent me the films saying she was going to report me and get me kicked out of halls.'

I didn't like the sound of this flatmate either. Saffy came

across as such a lovely young woman and threatening her like that for something she hadn't personally done seemed particularly harsh.

'There's obviously still a lot to sort out with your parents, but how are you feeling now that you've officially left and collected your belongings?'

'So relieved. No doubts, no regrets. I'm not even worried about what to do next. Something'll crop up. I'm just disappointed in my parents for making this a million times harder than it needed to be, and for upsetting Grandma. I hope she's okay.'

'She'll be fine, Saffy. I know she will.'

'I'm thinking we maybe don't say anything about the pop-up shop today. It might be too much to throw at her. I'll give her a day or so to settle back in first.'

'That's a good idea.' I marvelled at Saffy's emotional maturity as well as how brave she was. She had no idea what to do next yet she was remaining positive about it, believing that everything would work out fine. I wished I'd had some of her self-belief when I'd been her age. My life might have gone in a completely different direction if I had.

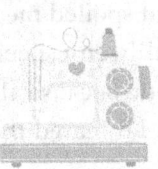

18

The village hall blinds were pulled down when I arrived for Cake & Craft Club the following Wednesday, which was unusual. I opened the outer door, walked through the entrance hall and stopped dead. There was paper covering the glass panels of the double doors into the main hall so I couldn't see inside. Confused, I pulled on the right door and shrieked at the yell of, 'Surprise!'

Party poppers exploded and paper streamers were unfurled in my direction as Veronica led a chorus of 'Happy Birthday'. There were sixtieth-birthday banners taped across the walls and a giant pink helium balloon with a silver '60' in the middle. How on earth did they know about my birthday? I caught Saffy's eye and she flashed me one of her wide smiles. Of course!

'Thank you all so much,' I said when they'd finished with three cheers. 'That was a lovely surprise.'

'There's more,' Paulette said.

The group parted, revealing a table on which there was a birthday cake and a stack of presents, some wrapped and others in gift bags. Tears pricked my eyes.

'All for me?' I whispered, struggling to force the words out over the lump in my throat. I'd never seen anything like it. Mum had always bought me gifts but, after she died, Dad never bothered. He didn't even acknowledge the day but Mrs Kellerman and Cliff signed a card, gave me some new sheet music and a box of chocolates and got me to blow out the candles on a birthday cake. After we married, Cliff had spoiled me on every birthday and the first one without him had been especially hard – not because I had no gifts and cards but because there was nobody there to make me feel special and I'd feared there never would be again. Until now.

'Can't let a landmark birthday pass unnoticed,' Veronica said. 'Happy birthday, Yvonne.'

I smiled at her gratefully before addressing the group. 'I can't believe you've done this. It's so kind of you all. I'm sure I'm going to love every single one of these gifts. Thank you.'

A little later, we'd all had a helping of birthday cake and were working on our individual crafts. I'd made some good progress on the cross stitch for Laughlin but I couldn't bring it with me without giving the game away so I was working on a floral spring-coloured patchwork quilt kit which I'd found in my craft room. Saffy was sitting with Laughlin and he was showing her how to do pyrography so I went over to join them.

'I can't believe you did that for me, Saffy. I'm so touched.'

'Birthdays are special and everyone's should be celebrated. I couldn't bear to think of you having no cards or pressies.'

'I think it's the kindest thing anyone's ever done for me so thank you.'

Paulette joined us and asked if she could have a quick word with me. We slipped out into the lobby.

'You look brighter than you did on Sunday,' I said, giving her a weak smile. One look at her red eyes when she'd collected Saffy and I could have cried for her.

'I'm not one for crying. I feel deeply but it's rare it spills over into tears. Probably comes from my career choice. The last thing a grieving family needs is for the professionals running their funeral to be blubbering wrecks. But what Andrew and Joanne said to me on Saturday hurt me so very deeply that it was like someone had turned a tap on. That's the real reason I had to pull over on the way home.'

'What did they say?' I asked.

Paulette glanced down the hall before steering me away from the door, which signalled to me that she hadn't told Saffy what she was about to reveal to me.

'You know I said Andrew's my stepson – my second husband's son? I've always treated him and his sister, Nicola, like they were my own. Their mum died when they were young and, bless their hearts, neither of them really remembered her. I never asked them to call me "Mum" and neither did Stephen, but they both wanted to and we've always been close. Joanne, on the other hand, is an acquired taste. She's opinionated and controlling and...' She closed her eyes as she took a deep breath.

'Apologies. I don't want to speak ill of her. Andrew clearly loves her and doesn't seem to be fazed by some of the concerning behaviours I see. She'd already told me to stop interfering several times but, on Saturday, she took it a step further – said I'm not allowed to get involved and I'm not entitled to have an opinion on the matter because I'm not Saffy's *real* grandma.'

I gasped. 'She actually said that?'

'Those exact words, followed up by me not being Andrew's *real* mum.'

'What did Andrew say?'

'Absolutely nothing and that hurt me even more. I thought

he'd tell her she'd gone too far but he just sat there nodding along to everything she said. Then she told me to leave and he *still* said nothing. It broke my heart.'

'Oh, Paulette. I'm so sorry.'

I drew her into a hug and could feel her shaking as she held me. How could anyone say something so cruel to such a lovely woman?

'That would break anyone's heart,' I said when we parted. 'Have you heard anything from them since?'

'Not a word. Saffy hasn't spoken to them either. She's being remarkably strong about it, although she doesn't know what I've just told you. She'd be disgusted and I don't want to poison her against her parents. As for what happens next, the ball's in their court. Saffy's welcome to stay with me as long as she wants and, as she's officially an adult, they can't stop her. I'd just rather she was here with their blessing.'

'I'm sure they'll see reason eventually.'

'I hope so. She's their only daughter! I don't understand why they're behaving like this. Anyway, I wanted to thank you for everything you did last weekend. Saffy had a wonderful time with you, she's completely in love with Trevor and she's bursting with excitement about this pop-up shop idea which, incidentally, I think is brilliant. I'd love to be involved. Things have been a bit chaotic so far this year but I haven't forgotten my promise about a raincheck on the Chinese. I was thinking that, as soon as Veronica has news about Willowdale Gifts, we should all get together round mine and do some planning.'

I smiled at her. 'That would be great. But are you sure you're all right?'

'I'm a great believer in the power of time and space for resolving problems. Saffy's the important person in all of this and I think she's exactly where she needs to be to plan the next stage of her life. Andrew and Joanne will come round eventually and they'll make their peace with her.'

'Will they make their peace with you?'

She shrugged. 'I hope so, but things won't be the same. I don't hold grudges, Yvonne, but Joanne said some things that were unforgivable. It appears she's never liked me and she unleashed two decades' worth of contempt. We can't recover from that and, sadly, I can't envisage a scenario where Andrew can be in my life without it causing a rift between them so it looks like...' Paulette had managed to keep her voice steady until that point, but it broke. 'It looks like I've lost him,' she whispered, tears pooling in her eyes.

I pulled her into another hug. 'I know I don't know him but I'm sure he'll find a way to have you in his life because who wouldn't want you to be? You're amazing, Paulette, and I'm here for you to help you through this.'

She squeezed me tightly and wiped her eyes as she pulled away and nodded her head towards the outer door. 'I remember seeing you out there last September looking like you were about to do a runner. I'm so glad you didn't.'

'Me too.'

We smiled at each other and I felt the warmth of friendship. And I felt as though I could definitely let Paulette into my secret. I just needed to find the right moment.

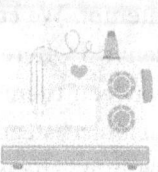

19

The raincheck on a Chinese came sooner than anticipated. Paulette rang me the following morning to say that Veronica had news about Willowdale Gifts and wanted to share it with us all over a takeaway.

'I'm meeting my friends for tea tonight,' I told Trevor as he preened himself in front of the mirror. Friends. Plural. I'd never in my whole life made a statement like that and now here I was at sixty years old with the most lovely group of friends. I'd never expected that. And if it wasn't too late to make friends at my age, it wasn't too late to find love either.

'Pretty bird!' Trevor called, followed moments later by, 'Visitor!'

I glanced out of the window where a car had stopped.

'That's the estate agent to value the house. I'll pop you back in your cage for the moment but you can come out again when he's gone.'

Having made the long-overdue decision to move, I saw no point in hanging around. I'd arranged for three estate agents to visit at intervals across the day and first up was the one who'd sold Betsy's house.

It was the third estate agent who I warmed to the most – a woman in her forties called Lorna who made a beeline for Trevor.

'Who's this beauty, Yvonne?' she asked, crouching down beside Trevor's cage.

'Trevor. He's thirty-eight.'

'Aren't you a stunner, Trevor?'

'Pretty bird!' Trevor agreed.

Lorna turned to me with a wide smile. 'I'm totally in love and I could spend hours chatting to him, but I'd better do my job. Should we start upstairs?'

After she'd gathered measurements and photos, I signed the sales agreement with a smile. It was really happening and, while I was sure I'd have a few emotional moments saying goodbye to the house I'd shared with Cliff, my gut told me it was the right thing to do.

'It'll be a pleasure to sell your home for you, Yvonne,' Lorna said when I walked her to the door. 'It's in a beautiful condition and these houses are a good size in a great location so I don't anticipate it'll stick around for long. I'll have it up on the website by the weekend and a "for sale" board up within the next couple of days.'

I waited on the doorstep for her to get into her car and was about to close the door when Christian cycled into the cul-de-sac, heading for his house. He changed direction and pedalled across to me as Lorna pulled away.

'Don't tell me you're moving too,' he said, standing astride his bike.

I nodded. 'The house is too big for just Trevor and me. If feels like time to move on, especially as...' I stopped myself before I could speak ill of my new neighbours but I hadn't managed to avoid a glance next door and Christian had clearly noticed.

'Not going too well with the new neighbours?' he asked.

'I miss Betsy,' I said, hoping that would be enough.

'If it's any consolation, I've tried to engage with them several times and they're not interested.'

I smiled gratefully. 'It's not just them. I don't feel like I belong here anymore. Most of the neighbours are really young and have families.'

Christian glanced around the houses, frowning. 'I'd never thought about it before but you're right. It'll be thirty years or so before any of this lot are eligible for bus passes. So where are you moving to?'

'Staying in the area – hopefully Willowdale – but I've just started looking. Do you think you'll ever move?'

'I don't know. It's interesting what you say about the house being too big for you. I never felt like that about my place until Emma moved out to live with Killian. Now I feel like I'm rattling around on my own and it's far too quiet.'

'I did wonder about Emma,' I said. 'I haven't seen her around for a while.'

'They've bought an old barn and are doing the conversion themselves so, when she's not working, she's there. She was asking after you the other day and I realised I'd barely seen you. I've been helping them at the barn so I've not been around much. I wondered if you'd like to come over for a coffee at some point.'

'That would be great. Any day except Wednesday works for me.'

A sudden gust of wind made us both shiver.

'We'd better get out of this cold. I'll find out when I'm needed at the barn over the next couple of weeks and give you a shout.'

Christian hopped back onto his bike and pedalled across the road to his house. Had he just asked me out? No! Of course not! He was a friendly neighbour offering a catch-up over a coffee. But we'd never done that and he had just admitted that he was rattling around in his house on his own which could suggest he was lonely. I shook my head, tutting to myself as I reached for the front door handle. Christian Wynterson was a handsome man and there was no way he'd ever be interested in me. Would he? As he wheeled his bike across his drive, he turned back and smiled and waved in my direction, causing the butterflies in my stomach to stir. I stared into the space he'd left, my brain racing. Was I attracted to Christian? Surely not! So why the butterflies? Closing the door behind me, I hugged myself and rubbed my arms to try and warm them up.

'What do you think of Christian Wynterson?' I asked Trevor as I released him from his cage. He shuffled along my forearm and looked up at me, as though waiting for me to continue. 'Could you see us together?'

I glanced across the road towards Christian's house and the butterflies stirred once more.

'I don't understand, Trevor. Why now?' We'd had plenty of conversations before and I'd never reacted like that.

'Pretty boy,' he said, making me laugh.

'Yes, he's very handsome, but I've always thought that and it's never affected me before.'

'Come in!' Trevor cawed. 'Pretty boy, come in!'

'Is that you giving me permission to let Christian into my life?' I said, stroking Trevor's plumage. I was joking but something about permission resonated with me. I gently placed Trevor in front of his mirror and wandered through to the dining room where my journal was open on the emotions section. Could that be the reason for the butterflies? That I'd given myself permission to feel love? The idea both thrilled and terrified me... but more of the former.

20

'I have some news,' Veronica said after we'd all arrived at Paulette's house and gathered round the dining table with drinks. 'Some *good* news.'

'We can have the shop?' Milly asked.

'We can. Ava and Graeme – her solicitor and former school friend – are now married so I arranged to meet them both. Ava couldn't face going into another year battling with her sister so they agreed a price and, shortly before Christmas, Ava became the sole owner of the building. The plan was to reopen the gift shop but Ava's mother's about to start chemo so Ava's putting things on hold to support her. They loved the idea of a pop-up shop and would be willing to start with a three-month lease and take it from there a month at a time.'

'If it does well, we'd probably want to stay open for the Christmas trade,' Paulette said. 'Would Ava want to be back in before then?'

'No. Her plans are on hold for at least a year so Christmas would be fine.'

Christmas? It seemed so far away but it would, of course, be the perfect time of year for sales. I could already picture my festive patchwork quilts, quilted advent calendars and placemats alongside pyrography *Santa stop here!* signs and crocheted Christmas decorations. Looking at the excited expressions around the table, I suspected I wasn't the only one drifting into the season of festive crafts.

'What if it did so brilliantly that you wanted a permanent shop?' Saffy asked.

'That might be jumping a little far ahead,' Paulette said.

'Perhaps,' Veronica said, 'but perhaps not. I think this idea of Saffy's is wonderful and you never know. Some businesses fly and, with the right branding and marketing, there's no reason why ours won't be one of them.'

'Can I show you something?' Saffy asked, opening the laptop she'd had in front of her. 'I know we haven't talked about names yet so this is just for illustration, but I've been tinkering this week.'

She turned the laptop round, eliciting a collective gasp. Saffy had designed a logo and signage for a shop called Created With Love. The 'T' in 'Created' was formed from buttons, the 'I' in 'With' was a needle and the 'L' in 'Love' was made from mosaic letters. The three words were then captured within a heart, the outline of which was made from various crafting materials and equipment.

'That's stunning,' I said, taking it in. 'That must have taken you ages.'

Saffy shrugged. 'Not really. I've always been quick at drawing.'

'What do we think of Created With Love as a name?' Veronica asked. 'I personally think it's lovely. Only three words but it says exactly what we do.'

Everyone agreed that Saffy had cracked the name and the

logo. She insisted she was happy to 'take notes', but nobody had any suggestions. What she'd done was exceptional.

Our takeaway arrived and we tucked in, the conversation dominated by our new business venture. Veronica, Paulette, Laughlin, Milly and I agreed that we wanted to give Created With Love our best shot and were happy to equally split the up-front rent. There were so many other decisions to make including the opening hours and how we covered them fairly, bearing in mind Milly worked and Veronica and Paulette both had several diary commitments each week.

'I don't mind working more hours,' I said.

'I don't either.' Laughlin caught my eye and I had a feeling he was thinking the same as me – gratitude at filling the empty days without our spouses.

'You've got Lancelot to look after, though,' Veronica said.

'And Yvonne's got Trevor,' Saffy said.

I smiled at her. 'I'm sure we'll be able to work something out.'

'I've done some research on how craft collabs like this work,' Saffy said. 'The most commonly used model is for the crafter to take a percentage of the asking price and for the shop to take the rest. The rent, overheads and any wages would be paid from the shop's percentage.'

We fired questions at Saffy and laughed as Veronica raised her hands to silence us.

'I have a suggestion. Why don't we take the rest of the week to think carefully about this? Consider the hours you'd be willing and able to work each week and also think about the crafts you've made and the price you'd need for them to cover materials, labour and some profit. The village hall's free from noon on a Wednesday so we could have a couple of hours together next week before Cake & Craft Club. I love this idea and I want to be part of it, but it's important we do some number crunching first to see if it's viable.'

'That sounds like a good plan.' Paulette reached for a spring roll and dipped it in a pot of hoisin sauce. 'Looks like we all have some homework to do.'

Every time we tried to steer the conversation away from Created With Love, somebody threw in an idea and talk focused back on our proposed business. Yes, we had some work to do and Veronica was absolutely right to ensure we considered the practicalities, but if enthusiasm could have any influence on the success of a business, Created With Love would soar.

After we'd cleared away and moved into the lounge with hot drinks, Saffy's phone rang.

'It's my bestie!' she announced, her eyes sparkling as she excused herself and rushed upstairs.

'My goodness, your Saffy's brimming with talent,' Veronica said, her voice full of admiration. 'You must be so proud, Paulette.'

'I am. She's always been artistic. I assumed she'd go to art college rather than sixth form and I was surprised when none of her A levels were art-related. I suspect now that it was her mum's influence and not what Saffy wanted.'

'What sort of things does she like drawing?' I asked.

'Anything and everything. She's pretty versatile. I don't think she's found her preferred style yet.'

'Is she staying for long?' Veronica asked. 'Because, if she is, she might like to consider one of the art classes at the village hall or perhaps an evening class at the art college.'

'You know who she should speak to?' Milly said. 'What's the name of that illustrator who got a book deal with her fiancé? It was in the paper. They live in Willowdale. His aunt and uncle own The White Willow.'

'Oh, I know who you mean!' Paulette said. 'I think her name's Autumn.'

Veronica nodded. 'Autumn Laine. I was having a senior moment then but when you mentioned The White Willow, it fell into place.'

'I'll take Saffy to The White Willow for lunch tomorrow and ask Kelly and Aled if they can put her in touch with Autumn,' Paulette said. 'It would be great for her to chat to someone who's made a career from their art.'

'I wonder how many people end up doing jobs they don't want to because they were pushed into it by their parents,' Laughlin said. 'I wanted to be an artist when I was at school but my dad was a mechanical engineer so three guesses what I became?'

'A circus clown,' Milly joked.

'Brain surgeon,' Veronica suggested.

'Stripper,' Paulette cried.

Laughlin's eyes widened before he spluttered with laughter and flexed his biceps. 'Oh, yes! I can see why you'd say that.'

The conversation moved onto how we'd fallen into our careers and the jobs we'd loved or hated.

'I wouldn't say I had a career as such,' I said when it was my turn. 'I got a job in the typing pool at the council when I left school and I did that for several years until Cliff set up his own business. I then helped run that, making appointments, keeping the books, ordering supplies. I can't say it was a dream job but it was easy work and home-based so I could do my crafts around it.'

'There must have been something you'd have loved to do, though,' Milly said. 'Even if it was only one of those fantasy jobs kids have like being a firefighter or driving a train.'

I pondered for a moment and a dream popped into my head that I'd forgotten about long ago.

'There was something, but it really was the stuff of fantasies. I wanted to be a concert pianist.'

'You play the piano?' Veronica asked. 'I didn't realise.'

'I haven't played for years. I had lessons with Cliff's mum from age ten and I passed grade eight, which is the highest grade you can get without going on to complete a diploma.'

When I was awarded my eighth distinction in a row, I told Mrs Kellerman that I was going to be a concert pianist, expecting her to laugh, but she'd looked at me solemnly and said, 'You could be if you really wanted to, if you really believed,' and then she changed the subject and I wondered if I'd imagined that she – the woman who barely ever praised, only sporadically muttering a nondescript *good* or *well done* – had given me the most enormous compliment.

'Grade eight?' Laughlin's eyes widened. 'You must be exceptionally talented. Noreen used to play. She made it to grade six and attempted seven a couple of times before giving up on the exams. She said it took considerable dedication and talent to get all the way through.'

'Why don't you play anymore?' Milly asked.

My heart was pounding. What had possessed me to share that particular childhood dream? Of course it was going to lead to questions. Why couldn't I have said something generic like wanting to be a nurse or a teacher? Everyone would have accepted that and moved on. I was ready to talk to them – but not as a group. When I shared my story, it needed to be one at a time, probably starting with Paulette or Milly. An audience was far too intimidating.

Everyone's eyes were on me and I shuffled in my chair. 'Erm, I just... Life, you know. I got married, Cliff set up his business, we moved house, and there never seemed to be enough hours in the day.'

Paulette caught my eye and gave me an almost imperceptible nod. Nobody else seemed to have picked up on my discomfort but I knew she had.

'Did I ever tell you all that I used to play the violin?' she asked, addressing the group. 'I use the word *play* loosely. Bet my parents wished there weren't enough hours in the day for me to play it.'

'Were you bad?' Milly asked.

'*Bad* would have been a compliment. I was dire. No musical ability whatsoever. I sent cats fleeing, made dogs howl, made small children cry as their ears bled...'

Everyone laughed as Paulette continued her tale of musical incompetence. She caught my eye once more and I gave her a grateful smile. For the first time ever, I felt as though I had somebody in my life who I could talk to about why I didn't play the piano anymore and I wanted to tell her sooner rather than later. Hopefully an opportunity would present itself.

Saffy rejoined us shortly after and, from her big smile, it had clearly done her good to catch up with her best friend. The conversation was still about music and Milly had surprised us by sharing that she was one of the few kids at primary school who'd been able to make the recorder sound pleasant. She'd graduated to a larger tenor recorder and she still played it most days to give her a break from her editing.

'Saffy can play the guitar,' Paulette declared, pride obvious in her voice, 'and she's got a beautiful singing voice. She was in a band at school and college.'

When we discovered Saffy had her guitar with her, we were eager to hear her play and sing, and she treated us to an impromptu concert which culminated in us all singing along to 'Hey Jude'.

Driving home at the end of the evening, I couldn't stop smiling. A year ago, I'd never have imagined a scenario where I spent an evening with a room full of people discussing going into business together and singing to The Beatles. When I'd written *living* in my journal as one of the things I wanted to start doing, I hadn't been sure what that might look like. This was it! I *was* doing it right now!

I spent the early part of Saturday morning continuing with my cross stitch for Laughlin before driving over to The White Willow to meet Paulette, Saffy and another two of Paulette's grandchildren for lunch. Paulette's youngest daughter, Julia, and her husband were at a wedding but the invitation hadn't included children so their two girls – fifteen-year-old Mila and thirteen-year-old Naomi – were spending the weekend with their grandma.

When she'd rung to invite me first thing this morning, Paulette had told me she wouldn't be offended if I said no because, now that she'd spoken the words out loud, she could appreciate that spending time with someone else's grandchildren perhaps wasn't that appealing a prospect. I assured her I was flattered to be asked and if Mila and Naomi were anything like Saffy, it would be a pleasure to meet them.

It would fit well with two of my journal entries to *stop hiding myself away* and to *see more of the local area with my new friends.* I'd wanted to dine in The White Willow so this was the perfect opportunity. As it was a dry and bright day, Paulette had told me the girls were planning to walk into Keswick afterwards and suggested the two of us go for a walk alongside the lake. I dressed in suitable clothes and put some thick socks, my walking boots, a waterproof coat and my hat in the car.

As I approached The White Willow, nervous butterflies fluttered round my stomach. I hated that I felt that way but I couldn't be too hard on myself about it when the sensation came from so many years of hiding away from people and feeling anxious about meeting anyone new. It didn't matter that they were a couple of teenage girls – they were still unknown.

I managed to find a parking space right outside the café and could see Paulette and her granddaughters already at a table perusing menus. Within minutes of joining them, the butterflies had settled. Mila and Naomi were as lovely as I'd anticipated and it was touching to see how close they were to Saffy and how much they looked up to her.

I recognised the woman who came over to take our order as the one who'd taken my cake order on New Year's Eve. She greeted Paulette warmly and they commented on how quickly the first few weeks of January had flown by.

'Yvonne, this is Kelly. She owns The White Willow with her husband, Aled,' Paulette said. 'Kelly, this is my good friend Yvonne. She lives in Pippinthwaite but is hoping to downsize and move to Willowdale so if you hear of anyone about to put their house on the market, do let us know.'

'I will,' Kelly said, smiling at me. 'You look familiar. Cake? New Year's Eve?'

'That's an impressive memory.'

'I never forget a face but I'm not so great with names so please forgive me if I need prompting a few times before it sinks in.'

'And these are three of my grandchildren,' Paulette said.

'Saffy's staying with me for a while, and Mila and Naomi are here for the weekend. Saffy has a favour to ask.'

'Fire away,' Kelly said.

'Grandma tells me that your nephew and his fiancée have a children's book coming out later this year and that Autumn's the illustrator. I love drawing and it would be amazing to talk to her about how she got into illustrating. Could you give her my phone number?'

'I can do one better than that. Dane and Autumn have a table booked for lunch in half an hour so I can introduce you then and you can sort out a time to chat to her.'

'Awesome! Thank you.'

'You're very welcome. She's lovely and extremely talented.' Kelly took our order and told us she'd be back shortly with the drinks.

When she returned, she looked directly at Saffy. 'When your grandma said you had a favour to ask me, I thought you might be looking for a job. We've had a couple of waiting staff leave unexpectedly without working notice so we're a bit stuck. I don't suppose you'd be interested?'

Saffy looked at Paulette. 'What do you think, Grandma?'

'It's up to you, love,' Paulette said. 'If you're sticking around, it makes sense to get a part-time job. This is a lovely place to work and it's handier than traipsing into Keswick.'

'I've just realised I should have asked if you have any experience first,' Kelly said. 'My brain's not in gear today.'

Saffy laughed. 'I had a job at the cinema while I was at college so drinks prep and serving hot dogs, nachos and popcorn if that helps.'

'That would be perfect. Have a think and, if you're interested, give me a shout and we can talk hours and pay. Your food will be out shortly.'

My lunch was delicious – a brie, bacon and cranberry ciabatta with curly fries followed by a slice of salted caramel sponge cake – and the company was great too. So many television programmes conveyed teenagers as uncommunicative individuals with their mobile phones stuck to their hands but, while I was sure there were many who fit that description, the only time any of Paulette's granddaughters dug out a phone was to snap photos to send to Mila and Naomi's parents. I took a photo of the three of them together and another of them with their grandma but was touched when they called one of Kelly's team over to take a photo of all five of us.

'You're an adopted member of the family now,' Paulette whispered to me, creating a lump in my throat. I'd almost forgotten what it felt like to be part of a family but having Naomi link her arm through mine as we smiled for the photo reminded me of how Mrs Kellerman and Cliff used to make me feel on my birthday.

When Kelly came over to clear our dessert plates away, she brought Autumn and Dane with her and made the introductions. I'd never met either of them before but I remembered seeing their photos in the newspaper. Autumn asked Saffy about the artistic styles she was most drawn to and, after a quick chat, arranged a date to meet up.

'When's your first book out?' I asked them.

'Not until the end of the year,' Dane said. 'We finished the series ages ago but it's a lengthy process to get to publication date.'

'You must be so excited,' Paulette said.

Autumn nodded. 'It still feels like a dream. I don't think either of us will fully believe it until we're holding a copy in our hands and, even then, I think someone might have to pinch me.'

'Your ring's really pretty,' Mila said, pointing at Autumn's sparkling engagement ring. 'When are you getting married?'

Autumn and Dane exchanged smiles. 'We wanted to make the books our priority for this year,' she said, 'but we're thinking next year for the wedding. We haven't looked at any venues yet, so we really need to get cracking with that.'

They settled at their own table and Kelly returned with the card reader so we could pay.

'I'd love a job, please, Kelly,' Saffy told her. 'I like it here. It's got a good vibe.'

Kelly smiled widely. 'Aw, bless you. If you scribble me down your email address and phone number, I'll send you the details and we can talk hours.'

'I'm really flexible,' Saffy said. 'If possible, I'd rather not work a Wednesday afternoon because I go to Cake & Craft Club with Grandma but, if you do need me then, that's fine.'

Bill paid and job secured for Saffy, we headed outside.

'Have a nice time in town,' Paulette said. 'I've transferred some pocket money into each of your accounts.'

To cries of, 'Thank you, Grandma,' they all launched at her with hugs.

'Thank you for letting me have lunch with you,' I said, smiling at them all, and was rewarded with hugs too.

As they crossed the road, I turned to tell Paulette she had a lovely family but I couldn't get any words out over the lump in my throat.

'Told you you'd been adopted,' she said, linking her arm through mine. 'Come on, you can drive me home to change our shoes then we'll have a walk by the lake to work off that incredible cake.'

It was a very short journey back to Paulette's and she chatted the whole way about how proud she was of the girls and the way they all stayed in contact despite only seeing each other every Christmas and perhaps once more during the year. I nodded and smiled but my thoughts were elsewhere. If I'd made different choices, would I have had grandchildren like Paulette did? Would I be the one slipping them pocket money and being crushed in grateful hugs? Would I be the person they turned to in their hour of need like Saffy had turned to Paulette? It must be incredible to be so loved, wanted and needed.

22

Having donned our walking boots, waterproofs and hats, Paulette and I set off on our walk. As we wandered through the village, I asked if there was any news from Saffy's parents. Paulette hadn't spoken to either of them but they'd phoned Saffy a couple of times, both calls ending in tears.

'I just can't understand why anyone would push away their only child like that,' she said, shaking her head. 'Saffy's so hurt by it all that she says she can't imagine ever living at home again. As you might have gathered from the job conversation earlier, she's asked if she can stay with me permanently.'

'Oh! That's a pretty big deal.' And one I could personally relate to. Although the scenarios were different, the outcome was the same and, no matter how brave a face Saffy put on it, her heart had to be broken. Mine had been and I hadn't been close to Dad or Marianne.

'Isn't it?' Paulette said. 'I've no problem with her staying – I'm loving the company and she's a delight to have around so I told her she's very welcome – but I'm concerned about the impact on her relationship with her parents. What if it causes a rift that can't be healed?'

'Surely they'll come round when they've had some more time to think about it.'

'I hope so, Yvonne. I really do. Families should be there to heal each other – not to be the ones causing the wounds.'

Absolutely that, but life was rarely that straightforward.

A little later, we arrived at Willowdale Hall and peeked through the wrought-iron gates into the estate, but couldn't see anything as the old manor house – owned by Christian's son, Oliver – was set way back beyond the sweeping driveway. It had been going through a major conversion since the start of last summer to make it part home, part luxury holiday apartments.

'My neighbour's daughter runs the alpaca-walking business,' I told Paulette as we continued our walk alongside the estate grounds, spotting a few alpacas in the field. 'I keep meaning to book a walk.'

'Me too. You know what? I bet Saffy, Mila and Naomi would love it. Why don't we see if we can all book one for tomorrow? I don't imagine all the slots will be filled at this time of year.'

'Much as I've loved spending time with you all today, you don't see your granddaughters that often so I think you should do it together, but let me know how you get on and maybe you and I can book a walk together another day.'

'That's a plan,' Paulette said. 'How are you getting on with your journal, by the way?'

'It's finished. I really enjoyed doing it.'

'That's good. Saffy mentioned accidentally seeing a couple of your entries when she stayed over – something about Trevor wafting a piece of paper across to her? She hasn't broken any confidences but she did ask a bit later if I'd be interested in meeting anyone and whether I thought it was ever too late to find love. I put two and two together and might have got five, but if I got four...'

I couldn't be annoyed with Saffy as she clearly hadn't told Paulette what she'd seen and, even if she had, I wouldn't have minded.

'You got four,' I admitted. 'I used Saffy's questions and followed my gut like she suggested. Love came up and that's what Saffy saw, although I told her I wouldn't have the first idea how to meet anyone at my age.'

'To be honest, I don't think it's easy at any age, but sometimes the unexpected happens. After Hector died, I never expected to meet someone else but I did.'

'What happened to Hector?' All I knew was he'd died young.

'He'd been on a work trip to South America and came back with what we thought was a bout of flu but he began really struggling for breath. At the hospital, they told me his organs were shutting down and I should prepare myself for the worst. Within twenty-four hours, he was gone. He was only thirty-four, for goodness' sake.'

'That's so young. Must have been a heck of a shock.'

'I wouldn't believe them at first. I was convinced they'd mixed up patient records but there I was, widowed in my mid-thirties thanks to some rare virus and suddenly a single parent. Martha was sixteen, David thirteen and Julia nearly ten so they were my only focus. The thought of meeting someone new never even crossed my mind.'

We'd reached a bench overlooking Derwent Water so we sat down while Paulette continued her story.

'Meeting Stephen was one of those things that happen unexpectedly. His wife had had a short battle with cancer so, like me, he was adjusting to life as a single parent. His daughter, Nicola, was in the same class as Julia at primary school and Stephen and

I both got roped into being the parent helpers on a school trip to Blackpool. We'd never met before but we sat together on the coach and talked non-stop.

'We were friends for a couple of years but realised one day that we both felt more. I'd never imagined I'd fall in love again but we had thirty-eight wonderful years together – nearly twice as long as I had with Hector.'

'Stephen died recently?' I prompted when Paulette fell silent, her gaze directed across the lake to the fells on the east side.

'Two and a half years ago – heart attack while he was descending Walla Crag.'

I realised it was Walla Crag Paulette was looking at – a lovely walk which I'd completed with Cliff on several occasions with stunning views over the lake and surrounding area.

'Were you with him?' I asked.

'No. I stopped walking up the fells maybe a decade back. Going up was fine but the descent was too much for my knees, even with poles. Stephen and a couple of his friends had decided to do a final hike up several of the smaller fells that summer and Walla Crag was the last one.' She sighed heavily. 'Really was the last. I'm so grateful he wasn't alone and that it was quick. He'd told his friends he was feeling a little lightheaded partway down so they stopped for a drink and he said he was going to close his eyes for five minutes. He never opened them again.'

'Oh, Paulette. I don't know what to say.'

She turned to me with a gentle smile but there were tears in her eyes. 'You don't need to say anything. We're not here forever and nobody knows when our time will be up. I could spend my remaining days being angry at losing two husbands but, instead, I focus on how fortunate I was to be blessed with true love not once but twice, bringing me my children and grandchildren.'

'Would you be interested in meeting someone else?'

'If you'd asked me that question at any point last year, I'd have said a resounding no but, lately, I have been wondering whether lightning could strike three times. I miss having that special someone in my life. I don't think anyone's too old but I agree that it *is* probably a bit harder to meet someone later in life. Harder but not impossible. For me, the hardest part is what goes on up here...' She tapped her head, 'and in here...' She placed her hand over her heart. 'We might think we're ready but it's not easy letting someone new in after the love of your life has gone, especially after so many years together.'

I had a question circling round my mind, desperate to be voiced and, if I asked it, there'd be no going back. This would be the moment I told Paulette everything. But I'd previously told myself that it was time and that she or Milly were the ones I'd tell first when the right opportunity presented itself. Could there be a better moment than now?

I took a deep breath, trying to still my nerves. 'What happens if they weren't the love of your life?'

Paulette's brow creased. 'Are you talking about Cliff?'

I lowered my eyes, my stomach in knots, knowing I'd cranked the handle too many times and the Jack-in-the-box was poised to spring whether I wanted it to or not.

'You've always talked so warmly about Cliff,' Paulette said after I nodded.

'Because that's how I felt. He *was* a wonderful man – my best friend – but...' I whipped my hat off my head, suddenly feeling very hot.

'You can tell me,' Paulette said, her voice gentle and reassuring.

I studied her face and had the strongest feeling that I could trust her completely. There was only one person who knew the truth about Cliff and me and I'd never imagined I'd open up to anyone else but, ever since I'd joined Cake & Craft Club, my life had moved in a new and exciting direction. If I was going to continue that momentum, I was going to have to be honest about the past. I needed to in order to move on and, truth be told, I didn't want to keep it inside anymore. I wanted that Jack-in-the-box to have its freedom.

23

THIRTY-NINE YEARS AGO

The ninth anniversary of Mum's death fell on a Sunday and I wondered if I was the only one who'd even registered the date. I'd risen early to make Dad a cooked breakfast as usual, which he'd eaten in silence before pulling on his work boots and heading out. As the door slammed shut, I sank into the seat he'd vacated, pushed his plate aside and lowered my head into my arms.

Even though Dad was out and Marianne was in her bedroom, I could feel the heavy atmosphere of despair closing in on me. If it hadn't been for Cliff, it might have pulled me under. His friendship had been the only brightness in an otherwise dreary and monotonous existence. His home next door had become my retreat. We talked, played Scrabble or cards, watched television or read books in companionable silence. But all that was about to change. Cliff had secured a new job working for a kitchen fitter in Keswick and it made no sense for him to commute from our hamlet every day so he'd sold the cottage and bought a terraced house near Keswick town centre. The sale and purchase were set for completion next week. I was dreading it and wished I could leave home too, but I didn't have the financial means and I feared I never would.

I'd turned twenty-one in January and was feeling more trapped than ever. My job didn't pay well enough for me to leave home, especially when Dad insisted on me handing over half my wages to cover my keep. By the time I'd paid my bus fare to work from the nearest village (which I had to cycle to and from) and covered an occasional trip to the cinema with Cliff, I had very little left so there was no way I was ever going to manage to save enough for a rental deposit. I didn't need anything flashy – a small bedsit would be better than here – but I couldn't see a way of it happening.

'Wish you were still here, Mum,' I muttered before reluctantly pushing my chair back and clearing the table.

Dad never talked about Mum. He barely talked full stop. He was an advocate of *real men don't cry* but I knew he did it in private. I'd shed enough tears of my own to recognise the redness of his eyes, the haunted expression, the hunch of his shoulders.

We had a roast with all the trimmings every Sunday lunchtime and Dad insisted on us sitting down as a family to eat. The whole thing was a joke as there was no conversation – just the scrape of cutlery and the occasional request for someone to pass the salt or gravy. On today's menu was roast lamb and I'd already prepared the meat and vegetables. I usually put the oven on while I was peeling the potatoes but my thoughts of my final months with Mum had distracted me and it was only when I opened the oven door to insert the roasting tin that I realised I'd forgotten. Cursing under my breath, I closed the door and switched the oven on but the wait for it to get up to heat made me feel restless. The door between the kitchen and dining room was open and the piano enticed me. Playing a couple of Mum's favourite pieces would soon pass the time.

* * *

I was so lost in Beethoven's 'Moonlight Sonata' that I didn't even hear the kitchen door opening and closing.

'What the hell's going on?' Dad's voice was loud and gruff as he burst into the dining room. I stopped playing and stared at him in horror. Why was he back? It couldn't possibly be lunchtime.

'Why's the lamb on the side?' he demanded.

'I erm... I lost track of time. It's Mum's anniversary and I was playing her favourites.'

My fingers were still poised over the piano keys as Dad strode across the room.

'Why? She's not here to hear them, is she?'

That was harsh. 'I know, but I still wanted to...' I gulped. My brain told me to stop talking and make a dash for the kitchen to cobble some lunch together and have the lamb for tea instead, but my fingers sought out the keys and, in a moment of insanity, I played the chorus of Simon & Garfunkel's 'Bridge Over Troubled Water'.

'Are you taking the piss?' Dad yelled.

I continued to play. 'It was one of Mum's favourite songs.'

He lunged for the piano and slammed down the lid over the keys. If I hadn't had speedy reflexes...

Even Dad looked shocked for a moment as I held my hands up, palms towards him, fingers splayed, shaking but intact. Moments later, he unleashed what I suspected was years of pent-up fury on me. I was still reeling from what had just happened and barely took any of it in but certain words and phrases jumped out at me between expletives. *Useless, unwanted, ruined my life, needy, stupid, worthless.* Then he was gone, slamming the door behind him so hard that it felt as though the whole building shook.

I was still sitting on the piano stool, my arms crossed over my body with my hands tucked protectively under my armpits, when the door from the lounge opened and Marianne appeared.

'What happened?' she asked, her voice small.

'I forgot to put the lamb in the oven.'

'Oh.'

'And Dad slammed the piano lid down when I was playing it and he nearly—' I burst into tears as the reality hit me of the damage he could have inflicted if I hadn't moved my hands quickly enough.

Marianne crossed the room and, for the first time ever, gathered me in a hug. And then she let go and left, making me wonder if I'd imagined it.

I didn't know what I was expected to do about lunch. All I knew was that I didn't want to be in the cottage when Dad returned. I pulled on my coat and boots and walked up to the field Mum and I used to lie in when spotting shapes in the clouds. There'd been a lot of rain recently so the field was boggy. Dad apparently thought I was *stupid* but I wasn't daft enough to lie down, no matter how much I wished I could.

A drystone wall ran around the perimeter and there was a section in need of repair where several stones had fallen over, creating a seat. I hadn't been there long when I spotted a figure coming towards me. My stomach clenched, fearing it was Dad until the figure waved and I realised it was Cliff.

'Are you okay?' he asked when he reached me.

'No.'

I shuffled up a little and he squeezed in beside me.

'I heard shouting. He hasn't hurt you, has he?'

I told Cliff what had happened and he took my hands in his, shaking his head as he checked for scratches.

'How did you know I was here?' I asked.

'I heard you playing and then I heard your dad shouting and wanted to check you were okay. Nobody answered the door but I knew what date it was so figured you'd be here with your mum.'

'How is it you remember the date and my dad and sister don't? Or act like they don't. Mind you, they're both so down all the time that I doubt I'd notice the difference.'

'It's getting worse at home, isn't it?' Cliff asked.

'I don't know how much more I can bear. I wish there was someone out there who wanted to marry me but there's fat chance of me meeting anyone. I work exclusively with women, we're not allowed to talk at work, and I can't get to know them after work because I have to run for the only bus that comes anywhere near home.'

'You've never talked about wanting to get married before.'

'If your only role models for marriage were my parents, would you want to walk up the aisle?' I exhaled heavily. 'I don't know, Cliff. Right now it feels like it's my only way of escaping and that scares me because I can't see it ever happening. You know what my biggest fear is?'

His eyes met mine. 'What?'

'That I'll still be here in ten years, twenty, thirty and I'll have turned into my sister. It's no way to live. I don't really want to get married but I need to.'

I nearly added how much I was dreading him moving away and how I feared our friendship would dwindle when he was no longer next door, but I didn't feel it was fair to lay any guilt at his door. He was doing the right thing for him and I was fully supportive of his move – just envious I couldn't do it myself.

* * *

The following Saturday, Cliff took me to a matinee showing of *The Color of Money* at the Alhambra in Keswick. He insisted on paying for my ticket and told me he'd purchased the film poster for me to put up with the *Top Gun* one he'd given me last year. To thank him, I bought us both a bag of chips afterwards and we sat on the pebbly beach at the edge of Derwent Water, eating our chips and discussing the film.

'I liked it but I preferred *Top Gun*,' I said.

'Yeah, *Top Gun* wins for me too. You know you said you didn't want to get married? I bet you'd change your mind if Tom Cruise came along and swept you off your feet.'

'Funny you should say that because he did turn up at home this morning wanting to whisk me off into the sunset, but I told him I had a cinema date with my best friend so I'd have to politely decline.'

Cliff laughed. 'I'm your best friend, am I?'

I gave him a gentle nudge. 'You know you are. Best friend. *Only* friend. I don't know what I'd have done without you.'

He put his arm around me and I rested my head on his shoulder. 'You're my best friend too.'

We sat there in silence for a while, watching the gentle lapping of the water on the shoreline, but darkness was falling and the temperature had dropped so we agreed it was time to retreat.

As we walked back towards town to where Cliff had parked, his pace slowed. He fiddled with the cuff on his coat and then his watch strap.

'Are you okay?' I asked, stopping and facing him. 'You seem nervous.'

'I've been thinking a lot about our conversation on Sunday –

about how desperate you are to get away from your dad and sister and how marriage feels like the only escape plan. I... erm... well, there's something I want to ask you.'

My stomach lurched. He wasn't going to propose, was he? I adored Cliff but my feelings didn't extend beyond friendship. He was like a big brother to me and I'd always been certain he never felt anything more than friendship in return. I had to put a stop to this.

'Please say you're not going to ask me to marry you.'

His silence answered that.

'Cliff! We're friends. I don't feel that way about you.'

'And I don't feel that way about you either.'

'Then why?'

He looked furtively around. 'There's too many people here. Can we talk about this in the car?'

We reached his car but he wanted to be somewhere we wouldn't be disturbed so we drove towards Whinlatter Forest, parked up a deserted track and twisted in our seats to face each other and I waited for Cliff to speak, bewildered by what was happening.

'There's something I've never told you because, even though I think you'll be all right with it, there's this fear of losing you if you're not. At work, there've been rumours that I'm a homosexual. Working in an alpha male environment is *not* a good place for a gay man to be, especially when there's so much fear and ignorance at the moment about AIDS.'

Gay? The thought had never entered my head, but why would it?

'Are you gay?' I asked. 'Because it wouldn't make a bit of difference to me if you were.'

He squeezed my hand. 'Thank you for that but, no, I'm not gay.'

'Then why do people think you are?'

'Because I don't have a girlfriend, I don't wolf whistle when women walk past the site, I don't leer at the page three models in the paper.'

'Have you ever had a girlfriend?' I asked, realising I'd never heard him talk about girls and that I'd never seen one visiting his cottage.

'No, and it's not because I haven't found the right person yet.' He ran his hands through his hair, nerves evidently getting the better of him once more. 'This is so hard.'

'Take your time,' I said softly. 'You can say anything to me.'

He took a deep breath and nodded. 'Okay. Here it is. I've never had a girlfriend – or a boyfriend for that matter – because I'm asexual.'

I shrugged, unfamiliar with the term.

'It means I'm not sexually attracted to anyone. I've never had sex, I don't want to have sex. I don't even want to kiss anyone. I can look at a woman and appreciate that she's pretty but it never develops into anything more than that.'

I had no idea such a thing existed. I wasn't aware of having met anyone who was homosexual or bisexual but I was familiar with those terms. This was new and I had so many questions, but Cliff was talking again.

'You looked shocked earlier when you thought I was going to propose, but that was because you thought I might have feelings for you that aren't reciprocated, right?'

I nodded. 'I didn't want things to get awkward between us. Like I said, I see you as a friend – love you as a friend – but not romantically.'

'Good. In that case, I think we can help each other. You're my best friend, I think you're an exceptional human being and there's nobody I'd rather spend time with so why don't we get married?

It'd be in name only but it'd give you the escape you need and take the heat off me. I promise to be the best husband possible. I'll treat you well, I'll support you with your career if you want to go to college to retrain, I'll make our lives together really comfortable. The only thing I can't offer is a sexual relationship.'

Cliff's revelation about his sexual orientation was surprising and the last thing I'd expected from him this evening was a marriage proposal, so my head was spinning. I was desperate to leave home but was a marriage of convenience really the answer? I'd meant it when I told Cliff last Sunday that I wasn't convinced I wanted to get married but that didn't mean I wanted to live my whole life without love, without ever kissing a man, without sex.

'I don't know what to say,' I managed eventually.

'Shocked?' he asked.

'Not the bit about you. Well, maybe surprised at that, but getting married? It's huge. I'm going to need time to think about it.'

'Take as much time as you need. I didn't expect an answer immediately. It's a big thing for me but I know it's way more significant for you. I've accepted who I am and what that means so I'm not giving anything up, but you'd be closing yourself off to true love and the opportunity to be a mum.'

My stomach lurched. I hadn't even thought about that one. Did I even want children? I wasn't sure.

Cliff clapped his hands to his cheeks. 'Oh, God! Babies! I hadn't even thought about that until I said it aloud just now. What was I thinking? Marrying me would get you out of Hayscroft Lane and away from your dad and sister but you'd be giving up so much and I can't ask you to do that.' He gripped the steering wheel, shaking his head. 'Can we forget I said anything? I can live with the rumours and jibes. I'm sorry.'

I placed my hand over his. 'I don't want to forget about it and I don't want you to regret saying anything. You say you wouldn't be giving anything up but you would be. Yes, the rumours might stop, but your life would change in ways I bet you've never considered. Why don't we both take a few days to think about it and we'll talk again?'

As Cliff drove me back home, I knew I'd think of nothing else but this.

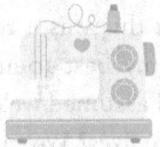

24

'I couldn't sleep that night,' I told Paulette. 'It was so unexpected but also such an incredibly unselfish thing to offer. Over the next few days, I kept blowing hot and cold on the whole thing. Finding true love wasn't high on my list of priorities. Escaping home was. Being a mum hadn't really been on my radar either and, the more I thought about it, the more I became convinced I didn't want a family. Even though my mum was great with me, I had no sense of what being part of a loving family looked like. I even began doubting Mum. She'd doted on me but her relationship with Marianne was broken so perhaps she wasn't a role model either. Cliff talked about me making huge sacrifices but I wasn't convinced they were that big after all. Hayscroft Lane was my prison and he'd just handed me the key to escape.'

'And that's why you said yes?' There was no judgement in Paulette's voice. She'd clearly been surprised by my revelation – who wouldn't be? – but there was no indication of her thinking ill of either of us.

'The sale of his cottage went through on the Wednesday and I got home from work that evening feeling sick at the thought of him not being there anymore. I missed him so much and the future without him next door felt so bleak that I wanted to say yes that very evening. I made myself take until the weekend to think everything through then caught the bus into Keswick, bought a pot plant and took it round to his house as a housewarming gift. His new place needed some work and it needed decorating but it exuded a warmth I'd never felt before, even when Mum was around. It struck me that this was a real home and I could see myself living there with my best friend so I asked if we could discuss the practicalities. I assumed we'd have separate rooms but would we also live separate lives? We came up with a way forward that worked for both of us – separate rooms but joined-up lives. Cliff insisted on one more *rule*. He said that, if I ever met someone who I wanted to be with romantically or even just physically, I only had to say the word and he'd release me from the marriage without hesitation. All that was left was for Cliff to ask my dad for his permission. We thought it would add plausibility to it all and I assumed Dad would agree.'

'But he refused?' Paulette asked.

'Yes, so I tried. He kicked me out and I never saw him again after that.'

'Doesn't sound like much of a loss.'

'It wasn't. I never understood what I did to make him hate me so much.'

'From what I'm hearing, you did *nothing*. It was all on him, Yvonne, and the fact that you entered into a marriage of convenience to get away from him and your sister speaks volumes. But it sounds like you and Cliff had a good marriage, even if it wasn't a conventional one.'

'Oh, we did. I suspect our sex-free marriage was better than a lot of regular marriages! I was married to my best friend who made me laugh so much and we travelled and saw so many incredible places.'

'It's a big thing you did for each other, although I agree with Cliff that the sacrifices you needed to make were far greater. I'm assuming you aren't asexual?'

'No. I was and still am attracted to men.'

'But you stuck with your marriage despite that. Did you ever consider taking Cliff up on his offer of a get-out-of-marriage-free card?'

Yes! I pictured Will's smiling face, the tender look in his eyes... Paulette had shown no judgement so far and I was pretty sure she wouldn't for the next part either, but sharing it required even more courage. I'd never told anybody what happened that weekend. Not even Cliff.

I looked at Paulette and bit my lip.

'Once. And I still think about him all the time.'

25

THIRTY-NINE YEARS AGO

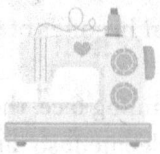

I'd been too scared to touch the piano at home after the lid-slamming incident and, given that I'd been shooed out of the cottage and told never to return, I hadn't dared go back to collect my beloved instrument. But then Mum's sewing machine had turned up on the doorstep of my new home a couple of weeks after I'd moved in with Cliff. Somebody had pressed the doorbell and scarpered, leaving the machine and my sewing box behind. Marianne barely left the hamlet so there was no way she'd have walked or cycled to the nearest village to catch the bus all the way to Keswick on her own, so Cliff and I reasoned that Dad must have had a change of heart.

'He might let you have the piano,' Cliff said.

'I doubt it.'

'It's worth a try. He said you couldn't have the sewing machine but you have it now and it's not damaged. Let's go and ask him.'

Marianne answered the door. 'He's not here.'

'I wanted to ask him if I can have the piano.'

'I don't think you'll want it.'

We followed her through to the dining room and I released a

strangled sob when I saw it – or rather what was left of it. 'What did he do?'

'Took an axe to it.'

My beautiful piano had been hacked to pieces. Some of the keys were scattered on the floor and others had chunks out of them. The top board which protected all the inner workings had been ripped off and the strings slashed and there were chunks of wood missing from the side and front panels. I felt sick and grabbed onto Cliff's arm to steady myself. Why had he done something so brutal, so destructive, so hurtful?

'You might be able to salvage your music,' Marianne said. 'He'd run out of steam by then.'

I had stacks of sheet music and books, having inherited all of Mrs Kellerman's to add to my own collection. I kept my favourites in the storage compartment of the piano stool and the rest in the sideboard. Dad had taken his axe to the stool too. The cover was ripped, stuffing was spilling out, and there was a leg missing, but the music spilled across the floor looked relatively unscathed. Cliff gathered everything together while I retrieved the rest from the sideboard, determined not to cry and desperate to get out of there.

'Are you okay?' I asked Marianne, worried for her safety. 'Why don't you come with us?'

'I'm fine,' she said, her voice small. 'I don't want to be out there with all the people. It's too much.'

'But what if he—'

'He never has before and he won't now.' She headed for the door. 'You should take your music and go. He'll be back soon.'

We took her advice and beat a hasty retreat. All the way home, I stared out of the window, my throat on fire, my eyes burning with unshed tears because I was determined not to let that man make me cry. As soon as we arrived home, all it took was for Cliff to put his arms out and I was a goner. It wasn't just about the piano; it was about *everything*. Mum dying, Marianne's indifference, Dad's hostility, the misery of the past decade, my unsatisfying job. Every time I felt like I might have it together, another memory or injustice hit me and Cliff held me and whispered reassurances that everything would be all right.

'I'll buy you a new piano,' he said when I'd finally run out of tears.

'I don't want one. It wouldn't be the same.'

'I know, but you love playing. If only I hadn't sold my mum's.'

'It's not just the piano, it's the memories. They're too sad. I need to move on.'

Even though we'd salvaged all my music, I doubted I'd ever play again. Having Dad destroy my piano like that broke my heart so badly. I felt deeply that, instead of bringing me joy and making me think of my beloved mum, playing the piano would remind me how much my dad hated me. I didn't want to keep feeling that pain. Better to walk away.

26

TWENTY-THREE YEARS AGO

Cliff and I got married in the October of the year he proposed with only his boss and wife, Ernie and Joan, in attendance. It was very low-key – a registry office wedding after which the four of us had a pub lunch. We'd been married for four years when Ernie sold the business and Cliff decided it was time to set up on his own. He was a skilled joiner, reliable and personable, so it didn't take long for him to get established, at which point I left the council and became his assistant. The offer remained for me to go to college and retrain but there was nothing that appealed. As long as I had time for crafting, I was content and fulfilled.

The years sped past through my twenties and early thirties and I never once regretted accepting Cliff's proposal. Our friendship grew stronger and stronger and I couldn't imagine my life without Cliff in it – my best friend who made me laugh, who understood my difficult relationship with Marianne and supported me after every challenging phone call, who radiated positivity and who made me feel so loved, albeit platonically. Every year as our wedding anniversary approached, he asked me if I was still happy and reminded me of the promise he'd made to release me from our marriage if I ever met someone I wanted to be with romantically or physically. I always smiled and assured him that, as long as he remained happy with our arrangement, I was still fully committed to making our marriage work. I meant it. Cliff had promised to be the best husband possible and he'd fulfilled that promise in so many ways.

But something happened shortly after my thirty-seventh birthday which made me so much more aware of the ways in which Cliff couldn't be a husband. It was a chilly Saturday afternoon in early February. After a morning of work, Cliff and I had planned to go into Keswick to buy some fabrics and thread, get an early pub tea then go to the cinema. As we were preparing to leave the house, a call came through from a potential new client who I'd been trying to pin down for a quote appointment for weeks.

'He's free now,' Cliff mouthed to me, grimacing.

It would be a huge project and great for the business so I nodded vigorously.

'But that messes up our plans,' Cliff said after he'd hung up.

'The quote's more important. I can do the shopping on my own and meet you in the pub for tea.'

It didn't take me as long as expected to get what I needed in town and I was bitterly cold so I went to the pub early and made my way to our reserved table, clutching a large glass of wine. There was a man sitting at the table beside ours with a sleeping toddler in a pushchair next to him. I gave him a half-smile in greeting as I passed, then settled into a chair and retrieved a book from my bag. I'd only read a couple of pages when I had a strong sensation of being watched.

'Sorry,' the man said when I looked up questioningly. 'I didn't mean to stare but I'm sure I know you.'

I took him in – tall, good-looking with a mop of dark hair and bright blue eyes – and searched my memory bank. I couldn't place him, but there was something about those eyes...

'It's Yvonne, isn't it? Yvonne Lambert?'

'Erm... Kellerman now, but yes.' He clearly knew me from way back to have used my maiden name.

'We were in the same French class at school. Brett Palmer.'

And suddenly I knew exactly who he was. I apologised for not recognising him and he laughed and said most people wouldn't after so long but he had an uncanny ability to remember the faces and names of everyone he met.

'It freaks my wife out,' he said, 'but she does find it funny when people clearly don't have a clue who I am but play along anyway.'

'I *definitely* remember you now that you've mentioned French class.'

I told him who he'd sat next to and the hairstyle he'd had at the time and we fell into easy conversation about what we'd been doing since school. The longer we talked, the more aware I became of how attractive he was. He'd told me he was happily married and that his wife was going to appear at any moment with another two children, but that somehow didn't stop me focusing on the sparkle in his eyes, the way one of his eyebrows curled up at the end, how he spoke with his hands, or how kiss-able his lips looked. A longing that I'd buried deep down inside of me clawed its way to the surface and suddenly my thoughts about what it might be like to kiss Brett became a lot more X-rated. Heat flowed through me and I grabbed at the menu on the table to fan myself, making a joke about the thick jumper being a mistake for a warm pub.

I didn't know what had come over me. I'd had fleeting moments of attraction before but the intensity of this was something else. I hated that I was feeling this way about a married man although it wasn't as though I was about to act on it. This was a friendly catch-up between two former classmates and nothing more.

Brett's wife arrived with a young boy and girl and Brett hugged his kids before giving her a soft kiss. A look of such deep love passed between them and then they focused back on the children, helping them out of coats and settling them at the table with colouring books and felt tips.

Cliff arrived moments later and we exchanged introductions and I wondered how on earth I was going to be able to act normal and force a meal down my neck with Brett sitting so close and a fire burning inside of me. Thankfully a group nearby vacated a larger table and Brett and his family moved over to that so I was able to relax. But, every so often, I found my gaze drawn to them and another longing emerged. The toddler had woken up and Brett's wife was bouncing him on her knee, eliciting the most adorable giggle.

'Everything all right?' Cliff asked. 'You seem a bit distracted.'

There was no way he could have failed to notice me repeatedly looking over to Brett's table so I told a part-truth. 'It's weird seeing Brett again after all these years. I knew him when Mum died so there's all sorts going on up here.' I pressed my finger against my forehead with a sigh.

* * *

That night, I lay awake with the curtains open, staring out at the darkness, thinking about all the dormant feelings Brett had awoken inside me. Cliff and I were tactile, hugging all the time, so I hadn't felt like I'd missed out on affection, but now I wanted more than that. I wanted intimacy. I wanted *real* love. Not with Brett, of course. Even if he hadn't told me he was happily married and even if I hadn't seen that for myself, I was sufficiently in tune with my feelings to know that my reaction towards him had been purely sexual rather than emotional, but it was enough to trigger some doubts. Did I really want to go through the rest of my life without ever experiencing sexual intimacy? But to get it, Cliff and I needed to split up. After everything he'd done for me, after the wonderful years we'd spent together so far, was that a sacrifice I wanted to make?

27

TWENTY YEARS AGO – JANUARY

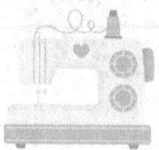

The rest of my thirties passed and, most of the time, I was really happy with Cliff and our life together but, with increasing frequency, that longing for more stirred and, along with it, the awareness of my biological clock ticking. Everywhere I went, I found myself drawn to children, noticing things I'd never thought about before – how cute sleeping babies looked, how adorable the unsteady steps of toddlers were, the joy on a young child's face when being pushed on a swing. I thought about the close relationship I'd had with my mum and imagined having the same with my own son or daughter.

Cliff knew something was wrong and kept trying to get me to talk to him, but I insisted everything was fine and I was just a bit tired. He offered to take on another assistant, to get a cleaner, to do even more of the cooking and I started to resent him for always trying to fix everything. What was going on in my head could *not* be fixed.

We started arguing or, rather, I started arguments over stupid little things. I hated myself for doing it, knowing how unfair I was being. I'd chosen this life, gone into our marriage with my eyes open, and he'd kept every single promise he'd made to me. I knew that he'd stand by his final promise to release me if I met someone I wanted to be with instead, but that was the problem. I *hadn't* met someone. I'd barely given Brett a second thought since that day in the pub and there hadn't been anyone specific since bumping into him, but there had been the possibility of someone. A possibility of passion. Of love. Of a family.

As my fortieth birthday approached, my mood darkened. I felt as though I'd reached a major crossroads in my life, looking up at a sign with *Friendship* pointing one way and *Family* pointing in the opposite direction. If I chose the *Family* route, there were no guarantees. I might not meet anyone and, if I did, what were the chances of them wanting children too? And quickly! What if I'd left it too late and couldn't conceive? Or what if all that was fine but our relationship wasn't as strong as the one I had with Cliff? Sticking to the *Friendship* path was safe, comfortable and something I already had. That old proverb kept popping into my mind: *A bird in the hand is worth two in the bush.* The thought of losing everything special I had with Cliff to pursue something that could be worse terrified me.

My fortieth birthday fell on a Wednesday. Cliff took the day off work and knocked on my door first thing to deliver breakfast in bed. He showered me with gifts and took me to a heritage railway line for afternoon tea on board a beautiful steam train. I looked around the carriage at couples holding hands, celebrating birthdays, anniversaries or simply having a day out, and felt resentment that I was doing something incredibly romantic... with my platonic husband.

I'd probably have managed to smile my way through the day if Cliff hadn't presented me with one more gift. I opened the small package to reveal a guidebook to Venice and, with a churning stomach, unfolded an itinerary with details of flights, a hotel and a gondola trip. Spring in Venice, just as I'd always dreamed. But with the wrong person. This was my dream romantic destination and I'd deliberately never mentioned that to Cliff because of our situation.

'I know you've never suggested Venice for a holiday but you always seem to be drawn to it when you're flicking through holiday brochures.' Cliff's voice was full of excitement and I didn't want to burst his bubble. I loved that he'd noticed. I loved that he wanted to surprise me. But...

'I need you to cancel it,' I murmured, pushing the book and itinerary back across the table. 'I'm sorry.'

'Why?'

'Please just do it.'

'There has to be a reason.'

I glanced around the carriage. This wasn't the time or place. 'Can we talk about it later?'

We spent the rest of the journey staring out the window and drove home from the station in silence, the atmosphere between us unbearably tense.

'I don't understand what's going on with you at the moment,' Cliff said as we hung up our coats at home.

He followed me into the lounge. 'Talk to me, Yvonne! You keep saying nothing's wrong but it has to be.'

He looked at me beseechingly but I couldn't seem to form any words because I didn't know what I wanted to say. Did I want out? I wasn't sure I did but I equally knew we couldn't continue like this. I didn't want to take out my frustrations on him because he didn't deserve it at all, but I was all fired up and I had a feeling I wasn't going to be able to stop myself.

'I thought Venice would be perfect,' he said, the frustration clear in his tone. 'It's the sort of place you love – beautiful, historical. One of the most romantic cities in the world.'

That was it! 'Romantic?' I practically spat the word out. 'You really think I'd want to go to one of the most romantic cities in the world with you and our... our... completely unromantic situation?'

His face paled and his body seemed to deflate. 'You've met someone else.'

'I haven't.' But I could feel my cheeks burning.

'You have. It's okay.' His voice was so gentle, so full of under-standing and my heart broke for him. 'I knew it would probably happen one day.' He sank down onto the sofa. 'What's his name?'

I shook my head, tears burning my eyes, guilt consuming me. 'There isn't anyone. I promise you.'

'Then what is it?'

The tears broke free. 'The possibility of someone. I love you. You know I do, but...'

'You're not sure if it's enough anymore,' he said when I tailed off.

Next moment, he had his arms around me, comforting me. Where did he find the strength? I'd hurt him but he was the one making me feel better.

Over the next couple of hours, it all tumbled out – everything I'd been thinking and feeling since that unexpected encounter with Brett in the pub and how confused I was about the future. Cliff truly was the best of the best, asking questions, properly listening, empathising.

The following day, when he got home from work, Cliff sat me down at the dining table and presented me with a new proposal.

'I've cancelled Venice. I should have thought about what it symbolised and I'm sorry for being insensitive.'

'Oh, Cliff, you're not that. It's me being overly sensitive, but thank you for cancelling.'

'You're welcome. So, we're not going to Venice, but I do think we need a break. From each other.'

My stomach lurched and I opened my mouth to object, but he shook his head. 'I'm not saying we should split up. I'm saying you need some time to think and to decide what you want to do next. We already know that's impossible while you're here – seeing me every day and working together – so my proposal is that you take the money we would have spent on Venice and go away somewhere by yourself. It's completely up to you where you go and for how long, but I think it's important for both of us that you take that time. Do what you want with it. Hide yourself away and craft or read, do some yoga, go out clubbing, kiss a stranger…'

'Cliff! You can't—'

'I *do* mean it. Kiss ten strangers, have sex…'

'Cliff!' I cried, louder this time. What had got into him?

He took my hand across the table. 'You need to do whatever it takes to make a decision about whether or not you want to stay married to me because, being completely honest, I've found the last few years really tough. I remain fully committed to this marriage. You always have and always will mean everything to me, but I said all along that you were the one making the big sacrifices, not me. If you decide to call time, I'll make it happen quickly, just as I promised. But if you want to stay, you have to be fully in because I can't do this again. I can't live with the dark moods and the arguments, you not talking to me, pushing me away. It's too painful.'

I nodded, my heart breaking at how much I'd unwittingly hurt him already, without even acting on any of my feelings. I had a question that I was afraid to ask, but knew I had to.

'If I did walk away – and it's a huge *if* – would we stay friends?'

Cliff squeezed my hand then released it with a sigh. 'I don't know. In a perfect world, of course we would, but in a practical world... who knows?'

'But you're my best friend. I love you!'

'And I love you too, but how would a new partner feel about our friendship? Even if you and I made it through unscathed, would they be supportive of us? I can't imagine many men would be.'

I doubted they would be either, but the idea of losing Cliff from my life terrified me.

'Do you accept my proposal?' he asked.

I didn't need to think about this one. He'd been so good to me and it wasn't fair to keep going like this. There was only one answer I could give.

'I do.'

28

TWENTY YEARS AGO – FEBRUARY

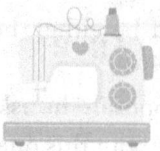

Although the thought of going away on my own was scary, I knew it was essential for properly getting my head together. Travelling overseas on my own felt like a step too far and, as I needed time rather than significant distance away from Cliff, I decided to stay somewhere relatively local and familiar. I booked a two-centre break in Manchester – five nights in a country hotel with a spa where I'd have plenty of time to relax and think, followed by a weekend in the city centre where I could take the intensity off the thinking time with a visit to the theatre and a few museums.

The country hotel was everything I'd hoped it would be. I swam each morning, had massages and facials, read, worked on a cross stitch, wandered the grounds and thought, thought, thought. By the time I checked into my city-centre hotel on the Friday afternoon, I felt rested, relaxed and reasonably sure that my decision would be to stay with Cliff. Yes, it meant sacrifices, but I'd already had the best part of two decades making them and they'd been happy years. I loved his company and the lifestyle we had. I wanted to travel more so perhaps we could do that, exploring further-flung places together.

I'd booked a ticket to see a musical that evening – something I'd done quite often on my own because, while Cliff loved the theatre, it was plays he favoured and he wasn't a musicals fan. After dining in my room, I felt restless and decided that, as it was a cool, calm evening, I'd kill some time before the show by wandering round the streets near the theatre.

Commuters on their way home from work jostled for pavement space with those dressed up for an evening out and, even though I preferred the gentler pace of life in the countryside, a brief visit to the city always gave me a buzz of excitement.

A little way ahead of me, a shop sign caught my eye – Pianos of Distinction – and my pace quickened. Showcased on a plinth behind a large window was a gleaming black grand piano with the lid propped up. Spotlights illuminated the keys and the workings beneath the lid and I drew a sharp intake of breath, marvelling at how beautiful it was. Debussy's 'Clair de Lune' – one of Mum's favourite classical pieces – was open on the music stand and my fingers twitched as I heard the tune in my head and imagined playing it.

'It's a stunner, isn't it?'

I hadn't even noticed the man approach and jumped as he spoke.

'Sorry,' he said. 'I didn't mean to startle you.'

I looked up at him and guessed he was a similar age to me. He had thick dark hair, a five o'clock shadow across a strong jawline and the warmest smile.

'It's okay. I was miles away.'

'You play?' he asked.

'I used to.'

'Were you playing that piece just now? Your fingers were moving.'

I glanced back at the music. 'I couldn't help myself. It's been a long time but the memory's still there.' I looked up at him once more. 'Do you play?'

'I do but, lately, I haven't been feeling it.'

I nodded, totally relating to that.

'My mum loved "Clair de Lune",' I said. 'She cried every time I played it. She said it made her imagine she was floating across a lily pond, the sun kissing her cheeks, the breeze ruffling her hair, feeling completely at one with nature.'

I bit my lip, unsure what had made me share such a precious memory with a stranger, but he looked captivated by it.

'That's beautiful. I can hear it in my head and picture exactly that.'

'Makes me want to play it again.'

He glanced around us and leaned a little closer. 'I think there might be too many people about to get away with throwing a brick through the window tonight,' he said, making me laugh. 'But you could always come back tomorrow when the showroom's open and give it a go.'

'I couldn't do that, could I? Not when I'm not buying a piano.'

'They don't mind. I've done it before.'

I turned my gaze to the window. Beyond the grand piano, I could see rows of uprights and a couple of baby grand pianos. Excitement flowed through me at the thought of playing any of them.

'I was going to go to a couple of museums,' I said, 'but maybe I'll come here first.'

'If you haven't played for a while and you don't want much of an audience, mornings are quieter.'

I smiled at him gratefully. It was one thing playing the air notes just now and quite another actually putting my fingers to the keys but, at that moment, I didn't just want to play the piano. I needed to.

'I'll do that,' I said. 'Thanks...' I added an inflection to the word, searching for his name.

'Will,' he said, proffering a hand to shake.

'Yvonne.' As I took his hand – cool and strong – and looked into his eyes, I felt a jolt inside me, stirring the butterflies in my stomach.

'Lovely to meet you, Yvonne.'

His warm smile sent the butterflies soaring and I felt strangely disappointed when he released my hand.

'I've got to shoot, but I hope you do come back tomorrow and play "Clair de Lune" and anything else that calls to you.'

I nodded. 'I will. And I hope you feel the music again really soon.'

'I hope so too. Bye.'

Will disappeared into the night and I stood by the piano, my heart pounding, my hands shaking because meeting him just now had thrown everything I'd concluded over the past week into disarray. I'd felt something for him. Cliff had told me to *kiss a stranger... kiss ten strangers, have sex*. As if! But maybe that was what I needed to do – or at least the first part.

Without pausing to decide whether it was a good idea or not, I raced after Will. He'd gone down a side street but, when I turned down it, it was deserted. I sighed heavily, disappointment flowing through me at the missed opportunity.

Returning to Pianos of Distinction, I took one last longing look at the grand piano in the window then set off towards the theatre. Probably just as well Will had gone. What would I have said if I'd caught up with him?

* * *

The following morning, I stood outside Pianos of Distinction, debating whether or not to go in. I no longer feared the memories that playing the piano would evoke but I did fear placing my fingers on the keys after twenty years and being unable to play competently. My head told me that I knew all my favourite pieces off by heart and those memories would rapidly return, aided by the muscle memory in my fingers. Last night, my fingers had definitely remembered 'Clair de Lune'.

My heart raced as that train of thought took me to Will and the steamy dreams I'd had about him, which seemed ridiculous when I'd only spent a few minutes in his company.

One more glance at the piano and I took a deep breath, told myself that nobody inside the showroom knew me, they wouldn't be expecting a grade eight-level piano recital, and that I could play some scales or arpeggios with ease and without judgement.

A smartly dressed sales assistant caught my eye and smiled. 'Can I help you?' he asked.

'Yes, I, erm... I haven't played for a couple of decades and I'm thinking it's time I got back into it. I'd love to try one of the pianos, but I'm not in a position to make any buying decisions today. Playing again is a big thing for me.'

'I completely understand, and a piano isn't an impulse purchase anyway. Most of our customers like to come back several times before they decide to buy and some don't buy at all. What type of piano interests you?'

'An upright, but if there's any chance of also playing a grand piano, that would be incredible. I've never played one before.'

'Consider it done! My name's Michael and I'll look after you this morning. How about you warm your fingers up on a few of the uprights before your grand piano debut?'

He took me over to the first row of upright pianos and pointed out some of the key differences. 'I can rattle off all the details for you but, if you haven't played for twenty years, my guess is you just want to crack on. Choose your instrument and enjoy it. You can take as long as you want and ask as many questions as you need. There's a selection of music on that table you can help yourself to.'

My hands actually shook as I placed them over the keys. I decided to start really simple with a C-major scale, right hand only. I pressed middle C with my thumb and scarcely made a sound. Clearing my throat, I pulled the piano stool a little closer and played two octaves of the scale before adding in my left hand. Mrs Kellerman had drummed the scales into me and I played them as easily as breathing so why was I wasting my time on beginner activities?

I glanced over to the table of sheet music Michael had pointed out and rummaged through it, my mind buzzing with each of the melodies. An allegro piece – the musical term for fast and lively – might be a little too challenging for my fingers after such a long absence. I settled on 'Gymnopédie No. 1' by Erik Satie – a slow and tranquil piece some would recognise from a television advert for dark chocolate – and sat down at the piano, my fingers poised over the keys. *You know this piece so well. You can do this!*

And I could. My fingers knew exactly what they were doing. I told Michael I'd spotted the sheet music for 'Clair de Lune' in the window and he swiftly retrieved it for me to play next, my fingers drifting across the keys with ease, happy thoughts of my mum floating across a lily pond in my mind.

Before long, I was playing faster, more demanding pieces, my heart soaring with the joy of creating such beautiful music. I'd forgotten how incredible getting lost in the music could feel, like soaring through the heavens, feeling so alive.

'It's like being at a concert,' Michael said, beaming at me. 'Did that feel good?'

'Fantastic. I can't believe how quickly it came back to me.'

'I think the grand piano calls, don't you? And perhaps this?' He handed me the sheet music for Mozart's 'Ronda Alla Turca (Turkish March)' – a fast, fun and dramatic piece which featured in the BBC's adaptation of *Pride and Prejudice*. I smiled as I pictured the scene at the Netherfield Ball in which Bingley's sister, Mrs Hurst, played it while Miss Elizabeth Bennet was humiliated by the outlandish behaviour of her mother and younger sisters.

Playing the grand piano blew me away. The sound was out of this world. As the piece ended, I felt both joyous and tearful. Had I really just played the 'Turkish March' on a grand piano, note-perfect?

The sound of applause pulled me from my daze and I gazed around the room, astonished to see I'd drawn a crowd. I'd only ever played to Mum, Cliff and Mrs Kellerman before, and nerves tingled in my stomach at roughly a dozen staff and customers smiling and clapping.

Blushing, I bowed my head in thanks before gazing around the room once more. My eyes caught those of a dark-haired man seated by a baby grand piano nearby and my heart leapt. Will! In the dim light last night, I'd thought he was good-looking but now that I could see him properly, he had to be the most handsome man I'd ever seen in real life. My heart pounded even faster and a shiver of delight rippled through my body as he smiled at me.

'That was stunning,' he said, his voice velvety, sending butterflies soaring as he approached me. 'Hello again, Yvonne.'

'Will! I didn't think I'd see you again.'

'I couldn't resist.'

I wasn't sure what he couldn't resist – the chance to play, to hear me play, or simply to see me again. I couldn't help hoping it was the latter.

'I don't suppose I could tempt you with a duet?' he asked.

'A duet? I don't know. I've never played one before. Have you?'

'A few times.'

'I've got just the piece,' Michael declared, 'but let me change the stool first.'

I stood up as Michael swapped the single stool to a longer one to seat us both. As he rummaged through the racks of music, Will sat beside me, his pine-scented body spray tantalising my senses.

'You play with such emotion,' he said, his eyes fixed on mine, his voice full of admiration. 'I could listen to you all day.'

'I was so nervous about playing after such a long break.'

'How long?'

'Nearly twenty years.'

His eyes widened. 'You're not serious? Oh my word, Yvonne, that's one heck of a talent you have.'

'Here we go,' Michael declared, bounding over to us and placing the sheet music for a duet of 'Fly Me to the Moon' on the music stand.

Will and I took a moment to familiarise ourselves with the piece, picking out and playing a couple of trickier parts before settling into the duet. I hadn't played that many contemporary pieces and loved the jazziness of this one. I'd never imagined that playing a duet could be so much fun and I couldn't stop smiling.

As soon as we'd finished, Michael replaced the music with an arrangement of Billy Joel's 'Piano Man' which was even more fun to play.

Five duets later, Will and I agreed it was time to let other customers have a go.

'Thank you so much for that,' Will said, shaking my hand once more. 'The piano and I have had a difficult relationship recently, and you've just made me fall back in love with it.'

'Really? I'm so pleased.'

As we smiled at each other, the butterflies in my stomach chased each other, making me breathless. I didn't want to say goodbye to Will. I wanted to know about his *difficult relationship* with the piano and, surprisingly, I wanted to tell him about mine.

'I don't suppose you have any plans for the next hour or so?' he asked.

'Nothing special. A museum, perhaps?'

'Care to trade the museum for a drink? We could swap our sad piano stories.'

* * *

Will clearly knew Manchester well as he led me up various side streets until we arrived at a cosy pub with beamed ceilings, wooden floors, leather high-backed armchairs and chilled music playing. It was only late morning so we ordered a pot of tea for two to start with.

'I can't get over how beautifully you play,' he said, shaking his head at me. 'You play with your heart. You don't just read the music, you feel it too. That's such a gift.'

I stared at him, mouth open, stunned at such incredible feedback, especially when Will was an exceptionally talented pianist himself.

He laughed lightly. 'I gather you haven't had much feedback on your playing.'

'Barely any. What about you? Why the *difficult relationship* with the piano?'

'My wife left me,' he said. 'She wanted to be with someone

else – an acquaintance of mine, actually – which wasn't great. Apparently guitarists are sexier than pianists and pianists are boring.'

'Oh, Will, I'm so sorry. How long ago was this?'

'Four years back. I'm over it now but it completely blindsided me at the time. She said we'd been having problems for ages and couldn't understand why I was so shocked, but I honestly thought we were fine. We had the occasional niggle – usually a difference of opinion over parenting – but nothing serious enough to constitute a problem. Not in my eyes, anyway.'

He was a dad? Somehow it endeared him to me even more.

'How many children do you have?' I asked.

'Two. Liberty's fourteen and Mackenzie's eleven, so they were ten and seven when Eleanor and I separated. They took it all in their stride and I'm so proud at how resilient they've been.'

Will told me more about his marriage break-up and his children. His eyes shone when he spoke about them and it was obvious to me that he was an amazing dad. He told me he'd have loved a third child and perhaps even a fourth and my mind drifted off into a fantasy where I was the mother of those children.

The insults his wife had hurled at him about pianists being boring had massively impacted how he felt about playing, which wasn't ideal considering his job as a music and drama teacher.

'I couldn't escape from the piano,' he said, 'but my love for it had gone. I was playing the notes but I wasn't feeling them. It was like I'd forgotten how to and then I met you, heard you play, and felt the passion and the love I had for the piano flooding back. It was as though everything I'd felt about it before had been trapped in a bubble above my head and your playing was the magic pin that burst it. Thank you.'

'I'm so sorry you went through that, but I'm honoured to have played a part in helping your love for music return. Perhaps we were destined to meet.' My heart pounded as I said the words.

'I believe we were,' he replied, his voice husky. 'Last night, I was picking Liberty up from a dance class. I do it every Friday evening and I've never once walked past Pianos of Distinction. It's out of my way. But something drew me there last night and there you were.'

His eyes held mine and the chemistry sizzling between us was unmistakable.

'You're going to tell me you're married, aren't you?' he said.

I'd taken my rings off when I arrived at the country hotel – something Cliff had suggested I do to help me think about a single life – and I self-consciously looked down at my naked ring finger.

'I am, but it's complicated.' I stroked the space where my rings had been. 'I'm here on my own because we're having some time apart while I decide whether I'm in or out.'

'That's a big decision,' he said.

I looked at him. 'Huge. And I thought I'd made it, but...' I bit my lip as I held his gaze once more, convinced he knew the end of that sentence without me needing to say anything.

He nodded slowly. 'Something stronger than tea next?'

'Yes, please.'

Across the afternoon and over a couple of bottles of wine, I told Will everything – about my childhood, my early friendship with Cliff and the conversation that led to his proposal. I talked about Dad throwing me out and how destroying my piano stopped me playing, and I shared how confused I'd been over the past few years, questioning what was missing in my marriage balanced against how good our relationship was. Will could have acted shocked or perhaps even been freaked out that I had no experience at all of sexual intimacy, but he wasn't. He listened, asked questions, showed absolute understanding of the situation I was in and why the decision to stay or go was so difficult. All the while, the chemistry fizzed between us.

We talked about so many other things from what had drawn us to the piano and the pieces we loved the most to the countries we'd visited and those we longed to see. Will shared that, having visited Venice with friends, it was on his bucket list to revisit with the right person, and I headed into another fantasy world where I pictured us there together, having a romantic meal by the canal, holding hands in the opera, kissing on a gondola. We had so many favourite things in common – bands, books, films and musicals – and shared the same values. I liked everything about him, from the way he leaned closer when I shared something deeply personal to the adorable way one of his fingers circled the back of his hair when he was nervous.

The afternoon merged into the evening and, as we'd skipped lunch, Will suggested dinner. I was starving and desperate to prolong our time together. He led me down another backstreet to a quaint Italian bistro and we slipped into a small candlelit table right at the back. Our legs were almost touching and, every time I reached for my drink, my hand brushed against his, sending desire flowing through me.

All too soon, we were the only customers left and it was time to leave. I didn't want to go. There was still so much I wanted to learn about Will but we couldn't stay there forever. Will insisted on paying and, as the waiter opened the door for us to leave, we both gasped. Being so far from the window, we hadn't noticed the turn in the weather.

'I think it might be raining,' Will joked as we huddled under the canopy, staring at the torrential downpour.

'We're going to have to make a run for it,' I said.

'Okay. One... two... three...'

Will grabbed my hand and, laughing, we ran along the street, splashing through the puddles as the rain hammered down on us. I was only wearing a showerproof mac and it was soon clinging to me. My jeans had absorbed the water and were cold against my legs and my feet were squelching in my boots.

It wasn't easy running after a big meal and lots of wine and Will pulled me into a sheltered doorway while we tried to catch our breath. We looked at each other, laughing as the rain trickled down our faces and backs.

'Your hair's a bit wet,' he said, gently pushing a dripping lock back from my cheek. The touch of his hand against my skin was too much to bear. Our eyes locked and, next moment, our lips met and it was everything I'd ever dreamed of and a whole lot more. I ran my fingers into his hair, pulling him closer, never wanting to let him go.

When a group of lads ran past and one of them jeered, 'Get a room!' we broke apart, out of breath, eye contact held.

'I don't know where my hotel is,' I murmured.

'I do.'

'Let's go there.'

'You're sure?'

I nodded, never more sure of anything in my whole life. As we ran back to the hotel, sparks flying between us, I had no doubt that this was something I needed to do. Even if Will and I didn't see each other again, I'd have experienced some of what was missing in my marriage and could make a far more informed decision about what happened next. Could it be classed as adultery when the marriage had never been consummated? Was it a bad thing when Cliff had given his blessing? Even though my head and heart told me no, it didn't stop me from feeling guilty.

As we stopped outside my hotel room, I paused with the key in my hand.

Will placed one hand on my shoulder and tilted my chin upwards with the other.

'I don't have to come in.'

'You're drenched. I can't let you go home like that.'

'And I can't let you do anything you don't want to do.'

'What if it *is* what I want?'

He smiled gently. 'Or anything you aren't ready to do. It's a no-brainer for me. I'm single, you're gorgeous, and if it's possible to fall for someone after only one day together...'

He lightly kissed my forehead, sending ripples of desire through me once more.

'...but I know it's much more complicated for you.'

'You really think you're falling for me?' He didn't seem to be the sort who'd use that as a line but I needed to hear him say it again while I looked him in the eye because I felt the same way myself.

'It started last night when I saw you looking in the window, your fingers playing "Clair de Lune", and I haven't stopped falling since.'

The tenderness in his eyes. The sincerity in his voice. He meant it.

'I feel the same,' I whispered as I placed the keycard against the lock and pulled him into the room.

* * *

When I woke up next to Will the following morning, I had no regrets. Cliff had given me the best birthday gift possible – the space and freedom to decide how I wanted to live the rest of my life. It had been the best night of my life and it wasn't just about sex. I'd never have invited Will inside if that was all it was. We'd had such a strong emotional connection too. He was everything I'd ever dreamed of – friendly, funny, romantic, attentive – and there was no doubting it was the real thing for both of us, even though it stunned us both how quickly it had happened.

Looking at Will propped up on his elbow, smiling tenderly at me, my decision was definitely made. It broke my heart that it would hurt Cliff, but it was time to tread a different path.

'How are you feeling this morning?' he asked.

'A bit fuzzy-headed, but happy.'

'Me too. Destiny knew what she was doing on Friday night, bringing us together.'

He kissed me slowly and tenderly before reluctantly pulling away.

'I hate to leave you, but I need to pick up Mackenzie from his karate class. Eleanor doesn't drive so, even when it's her weekend with the kids, I'm often roped in as taxi service.'

'I understand,' I said, trying not to sound disappointed that this was going to be goodbye.

'What time do you need to check out?' he asked.

'By noon.'

'Okay. What if I meet you in the lobby at noon and we spend the afternoon together? We can talk about how we make this thing between us work or, if that's too much for the moment, we can just enjoy each other's company.'

I loved how understanding he was, not trying to rush me into anything I wasn't ready for. 'I'd like to talk about how we make it work.'

'Music to my ears!' He pulled on his clothes, wincing as they were still soggy and, with a final long, lingering kiss, said a temporary goodbye.

I stayed where I was for a moment, replaying in my mind every part of our time together, before showering.

After I dressed, I realised my phone was still in my handbag. It was out of charge so I plugged it in and, moments later, it pinged with a voicemail. And that's when the course of my life changed once more.

29

PRESENT DAY

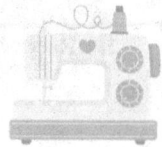

'What was on the voicemail?' Paulette asked after I fell silent.

'It was the hospital. Cliff had been involved in a serious car crash.'

'Oh, Yvonne! No!'

'Listening to that message was horrendous. I felt like the bottom had just dropped out of my world. I phoned the hospital but all they could tell me was that Cliff was in surgery and that it was *critical*. What did that mean? That it was a tricky operation? That he was about to die? I stuffed everything in my case and got out of there as fast as I could. All I could think about was what would happen if I was too late. I've never felt so scared in my whole life.

'I found out more about the accident when I got to the hospital. A courier had pulled out of a side road at speed, straight into the side of Cliff's van, knocking him into the path of another vehicle. He'd incurred serious abdominal injuries including a perforated bowel and needed a colostomy so it took a while to recover and make some lifestyle adjustments, but he got there.'

'And you were with him every step of the way,' Paulette said.

'How could I not be?'

'What happened to Will?'

I shook my head. 'I don't know. We hadn't exchanged phone numbers and I was in such a panic to get to the hospital that I wasn't thinking about him and it never entered my head to leave a message with reception. He'd have turned up at noon and probably waited for a while before asking after me, and he'd have discovered I'd checked out and gone. He probably thought I'd changed my mind.'

'Did you ever try to find him?'

'I didn't know how to. Stupid as it sounds now, we'd talked for hours about anything and everything – except those vital little details that would have helped me trace him. I didn't know his surname and he didn't know mine. I didn't know where in Manchester he lived.'

'But you knew he taught music and drama.'

'It wasn't a lot to go on but it was all I had and I'll admit I did a bit of searching when Cliff was back at work and life was back to normal but I drew a blank. It clearly wasn't meant to be.'

Paulette placed her hand over mine. 'I'm so sorry. I can hear the regret in your voice.'

'I regret losing Will, but I don't regret the time I spent with Cliff.'

'I fully get that when you had such a happy life together. But that doesn't mean you can't regret walking away from the possibility of a *different* life, or at least feeling wistful about what might have been. Regret's maybe too strong a word.'

We sat in silence for a while but I could feel the cold seeping into my bones and suggested we wander back.

'Did you ever tell Cliff about Will?' Paulette asked.

'No. I had no way of contacting Will so I knew that was over and, after the trauma Cliff had been through, what was the point in laying that on him? Besides, I'd made the decision to stay. When I got that message, spoke to his surgeon, saw his wrecked van, it broke me. The thought of losing Cliff... It might not have been romantic love but it was still love.'

Paulette linked her arm through mine. 'You've been through so much.'

'You have too.'

'Maybe that's why we're such good friends. We recognised each other's hurt.'

I squeezed her arm, loving the idea of that connection.

'If you had exchanged numbers with Will or you'd had another way to find him, would you have stayed with Cliff?'

'I've asked myself that question so many times over the years and I honestly don't know.'

'One more question,' Paulette said. 'If Will was walking towards us right now, what would you do?'

'Die of shock,' I quipped, but the pounding of my heart gave me the real answer. Being too old to find love again and not having a clue where to meet someone were just excuses to cover up the real reason I was uncertain about putting myself out there – that I couldn't imagine meeting anyone who made me feel like Will the Piano Man had made me feel. Paulette's experiences with two amazing husbands had led her to conclude that there wasn't just one right person out there but several and Milly thought the same. I still believed there was only one and, no matter how many times I'd pushed him out of my thoughts and told myself that it was impossible to conclude that someone was your one true love after one weekend together – a short one at that – I was as convinced as ever that Will and I had been meant to meet each other. As for why destiny had decided to tear us apart again, I'd never know.

30

When I arrived back at Mallard Close feeling so much lighter for telling Paulette everything, the 'for sale' board was up. Inside the house, I released Trevor, misted him, then stood by the window for a while looking at the board and thinking about the enormous change ahead of me. Moving house was huge but I had no doubt in my mind about it.

Trevor joined me at the dining table and I opened my journal to the page signposted *a new home for me*. I placed a sticker showing a 'for sale' sign on it and wrote today's date beside it. I turned to the next page – *see more of the local area with my new friends* – and rummaged through my stickers until I found a mug of coffee and a willow tree. I placed them on the page and added the words *The White Willow with Paulette* and the date. The next page was *Venice*. The timing wasn't right with the house move and establishing Created With Love, but I was going to believe that it would happen eventually.

I flicked back a few pages to the section about things I'd start doing. The third entry was still blank but I knew what it needed to be. I opened up a sticker pack devoted to music. Among the illustrations of record players, speakers, stereos and headphones were several musical instruments and notations. I removed a grand piano, a treble clef and a line containing four bars of music, and added them to the centre of the page. This year I was going to start playing the piano again.

Even though my experience in Pianos of Distinction had been truly wonderful, there was no way I could play the piano without thinking about Will so, yet again, I had to shut myself off from my beloved instrument to protect me from the memories. I didn't tell Cliff about visiting the showroom as I didn't want him to encourage me to return to the piano when I knew that playing would evoke too many painful memories of a love I'd had to let go.

Today, I didn't feel that way anymore but, if I was going to return to playing, I needed an instrument. I wasn't aware of there being any piano showrooms locally but a search on my phone brought up one in Carlisle called Celestial Sounds. It was closed on Sundays but I could see if Paulette or one of the others fancied joining me in the next week or so.

Lorna the estate agent called as I was making myself a mug of tea to tell me they'd had lots of clicks on my listing and already had two viewings lined up on Monday and Tuesday. That made the move feel more real in a way that signing the paperwork hadn't. I didn't need to do a panic clean and tidy because I never let the house get into a mess, but there was something I'd been putting off for years that did need tackling.

I retrieved a roll of bin bags from the kitchen and, upstairs, opened the door to Cliff's bedroom at the front of the house. It was slightly larger than mine but he'd given me first dibs and I'd preferred the one at the back overlooking the garden. I regularly aired it, vacuumed and dusted, so there was no problem with the room itself. The issue was what lay behind the wardrobe doors.

Ripping off one of the bin bags, I billowed it out before opening the nearest wardrobe door. As the bin bag deflated, so did I. How could looking at a hanging rail of shirts evoke so many memories? I ran my finger along the different fabrics with a sigh then closed the door, dropped the bag on the floor and returned to Trevor downstairs. It had been an emotional day for me with opening up to Paulette and I didn't need to do this too. I was already swamped with thoughts of what might have been with Will if only that courier hadn't pulled out of the junction at the exact moment Cliff was passing, if only we'd exchanged phone numbers or surnames or any details that could have helped us find each other. What ifs and maybes seemed to rule my life. I'd make something to eat and relax in front of a film instead.

* * *

The following morning, I woke up with fresh determination to tackle Cliff's bedroom. I opened the wardrobe door and ran my fingers across his shirts once more. I should have cleared them out before now. At first it had felt too soon, and then it had felt too hard. And now...

I lifted out what had been my favourite shirt on him – a short-sleeved blue checked one with a subtle pink thread running through the checks. He'd been a good-looking man but he'd looked extra handsome when wearing that. He'd worn it on our first night in Madeira. I pressed my nose to the collar and, even though it had been worn and washed several times since that holiday, I could smell his body spray on it. Or perhaps that was my imagination.

Lying the shirt on the bed, still on its hanger, I reached for another one – long-sleeved with dark grey stripes – which he'd worn on Christmas Day. Each shirt I removed triggered special memories and, before I knew it, I was slumped on the bed cradling a stack of shirts to my chest, hangers digging into me, sobbing for my loss. I might not have been in love with Cliff but I'd loved him deeply and missed him so much.

I let the tears flow – no point in trying to dam my grief as it would only find another way out. When the wave passed, I laid the shirts down and removed the first one from the hanger but I couldn't bring myself to fold it up and place it in the bin bag. Had I made this task more difficult by leaving it for so long?

I rang Paulette, figuring she must have done this twice and perhaps she had some advice. I suspected it would be a case of *you just have to rip off the plaster* but I was hoping there'd be something more helpful she could offer. When my call went to voicemail, I remembered our conversation about booking an alpaca walk. Paulette was probably doing that with the girls right now and would have her phone on silent. Even if she hadn't managed to book a slot, I'd said no to the alpaca walk so she could spend some quality time with the girls so it wasn't fair of me to call her and demand her time just because I was upset. Not wanting her to spot the missed call and ring me back, I sent her a quick text saying I'd called in error and would catch up with her next week. Paulette couldn't help me now, but I could think of someone else who might be able to.

* * *

Half an hour later, Veronica arrived.

'It's a dreadful task,' she said as we stood in the bedroom doorway. 'It can stir up all sorts of emotions but it needs to be done and my advice is to do it with someone else. Paulette's mother helped her after Hector died and one of their daughters helped sort through Stephen's belongings.'

'Did your daughters help you?' I asked, thinking it was odd that she'd mentioned Paulette's situation but not her own.

She sighed heavily as she shook her head. 'Felicity offered but wouldn't commit to a date. Rebecca offered instead but that riled up Felicity who said I'd already agreed to her support. I couldn't face the thought of them both turning up and fighting when I was already dreading the task so I told them I'd bitten the bullet and done it myself. I hadn't. A friend helped me.'

'Your daughters fought over clearing out their dad's wardrobe too?' I asked, feeling Veronica's pain.

'As I said, it's all a competition and, frankly, it's exhausting. Let's focus on you, though. What specifically is stopping you from saying goodbye to Cliff's belongings?'

'All the memories.' I grabbed a couple of shirts and shared what they triggered.

'Rather than donating his shirts, what about repurposing them into a patchwork quilt? That way you can retain the memories but gain your wardrobe space back. There's a wonderful mixture of plain and patterned shirts and a strong colour scheme of blues, greys and purples.'

While Veronica searched on her phone for alternative ideas, I considered her suggestion of a quilt. She was right about the complementary range of fabrics and colours but making a quilt was a big project and, if I was finding it hard seeing all of Cliff's shirts right now, would I only be prolonging my grief? And what would I do with it anyway when it was complete? The colour scheme wouldn't work in my bedroom and I wasn't sure I'd want to wrap a quilt around me made from my dead husband's shirts.

'If you fancied making something smaller, what about a memory bear?' Veronica handed me her phone and I scrolled through some of the images of teddy bears, large and small, made from the clothing of a loved one. It would be perfect. I'd never made a teddy bear before so that could be the new craft I learned this year, and a bear made from Cliff's shirts would be small, subtle and special.

'I love that idea,' I said, smiling at Veronica.

'Wonderful! I'd suggest you start by selecting your favourite shirts – the ones which will blend well together – and then we pack the rest away for charity.'

'Thank you for doing this with me. It's so good of you to give up your Sunday like this.'

'Yvonne, I've been where you are. I know how much it hurts and, if I can take even a small part of that pain away, my Sunday will have been well spent. Although I wouldn't say no to us taking a break for a carvery at The Fox and Rabbit if you don't have any lunch plans.'

I smiled at her. 'I'll make the booking.'

In some ways, I was glad that I hadn't been able to get hold of Paulette as it gave me a chance to spend some quality time with Veronica. How lucky was I to have found so many kind friends who were helping me heal and get my life back on track?

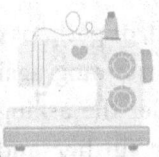

31

At noon on Wednesday, Veronica, Paulette, Milly, Laughlin, Saffy and I all met at the village hall to go through our Created With Love homework before Cake & Craft Club. I'd wondered if anyone would have changed their mind after they'd had time to properly think about it but we all remained fully committed and had similar thoughts about how everything should work, so it didn't take long to finalise everything. Saffy, who'd started a part-time role at The White Willow on Monday, offered to set up a website as well as being our social media guru – a role she said she could easily manage around her shifts.

Shortly before 2 p.m. the other group members started arriving and we agreed not to say anything to them about Created With Love until we'd definitely secured the premises. No point getting anyone excited about a place to sell their crafts if we fell at that final hurdle.

We were half an hour from the end of the session when Lorna's name flashed up on my phone. It was noisy in the hall with the whirr of sewing machines and general chatter so I nipped out into the entrance lobby.

'I've got some great news for you,' she said. 'Both couples have called me today with offers. They're in the same strong position – chain-free with mortgages lined up – and both want speedy completions, so my suggestion is to go back and ask for best and final offers. Do I have your permission to do that?'

'Yes, please. Do you think they'll come back with the asking price?'

'I'm confident they will, or perhaps even above it.'

Ten minutes later, Lorna rang again. One couple had come back with one grand under the asking price and apologies that they couldn't stretch any further and the other offered three grand above on the proviso that the house was removed from the market immediately and we aimed for completion at the start of the Easter holidays.

'They've got a deal,' I said.

'Everything okay?' Milly asked when I returned to the room.

I sat down at my table, feeling dazed that it had all happened so fast. 'My house has just sold.'

She offered me her congratulations and Paulette, Veronica and Laughlin all chipped in with theirs.

'You look like you're in shock,' Laughlin said.

'I am. And I'm panicking a bit. I need to be out by Easter and I haven't got anywhere to go. There's nothing on the market I like at the moment. Should I have waited until I found somewhere before I accepted?'

'No!' they chorused.

Next moment, I was flooded with offers of spare rooms if I either hadn't found anywhere by the time my sale completed or I'd found somewhere that would complete after my sale. Looking round my new friends, I felt overwhelmed by their kindness and counted my blessings once again that I'd stepped out of my comfort zone to join Cake & Craft Club.

* * *

I arrived home to a 'sold' banner across my 'for sale' board. Lorna and her team were impressively efficient. Christian must have been watching out for me because, as soon as I exited the car, he jogged across the road.

'Sold already? That was quick.'

'Way quicker than expected. Guess who'll be spending this evening searching for houses online?'

'I don't suppose I could interest you in joining me for tea between house-hunting? Emma was meant to be coming over but one of the alpacas has a mouth infection so she's waiting for the vet. I've made beef and ale pie and it's way too big for one.'

'Tea would be lovely, thanks. Hope the alpaca's okay.'

We agreed on six o'clock so I showered and changed. As I dried my hair in the mirror, I frowned at the state of it. It needed some major care and attention. I'd call into the hairdresser in Pippinthwaite this week and make sure I wasn't a lost cause before I booked an appointment. Running a brush through it, butterflies stirred in my stomach. Christian had invited me to his house for a meal. He'd never done that before. Was that a date? Did I want it to be? I chewed on my lip, debating my feelings. I liked Christian and I did find him attractive, but could I see us together as a couple? I wasn't so sure. As I replayed our brief conversation, I nearly laughed out loud at my train of thought. Of course it wasn't a date! Emma couldn't join him and he'd prepared too much food for one – simple as that.

* * *

'That was delicious,' I told Christian as I placed my knife and fork down on my empty plate. 'You're a good cook.'

'Thank you. I never used to be but Oliver's mum, Kathryn, was really into cooking and she inspired me. I don't know about you, but I find it a bit tedious cooking for one so I enjoyed experimenting when Emma was living here.'

'I enjoy cooking but I agree with you about meals for one. I tend to batch cook and eat more ready meals than I should. Cliff used to help me.' I laughed lightly. 'Or rather he tried to. He usually got in the way and created way more mess than should have been humanly possible, but I enjoyed the company.'

Christian gave me a sympathetic smile. 'I was thinking about you over New Year.'

Butterflies stirred in my stomach. 'You were?'

'Yes. I'm thinking it would have been five years since Cliff died.'

'That's right.' I was so touched that he'd remembered that.

'It's been over thirty years since Kathryn died.' Christian paused and frowned. 'Crikey! It'll be thirty-six years this October. I've no idea where that time has gone.'

'You and Kathryn – you weren't married, were you?'

'No. It's a long and complicated story.'

'I'm happy to hear it over a cuppa. Only if you want to share.'

Christian smiled and nodded. 'You're on.'

He made some drinks and we settled in the lounge as he told me about meeting Kathryn as a teenager, that she'd been the love of his life and how a stupid argument had torn them apart. He'd got together with Emma's mum, Liv, marrying her when she was pregnant and had tried his hardest to make the marriage work but Liv knew he loved her as a friend rather than romantically and they split up after eight years. He'd never expected to have a second chance with Kathryn as she was married but he kept seeing her around and it transpired that her husband, Hubert, was emotionally and physically abusive. He'd also had a string of affairs and didn't even try to be discreet about them.

'Hubert gave Kathryn every reason to leave him,' Christian said, 'but she could have lost Willowdale Hall. Her ancestors built it and she loved it so much. She couldn't bear the thought of that man owning it.'

Although he didn't go into much detail about his relationship with Kathryn, I could hear in his voice how uncomfortable he felt about having an affair, despite him not cheating on anyone himself and despite Kathryn's husband being a serial adulterer. I couldn't bear the thought of anyone cheating on their partner – such a hurtful and disrespectful thing to do – but I knew from personal experience that it wasn't always that black and white. It sounded as though Kathryn's marriage had had its own complexities, albeit in a different way to my own. My thoughts strayed to Will – something they'd done with even greater frequency than usual since opening up to Paulette on Saturday – and the debate I'd frequently had with myself as to whether I'd really cheated on Cliff. Even though I liked Christian and I was enjoying this deeper conversation with him, I didn't feel any desire to open up to him about my own situation.

'When Oliver was born,' he continued, 'it was so hard knowing that he was my son and I couldn't be his dad.'

'You always knew Oliver was yours? I assumed that was a recent discovery.'

Christian shook his head. 'Only for Oliver. He found out roughly eighteen months ago, and I told Emma shortly after. I probably shouldn't talk about that part as it's more about them than me.'

'I understand. But you're close to them both now?'

'Really close. You know, I spent decades feeling like such a failure because I wasn't a proper dad to either of my kids and I'm so grateful that I've had the chance to start over with both of them.'

We both took a sip of our tea and then he hit me with the question that I always dreaded being asked. 'You and Cliff never had kids?'

I shook my head and reeled off the standard reply. 'Neither of us particularly wanted them.' Will had wanted more kids. Would that have happened? It was pointless torturing myself with another what if or maybe. I'd chosen my path and it had been a child-free one and I'd had to come to terms with that. If it hadn't been for Cliff's accident, it might have been different but... Feeling myself welling up, I gazed around the room seeking out a distraction and my eyes landed on a wooden bowl on the coffee table.

'That's beautiful,' I said. 'Lovely quality wood. Is it oak?'

'It is – oak from your husband's supply.'

I whipped my head up. 'You made it?'

Christian smiled. 'I did. Give me a second.'

He left the lounge, returning moments later with a similar bowl. 'This is for you. I've kept meaning to bring it across.'

I turned the bowl over, admiring the grain and the smooth finish. 'You've been using Cliff's lathe?'

'I'd run out of room for storing the big carvings but I wasn't ready to stop working with wood. I saw this article about a wood-turning course in the village hall newsletter so I signed up for that.'

I had a flashback to that August day when the newsletter arrived. I'd been at my lowest point then and it was amazing to think how much had changed in the space of five months.

'I spotted that and wondered if you would too. Have you enjoyed it?'

'Loved it. Wood carvings still have the edge for me – I like the bigger scale – but I'm learning all the time on the lathe so who knows? Do you want to see what else I've been making?'

I slipped my coat on and followed him outside to his workshop – an enormous extension to the back of his double garage. He flicked the light on and the first thing I noticed was the metal racking down the side walls, packed full of his chainsaw carvings.

'So many!' I exclaimed.

'I might have a bit of a problem,' he admitted. 'Hello, my name's Christian Wynterson and I'm addicted to carving animals from wood.'

I stepped a little closer and ran my fingers down the plumage of the most adorable owl. 'They're spectacular.'

'Thank you. My lathe work's on the other side.'

He showed me bowls of varying sizes, salt and pepper shakers, tealight holders and clocks, all of which exhibited considerable skill.

'What are you going to do with them all?' I asked.

'Emma keeps telling me I should sell them. She sells the alpacas through her website but I've never got round to looking into the rest of the animals.'

'I might have a solution for you but do you mind if we go back inside? It's chilly in here.'

We returned to the lounge and I outlined our plans for Created With Love. Christian loved the sound of it, even offering to cover some shifts while we got established if we found ourselves stuck.

'I love the idea of a shop for creatives being run by creatives. I know you sew but I've never asked you what you make.'

'Patchwork quilts mainly...'

The conversation flowed as I talked about my sewing, the quilt I'd given to Paulette and the memory bear I was going to make from

Cliff's clothes. Christian talked about the favourite pieces he'd made and how easy it was to look up from his work thinking a couple of hours had passed only to realise he'd been working for four.

This was by far the longest I'd spent in Christian's company and I liked it a lot. He was easy to chat to, he was open about his past, and he was interested in finding out more about me. I couldn't read Christian – couldn't tell if he was being flirty or just friendly. When I'd been with Will, the electricity had crackled between us and I'd never doubted for a moment that he was interested in me so I suspected that, with Christian, it was the latter and that suited me just fine. As nine o'clock approached, I struggled to stifle a yawn, which made us both laugh.

'Is my company really that bad?' Christian asked, his tone teasing.

'Your company has been brilliant, I promise, but my day has been long so I'd better make my move.'

He helped me back into my coat and walked me to the door.

'Thanks again for the delicious meal,' I said, stepping out into the cold night air. 'And for this beautiful bowl.'

'You're welcome. Thanks for the great company. We'll have to do it again sometime.'

'My turn next. How about I cook for you one day next week?'

'Sounds good to me. Good night, Yvonne.'

He leaned forward and I tensed. Was he going to kiss me? A wave of panic swept through me. The only man I'd kissed was Will and I wasn't convinced I wanted to kiss Christian. But his lips lightly brushed my cheek and he pulled away, smiling at me. 'See you soon.'

'Night,' I murmured. 'Sleep well.'

But as I dashed across the road, I frowned. I'd expected to feel relieved that Christian had only given me a friendly peck on the cheek but, for some reason, I felt disappointed instead. How could that be? Why were my feelings towards him all over the place?

I placed my key in the lock and glanced back. It was touching to see Christian still on his doorstep, as though making sure I made it inside safely. He raised his hand in a wave and I did the same before ducking inside, hastily locking the door and releasing a long breath.

After my heart rate steadied, I went into the lounge to place the bowl on the coffee table and check on Trevor.

'I was longer than I thought,' I told him. 'I'm sorry you've been on your own all evening. I promise to spend some time with you tomorrow but it's bedtime now.'

'Bedtime!' he repeated. 'Bedtime!'

As I draped the cover over Trevor's cage, he fell silent, and I completed my usual nighttime round of the house, closing blinds and curtains and checking the locks downstairs before heading upstairs. I paused in Cliff's doorway for a moment then, without switching on the light, made my way over to the window, my eyes focused across the road. I knew Christian's bedroom was at the front of the house but it was in darkness. I was about to leave when his room illuminated. The blinds were raised and as he walked towards the window, I gasped at the sight of his bare chest. I ducked behind the curtains, my heart pounding and, moments later, the blinds were lowered and tilted. Releasing another long breath, I shook my head. We'd been talking about our ages earlier as I'd mentioned how kind my friends at Cake & Craft Club had been after discovering my sixtieth had passed unnoticed. He'd mentioned that his sixtieth had been a non-event – just a couple of drinks with some of his teacher colleagues – but he was hoping to do something special for his seventieth birthday in December. Seventy! I knew he kept himself fit and that flash of his naked torso had proved it.

I liked Christian a lot and the age gap didn't bother me – not that much more than the one I'd had with Cliff – but could I see us together? I still wasn't convinced but stranger things had happened. But as I settled down to sleep, it was Will who occupied my thoughts, not Christian.

32

'Harry's coming back on the 15th,' Milly said after we'd sat down with our drinks in The Fox and Rabbit on Sunday, the first day of February. 'I'm going to tell him I want a divorce then.'

'Only a fortnight away! How do you feel about giving him the news?'

'Pretty scared. What if he refuses?'

'Do you think that's possible?'

Milly shrugged. 'I don't know. You'd think I'd know him after twenty-five years together but he's spent so much time abroad that it's probably only a fraction of that in real terms. Sometimes he says and does things that surprise me. My mum says he's a funny onion.'

I loved that phrase and it sounded perfect for what I'd heard about Harry.

'He certainly sounds it. Will you tell him straightaway?'

'It depends when his flight lands. It's Veronica's party that day and I don't want to miss that, but I can hardly give Harry the news then bog off to a party without talking it through. I usually pick him up from the airport but I'm going to ask him to get the train this time and I'm hoping the timings will work out so I can tell him *after* the party.' She held up crossed fingers on both hands. 'It feels a bit harsh doing it immediately – *welcome home and, by the way, I want a divorce* – but it doesn't feel fair keeping it from him either. I guess there's never a right time to drop a bombshell like that. Kind of gives me an insight into why it took Rob so long to tell me he was leaving me. I just hope he takes it well and doesn't decide to fight me every step of the way.'

I hoped Harry would respond positively and make the process smooth for Milly but I could understand her fear that he wouldn't. The thought of ending my marriage had terrified me and our situation had been completely different.

Milly and I had a delicious meal and a great chat. I told her that I was thinking about getting a piano and would be driving to Carlisle on Saturday if she fancied a day out.

'Can I let you know later in the week?' she said. 'Coral said something about coming home to collect something but it was all a bit vague. I haven't told her Harry's coming home yet. She might prefer to time a visit to see him.' She laughed and rolled her eyes at me. 'Although the weekend I tell her father I want a divorce might not be the best one to come home.'

'Are you going to warn her?'

'I can't decide. On the one hand, I think it's only fair that Harry's the first to know but, on the other, I'd quite like her to be prepared. I don't think she'll be bothered. They're not close. She's even said before that she doesn't get why I've stayed married to him, but saying something in theory and meaning it in reality are two different things.'

Didn't I know it? Even though Cliff had been sincere each time he'd asked if I wanted to be released from our marriage and especially when we had our break, the reality was that ending things would have broken his heart and mine too.

'Enough about me,' Milly said. 'Do you think you'll buy a piano?'

'I hope so. I've been thinking about it a lot recently and my fingers are restless. I need to play.'

'There's a piano in the village hall here, you know. They had a fundraiser to buy one in Willowdale a few years back but there was a hole in the roof so the funds had to be redirected. I'm sure nobody would mind you using the one in Pippinthwaite's hall.'

I loved that idea. 'Who would I ask?'

'Trudy Eccles. She's the current chair of the village halls committee. I'm pretty sure her number's on the noticeboard. We can take a look after we've eaten.'

* * *

Trudy's number had been on the board and she'd said it was no problem me using the piano. She only lived a few doors down from Pippinthwaite Village Hall so it was easy to collect the key from her house and drop it off when I was done. Across the following week, I managed an hour a day when the hall was free, confirming to me that I definitely wanted and needed a piano back in my life.

Milly let me know that Coral wasn't coming home, leaving Milly free to come to Carlisle with me. At Cake & Craft Club on Wednesday, I extended the invitation to our friendship group, emphasising that they didn't have to come to the piano show-room and could do their own thing. Laughlin's brother was visiting and Veronica had plans with another friend but Paulette was free to join Milly and me.

Going out in a group was new to me and I had a brief flutter of apprehension about being the third wheel in a longer-standing friendship but I needn't have worried as the conversation flowed easily between the three of us. Milly told Paulette about her plans to ask Harry for a divorce which earned her an *about time too* comment and Paulette updated us on the latest with Saffy's parents.

'Andrew phoned one evening when Joanne was out and apologised for the comments about me not being his *real* mother,' she said, 'but, as we chatted, it was obvious that Joanne had no idea that he was apologising on her behalf and wouldn't be impressed. I told him to get back in touch when he'd grown a backbone.'

'How did he react to that?' I asked, giving her a sideways glance, impressed by her no-nonsense approach.

'He told me Joanne's a complex woman and I don't understand so I told him he was right, I don't. I don't understand why he'd let her speak to me like that when we've always enjoyed a great relationship full of love and respect and I particularly don't understand why he'd let her destroy their relationship with their only daughter, especially over something that was making her miserable.'

'Good for you,' Milly said from the back seat.

'I didn't like having to lay it out there but he needed to hear it. I've no idea what the *complex woman* thing was all about – sounds like an excuse to me and I told him that too. I said *if she has some mental health issues, I'm sympathetic to that, but it's the first I've heard of it and it doesn't excuse what she's doing to Saffy. The girl dropped out of university, for goodness' sake. She didn't rob a bank or murder anyone!* I don't want Andrew to hate me but I'll gladly take that hit if it gets him to see sense about Saffy.'

I was in awe of the way Paulette continued to stand up for Saffy and fight her corner, no matter what it cost her personally. What a privilege to have a friend like that.

We arrived in Carlisle and they were both keen to join me at Celestial Sounds but said they'd understand if I preferred to do it on my own, knowing I might not want an audience while I tested out the pianos. It was so kind of them to acknowledge that, but I wanted them with me.

Celestial Sounds was completely different to Pianos of Distinction. It was inside a converted church – presumably the inspiration behind the name – and there were so many nods to its heritage. The pipes for the church organ remained and had been beautifully restored although the owner, Mervyn, told us that the organ had regrettably been removed and destroyed before their time. Beneath the pipes, a plinth had been created for a beautiful white grand piano. The backs of the pews had been made into shelving units housing music books for sale in the spaces where hymn books would have been, and a couple of the windows were stained glass although they'd clearly been purpose-made more recently as they depicted musical notations and piano keys.

There were several beautiful upright pianos and, although it had been great playing the one in Pippinthwaite Village Hall, the sound from the first piano I played in Celestial Sounds was far superior, partly due to the quality and condition of the instrument and partly due to the exceptional acoustics in the former church.

After I'd played my first piece, I turned to my friends. Milly was bouncing on the spot clapping frantically and, although Paulette was clapping too, she had tears in her eyes and I knew why. She knew my story. She knew why I'd stopped playing.

'I knew you'd be good,' Milly said, 'but that was off the chart.'

'It was exceptional,' Paulette agreed. 'There's something about your playing I can't put my finger on.'

'Oh, I can,' Mervyn said. 'It's the difference between a good pianist and a great one. A good pianist is technically gifted, playing the piece with precision – exactly as it's written. A great pianist does that but they also feel the piece. They read between the lines, quite literally, interpreting the music with their heart rather than just their brain. Your friend does that.'

I smiled at him, grateful for such kind feedback, but I also felt a jolt of sadness as it had strong echoes of what Will had said about my playing.

'Please try as many as you like,' Mervyn said. 'It's a pleasure to hear such beautiful playing.'

I moved to the next piano and played another classical piece before asking Milly, Paulette and Mervyn if they had any requests, playing each on a different instrument. When I was done, I'd narrowed it down to two favourite pianos and asked Mervyn if he'd mind me coming back after lunch to make my final decision.

'Before you go for your lunch, I know you're not looking for a grand piano but you're more than welcome to give our showcase grand a play.' He swept his arm towards the white grand piano.

As Mervyn ran through the details, I gazed up at it looking spectacular on its plinth beneath the colourful organ pipes. I'd regret it if I didn't but, as I lowered myself onto the piano stool and poised my fingers over the keys, I found myself glancing towards the door, half expecting Will to come in. Perhaps if I played the same piece I'd first played on the grand piano in Pianos of Distinction – Mozart's 'Turkish March' – I could somehow conjure him. The door opened at one point and my heart leapt but it was a young couple who paused by the doorway to listen. It opened again a little later, but it was only a postal worker who waved a couple of envelopes in Mervyn's direction and placed them on the side before leaving. No Will, obviously.

* * *

'I'm still in shock about your unbelievable talent,' Milly said as we settled into a booth after we'd placed our orders for a pub lunch a little later. 'Here was me making out that I'm good on the recorder and I sound like a total amateur compared to you.'

'Ah, but I can't play the recorder!'

Milly laughed. 'I'd trade my recorder skills for your piano ones any day.'

'It was a privilege to hear you playing,' Paulette said. 'I'm glad you've returned to it.'

'You kept looking over to the door while you were playing that grand piano,' Milly said and my stomach lurched. Had I made it that obvious? 'How did you manage to keep playing seamlessly?'

I glanced at Paulette and, evidently reading the question in my mind, she gave me an encouraging nod.

'It's a bit like touch-typing,' I said, answering Milly's question. 'My fingers know what they're doing. But there's a reason I was looking at the door...'

I shared with Milly the same details I'd shared with Paulette about Cliff and about Will. I valued all my new friends so highly and didn't want to have secrets with some and not others. While I didn't see quite as much of Veronica or Laughlin, I would eventually tell them when the moment felt right. Milly's reaction was exactly what I'd expected from her – a mixture of surprise and empathy. It struck me that, just a couple of months ago, I wouldn't have imagined me sharing my past with any of my Cake & Craft Club friends but everything had changed this year. As well as feeling lighter for telling them and for not getting a negative reaction, I felt steadily more confident about the future and placing even more ticks against the entries in my journal. Including finding love again.

After we'd eaten, I told them about my meal at Christian's. I'd returned the favour a couple of nights ago and it had been a great evening which had ended, once more, in a kiss on the cheek from him, leaving me confused as to his intentions.

'I'm so clueless,' I said. 'Does a kiss on the cheek suggest he's interested or is he just being friendly?'

'I'd say probably interested,' Paulette said, but the use of the word *probably* and the catching of her lip with her teeth suggested she wasn't convinced.

Milly shrugged. 'How did you leave it? Any plans to get together again?'

'None.' I rolled my eyes at them. 'He'd have asked me out if he'd wanted more than friendship, wouldn't he?' They didn't need to answer that. It was written all over their faces. 'It was nice to imagine it could be something more if only fleetingly.' But as I said the words, I couldn't help feeling that imagining it was the best part and that I still wasn't convinced it was what I wanted.

'You like him?' Milly asked.

'I've always liked him. As to whether I like *like* him, there's something there but I'm not really sure what it is – friendship, gratitude or something else.'

'The very fact that you're feeling something suggests to me that you're ready – or nearly ready – to let someone in again,' Milly said, 'even if that someone isn't Christian. I know I am. I've been checking out some dating apps. The idea still fills me with horror but I was watching this really romantic film the other night and I thought *that's what I want and I'm not going to get it unless I make it happen* so I decided to do some research. I'm not saying I'll be uploading my profile five minutes after I give Harry the divorce news but there's no harm in being prepared.'

'You'd be perfectly justified in putting a profile up thirty seconds after you tell him,' Paulette said. 'In fact, I don't think anyone would blame you if you did it now.'

I nodded. 'I agree with Paulette, but I get the guilt. Moving on isn't easy.'

We finished our drinks and returned to Celestial Sounds. I played my two shortlisted pianos once more – same piece on each this time, which helped me make my final decision. I placed my order and selected a few books with contemporary music in them which I couldn't wait to play, but which I'd save until I had my new piano. After I explained my house situation to Mervyn, he said it was no problem to store it for me if I hadn't moved by the time it arrived.

On the drive home, I felt uplifted from our day out. Choosing the piano had been a special moment for me but spending the day with two friends who I'd let into my life had been monumental. I told them how much I appreciated how supportive and non-judgemental they'd both been.

'I don't think anyone has a right to judge anyone else until they've walked a hundred miles in their shoes and, even then, they can never truly know what it's like for that person,' Paulette said. 'Unless the person they're judging happens to be called Joanne. I can't help judging her for her current behaviour.'

'How's Saffy holding up?' Milly asked.

'Surprisingly well. It helps that she's feeling so settled in Willowdale. Joanne's blaming me for keeping her here, of course, but I'm beyond caring. Saffy's the one that matters here.'

'She's a special person,' I said, smiling at Paulette. 'It's thanks to her journalling lesson that I've sold my house, bought a piano and shared my past with you two.'

'And it's thanks to her journalling lesson that I've decided to take control of my life too and get the long-overdue divorce,' Milly said.

'I made a photo album of the grandkids,' Paulette said, 'but you two have inspired me. I think it might be time to start a new one and answer those four questions but think about what *I* want. I've always been so focused on my family that I've never really thought about me.'

'It's been life-changing,' I said. 'You should definitely do it.'

'I agree,' Milly said.

'I'll do it. It's fabulous seeing the pair of you so invigorated and excited about the future. I want a piece of that too. It's time to take control of my life. Tomorrow starts today.'

'Ooh, I like that,' Milly said.

'Me too,' I agreed.

In fact, I liked that statement so much that, when I got home, I wrote those three words in chunky capitals across the front cover of my journal, accompanied by an exclamation mark.

TOMORROW STARTS TODAY!

It wasn't just a statement – it was a mindset which echoed what Laughlin had said to me when we'd been talking about Venice and not putting off until tomorrow what could be done today. It was about spending each day making the decisions and choices which laid the foundations for what my heart desired. It was about truly committing to those *START, STOP* and *SEE* question responses in order to achieve the *FEEL* ones. It was how I needed to live my life from this moment on.

I stroked my fingers over the letters, excitement and anticipation flowing through me.

'Tomorrow starts today,' I whispered, and I believed so strongly now that it did. Great things lay ahead for me, for Milly and for Paulette once she'd searched her heart and answered those four questions. We all deserved it, but we were the only ones who could make it happen and I needed to make sure I didn't lose sight of that.

33

Valentine's Day arrived and could there be a more appropriate day for the next phase of Created With Love? Veronica, Laughlin, Milly, Paulette and I – or The Fabric Five as Paulette had christened us – met Ava to look inside the former Willowdale Gifts.

'Apologies for not being able to meet you sooner,' Ava said, placing the key in the lock. 'Bear in mind it's been empty for over three years so it's cold, dusty and a bit on the whiffy side.'

She pushed open the door and we bundled inside and spread out. I'd expected to find some shelving and a shop counter but the place had been stripped bare.

'We cleared it out last spring,' Ava said, as though reading my mind. 'We knew someone who could make use of the shop fittings. The upside is that you have a blank canvas for creating exactly the space you want. The downside is you're going to need to buy some fittings, although there's no need to break the bank. When I started out, I had a couple of pasting tables covered in cloths and built up to better displays when the shop started making money.'

She pointed out a damp patch by the front window where the

rain had seeped in through a rotten window frame and advised us that she'd booked a builder for next week to sort out the damp and replace the window.

'As I own the building, it's my responsibility and in my best interests to ensure the building's sound. Internal décor is usually down to the tenant but I'm conscious the shop's not in great condition. It needs painting and a thorough clean. With my mother being ill, I don't have the time or inclination to do that myself, so I have a proposal for you. What would you say to having this place rent-free for the month leading up to the Easter holidays, during which time you clean and paint it at your expense?'

'Rent-free?' Laughlin asked. 'That sounds like we're getting the better end of the deal.'

'If you do it yourselves, you would be, and it won't take you a month so it means you can bring in your shop fittings and your stock and be ready to open as soon as the schools break up.'

Accepting Ava's offer was a no-brainer. At the back of the shop there was a stud wall with an opening the size of a doorway but without a door. On the other side was a small storeroom which had metal shelving units around three sides. Some of them were a bit bashed but they'd be perfect for our needs. There was also a kitchenette, a toilet and the stairs up to the flat. The flat had two double bedrooms, a small bathroom and an open-plan kitchen and living space. Although the style of bathroom and kitchen were dated, they looked as though they'd never been used and I questioned Ava about it.

'When we bought the building, the flat was a mess so we had it refitted but never ended up using it other than for storage. The rent we've discussed is for downstairs but you can use the flat for storage if you want, free of charge. I can't rent it out to anyone else because there's no separate entrance. However, if one of you or a family member were interested in a temporary lease while you're running the shop, I'm happy to have a separate conversation about rent.'

We returned downstairs and Ava handed Veronica a cardboard folder containing the floor plans and a draft contract to peruse.

'It's been lovely to meet you all,' she said. 'I'd love to be your landlady but retailing is tough. I think this pop-up idea is sensible but it still comes with costs and risks so do take some time to discuss it as a group and be sure it's what you all really want to do.'

I certainly wanted to do it and, if I was correctly interpreting the expressions of the others, they did too. Veronica suggested we retreat to The White Willow for drinks, cake and decision-making so we thanked Ava and told her we'd be in touch next week.

It was only a short walk to the café but, by the time we'd reached the door, we had a unanimous decision about going ahead. We settled in our table, talking over each other. *It was bigger than I expected inside. It's going to look fantastic. What colour should we paint the walls? Where should we put the counter?*

Veronica held her hands up, laughing. 'The enthusiasm is wonderful, but might I suggest we get the drinks in and then take it in turns to share our thoughts?'

Saffy joined us to take our order and was eager to hear how it had gone. We told her we were definitely going ahead but had lots to discuss.

'Kelly says I can take my break now,' Saffy said when she returned with our drinks and cakes. 'Do you mind if I join you?'

Milly had taken lots of photos on her phone so Saffy scrolled through them as we updated her. All too soon, her break was over and she stacked our empty plates to clear away.

'How's it going working here?' I asked her.

'It's great. Everyone's so nice and the chef's really fit so that helps.'

'What's his name and how old is he?' Milly asked.

Veronica craned her neck towards the kitchen. 'What does he look like?'

'And is he single?' I added.

Saffy laughed. 'Is this an interrogation? His name's Felix, he's twenty-two, he's Kelly and Aled's son and Kelly has told me several times that he *is* single so I think she'd approve if anything happened. Looks-wise he's tall, with dark hair and twinkly brown eyes. Pretty lush really.'

When she'd gone, Paulette told us that Saffy had been round to Autumn's cottage and had been massively inspired by what Autumn had said. She'd since enrolled for an art class at the village hall and was looking into courses at the technical college starting in September.

'She's planning to stay in the area long-term?' Veronica asked.

Paulette nodded. 'It looks that way. Willowdale's good for her. Being here seems to be helping her discover who she really is and what she wants for her future.'

'I think you need to take some credit for that,' Veronica said, smiling at Paulette. 'You've given her the space, freedom and support to find that out.'

The rest of us added our agreement and Paulette radiated happiness as she thanked us.

We had another round of drinks during which we talked about everything from paint colours to where we could place the counter to whether the doorway to the back of the shop should have saloon doors added to it. We didn't necessarily make any decisions but it was fun throwing around ideas.

Bill paid, we pulled on our coats and headed outside. Milly

had picked me up and her car was parked opposite The White Willow but the other three, all being Willowdale-based, had walked.

'We'll see you for your party tomorrow,' I said to Veronica. 'Are you looking forward to it?'

It was a standing joke that she wasn't. When she'd presented me with my invitation, she'd explained that she'd had a party booked for her sixtieth birthday but had been rushed to hospital with appendicitis days before so it got cancelled. Rebecca and Felicity had insisted she have it the following year instead and she'd refused but it had cropped up every year so she'd finally relented. The others had all been invited to her sixtieth so knew the story already.

'Oh, I'm so looking forward to it,' she said with over-emphasis as she rolled her eyes. 'Turning sixty-three is such a landmark birthday.'

'But you must be looking forward to having your daughters here,' Milly said.

There was a beat before Veronica answered, 'Of course!' but I could see the tension in her smile.

'Did you notice Veronica's expression when I asked about her daughters?' Milly asked after we set off towards Pippinthwaite.

Milly evidently didn't know about the tension between Veronica and her girls and I wasn't going to betray anyone else's confidences.

'No. What did I miss?'

'I thought she looked tense when I mentioned them, but maybe I'm imagining things.'

'Wasn't it her daughters who insisted on her having the party when she didn't want one? That's probably it.'

'Yeah, that would make sense. I wonder if they'll get some decorations for her after all.'

'Better to have double than none at all,' I said.

Laughlin had told us that, although Veronica hadn't wanted the party, she was a great believer in the idea that *if you're going to do something, do it properly*. Her daughters didn't seem to share that philosophy and had done little more than book the venue and confirm the menu. Veronica had bought and sent the invitations and had even organised her own cake but was loath to organise decorations, despite her discomfort at the small but special details being overlooked. Milly, Paulette and I had therefore been fully supportive of Laughlin's suggestion that we form a decorating committee and surprise Veronica with balloons, banners and table decorations. Even though she'd said her sixtythird birthday wasn't important, it was really her belated sixtieth and we wanted her to have the party she should have had back then. Milly was driving into Keswick to collect everything as soon as she'd dropped me off.

As Milly pulled onto my estate, Christian was pulling out in his car. I was about to raise my hand in a wave but stopped myself, realising that he wouldn't recognise Milly's car. She dropped me off outside my house before turning round in the cul-de-sac and I was putting my key in the lock as she drove past.

'Happy Valentine's Day,' she called out of her open window.

'And to you!' I called back, laughing.

Valentine's Day. Cliff and I used to make it a fun day. We'd give each other cards, carefully chosen with messages which worked for love between friends and we'd try to out-cheese each other by finding the funniest or tackiest Valentine's gift. What must it be like to receive a card sent with genuine romantic intentions from a secret admirer or a loving partner?

I pushed open the door and my heart leapt. There was an envelope on the doormat with my name handwritten on it. A Valentine's Day card? The only person I could imagine hand delivering me one was Christian. I ripped open the envelope with shaking hands, my heart pounding as I took in the entwined hearts on the front. And then it sank as I read the words: *Engagement Party!*

Opening the card, my disappointment at it not being a Valentine's card was replaced with happiness for Emma and Killian. I was delighted for them and wondered when Killian had proposed and how he'd done it. Emma had told me he was a true romantic so I figured it would have been something pretty special. My instinct was to dash over to Christian's to ask for details but that would be pointless when I'd just seen him leaving the estate. It struck me that he might be heading off to meet a Valentine's date. Would it bother me if he was? I wasn't convinced it would.

34

Veronica's party the following day was being held in Lakeside Inn in Willowdale – a large hotel, bar and restaurant which overlooked Derwent Water and stretched from opposite The White Willow to just beyond our proposed pop-up shop. Milly picked me up as agreed and I smiled at the clear bags full of balloons bobbing about on her back seat. We'd arranged to meet Laughlin and Paulette an hour early and waved at them crossing the road by the corner shop as we pulled into Lakeside Inn's car park.

'They've got the conservatory booked,' Laughlin said as Milly distributed bags. 'Oh! Looks like she's beaten us here.'

We all looked towards the large conservatory at the back of the building. The vertical blinds on the windows weren't fully open but there was enough space between them to see Veronica in there.

'Who's she with?' I asked. There was at least one other person in there but I couldn't see them properly.

'I can't tell,' Laughlin said. 'Could be one or both of her daughters but could be staff. We'll soon find out.'

The conservatory was accessed from a wide corridor inside

the hotel. The double doors were closed and Laughlin was about to reach for the handle when Milly grabbed his arm and pulled him back. At the same time, I heard raised voices inside but wasn't close enough to the door to hear what was being said.

'It's her girls,' Laughlin whispered. 'Felicity's coming!' He ushered us all backwards.

The door opened a few inches and Veronica's voice came across strong and clear. 'Don't walk away! Please, Felicity, we need to talk about this.'

'There's nothing to talk about.'

'There is!' Veronica called. 'I'm not stupid and I'm not blind. Something has soured between the two of you and it's affecting all of us. I want to know what it is.'

We were trapped. The door to the corridor had a loud squeak so if we opened it to try and beat a hasty retreat, we'd alert them to our presence and possibly make a bad situation worse.

'Then ask Rebecca,' Felicity snapped.

'I don't care who tells me but one of you has to. You used to be so close but something changed and I've had my fill of it. Talk to me! Whatever it is, we can work it out together.'

'Just leave it, Mum.' That voice had to be Rebecca's. 'It's your birthday. Enjoy it!'

'No! This ends now. Call it my birthday gift. So who's going to tell me what went wrong? I know when it happened, but I don't know why.'

'Does there have to be a reason?' Rebecca cried. 'Why can't you just accept that we got on as kids and we don't as adults?'

'Because I don't believe that's the problem,' Veronica responded, her voice strong but controlled. 'So what's *really* going on?'

A pause before Felicity said, 'I think we should tell her.'

'Don't you dare!' Rebecca yelled.

'She has a right to know.'

'Felicity! I mean it! Don't even think—'

'Stop trying to be the boss of me!' Felicity yelled back. 'I listened to you then because you were my big sister and I looked up to you but you were wrong then and you're still wrong now.'

The pair of them hurled words and insults back and forth, Rebecca clearly trying to stop whatever her sister was about to reveal and Felicity insisting their mum knew *the truth*. And then the truth spewed out.

'Dad was having an affair!' Felicity shouted. 'She told me I couldn't tell you but I thought you had a right to know.'

My stomach plummeted to the floor and my heart shattered for Veronica. Looking at the expressions on the faces of my friends, this was as much of a shock to them as it was to me. I could hear voices, but not raised this time so I couldn't tell what was being said. Next moment, the door was shoved wide open and Veronica stormed out. She paused in front of us, an expression of confusion flickering across her face. What a sight we must look blocking her path with brightly coloured helium balloons when the bottom had just dropped out of her world.

'I'm so sorry,' Paulette murmured.

Veronica shook her head. 'I need to...'

We parted to clear her route. There'd been further shouting in the conservatory but I'd been too concerned about Veronica to tune into it. Rebecca rushed out and headed towards the door but Laughlin blocked her way.

'I think your mum needs some time, don't you? I'll check on her.' He passed me his bag of balloons and went after Veronica. Paulette, Milly and I instinctively closed the gap so Rebecca couldn't follow.

'Oh, for God's sake, let me through. I'm not following her.'

We couldn't exactly keep her trapped so we moved aside.

'Anyone else feel ridiculous holding these now?' Milly asked, grimacing at us. 'Might as well dump them in there.'

Inside the conservatory, Felicity was slumped on one of the chairs, sobbing. Paulette indicated with a nod of her head that we should ditch the balloons while she comforted Felicity. I hoped Laughlin had managed to catch up with Veronica and that he could be of some comfort to her.

It didn't feel appropriate to decorate the room as planned so Milly and I placed everything at the end of the conservatory and hastened to the bar.

'Well, that was unexpected,' Milly said when we sat down with drinks. 'Poor Veronica.'

'I can't even begin to imagine what she's going through right now.'

The bar was filling up and, as they could well be guests, we decided it was best not to discuss what had just happened. Milly sent a text to Paulette asking her to let us know when Felicity had gone as we'd join her then. Ten minutes later, Paulette texted back to say the coast was clear and she needed wine.

'How was Felicity?' Milly asked as we joined Paulette in the conservatory and handed over her drink.

Paulette took a gulp of wine before answering. 'Devastated. She's scared her mum won't ever speak to her again. I've assured her Veronica wouldn't do that, but she might need some time to process the news. She clearly wanted to spill out the full story but I told her it wasn't fair to Veronica that I hear the details first. I felt bad closing her down like that.'

'It was the right thing to do,' I said, and Milly threw in her agreement.

'Where is she now?' Milly asked. 'Is she coming back?'

'She's gone back to her room, but she says she won't be returning for the party. How can she after that? I doubt Rebecca'll return either. Felicity saw her leaving in her car and told me her family are staying somewhere in town.'

I sighed heavily. 'What a mess. Do you think Veronica will come back?'

'Would you?' Paulette asked.

'Not a chance.'

* * *

A birthday party with no guest of honour was an unusual experience. We'd still been in the conservatory when Laughlin phoned Paulette to say that Veronica had headed home but he'd managed to catch up with her halfway and she'd let him accompany her inside. She hadn't said much as she was clearly in shock but she'd let him make her a sweetened tea and said he was welcome to stay so long as he didn't try to get her to talk as she wasn't ready for that yet. Her request was for us to go ahead with the party without her and to apologise to her guests for her absence again. We were to say that it was a family emergency which, given the absence of Rebecca and Felicity, seemed plausible. With heavy hearts, we displayed the balloons, put the birthday banners up and sprinkled the table confetti to make everything look as 'normal' as it possibly could.

Paulette made the announcement and the guests were clearly disappointed but it didn't stop them enjoying the food and having a great afternoon. They had no idea what had gone down earlier. It was only Milly, Paulette and I who struggled to relax, worried about our friend.

'It feels like such a waste,' Paulette said as we burst the balloons after everyone had left, 'but we can hardly show up at Veronica's with these.'

We loaded the cards and gifts into the boot of Milly's car and, when we dropped Paulette home, we took everything into her house for when Veronica felt ready to collect them.

'Out of the frying pan and into the fire,' Milly said as she pulled up outside my house a bit later.

I stared at her, not getting her meaning for a moment. 'Oh, my gosh! Harry's at your place.' It had completely gone out of my head thanks to the unexpected turn of events at the party. 'How are you feeling?'

'More churned up about Veronica than I am about asking my husband for a divorce. I thought I was going to spend today fretting about it but that was one heck of a distraction.'

'I hope he takes it well. If you want to talk about it later, you're welcome to come round.' It had been a heavy day, so I decided to lighten the mood. 'Trevor's a good listener. All you have to do is tell him he's a pretty boy and slip him a slice of fruit.'

'I might take him up on that,' Milly said, smiling.

She did. The doorbell rang shortly after 7 p.m. and Milly thrust a bottle of wine at me the moment I opened it. 'Don't know about you, but I could do with this after today.'

'How did it go?' I asked, returning from the kitchen and handing her a large glass of wine.

'Remember how I said before that my biggest fear was that he might refuse? Turns out the thing I should really have feared was him saying an immediate yes.'

'Immediate?' I asked.

'Immediate. I got home and he had the telly on watching a football match. I said *hello* and asked how his flight was and do you know what he did? He put his finger up to silence me. The game was nearly over and he wanted to watch the ending uninterrupted. Four months abroad and another five minutes of football was of more interest to him than his wife.'

'Oh, Milly, that's awful.'

'Isn't it? So I grabbed the control, switched it off and told him we needed to talk. I had this speech all prepared about how unhappy I was and had been for a while because we barely ever saw each other and, when we did, I felt like we'd grown apart. After I delivered it he said, *so I'm guessing you want a divorce?* I said *yes* and he said *okay* and took the remote back from me, switched on the telly and watched the final minute of the game.'

She paused to take a large glug of wine. 'I'm lost for words. I mean, I didn't expect him to beg me to reconsider but I did anticipate at least talking about it. I thought he'd have questions. I stupidly thought he might apologise but he didn't seem to care. Honestly, Yvonne, I have *never* felt more insignificant in my entire life.'

'I'm so sorry he reacted that way, Milly. That's really hurtful, but I can assure you you're anything but insignificant. If he can't appreciate you for the smart, funny, beautiful, kind woman that you are, he clearly can't appreciate anything.'

She gave me a weak smile.

'What's he doing now?'

'I've dropped him off at Lakeside Inn and he's coming back to pack up his stuff tomorrow. His brother's collecting him and his belongings tomorrow and he'll stay with him for a while. Can I ask a huge favour? Can I work from here tomorrow? I won't be able to work while he's clattering about and I don't really want to be there anyway.'

'Of course you can. I can clear the dining table for you.'

'Thank you. He's said I can keep the cottage and he'll keep the Manchester flat. Assuming he doesn't change his mind about that, the divorce should go smoothly.'

'That sounds really positive to me, but you don't look too enamoured.'

She sighed. 'It *is* positive. I love my cottage and I'm thrilled I get to keep it. It's just that it was all too easy, like we were dividing up our CD collection or something.'

'And you'd have preferred him to put up a bit more of a fight?' I suggested.

'I guess. It's daft, isn't it? I want a divorce and now I'm moaning because he's granted me one.'

'It's not daft. Your marriage is ending and, even though that's the right thing for you, you're bound to be feeling all sorts of emotions about it. This is the man you loved who you chose to spend the rest of your life with. He's the father of your daughter. Your feelings for him might have changed but that doesn't mean that calling time on your marriage isn't going to hurt. You're grieving for what you used to have and what you hoped you'd have in the future and it's only natural to want him to grieve for it too.'

Milly smiled at me. 'You missed your calling in life. You should have been a counsellor or a life coach.'

'I think I'll stick to patchwork quilts but thank you. So what else do you have in your journal to look forward to? Let's focus on the good things ahead. Tomorrow starts today, just like Paulette said.'

'Absolutely that!' she said, clinking her glass against mine. 'This is a good day. Well, not for Veronica, but it *is* a good day for me. I should have done this a long time ago.'

'But you've done it now and that's the important thing,' I assured her. It was never too late. I knew that now.

35

A week passed with no sign of Veronica. My concern for her was eased a little by the knowledge that Laughlin and Lancelot visited every day. At my suggestion, Milly, Paulette, Laughlin and I had clubbed in for a bunch of bright, cheerful flowers and had signed a *thinking of you* card which Laughlin had taken round on the Tuesday. She'd sent us all a lovely message that afternoon.

FROM VERONICA

Thank you all for the gorgeous flowers and card. That's so kind of you. Thank you also for your kindness in giving me space to come to terms with that shocking and unexpected revelation. Your friendship means the world to me and I'd hate you to think I'm pushing you away. I'm just not strong enough to talk about it at the moment. I'm giving all my clubs and activities a miss this week but I hope to be back next week. Much love to you all x

TO VERONICA

I'm so sorry for what happened and completely understand the need for some time and space to process things. Thinking of you and here for you whenever you're ready – even if that's just for some mindless chatter about the weather over a slice of cake x

On Thursday, we had an update about the shop.

FROM VERONICA

In the midst of a dark week, I have some exciting news! Ava says we can have the keys on Monday. The builders have finished and she sees no reason for us to wait another week before we get in. If we open on 28 March as discussed, we have five weeks to get organised which should be more than enough time. Created With Love will soon be open for business!

When Monday morning came round, we'd hoped Veronica would meet us for the key handover but Laughlin arrived shaking his head and making a zipping motion across his mouth which I took to indicate that he'd tell us more later. Saffy had joined us for a quick tour before her shift at The White Willow and she wasn't aware of what was going on.

'No Veronica today?' Ava asked.

'She's feeling under the weather this morning,' Laughlin said. 'Sends her apologies.'

'That's a shame. Well, here's two sets of keys but feel free to cut a set each. See how you get on with the cleaning and decorating. If you want to open earlier than planned, that's fine, but your rent would start from that point. Just keep me posted.'

We thanked her for being so accommodating and she wished

us luck before leaving us to it. Ava had given the keys to Milly so she did the honours and opened the door to *our* shop. We were really doing this!

Even though the unit still needed a deep clean, the treatment of the damp patch and the replacement of the window had already made a huge difference. That musty smell wasn't nearly as strong and, if we kept the windows open while we worked and spread a few air fresheners around, it would soon clear.

Saffy snapped photos on her phone. She'd asked if she could design a display concept and, as none of us had a clear vision, we were happy for her to give it a go.

'If you're free for a drink in The White Willow afterwards, I'll give you an update on Veronica,' Laughlin said in a hushed voice while Saffy was exploring upstairs. 'She's given her permission.'

There wasn't much we could do in the shop today. Milly needed to work this afternoon and Paulette had a dental appointment so we'd agreed to start on the cleaning tomorrow. We therefore locked up once Saffy had finished investigating and wandered over to The White Willow with her.

'Veronica's not quite ready to see anyone but she wanted me to give you an update,' Laughlin said after Saffy started her shift and we'd placed our order. 'She's humiliated about the affair. She knows nobody's judging her but she can't help feeling like a fraud for talking so positively about Carson when it seems their marriage wasn't as strong as she believed. She's angry that he isn't here to answer all the questions like why, who, how long? On top of that, she's devastated about the affect this secret's had on her daughters and their relationship with each other and with her. She feels like she gave up everything to support Carson and his career and, while she chose that life and loved what she did, this feels like a slap in the face and she's reeling from it. You know Vee. You know what a proud and proper woman she is.'

We all expressed our understanding but nobody mentioned that Laughlin had just affectionately referred to Veronica as Vee. Was I the only one who'd noticed?

'You're probably wondering why she's talking to me and not the rest of you. The thing is...'

Saffy brought our drinks and cakes over at that point so we paused the conversation while they were distributed.

'You were saying...?' Paulette prompted after Saffy left.

Laughlin picked up his teaspoon and stirred his latte, staring into the mug. 'The reason Vee's talking to me is that I know what she's going through because I've been through it myself. Well, part of it.'

Beside me, Paulette gasped. 'Surely not Noreen?'

Laughlin finally looked up and nodded. 'Noreen and I met later in life. I was forty-two and she was forty-six. Neither of us had been married before, neither of us had children – we'd both been unlucky in love and had thrown ourselves into our careers instead. A mutual friend introduced us, we clicked immediately and, for the first twelve years, our marriage was great. But then Noreen lost her job. She was fifty-eight and far from being ready to retire, but she had no success job-hunting. She was convinced it was because of her age but I kept telling her something would turn up and I'm ashamed to say I didn't appreciate how much each rejection broke her.

'We'd always planned to travel when we eventually retired so she proposed I retire early and we do that. I loved my job so I refused and unhelpfully suggested that the reason she was struggling to find a job was because she was being too fussy, wanting to be the same level as before, and she should consider more junior positions.'

He grimaced, evidently ashamed of the approach he'd taken. 'She bumped into an ex at a job club who was struggling with unexpected redundancy and...' He broke off with a sigh and stared out of the window for a moment, as though searching for the words on the wind.

'It was Veronica who spotted them together in a pub one day. When Noreen saw Vee, she knew the game was up. She asked her not to say anything and Vee said she wouldn't but encouraged Noreen to tell me herself, so she did. We went for marriage guidance and I learned a lot about myself. I thought I'd been supportive but all I'd done was throw platitudes at Noreen. I hadn't listened to her or understood her pain. In fact, I hadn't even realised she was in pain.'

'But that surely didn't justify her having an affair?' Milly said when Laughlin paused once more to sip his drink.

'No, it didn't, but it's not like she sought him out deliberately. They just happened to be in the same job club and she turned to someone she knew who gave her the support and understanding that she wasn't getting from me. She felt invisible in the workplace but she also felt invisible at home and the ex saw her. And even though I was heartbroken that she'd turned to another man, I saw her at that point too. I saw the woman I still loved and I wanted to try and rescue our marriage but there was no way I could do that if I was still working. So I did take early retirement and we started our travels around Europe. It was hard at first. There was a lot of resentment between us. I'd failed her but she'd failed me too. We made a decision to stop sniping at each other and enjoy our surroundings and properly talk when we felt calmer. Our European travels saved our marriage because we got to know each other again and, fortunately, fell in love all over again.'

Paulette placed her hand over Laughlin's. 'I'm so sorry. I had no idea.'

'We'd moved on and were in a good place by the time she

joined Cake & Craft Club. There was no need to talk about it and stir up difficult memories.'

'I'm sorry you went through that,' I said. 'I can see why it makes you the ideal person for Veronica to talk to.'

I'd finished Laughlin's cross stitch last week and had it framed. It was currently in my car but I wasn't sure whether it was appropriate to give it to him now after what he'd just revealed, although he had said that their travels had got their marriage back on track and he'd originally shared that photo with me as a happy memory. Paulette and Milly hadn't yet finished their drinks but Laughlin and I had so I saw an opportunity to steal him away momentarily.

'You know a bit about cars, don't you?' I said. 'Can I borrow you for a moment to look at a warning light on mine?'

Laughlin followed me to where my car was parked outside.

'There's nothing wrong with my car,' I admitted as I opened the boot. 'I made something for you but, after what you just told us, I didn't want to make you uncomfortable if I gave you it in front of the others. I won't be offended if you don't want it.'

I peeled back the bubble wrap protecting the cross stitch and tilted the frame towards him, watching his face carefully for his initial reaction. Thankfully, it was a positive one.

'That's never a cross stitch?' he said, his eyes wide.

'It is. I found this company who turn photos into patterns.'

'It's incredible! Thank you so much.' He couldn't seem to take his eyes away from it. 'I can understand why you'd be worried about giving me it but I love it, Yvonne. That particular moment right there in the *acqua alta* was extra special because it was the moment we both knew everything was back on track. I can't tell you how much this means to me.'

He turned to face me. 'You're so kind, you know. Vee and I

were talking about you yesterday and how glad we both were that you'd joined our club.'

Tears rushed to my eyes and I couldn't speak for fear I'd start sobbing. That meant the world to me so I hugged Laughlin and whispered, 'Thank you,' into his chest.

He patted my back. 'No. Thank you.'

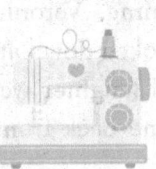

36

The following day, we met at the shop at 10 a.m. to start on the cleaning and, to everyone's relief, Veronica joined us. Pale-faced and subdued, she looked as though a feather could knock her down.

'It's great to see you,' Paulette said.

'I wasn't going to let you lot take all the credit for the refurbishment.' Veronica's words were jovial but her voice was strained and her smile awkward. I wanted to hug her tightly but I sensed it had taken every ounce of willpower to get here and that a demonstration of care like that would tip her over the edge. I suspected the others felt the same as the focus was jokes: *Damn right! No slackers on this watch!*

Paulette had purchased the cleaning products and she handed out yellow rubber gloves to everyone except Veronica.

'I've got something a little classier for you, Veronica.'

Paulette handed her a pair of bright pink gloves with feathered cuffs and fake pearls on them. Veronica stared at them for a moment then burst out laughing as she pulled them on and posed with them. It had been an inspired purchase because Veronica's mood completely lifted from that point.

We stopped at lunchtime, mindful of Milly needing to work but wanting to be as much a part of getting the shop ready as everyone else.

'I never imagined a scenario where I'd enjoy cleaning quite so much as I have this morning,' Veronica said, her smile genuine this time. 'Every time I looked down at my gloves, I couldn't help smiling. Your chatter and laughter were just the tonic I needed too. You've helped pull me back from a dark place and I'm so grateful.'

That was the appropriate point for hugs and, as I squeezed Veronica tightly, I marvelled at how long I'd gone without physical human contact and how powerful and restorative it could be. What had happened to Veronica had nothing to do with me, but her journey did. I was honoured to be part of her healing and it was healing me in return.

* * *

A couple of days later, Saffy presented us with some sketches she'd drawn on her iPad showing the most incredible vision for the shop décor.

'I agree with Ava about not wasting money on expensive shop fittings,' she said. 'You'll be stocking a mishmash of creative styles so I think the fittings should reflect that. I'm thinking distressed pine dressers, apothecary drawers, coat stands and racks for scarves and bags, wrought-iron bedsteads with Yvonne's quilts draped over them...'

We all loved her suggestions and were in awe of how talented she was. She hadn't just thought about furniture – she'd thought about the stock we could display on each item. Her illustrations were so detailed that I felt as though I could step into them and start serving a customer. I offered a couple of items of furniture from my house which would fit with Saffy's vision. My move symbolised a completely fresh start and I wanted new furniture – items I hadn't chosen with Cliff – in order to accomplish that so it made sense to donate what I could to the shop. We agreed a budget for sourcing the rest of the furniture and fittings and Paulette and Saffy took on the responsibility for that.

Over the next couple of weeks, we cleaned then painted, choosing a warm cream for three of the walls and a vibrant peacock green for the back of the shop where the counter and till would go. I loved how bold that feature wall was. There were usually only a couple of us at a time working a few hours each day, which worked really well for me as it meant I could spend the rest of my time clearing out my unwanted furniture and packing for my move.

As I was getting out of my car at home following an afternoon of painting, Christian pulled into Mallard Close and waved. I'd barely seen him recently, only managing a brief conversation during which I'd let him know that we were keen to stock his carvings and wood-turned products in Created With Love.

I waited for him to get out of his car. 'Have you got time for a coffee?' I called across the road.

'I'm parched, so yes.'

'I take it you're painting,' he said, indicating a large splodge of dried emulsion on my arm as I handed him his drink shortly after.

I gave him an update on what we'd done so far and Saffy's vision for the inside.

'If you'd like my help for any repairs, making shelves or attaching any fittings to the wall, just say. I'm not needed at

Emma and Killian's place at the moment as they've got the electricians in and I'm itching to get my power tools out again.'

His eyes sparkled as he spoke and I wondered for a moment whether it was an innuendo, but told myself that Christian wasn't that tacky.

'That would be fantastic, if you're sure you don't mind. None of us are particularly proficient at anything other than hammering in nails and, even then, I think there's room for improvement.'

The following week, Christian's skills were invaluable. He helped in the shop but also generously offered his workshop for stripping down and painting or varnishing the furniture Saffy and Paulette had found. He showed so much enthusiasm for what we were doing that we all agreed to invite him in as an investor if he was interested. He loved the idea and looked both surprised and flattered to be asked so, at the end of week three of our refurbishment, Christian became part of The Fabric Five, except there were now six of us, so Paulette renamed us The Crafty Crew.

Getting Created With Love ready for opening had gone so well that we contacted Ava and agreed on four rather than five weeks to prepare, opening a little earlier than planned. The main tourist season in the Lake District started with schools breaking up for the Easter holidays and we figured that opening on the Monday of the week before would give us the opportunity to iron out any teething problems while the area was a little quieter.

For me personally, life was feeling pretty incredible. I adored having such good friends and being part of something special with them. I'd heard people speak about loving their jobs or being passionate about their careers and, while I'd been happy enough as Cliff's assistant, it hadn't been a dream role. But now I had an actual job which filled me with excitement. I couldn't wait to get to the shop each day and my heart leapt every time I walked through the door and saw the improvement from the day before.

My house sale was progressing well and my solicitor couldn't see any reason why it wouldn't complete early on in the Easter holidays. The only fly in the ointment was that I still hadn't seen anywhere I wanted to buy. Mallard Close had been a practical choice – a head decision – but I wanted my next purchase to be chosen by my heart. I wanted to walk into the property and fall instantly in love, to have that special feeling that it was a home rather than a house. Milly or Paulette had accompanied me on a handful of viewings in and around Keswick but nothing had made my heart sing. I'd wondered if I was being too fussy but they'd assured me I wasn't and that the intangible feeling you got about the right property was just as important as size and location. Even if I had found somewhere, it was far too late to try and coordinate the sale and purchase. I'd promised my buyers a quick sale and I was sticking to that.

As kind as the offers of a spare room from my friends had been, Paulette had Saffy, Milly had her work, Laughlin had Lancelot and Veronica had so much going on with trying to fix her family that it wasn't really convenient to stay with any of them. I decided to rent the flat above the shop instead. Hopefully I'd have found somewhere permanent by the time our initial three-month contract ended.

Ava said I was welcome to paint the flat so long as I didn't go for anything garish. Garish wasn't me so there was no danger of that. Christian had already offered to help me paint as soon as the shop was ready, which I really appreciated. Having two of us would make the task so much quicker.

Mervyn at Celestial Sounds had been in touch to tell me my piano had arrived and reiterated that it was no problem to store it for me until I was settled in my new home. In the meantime, I purchased a second-hand keyboard on a collapsible stand. It wasn't the same as playing the piano but it meant I could work my restless fingers and switch off from thoughts about Created With Love, which were in danger of occupying every waking hour.

Everything I'd entered in my journal was coming together. I hadn't had much time to *see more of the local area with my new friends*, but that was because of the shop. I was confident I'd be able to work on that entry once we were open and had settled into a routine. I'd stopped all the *stop* entries, although I still felt some guilt about cutting Marianne out of my life. In quiet moments, an image floated into my mind of my sister surrounded by all that junk and my conscience pricked at me.

On the Thursday before we opened for business, I'd spent the morning putting out stock with Veronica and Paulette. Laughlin joined us in the afternoon, accompanied by Lancelot. Lancelot was usually exceptionally well-behaved but the buzz of excitement and the flurry of activity must have been too much for him because he kept helping himself to the stock and running up to the flat with his stolen property.

'I'd better take him home,' Laughlin said, 'before we have nothing left to sell.'

'Why don't I take him for a walk?' I suggested. 'I could do with some fresh air and it should tire him out.'

While Laughlin attached Lancelot's lead to his collar, I pulled on a thick purple coatigan. Spring would officially arrive tomorrow and, although the daffodils were in full bloom and the sky was blue, there was still a wintry nip in the air.

I walked Lancelot through the village towards the marina, smiling at the speed at which his little legs moved and the way he clasped Spud, his red panda, between his teeth the whole time. We walked past Willowdale Hall and as far as the jetty before turning round and retracing our steps. At first, my thoughts were focused on the shop – how fabulous it was looking with stock out and what we still had to unpack – but, as I headed back towards the village, they turned to Marianne. It was no good. I was going to have to ring her and there was no time like the present and I knew exactly where to go to make that call.

Between the marina and one of the lakeside houses, there was a narrow track which looked insignificant from the path but which Paulette had taken me down, describing the end of the track as *one of Willowdale's best kept secrets.* The track led to a grassy area which gently sloped down to the lakeside and delivered the most stunning views across the marina, the lake and the fells beyond. It was so tranquil there so I'd visited several times since, usually taking a picnic blanket with me so I could either sit and think or empty my mind, depending on what was needed. I didn't have my blanket with me today but it had been a dry week so I lowered myself onto the grass while Lancelot sniffed the clusters of vibrant yellow and pale lemon daffodils and took my phone out of my pocket. I'd call Marianne under the guise of letting her know that I was moving house.

'Why are you telling me this?' she asked, her voice slow and croaky after I'd updated her.

'I thought you should know.'

'And now I do. Was there anything else?'

I had planned to tell her about Created With Love but what was the point? It had been a bad idea to call her after all.

'Just wondering how you are,' I said.

'Don't start that again. You're not my mum or my doctor so leave me alone.' The line went dead.

I put my phone back in my pocket and sighed heavily. That was the end of it. From now on, I'd be sticking with my entry in my journal to *stop chasing a relationship with Marianne.* No more phone calls, no more visits. She clearly had no interest in being part of my life and I'd had more than enough of trying to force her, even though cutting her out completely made me feel sad. I was convinced she was ill or lonely or both, but she wasn't going to confide in me about any of it and I had to respect her choice.

* * *

The following day, The Crafty Crew minus Christian spent the afternoon displaying the last of the crafts and checking everything was priced up and I was so proud of what we'd accomplished. The shop looked incredible with an impressive range of gifts, all handmade with love.

Saffy had taken some candid photos of us doing our crafts which she'd told us were for social media, but she'd surprised us at Cake & Craft Club on Wednesday with a couple of boards, each featuring photos of three of us alongside a list of the things we were passionate about. My entries had made me laugh as, besides *sewing*, *patchwork quilting* and *playing the piano*, she'd put *eating cake* and *talking to her parrot Trevor*. She'd sized them to display on the walls either side of the bay window so anyone looking in could get a sense of the team behind the business. I'd told her she should have included herself but she was adamant that it should only be the owners, although she was happy to be featured on the website as part of the wider team of contributors. The whole window display looked amazing and the boards really finished it off.

Christian hadn't been able to join us this afternoon but he'd kindly offered to help me do some painting in the flat this evening.

'How did you get on today?' he asked when he arrived a little after five o'clock.

'All done. I can't believe it's ready.'

'It looks brilliant.' He completed a circuit of the shop, pausing to look at the ranges we'd added this afternoon. 'It's amazing what you can achieve in a short time with enough pairs of hands.'

The evening's task was painting the living space. I'd chosen a pale sage green for all four walls – quicker and easier than including a feature one. Christian and I made a great team as I enjoyed the precision work round the edges but he preferred the big work with the paint roller. We chatted as we painted and there was plenty of laughter. The more time I spent in Christian's company, the more I liked him but I still couldn't decide if that was in the romantic sense or more as a friend.

A few hours later, we'd finished a first coat in the lounge and, as the cutting in took longer, Christian had also painted the small bathroom white, at which point I declared our painting party over for the evening. I was transferring some green paint back from the tray into the tin and Christian was cleaning the white paint tray in the kitchen sink when the entire tap attachment came off and water spurted upwards and outwards like a geyser erupting.

'Flood!' Christian called, lunging for the sink and trying to ram the tap back into place. 'Where's the stopcock?'

'Under the sink,' I said, pulling open the cupboard and grasping for the handle.

I looked up sheepishly when I'd turned it. 'I'm so sorry. Are you okay?'

'You might need a new one of these.' He waved the tap before dropping it in the sink. 'And I might be a smidge damp.' He ran his hands through his hair, droplets of water spattering everywhere.

'Just a smidge,' I said, my lips twitching as I took in the soggy mess before me, his T-shirt dripping onto the wooden floor.

Next moment, we were both laughing helplessly. I ran to the bathroom to grab the hand towel from there and my breath caught when I returned. Christian had whipped off his T-shirt and was wringing it out in the sink and he was impressively toned. I meant to pass him the towel but I managed to keep hold of it and blot his chest instead. I looked up at him and he looked down at me and I was sure I picked up a flicker of something more than friendship passing between us. Without pausing to think about whether it was a good idea, I stood up on my tiptoes and pressed my lips against his. My mind skipped ahead in time, imagining him kissing me back and pulling me into a passionate clinch but what actually happened was that he stepped away and both the towel and his T-shirt dropped to the floor with a splat.

'Yvonne, I—'

'I'm so sorry.' I retreated several paces, my stomach churning. 'I don't know what... I didn't mean to... I shouldn't have... erm.'

He pulled his wet T-shirt back on, which must have felt disgusting, and looked at me, his expression sorrowful. 'It's my fault.'

'No, you weren't the one who...' I couldn't bring myself to even say the word *kissed* out loud.

'I know, but I might have given you the wrong impression and that was never my intention. I really, really like you, Yvonne, but as a friend. I hate myself for saying that because it's one of those awful excuses.'

'It's not an excuse. It's the truth and the stupid thing is I feel the same. I really value your friendship. Can we put it down to a misjudged moment and forget it happened? I really don't want things to be awkward between us, especially when we're in business together.'

'I promise you there's no harm done.'

We stood there for a moment, eyes held, atmosphere heavy. I

wanted the ground to swallow me up whole. What had I been thinking?

Christian finally broke the silence. 'So, erm, there's not a lot we can do now until you have a working tap so why don't I pick one up for you in the morning?'

'You don't have to do that. You've done so much already.'

'It's really no bother. So, I'll be heading off now – time for a hot shower.'

'I'll see you out and thanks again for the help.'

As I closed and locked the door behind him, I hung my head, cringing. How awful had that been? I sincerely hoped there'd be no awkwardness between Christian and me going forwards. Imagine if I ruined things for the rest of The Crafty Crew. I trudged back up the stairs, cursing my stupidity. At least one positive thing had come out of it. Even though my mind had raced ahead imagining the kiss progressing, my heart hadn't. I hadn't felt anything when I kissed Christian, confirming that I didn't want to be with him in a romantic way. Had him being dripping wet triggered my memories of being caught in that torrential downpour with Will? It was the only logical explanation for acting so irrationally. I just hoped we could move on from it.

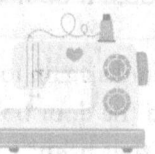

37

The following morning, I was spending some time with Trevor when a message came through from Christian.

FROM CHRISTIAN

Morning! I've been to the flat and fitted you a new tap which is working fine. I've also cleaned the paint trays. See you tonight

'It's lovely of him,' I told Trevor, 'but it sounds to me like he couldn't face seeing me. What do you think?'

'Feed me!' he responded so I passed him a piece of grape.

'I don't know if I can face Emma and Killian's engagement party.'

'Party!'

'I don't want to put a dampener on Emma's special night if things are awkward between her dad and me. It's a shame because Milly was really looking forward to it.'

I didn't know what to do for the best. I'd invited Milly as my plus one as I'd wanted to cheer her up after the non-reaction from Harry about the divorce. She'd understand if I cancelled but

I'd felt bad about it for her and for Emma. It had been really kind of her and Killian to invite me.

'Visitor!' Trevor cawed and I looked up to see Christian walking up my drive holding a bunch of flowers.

'I wasn't expecting to see you today,' I said when I opened the door.

'These are for you,' he said, passing me the flowers. 'They're to say sorry.'

'Sorry? You did nothing wrong. I'm the one who owes you the apology.'

'Believe me, you don't. I've been doing a lot of thinking about my behaviour around you over the past month or so and I've said and done things which, on reflection, were misleading. It was never my intention.'

I smiled at him. 'I'm off to the hairdresser's in twenty minutes but I've time for a quick cuppa if you'd like one.'

'I'd love one.'

Twenty minutes was ample time to clear the air. It transpired that Christian hadn't had any strong female friendships since his schooldays and that, accompanied by his limited dating experience since Kathryn died, meant he'd struggled with reading signals and with where to draw the line. I could relate to that and we both admitted to being a little embarrassed by that considering our ages but agreed that age didn't necessarily come with wisdom about absolutely everything, especially matters of the heart.

'It might have been easier if I'd made it clear from the start that I was only looking for friendship,' Christian said, 'but the truth is, I didn't know what I was looking for. You're an attractive woman, Yvonne, and I enjoy spending time with you. I wasn't sure whether that was as a friend or something more.'

'Same here. It felt like there should be something between us and I guess that kiss was to see whether there was, but...'

When I scrunched my nose up, he nodded. 'If the chemistry isn't there, it isn't there and you can't force it.'

'Agreed.'

Christian drained the last of his tea. 'I'd better let you get to the hairdresser's but thanks for listening and understanding. Friends?'

I smiled widely. 'Friends.'

'I will see you at the engagement party tonight?' he asked as I walked him to the door.

'Yes. I was toying with dipping out as I didn't want things to be awkward but I'll definitely be there now.'

'Good. Emma would kill me if she discovered you weren't there because I'd messed up.'

'Let's say we both messed up but it's sorted now and we're friends and business partners.'

He ran back across to his house and I grabbed my bag and set off to the hairdresser's in the village centre, feeling thankful that no lasting damage had been done between Christian and me and also relieved that things had come to a head. It had been confusing for a while, thinking I maybe liked him but not being quite sure, and it sounded like he'd felt the same. But at least I'd tried. I'd never have done that a few months ago.

* * *

'I can't wait to see what it looks like inside,' Milly said as I drove us through the gates to Willowdale Hall that evening. 'Coral and I did an alpaca walk in the summer so I've seen the outside and it's a stunning building.'

'I haven't even seen the outside. I was going to book an alpaca walk with my former next-door neighbour, Betsy, but she finally admitted that she's scared of alpacas and llamas so it never happened.'

'I'd love to do another walk. Maybe we can book one together to celebrate opening the shop.'

'That's a great idea. We should... oh! Wow!'

I eased my foot off the accelerator as I took in the stunning manor house ahead of us. Three storeys high and constructed from grey slate with sandy-coloured stones round the windows, it took my breath away.

'Beautiful, isn't it?' Milly said.

'It's even more impressive than I expected. Could you imagine getting married here? The combination of the house, the lake and the fells would be so special.'

Christian had told me that Oliver and his girlfriend, Rosie, had already hosted several events in the ground-floor function room where Emma and Killian's engagement party was being held. The room had been refurbished as part of the huge renovation project but they were still debating getting a licence to become a wedding venue, not that Emma and Killian would get married there if they did. The hall was important to them as they'd met through working there so it was the ideal venue for their engagement party, but they felt it would be a bit much getting married at their place of work.

Inside, Willowdale Hall was equally impressive with a sweeping dual staircase, an enormous sparkling chandelier and beautiful wooden panelling. An A-board to the right directed us through an open doorway, not that it was really needed as we could hear the music and chatter.

I spotted Autumn and Dane and introduced Milly to them. Milly mainly worked on novels but had edited a few children's books in her time. She knew a few authors who Autumn and

Dane had met so, noticing Christian nearby, I excused myself and left them deep in conversation.

'I'm glad you came,' Christian said, smiling at me.

'Me too. This place looks incredible.'

'Can I say that you do too? I love your hair. That really suits you.'

'It was long overdue.' I'd been thrilled with the miracle that had been worked on my dull hair. The hairdresser had taken several inches from it and added various colours to create a shiny, bouncy shoulder-length style which Milly had said made me look years younger.

Christian introduced me to Oliver and Rosie.

'You have a beautiful home,' I told them. 'How's progress going with the apartments?'

'We're almost there,' Rosie said. 'The boat house was ready at the end of last summer and it's been fully booked ever since. The apartments in the other wing are ready and we've got our first guests booked in from the start of the Easter holidays, which is both exciting and scary.'

'The rest of the apartments – upstairs in this wing – should be finished by the end of May,' Oliver said, 'but our home's on this floor and there's still work being done inside so we're not taking bookings until the summer when all the building work's finished.'

Rosie nodded. 'The whole project will have taken about a year which isn't bad considering the size of this place. I believe you have a project of your own, Yvonne, but I need to find my mum as she wants to chat to you about your patchwork quilts.'

Rosie introduced me to her mum, Alice, who told me she loved patchwork quilts and had one on her bed but it was old and worn and she'd love a new one so would definitely visit Created With Love during our opening week to make a purchase. It gave me a thrill to know that I already had a customer.

Across the evening, I was introduced to various guests including Alice's fiancé, Xander, and a lovely woman called Mel – the conservation architect who'd developed the plans for the building. When I discovered that she'd also been responsible for the interior design, I couldn't resist mentioning Saffy's name and whipping out my phone to show her the designs Saffy had done for Created With Love.

'You say she's had no formal training?' Mel asked as she flicked through the photos.

'None, although she's started art classes at the village hall and is looking into college courses.'

'She's got a raw, natural talent.' Mel looked thoughtful as she scrolled back and forth before returning my phone to me. 'I often get asked to do interior design and, while I enjoy it, it's not my core business so I usually have to turn it down. Willowdale Hall was an exception. I've loved this building since I was a little girl.'

Mel retrieved a business card and handed it to me. 'Tell Saffy to get in touch. I think it would be worth us having a chat. I might not be able to give her any work but I can offer some advice – maybe even a spot of mentoring.'

'That would be amazing. Thank you so much.'

It was a lovely evening which I was glad I hadn't missed. Emma and Killian's friends and family were so welcoming and they all passed on their best wishes for Created With Love's opening day on Monday, promising to visit. At various points across the evening, my eyes connected with Christian's and we smiled at each other but those butterflies which had previously paid me a brief visit didn't reappear. Milly thought that the physical reaction I'd had to him could have been the result of him being the first man to pay me any attention since Cliff died. That certainly made sense. I'd been flattered and got carried away with it. A positive from it was that spending so much time with Christian had given me the courage to be around other men. For now, the priority was opening Created With Love, completing on my house sale next week, settling into the flat and finding somewhere permanent to live but I'd do something about finding love once everything was settled. No idea what but I'd come up with something.

Milly seemed to be really enjoying herself which was great to see. I'd been worried about how subdued she'd been lately but getting dressed up and being out among people for a happy occasion seemed to have done her the world of good. My friends had all had a tough start to the year and, while Created With Love had provided us all with a welcome distraction, everyone could do with a little fun and a session walking Emma's alpacas could be just what we all needed.

38

'There's a queue outside,' Milly cried, her eyes shining with excitement on Monday morning. 'An actual queue!'

Although we'd all acknowledged that it was overkill having seven of us – The Crafty Crew plus Saffy – present for our ten o'clock opening time, it was too special a moment for any of us to miss out on. Kelly had given Saffy the day off especially but, when Saffy realised we were all going to be here, she'd offered to dip out. We'd said we wouldn't allow it after everything she'd done. The shop would never have looked as good as it did without her and the queue was down to her hard work too. She'd drummed up an impressive following across various social media accounts, had secured some coverage in the local newspaper and had organised a leaflet drop to all the houses in Willowdale and Pippinthwaite.

'It's time,' Veronica said, turning the key in the lock and opening the door wide. 'Good morning, everyone! You're our very first customers. Thank you so much for your support. Come inside!'

A group of maybe ten entered the shop, heading in different

directions. Veronica and Laughlin stepped behind the counter while the rest of us spread out to help and answer questions.

A woman who'd been looking at my quilts approached me. 'You're going to hate me. I love the quilts but I think the one in the window is my favourite. Would it be possible to see it?'

I gave her a reassuring smile. 'It's no problem at all. Just give me a moment to move a few things.'

We'd created an Easter display in the window which included a quilt I'd created from cream, yellow and green fabrics draped across a child's wooden chair. Paulette had joked that it was so pretty and eye-catching that it'd probably be one of the first items to sell. Fortunately, it wasn't difficult to retrieve and, when I held it out for the woman to see, she confirmed she wanted it. I had to contain a squeal of excitement that one of my quilts had sold during the first hour.

After the initial rush, there was a steady flow of customers across the morning. Some made big purchases, some small and others were just browsing but everyone we spoke to was complimentary about how perfect Created With Love was for gifts – exactly the feedback we'd hoped for.

As lunchtime approached, we agreed that there was no need for us all to stay for the entire day. Paulette, Saffy and I went upstairs for some lunch, after which the others headed home. Saffy had taken various videos that morning and wanted to edit them and share them on social media to keep the hype going so she remained upstairs to work her magic on her phone.

During the afternoon, plenty of people admired my quilts but there weren't any purchases. If we sold one a week, I'd be delighted but wasn't even expecting that. A pair of patchwork cushions sold and it was interesting seeing which other products were popular. One customer asked if we could provide thirty panda crocheted keyrings to go in party bags for her panda-obsessed daughter. A couple of customers asked whether the pyrography signs could be personalised and a quick call to Laughlin confirmed he could easily do that. Saffy had designed some lovely quotes and pictures which she'd printed off and framed and they'd proved popular. She'd also created some beautiful pictures using sections of old sheet music from my collection alongside musical notations and imagery the music evoked. I hadn't been sure about cutting up my music until she'd shown me what she was planning to do with it and I loved the idea of the aged pages being given a new, different lease of life.

In a quiet moment, I walked a lap of the shop, straightening up a few items and restocking. We really did carry an impressive range – something for all ages and tastes – and I hoped word would spread and Created With Love would take off. It would be a shame to close down after the three months we'd initially agreed.

As closing time approached, Milly, Veronica, Laughlin and Christian returned to see how the first day had gone. Sales were way higher than we'd imagined, helped by a couple of pricier purchases including my quilt and cushions.

'I think this calls for a celebratory drink,' Christian said. 'Over the road?'

I noticed Veronica stiffen and Laughlin evidently had too as he suggested The Hardy Herdwick instead. Presumably Lakeside Inn was a little too raw for Veronica after her disastrous birthday party. I wasn't sure whether Veronica had been in touch with either of her daughters since then and I didn't like to ask. I really hoped they were speaking and were finding a way to make their peace with each other.

* * *

The first week of trading went really well. Alice and Xander did stop by as promised and chose a beautiful blue patchwork quilt. I recognised other customers as guests from Emma and Killian's engagement party too. I'd worked the lion's share of the hours but I didn't mind because I'd finished my packing and had the time free. Christian helped me finish the painting in the flat so, when the sale on my house in Mallard Close completed on the Tuesday of week two of trading, it was ready for me to move into. I took the day off from the shop and thought I'd feel sad leaving the house where Cliff and I had spent so many years together but, as the removals van took my belongings away to a storage facility, I felt more relieved than anything. A fresh start was absolutely what I needed.

I'd kept only the essentials and a few home comforts for the flat so I spent the rest of the day unpacking and settling in. To my relief, Trevor seemed unfazed by his new surroundings. As long as he had his cage, his mirror and his misting spray, he was perfectly content.

I was back at work the following day. As we were now into the Easter holidays, I'd noticed more people walking round the village but the footfall in the shop hadn't necessarily increased, probably because so many friends and family had visited during the first week.

We'd agreed that it was okay to work on our crafts during quiet moments in the shop, thinking it added an element of authenticity when customers came in. Of course, that only applied to some of the crafts – Christian certainly couldn't start wielding his chainsaw. I'd barely done any sewing recently and I'd really missed it so, in a mid-morning lull, I dug out the memory bear I was making from Cliff's shirts. I'd reached the final stage of stuffing the bear's body and sewing up his back when a dark-haired woman entered the shop and glanced in my direction.

'Good morning,' I called to her.

'Morning! A friend told me you have some stunning patchwork quilts.'

I rose from my chair to join her. 'We've got one in the window and a few on display around the shop but I've got other colours and designs out the back. If you have a size or colour scheme in mind, I can dig out a selection for you.'

'It's for my mum. She's about to move into a retirement flat in Keswick and I want to get her a quilt as a moving-in gift. It needs to be a double and it has to be pastels. She doesn't do bright colours.'

I pointed out where the various quilts were on the shop floor and suggested the customer have a look through those while I brought some pastel-coloured ones through from the back. We spent about twenty minutes looking through them and the woman narrowed it down to a green-and-cream one and a multicoloured one.

'I can't decide,' she said. 'Do you mind if I take photos and send them to my daughters?'

'No problem at all.' I held up the quilts so she could take a full photo of each.

'How many daughters do you have?' I asked.

'Three – age twenty, seventeen and thirteen. My poor husband,' she said, laughing, 'but he says he wouldn't have it any other way.'

I returned to my bear so she could peruse the rest of the shop in peace while waiting for replies.

'My eldest says the green one,' she called to me as a text came through. 'I'm leaning towards that. It's Mum's favourite colour.' Her phone beeped a couple more times and she laughed again.

'That was no help whatsoever. The other two have said the multi-coloured one so it's two votes each. Which do you prefer?'

'I'm not the best person to ask as I'm a bit biased. I was the one who made them.'

Her eyes widened. 'Just these ones or all of them?'

'All of them.'

'You are *so* talented. I wish I was creative but I can't knit, sew, bake, draw... but I can change the oil in the car and fix the washing machine when it has a hissy fit.'

'I can't do either of those things so I'm in awe of your talents. It'd be a boring old world if we were all good at the same things.'

The woman smiled. 'Too right! I'm Fen, by the way.'

'Yvonne.'

'What are you working on because that doesn't look like a quilt to me?'

I turned the bear over so Fen could see him from the front. 'He's a memory bear. These were my husband's shirts.'

'Oh, I'm sorry. Recent bereavement?'

'Five years ago but I'd never got around to doing anything with his clothes. I've sold my house so I had to do a clear-out and a friend suggested making a bear from my favourites. I'm really pleased with him.'

'He's gorgeous. I don't suppose you take orders?'

'I hadn't thought about it but I don't see why not.' I did a swift calculation in my head. As the customer would be supplying the fabric, I only needed to charge for the stuffing, thread and eyes, but I needed to account for the labour, bearing in mind that the cutting up and organising of the patches did take a lot of time. I suggested a price, expecting a pass but she smiled.

'That sounds reasonable to me. My dad passed away recently and I reckon my mum would love a memory bear from his shirts. We've just bagged up his clothes this past week but haven't done anything with them yet so this is perfect timing. I think my girls would like one each too. Any chance you could make four? I've got a niece and nephew too but they're a bit older so I think I'd better ask them first. What do you need from me?'

'A pile of clean shirts and some guidance as to which are the favourites as I can make those ones more prominent and include them on every bear. Some insight into your dad's personality would be good too. I can attempt a facial expression that's more serious or a bit cheeky, depending on what he was like.'

'I love that idea. I live in Kendal but my brother lives in Keswick so I'll get him to drop them off but I'll scribble down some notes. Do you need a deposit?'

'Ten pounds per bear when your brother drops the shirts off.'

'That's fine. I'll send cash with James and, for now, I'll take the green quilt, please.'

When Fen left, I couldn't stop smiling. I'd sold yet another quilt *and* I had orders for four memory bears. It had never entered my head to sell them but I'd check the others were happy with it and, assuming they were, I'd get Saffy to make a sign and I'd display Cliff's bear in the shop.

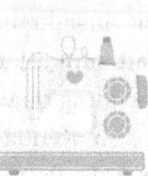

39

The following week, I was wrapping up a pair of Christian's wood-turned candlesticks when a man entered the shop and strode towards the counter. Evidently noticing I was serving a customer, he moved off to one side and stood with his back to me, looking at Saffy's pictures on the wall. My candlesticks customer was about to pay when she spotted some cute wooden toadstool keyrings on a stand by the till.

'I'll have one of these, but which colour?' she murmured, clearly more to herself than to me. While she was deciding, I glanced across at the man. He had a large bag with him which he'd placed on the floor and his right hand crept up to his short dark hair, his index finger swirling in a small circle. My breath caught and my heart leapt. Will? It couldn't be! I pictured him in the pub in Manchester, nervously twirling his hair exactly like that. I gripped the counter, my legs feeling suddenly shaky, but there was no way it could be him. Not now, not in my shop, not after all this time.

'I'll take this one,' the customer said, yanking my attention back to her and the lilac toadstool she was dangling from her finger. 'No! I'll go traditional with red. But purple's my favourite colour. Argh! I can't decide. Which do you like best?'

My favourite was actually a turquoise one but I wasn't going to confuse matters by throwing that into the mix. I was desperate for her to make a decision and go so the man could turn around and I could settle my now-pounding heart with confirmation that it wasn't Will. I mean, why would it be?

'If purple's your favourite colour, I'd go for your first choice.'

'Good idea. I'll take this one, please. No! I'll go for both.'

She then faffed about as to whether to pay cash or card, settled on card, then couldn't decide which of several accounts to use. Paulette didn't have a lot of patience for ditherers but they'd never bothered me – until now! She changed her mind back to cash and, while she made a rigmarole of counting out the exact money, I kept glancing across at the man. He had his phone out and whatever he was reading on it sent his finger back to twirling his hair.

'Thanks for your help,' the woman finally said, picking up her purchases and heading out with a wave.

The man picked up his bag and sauntered over to the till, his head bowed over his phone, his shoulders hunched. *Look up! I need to see your face!* He was the right height and build for Will – maybe a little more filled out across the stomach – but I couldn't be sure until he raised his head. Although if my pounding heart and swirling stomach were anything to go by, it was definitely him.

'My sister asked me to drop these off.' He placed the bag on the counter but still didn't look up. 'There's an envelope in there with some money and instructions.'

That silky smooth voice was unmistakable. I'd heard it so many times in my dreams. His dark hair was now salt and pepper on the top, giving him a distinguished air.

'Is there anything else you need?' My words sounded distant and I was surprised I'd managed to form any at all. Why was he here? How was he here?

He finally looked up and I swear my heart stopped beating for a moment. It was him! Older but definitely him. Except Fen had said her brother's name was James. Nothing was making sense.

'You're Fen's brother?' I asked, willing him to recognise me, but he only glanced at me briefly before a beep from his phone drew his attention downwards again and he released a heavy sigh.

'Fen's number's in the bag if anything's not clear,' he said, staring at his phone.

Why didn't he recognise me? Even a flicker of recognition would have been something. I felt foolish for thinking about him for twenty years when he clearly hadn't been thinking about me. Then it struck me that I'd given him ample reason not to want to remember me. I'd checked out of the hotel and abandoned him without any explanation. If somebody had done that to me, I'd have done my hardest to remove all memory of them from my mind.

Will's phone rang and he raised his eyes once more. My heart filled with hope. His glance had been far too fleeting before, but what about now? But he was clearly distracted by his phone ringing.

'Is there anything else you need?' he asked.

'No. I've got everything, thanks.' The words were laughable when the one thing I really wanted was standing right in front of me.

He nodded and left the shop, connecting the call before he reached the door. I watched in disbelief as he paced up and down in front of the window. Whatever the phone call was about, his stiff body language suggested it was an intense one. The call must have ended as he clutched his head in both hands. He looked to me like a man desperately in need of a hug but I could hardly dash out the shop and launch myself at him, no matter how much I ached to hold him in my arms again.

Next moment, Will lowered his hands and tilted his head to one side, something in the window evidently catching his eye. Veronica had been responsible for the most recent window change and I couldn't remember what she'd put in there.

His phone rang again and he pressed it to his ear, returning to his pacing. Then he stopped dead, staring into the window once more and, this time, I was in no doubt as to what he was looking at. From the angle of his head, it had to be the posters Saffy had created of The Crafty Club. My photograph and my interests were on the side of the window he was focused on. The call ended and he stood there for several minutes, just staring. I couldn't bear it. There was no reason for him to be so gripped by that poster unless he'd recognised me from my photo and realised I was inside the shop, but what was he going to do about it? Come in and politely ask if we used to know each other? Come in and demand to know why I'd run out on him two decades ago? Or walk away?

He turned his head away from the poster, cupped his hands round his face and peered into the shop. Panicking, I plucked a shirt from the bag and pretended to be preoccupied with it. The door remained firmly closed and, when I looked up, there was no sign of Will.

'Damn it!' I stamped one of my feet in frustration. What was wrong with me? I was a sixty-year-old woman who'd just behaved like a shy child. Why hadn't I spoken to him? Despite the name difference, there was no mistaking who he was. I'd been thinking about and dreaming of this man for twenty years. I recognised his stature, his face, his voice. Fate had delivered him to my door in the year I'd decided to get a life and search for love. Could the universe be any more obvious? And I'd let him slip through my fingers. If I could turn back the clock ten minutes, I'd do it all so differently.

A few minutes later, the door opened and Will strode up to the counter and I stared at him, dumbstruck.

'The picture of the music in the window – can I have a closer look?'

He held my gaze as he spoke this time but I still couldn't tell whether he recognised me.

'I'll get it out for you.' How I managed to keep my voice steady, I'll never know.

It was easily retrieved and, as I glanced down at the music, my heart leapt. It was Debussy's 'Clair de Lune' – the piece I'd played with my fingers outside Pianos of Distinction the evening we met.

'I'll take it, please. It reminds me of someone I met a long time ago.' He looked up from the picture and fixed his gaze on mine. 'She told me it made her mum think of floating on a lily pond, the sun on her cheeks, the breeze in her hair, at one with nature.'

He remembered! He recognised me after all! Tears pricked my eyes and my voice wobbled. 'I'm so sorry, Will.'

'I came back for you and you were gone.'

'I know. I never intended to leave you but—'

'You don't have to explain. I know your situation was difficult and I do understand. You were such a kind person, Yvonne, and it sounded like your husband was too. Of course it was going to be hard for you to walk away, especially to take a chance on someone you'd only just met.'

'It wasn't like that. It—'

The door opened and a couple of young women entered and headed over to the scented candles. Talk about bad timing! I grabbed one of the shop's business cards and scribbled my mobile number on the back.

'I'm not making excuses...' My eyes flicked towards the customers and Will nodded once more. 'Something happened – something bad – and I had to leave. I wish I'd thought to leave you a message but...' I shook my head. 'Please give me a call so I can explain properly.'

He glanced across at the two women but they were sniffing the candles and deep in conversation.

'Are you still married?' he asked, his voice low.

I shook my head. 'Widowed five years ago.'

His expression – which I hadn't been able to read so far – turned soft. 'I'm sorry.'

'Thank you.'

I held the card out towards him, my heart racing, praying he wouldn't reject me like he must have assumed I'd rejected him, but thankfully he reached for it. His fingers brushed mine, sending a fizz of electricity throughout my body.

'I'd like to hear the explanation but things are complicated in my life at the moment and I'm not at my best. I don't want what's going on now to cloud our conversation so it might be some time before you hear from me, but I promise I *will* get in touch. There's a lot to say.'

'There is.'

He picked up the framed music. 'I haven't paid you for this yet. How much is it?'

'No charge. I'd like you to have it. Small peace offering to remember a special weekend.'

'Thank you. Do you still play?'

'Only just started again. That weekend, you told me I'd helped you rediscover your love of music but what I did to you lost me mine.'

'I'm sorry.'

'Don't be. *I* did that – not you.'

He gave me a weak smile then left. I watched the door close behind him, my heart pounding and I couldn't leave it there. Locking the till, I ran down the shop and out the door.

'Will!' I called.

He halted and turned as I ran up to him, stopping about a foot away.

'I can't not tell you. The hospital rang. Cliff had been in a serious car crash. I wasn't thinking. I packed my case and raced home, terrified I'd be too late. After the crash, when I knew he was going to be all right, I didn't know how to find you. I should have tried harder, but I didn't know how to leave him either.'

The wind blew a strand of hair across my face and I imagined Will tucking it behind my ear, his fingers brushing against my skin, sparks of electricity zipping through us both as we united in a passionate clinch just as we'd done in a shop doorway that rainy night in Manchester. But it was me who pushed my hair aside. No sparks, no clinches.

'I will call,' he said. 'I promise.'

'Okay.'

'Goodbye, Yvonne. For now, anyway.'

'Bye for now.'

As he disappeared round the corner, my heart sank. I so badly wanted to chase him but I needed to let him go. I was ready for this but he clearly wasn't. What was that saying about letting go of someone you loved? Something about them coming back if they were yours but never being yours in the first place if they didn't. Was Will mine? Only time would tell.

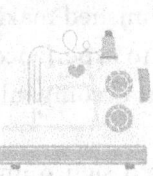

40

'Sorry about that,' I said as I returned to the shop, forcing a smile on my face and brightness into my voice. 'Customer forgot his change.'

They both looked at me, bewildered expressions on their faces, and I suspected they hadn't even noticed me leave.

'Can I help you with anything?' I asked.

'Just trying to decide which fragrance a friend would like best,' one of them said. 'We've narrowed it down to three.'

'That's a good start. Shout if you need me.'

They resumed their sniffing and I returned to the counter. Had that just happened? Had Will really just walked into my shop? Feeling shaken and needing to focus on something work-related, I retrieved the envelope from the bag he'd given me and found sixty pounds and a note asking for six bears rather than four, as well as the details about the favourite shirts and Fen's dad's personality. I had everything I needed and felt excited about creating six new memory bears.

The women finally made their choice and left. Across the afternoon, I replayed the encounter with Will on a loop in my head, thinking of so many better things I could have said. Could I have blown it by chasing him down the street and blurting out what had happened? He'd already told me he was interested in the full explanation but had too much going on in his life to hear it right now. I'd listened but I'd ignored him. That was disrespectful of me.

Between customers, I finished making my memory bear but I was too distracted by Will to experience the usual feeling of satisfaction and jubilation that accompanied the completion of any sewing project.

After turning the closed sign round and cashing up for the day, I went up to the flat and told Trevor about my day. The chicken casserole I'd set away this morning in the slow cooker smelled divine but I didn't have the stomach for it and, after pushing it round my plate for several minutes, I shoved it aside with a sigh.

Feeling restless, I put my boots on, grabbed my coat, hat and keys and left the flat. It was dark so a walk alongside the lake was out of the question but I could do a lap of the village. The wind was stronger than it had been this afternoon but it wasn't particularly cold. I turned right out of the shop and right again at the corner, taking me alongside the main road out of the village. There were streets on the left and the right so I wandered along each, picking out the houses I liked the most and imagining what they looked like inside. Try as I might to keep houses my sole focus, my thoughts kept drifting back to Will. He'd promised me he'd ring and I believed him but how long would he need? Days? Weeks? Months? What could his complications be? Had he remarried? Could he be going through a second divorce?

I passed The Hardy Herdwick and turned right into Paulette's street. A man walking a golden retriever said 'hello' as he passed and I paused outside the village hall. The lights were on but the blinds were down so I couldn't see what was happening inside. Reaching Paulette's house, I checked my watch. It was ten past seven so not an unreasonable hour to ring the bell.

Saffy answered the door, looking lovely in a pair of dark jeans and a sparkly top.

'Hi, Yvonne,' she said, beaming at me.

'I was out for a walk and I thought I'd drop in and see your grandma. But if it's a bad time...'

'Perfect timing as I'm about to abandon her for the evening.'

'Going anywhere nice?' I asked as I stepped into the hall. 'You look stunning, by the way.'

'Thank you. I've got a date with Felix.'

'The *fit* chef? Oh, Saffy, that's fantastic.'

'I'm so nervous. I've never dated anyone but Kyle.'

'You'll have a great time.'

We joined Paulette in the lounge and Saffy offered to make drinks, saying she was ready far too early and in need of a distraction.

'I met Mel for lunch yesterday,' Saffy said when she handed me a mug of tea shortly after. 'Thanks for giving me her card, Yvonne. It was so helpful chatting to her. She's given me a couple of interior design scenarios and asked me to share my ideas with her later this month. I know she'd said to you that she couldn't guarantee any work but that sounds promising, doesn't it?'

I nodded. 'It sounds like she was impressed with you during your chat and now wants to see what you're capable of. Do you think interior design's something you might like to do?'

'I loved designing the shop – probably my favourite worky thing I've done so far – so I'm keen to look into it.' She nervously checked the time on her phone. 'Are you ready for me to set you up on a dating app yet?'

I grimaced.

'You said you'd let me do it after the Easter holidays were over and we're more than halfway through.'

I smiled at her, recalling the conversation we'd had while setting up the shop.

'Nice try, but I told you I'd *consider* it after the Easter holidays. How about you focus on your own love life for now and I'll give you a shout if and when I'm ready to let you meddle in mine?'

Saffy grinned back at me. 'You're on!' The doorbell rang and she squealed. 'That'll be him. Wish me luck.'

'Good luck,' Paulette and I chorused and Paulette stood up to hug her granddaughter.

'Felix is a nice lad,' Paulette said when the front door closed. 'She was so excited when he asked her out. I think they'll be good together.'

'Another reason for her to stick around here,' I said.

Paulette nodded. 'How are we already a week into April and they haven't made peace?'

'Do they speak to her at all?'

'Andrew phones her every week but it's always the same day and time and Saffy knows that's when Joanne goes out so she's convinced Joanne doesn't know he's doing it, which means Joanne thinks they've severed ties and is clearly okay with that.'

'That must hurt.'

'It does. If she'd just finished three years at university, spent all her time going out drinking, skipped all her lectures and failed her finals, I could understand them being annoyed at spending a fortune for nothing, but she dropped out after one term and the punishment really doesn't fit the crime, especially when there's no crime committed.'

There was nothing I could say that hadn't been said already so I settled on a sympathetic eyeroll.

'If Saffy goes on too much about dating apps, you know you can tell her to button it,' Paulette said.

I laughed. 'It's fine. I'm just not ready, especially after what happened today...'

Paulette sipped on her tea as I filled her in on Will's appearance in the shop.

'What do you think the complications could be?' she asked.

'I'm not sure. I wondered if it could be a messy divorce. He wasn't wearing a ring. If he'd been widowed, I think he'd have shared that after I told him I was. There was a vulnerability about him which there hadn't been twenty years ago so I think that, whatever it is he's going through, it's big. Of course, his dad's passed away recently as that's why I'm making the bears but if it was connected to that, surely he'd have said.'

'You could tie yourself in knots speculating,' Paulette said. 'Do you wish you'd asked for his number?'

I pondered that for a moment before shaking my head. 'I think it's best I can't get in touch with him because, if I could, I'd want to and it would probably push him away. If he doesn't get in touch, that's his right, especially after I ran out on him. He said he needs time and, if anyone understands that, it's me. If it's meant to be, it's meant to be.'

'But you want it to be,' she said, her voice soft.

I didn't need to think about it. Seeing him again today had confirmed everything I'd believed over the past two decades.

'As much now as I did twenty years ago. Probably more. I know it's a strong statement to make but I can't help thinking that it's Will or nobody.'

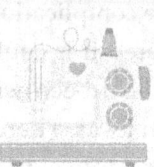

41

On the Friday evening of the following week, The Crafty Crew went out for a meal in Keswick to celebrate our first four weeks of trading. Saffy had been invited but Felix had asked her out on another date so, understandably, she'd ditched us for him. We were seated at a round table and, after our drinks arrived, Veronica led us in a toast.

'Congratulations to us all on a wonderful start to our pop-up shop. Created With Love seems to have gathered a lot of love from both tourists and the local community so far and I, for one, am delighted to have some storage space back at home.'

We all laughed and threw in our agreement.

'It's nice being in my workshop without dozens of wooden animals staring at me,' Christian said.

'There's something else I wanted to add,' Veronica said when the laughter and chatter died down. 'A huge thank you to you all for how supportive you've been during an exceptionally difficult couple of months for me. I have an update.'

She glanced at Laughlin and he gave her what appeared to be an encouraging nod.

'It feels a little uncomfortable holding an audience about my personal life but, as my business partners and good friends, I do want you to know what's been happening and it's perhaps a little easier to get it all out in one go rather than having several individual conversations. Is that all right with you all?'

There were murmurs of agreement coupled with reassurances that she didn't need to tell us anything that made her uncomfortable.

'I knew you'd all be lovely about it, but I think it's only fair that you have the full picture. There's still a lot to be resolved with Rebecca and Felicity and I'm going to need some time away from the business to do that. As you already know, it was my youngest, Felicity, who discovered what was going on...'

Veronica shared that a party had been held at the army base in Germany to celebrate her fortieth birthday. Felicity had been twelve at the time, Rebecca had recently turned sixteen and the sisters were close with just the occasional bout of sisterly bickering, mainly caused by Rebecca pulling rank as the eldest. After spilling a drink down her top, Felicity had told Rebecca she was going home to change and it was there that she found their dad with another woman, although she didn't see who. She ran back to the party to find Rebecca and ask her what to do. Rebecca had always been a daddy's girl and didn't believe her so Felicity dragged her back to the house to see for herself. As they drew close, the door opened and they ducked behind a wall, spotting their dad and the woman coming out and sharing a kiss. Both girls recognised her as Anita Westwood – the wife of another senior officer.

'Felicity wanted to tell me that night,' Veronica said, 'but Rebecca convinced her not to ruin my birthday. Felicity reluctantly agreed as long as they told me the next day. The next day, Rebecca asked Felicity to give her a bit longer to think. She wanted to get the timing right but how is the timing ever going to be right for news like that?'

'A difficult position for your girls to be in,' Milly said.

Veronica nodded. 'Absolutely! I don't envy either of them for that, especially at such a young age. They debated confronting Carson and getting him to come clean but the more time that passed, the more aware they became of hiding a huge secret, and the harder it became to say anything. Felicity remained adamant that I needed to know but Rebecca told her I wouldn't stand for it and we'd divorce. Felicity claims that Rebecca told her it would be all her fault if we did. Rebecca claims she said no such thing. Either way, the difference of opinion on something so enormous drove a wedge between them. Felicity admitted she never saw Carson and Anita in a compromising position again but she said it was obvious from the looks they gave each other that there was something still going on.'

'For how long?' Paulette asked.

Veronica shrugged. 'We returned to the UK fourteen years ago. I was forty-nine then and, for all I know, it could have been going on for the whole of my forties. Anita was at our previous base too and we knew her from the UK before that. They could have been seeing each other for the whole of our marriage – the whole of our relationship, even.'

The last part of the sentence was delivered with a croaky voice as Veronica blinked back tears, apologising for getting emotional. Laughlin gave her hand a squeeze and we all offered our condolences. I was devastated for her.

Veronica took a sip of her drink before continuing. 'I had questions – many, many questions, as I'm sure you can imagine. It didn't take long to track down Anita. She was back in the UK and I was all for getting in touch with her and demanding she tell me the details but Laughlin helped me look at the downsides of doing that. If I spoke with Anita on the phone or in person, she could say anything she liked. She could tell me that Carson never loved me and that he wanted to leave me for her. Truth or lie, where would it get me? Carson isn't around to corroborate or deny anything.'

She glanced at Laughlin who took over. 'I'm convinced that the only reason I was able to accept and move on from Noreen's affair was because she was there to answer questions and we had a professional to guide us through them. Vee wouldn't have that and I was worried it would do her more harm than good.'

'He was right,' Veronica said. 'Up until my birthday this year, my memories of my marriage were happy. I've taken the rose-tinted glasses off and I can see now that it wasn't perfect but it was still good. I'm shocked and saddened that my husband must have felt differently to me, but I can't change that so why torture myself with hurtful details? I'm going to focus on what I *can* control which is building bridges with my daughters. That can't be done effectively over the phone or a video chat so I'm planning to go to Scotland first to spend some quality time with Felicity then Germany to do the same with Rebecca. I'm not planning to stay with either of them. We need to have some honest, difficult discussions and I think we'll all need the space. It's bound to be upsetting so Laughlin has offered to accompany me as my emotional crutch.'

She turned her head to Laughlin and it was obvious to me that the smile they exchanged held more than empathy. I'd noticed them getting steadily closer since the incident at Veronica's birthday, although I wasn't going to embarrass them by voicing that. If something had happened and they wanted to share it with us, they'd do so when they were ready.

'So I need some time away from the business too,' Laughlin said. 'We appreciate the extra pressure that places on you all and that's not what you signed up to, so we're both happy to fund a part-time member of staff if that would work for you.'

'There's no need to do that,' I said. 'I don't mind working full-time while you're away.'

'I can work extra hours,' Christian said, and Paulette added that she could too.

'I can cover quieter days like Mondays,' Milly offered, 'provided nobody objects to me bringing in my laptop and doing some work when there are no customers in.'

Veronica held her hand to her chest, tears brimming in her eyes once more. 'What would I do without you all? Thank you so much. I promise I'll make it up to you when things are settled.'

'There's no need,' I said. 'If it was any of us who needed the time away, you'd step up. You take however long you need to get things back on track with your girls.'

Our starters arrived at that point and the conversation changed direction. Milly told us how much she was enjoying having Coral home for the extended Easter holidays and how she couldn't quite believe she was taking her back to university on Saturday for her final term when it felt like only yesterday that she'd dropped her off for her first. That led into a conversation about how far through the education system we'd each progressed, which then moved into some hilarious anecdotes from Milly's and Christian's years as teachers. They were both brilliant raconteurs and, by the time we'd finished our desserts, my sides were hurting from laughing so much and Veronica did give way to her tears, but they were tears of laughter this time.

'I needed that,' Veronica said over coffee. 'Laughlin and I do have one more piece of news.'

They exchanged glances and smiles and I held my breath. Were they going to admit that there was something going on between them? I hoped so. When I'd first met them, I'd never in a million years have put them together as a couple as they seemed like chalk and cheese but having seen how supportive Laughlin had been to Veronica and how his confidence had grown since spending more time in her company, I thought they were perfect together.

'We've been spending a lot of time together since my birthday and the connection between us has deepened and, well... it's... we're...'

I'd never seen Veronica struggle for words before and it was adorable the way she looked at Laughlin for help. He placed his hand over hers and kept it there this time.

'We want to take things slowly,' he said, 'but we do have feelings for each other – something neither of us ever expected. We're taking it a day at a time, ever so steady.'

'I'm thrilled for you,' Paulette said, and we all added our support and congratulations.

Looking at the pair of them side by side, the warm glow of love so obvious between them, my heart filled with joy. The drama at Veronica's birthday and the fallout from it had been awful but it had paved the way for Veronica to start mending her broken family and it had taken her down an unexpected but glittering path towards love. Laughlin and Veronica had both been through so much. They both deserved a second chance at love and I was delighted for them that they might have found it with each other. Although, as I drove home after the meal, I couldn't help hoping that I'd find my second chance at love too – with the first and only man I'd ever fallen for. I wished Will had called but patience was a virtue and I'd spent my whole life being patient. A few more days or weeks wasn't going to kill me, especially when I'd already waited for twenty years.

Back at the flat a little later, I wanted to spend some time with Trevor before going to bed so I put the television on and lay on the sofa with him strutting up and down my arm, half-heartedly watching a quiz show. My phone buzzed with a text notification from an unknown number and my pulse raced as I read it.

FROM UNKNOWN

> Hi Yvonne, it's Will. I really do want to talk but I'm still dealing with a lot of issues right now and I know they'll cloud what I think might be one of the most important conversations of my life. I appreciate that's really cryptic but it's the best I can do for now. Apologies again. Please bear with me

It was a relief to hear from Will and to know he hadn't ghosted me, but his text also brought frustration for a further wait as well as worries for him. *A lot of issues*, he'd put. When I'd seen him, he'd looked stressed and distracted and I hoped whatever he was going through could resolve itself without causing him much more distress. I re-read the bit about a conversation with me being *one of the most important conversations of [his] life*. That had to be positive. That had to signal thoughts of exploring a future together. Or did it simply mean closure for him after wondering what had happened for two decades?

There was nothing I could do until he was ready so I tapped in a reply.

TO WILL

> Great to hear from you but really sorry about whatever you're going through. I can offer you a listening ear if you need it so do let me know if that would help, but I otherwise respect your need for time

He responded with a thumbs up and I stared at my phone for several minutes, looking for the telltale dots that he was typing. Nothing came. Sighing, I switched my phone to silent, turned it over so I couldn't see any notifications and focused back on Trevor.

'Let's see if we can answer this question, eh, Trevor? I don't think that contestant's going to manage it.'

'Stupid!' he said, making me laugh.

'I agree. Not the sharpest tool in the box but a brave man for applying for the show and trying something different and exciting.'

Trevor turned his head to me. 'Stupid!'

He meant nothing by it. To him, it was just one of the many words he'd learned, but my heart sank at that moment. Was I being stupid about this whole thing with Will? Had a lifetime without romantic love made me cling on to the memories of one day and night – albeit incredible ones – and turn them into an epic love story when it wasn't that at all? But then I pictured Will's expression as he handed me the framed sheet music and shared what I'd told him about my mum. He'd never have retained that information if he hadn't still cared about me. If I was clinging on, so was he.

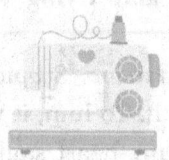

42

A fortnight later, it was the first Sunday in May – monthly Sunday lunch for Milly and me. She'd suggested that, now that I'd moved, we should alternate between The Fox and Rabbit in Pippinthwaite and The Hardy Herdwick in Willowdale which apparently also did a fabulous Sunday roast.

'It's busy in here,' I said, as we waited by the bar. 'Wonder if it's always like this or if it's because it's the bank holiday weekend.'

Milly shrugged. 'Good job we booked a table.'

The bar staff were quick and efficient and it was soon our turn to be served. We ordered our drinks and two lunches before being directed to our table.

'I've been dying to see you,' Milly said. 'I've got some news.'

'I'm guessing good news.' She looked like she was about to burst with excitement.

'Yes! I've met someone. I was in the supermarket on Thursday evening, putting some apples in a bag and they fell straight through. A man nearby bent down to pick them up and I realised it was Coral's old English teacher, Mr Sawdon. He recognised me and asked how Coral was doing so I told him about her being at university in her final year of performing arts. He said he wasn't surprised she'd gone down that route as he remembered seeing her in school plays and thinking how talented she was. He said he doesn't often get to hear about how his ex-pupils are doing and loves it when he gets snippets. Somehow he remembered that I used to be an English teacher too and was now a proofreader and he asked how business was and then we realised we were in everyone's way so he asked if I wanted to finish my shopping and grab a drink with him. We did that and got on really well and he asked me if I was free last night so we went on a proper date and it was brilliant. I'm seeing him again next week.'

Milly had barely paused for breath and it was so lovely to see her eyes shining like that.

'I'm so pleased for you. Does this Mr Sawdon have a first name?'

'Adam, although it took me a while to get used to calling him that.'

'I can imagine. What's he like?'

'Nothing like Harry so that's a good start. Aw, Yvonne, he's lovely. We talked pretty much non-stop and I realised how one-sided things had become with Harry. It was so refreshing to have someone ask about me and genuinely be interested. I got a bit emotional about it at one point and he was so supportive.'

'I'm assuming he's single?'

Milly nodded. 'Divorced four years ago. He married his child-hood sweetheart and they had two girls who are now in their twenties and when the second went off to university, they realised that pretty much the whole of their married life had been about the girls and not about each other. Left alone in the house, they had nothing to say, no shared interests, no reason to stay together.'

'That's sad.'

'Isn't it? He said they were like strangers under the same roof and I could relate to that because it was how I felt when Harry came home. She's since remarried but he wanted some space before he jumped back into anything and was just thinking he might be ready to dip his toe in the dating pond again when the mum of one of his former pupils dropped a load of apples in front of him.'

'There must be something in the water,' I said, smiling at her. 'Saffy and Felix, Veronica – or should I say Vee? – and Laughlin, and now you and Adam.'

'It's not the water. It's the journals.'

'Veronica didn't do one. She did some recipe books instead.'

'I know, but Laughlin did and he told me that one of the emotions he wanted to feel this year was love. It'll be you and Will next.'

I'd brought Milly up to speed with the Will situation when she'd taken over from me for an afternoon shift one day.

'I wish!' I said. And I really did wish it, every day, but I'd told him I'd respect his need for space. Much as I wanted to send him a friendly checking-in message I also didn't want to do anything to jeopardise things.

'I've finished the final memory bear so I'll be ringing Fen tomorrow to arrange for them to be collected. With any luck, she'll send her brother.'

'Did you find out why she calls him James?'

'No. He called himself Will when he texted me. If I do see him again, I'll ask.'

'You *will* see him. I'm convinced of it. You wished for it in your journal and the journals are delivering.'

I smiled at her. I felt as though I'd had a slight bump in the road with Will's reaction to seeing me again not being quite as enthusiastic as I'd hoped but hearing her news about dating Adam and hearing that Laughlin had completed a journal, my faith was fully restored. I was still going to get everything I wished for – just perhaps not as quickly or as smoothly as I might have hoped.

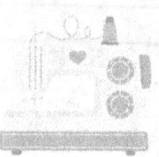

43

Even though the Monday was May Day Bank Holiday, we'd decided to open Created With Love because a warm, sunny weekend was expected, bringing lots of visitors to the area. We'd stayed open on Good Friday and Easter Monday too and the trade had been worth it. I was covering the morning shift and Milly was relieving me for the afternoon, although she'd told me she wasn't planning to go anywhere that morning and I should ring her if it got busy.

I awoke with butterflies in my stomach and I knew why – I was planning to ring Fen about her memory bears being ready for collection and hoping she'd send her brother for them.

After showering, I released Trevor from his cage and brought him into the bedroom, placing his towel and mirror on the top of a chest of drawers beside the two photographs of Cliff. Trevor strutted up and down, stopping every so often to admire his reflection and witter to himself.

I took extra care getting ready, carefully styling my hair, applying a little more make-up than I usually wore for work (making sure it didn't look overdone) and picking out a floral blue top I'd made which always drew compliments. Checking my appearance in a full-length mirror, I sighed.

'It's pathetic, isn't it, Cliff?' I said, rolling my eyes at Cliff's holiday photo. 'How old am I? I'm acting like a lovesick teenager. Worse! I don't imagine Saffy is mooning over Felix like this.' I glanced back at my reflection and considered removing my make-up. 'Is it too much?'

'Pretty Vonnie!' Trevor declared.

'What?'

'Pretty Vonnie! Pretty Trevor!'

Tears pricked my eyes and I blinked them away before I really did have to remove my make-up and start over. A feeling of calm flowed through me and I smiled at Cliff's picture. 'Thank you.'

My journal was on the small dining table and I opened it to the first section.

What 3 things will you STOP doing this year?

1. *Feeling sorry for myself*
2. *Blaming the past and hiding myself away*
3. *Chasing a relationship with Marianne*

We were four months into the year and the new life I'd created by throwing myself into my friendships through Cake & Craft Club, sharing my full story with Paulette and Milly, setting up Created With Love and selling the house had placed enormous ticks against the first two entries in the *STOP* section and I was so proud of myself for that. If Will didn't collect the bears or if he didn't make contact, I wasn't going to regress. I wasn't going to start feeling sorry for myself and I certainly wasn't going to live in the past and forever regret the decision to rush back to Cliff. Cliff and I had had a good marriage and I didn't regret the fifteen years we'd shared after I met Will. To say I did would be disrespectful to Cliff's memory. The past had happened and couldn't be changed but the future was mine for the taking and if that didn't include Will, it didn't include Will.

* * *

The shop was opening at ten o'clock and I decided to call Fen just before. My hands shook as I connected to her number.

'Hi, Fen, it's Yvonne from Created With Love in Willowdale. Just a quick call to let you know your bears are ready.'

'Fabulous! I can't wait to see them.'

'I'm really pleased with how they've turned out. I hope you will be too.'

'If they're anything like the one you were making when I bought the quilt, I'll be thrilled.'

'When would be best for you to collect them?' I asked. 'We're open today if that's convenient.'

'Possibly. I'm coming through to see my mum, although I might ask my brother to drop by instead.'

My heart leapt and I fought hard to keep my voice steady. 'Well, the bears are here for either of you whenever you're ready.'

When the call ended, I unlocked the front door and turned the sign round to open. There was a customer waiting already to collect a carved fox which she said Christian had put aside for her yesterday. He'd left me a note telling me where he'd stored it and that it was paid for so that was an easy transaction.

Across the morning, there was a steady flow of customers. Every time the door opened, my heart leapt into my mouth, but it wasn't Will or Fen. Milly arrived to relieve me at 1 p.m. and the bears still hadn't been collected. I wasn't in a rush to have my lunch and it was quite busy in the shop so I stayed downstairs in case Milly needed another pair of hands.

It was late afternoon when Fen arrived and I gave her a big smile, hoping it would mask my disappointment at her appearing instead of Will. While Milly was unfurling various bunting designs for another customer, I spread the six memory bears across the counter.

'Oh, my word!' Fen exclaimed. 'They're gorgeous.' She picked one up and twisted it in her hands, examining it from all angles. 'I knew they'd be good but, wow!'

'Every bear has the exact same pieces of fabric but, as you can see, they're all in different places so each one's unique. The favourite shirt appears on every bear's tummy so it has a prominent place.'

I picked up one of the other bears and pointed out the pocket I'd created on its chest. Fen was still holding the first bear so I told her to put her fingers in its pocket and lift out the contents.

'A heart! Oh, Yvonne!'

I'd made a small heart for each bear using the fabric from the favourite shirt and attached it inside the pocket with a satin ribbon so that it wouldn't get lost.

'The idea came to me when I was making yours so I added one to my own bear too. I thought it was a nice touch.'

'It's a lovely touch. And I love their expressions. They're warm and a bit cheeky, just like my dad was. I can't believe you've managed to capture that.'

'It took a few attempts but it's amazing what you can do by changing the angle of the stitching as well as the position of the eyes.'

'They're incredible. I can't thank you enough. My mum's now settled into her new flat and she thought the quilt was beautiful. I know she'll be delighted with her bear. They all will be. I hope you didn't mind me changing the number without checking first.'

'It was fine. You decided to give them to the older grandchildren after all?'

'Yes. The extras are for my niece and nephew. They're both going through a tough time at the moment, so I've taken a chance on getting the bears made without asking them. Mackenzie's lost his job and the timing is dire as his first baby's due this summer and Liberty and her husband have been trying for another baby and, well, let's just say that whatever worked for her two boys doesn't seem to be working this time round and she's a bit down about it.'

'I'm so sorry to hear that. Presumably that's why you've come to collect the bears instead of your brother.' Somebody needed to shut me up. It was obvious to me that I was fishing for information about Will and it had to be obvious to Fen too.

She scrunched her nose and wiggled her head from side to side. 'It's more complicated than that. You know that phrase about never having more thrown at you than you're strong enough to deal with? My brother must be a man of steel because he's had everything but the kitchen sink thrown at him recently. He's concerned for his kids, obviously, and our dad died a few months ago which has been hard. He'd sold his house but it's fallen through, and he has a major work situation which is horrific but which I can't talk about...'

I raised my hands. 'Completely understand. None of my business.'

'It's fine. I've started so I might as well finish. His ex-wife's divorcing the man she left him for and leaning on James way too much. She was never my favourite person but she's dipped to new lows, even for her. Who leaves their husband and still expects him to be there for them twenty-five years later, giving her lifts, holding her hand through her divorce, lending her money? And he's such a nice guy that he won't say no.'

'That sounds like a lot.' Poor Will. No wonder he wasn't in the right frame of mind for a conversation about me running out on him.

Fen was evidently on a roll. 'And, on top of that, he's unexpectedly bumped into a woman he met twenty years ago.'

My stomach lurched and I swear all the colour must have drained from my cheeks.

'They only spent a short time together,' she continued, her gaze fixed on mine, but her voice gentle, 'and he's been in love with her ever since. James is incredibly strong. He'll get through most of the bad stuff and he'll help the others involved get through it too so I'm not worried about any of that, but I *am* worried about this recent brush from the past because I think it's the one scenario which could break him.'

She knew! And I felt like I was being tested, as though she liked me but wanted reassurance that she hadn't made a bad character judgement.

'I never thought I'd see him again,' I said. 'I longed to so badly but what were the chances? And then he walked through that door with a bag of shirts. He didn't recognise me at first and I thought it served me right for abandoning him. I'd spent twenty years thinking about him and he'd forgotten about me.'

'He never forgot.'

'I know that now. I never meant to hurt him. I wanted to fully explain what happened but he said he has too much going on to hear it all right now and I need to respect that. It has to be on his terms.'

'He *does* have a lot going on but he's also protecting himself. As I say, this is the risky scenario. You're the danger zone, Yvonne.'

Me? I'd never have thought of myself like that. 'I don't mean to be.'

She gave me a gentle smile. 'I believe you. Nobody who puts as much love and care into creating something like these bears can be a bad person.' Fen picked up another bear and ran her finger across its face. 'You know, I've never been convinced it's possible to fall in love with someone you've only just met, but I always was the pragmatic one and James was the hopeless romantic.'

'It *is* possible.'

She looked up at me and nodded. 'James swore it was and, having met you, I think he's right.'

'It's also possible to stay in love with that person for two decades.'

She cuddled the bear to her as she studied my face. 'In that case, I'm rooting for you and will do what I can to convince him to meet you sooner rather than later.'

'You will?' I frowned at her. 'But you said I was the danger zone. And you must be angry with me for breaking his heart in the first place.'

'I'm still worried about the danger but, as for being angry at you for breaking his heart, you didn't. You actually fixed it. His ex, Eleanor, broke his heart. She did it so badly that he lost his way and, for a few years, I lost my brother. He even stopped playing the piano outside of school and that shattered the fragments of his heart into tinier pieces. Then he met you and heard you play and he came alive that day. Thanks to you, he not only found his love for music again but he found belief in himself and I got my brother back.'

I grabbed for a tissue from under the counter, wiping the tears away at her beautiful words.

'I didn't mean to make you cry,' Fen said.

'It's fine. I just can't bear to think of him being broken and I hate that I hurt him too.'

'But I don't think you meant to, did you?'

'Not at all.'

Fen gave me a gentle smile. 'There's a lot going on for him right now, like I said, and it's taken its toll on him. I've been worried but, since he saw you again, I've seen a fresh spark in him just like I saw twenty years back. You do something to my brother – something positive – so I'm on your team and I want it to work.'

I wiped at more tears. 'I promise I won't do anything to hurt him, or at least not intentionally. I can't control what he does next after I fully explain things.'

The door opened and another customer came in and it looked as though Milly's customer might have decided on her bunting.

'I'd better let you get on,' Fen said.

I carefully placed the bears back into a couple of bags and passed them to her.

'And here's the rest of the fabric,' I said, reaching for the bag of leftovers.

'Is there enough left to make any more bears?'

'If you want to include the favourite shirt, there's enough for two, maybe three.'

'In that case, keep the shirts and can you make me another two bears? I'd like one and I want James to have one too. I'll need to pay for these six by card, but I could ask James to drop a cash deposit off for the new ones.'

I smiled at her. 'I need to let him have some space. Card's fine for the deposit too.'

After I'd taken the payment, I let Milly have the till and walked to the door with Fen.

'Can I ask about the name? I'm really confused. You call him James but I know him as Will. Is that his middle name?'

She laughed. 'No. It comes from our surname – Wilson. Who's the most famous James you can think of?'

'James Bond?'

'Exactly. There was this kid at primary school who constantly plagued James with Bond references and theme tunes and it drove him mad but he was too nice to ask him to stop. He didn't want it to continue into senior school so his best mate, Aaron, started calling him Will and it stuck. He never introduces himself to anyone as James. He's Will to friends, colleagues and strangers but he'll always be James to family.'

'Mystery solved,' I said, opening the door for her. 'Hope everyone likes their bears.'

'They'll love them. Right, I'm off to have words with my brother.'

'Be gentle with him.'

'You too,' she said, with a wink.

Milly was still serving her customer and I caught her eye to indicate I was going upstairs for a moment. My make-up was likely smudged from crying so I needed to fix that, but I needed some time to process everything Fen had shared with me. I wanted to see Will even more badly now, wanted to support him through everything he was facing, but it had to be when he was ready. I loved that Fen was on my side but hoped she didn't push him too hard.

* * *

That evening, I was at the kitchen table cutting out the patchwork pieces for the two additional memory bears when a message came through. It was just a picture but it was perfect – one of the bears Fen had collected earlier holding a piece of paper across his tummy containing the words:

Thank you for bearing with me
Tomorrow at 7pm?
Drinks at The Olde Oak?

It seemed Fen had worked her magic.

TO WILL

I'll be there. Thank you

I released a shaking breath. Fen had said she was rooting for Will to meet me sooner rather than later and she certainly hadn't hung around. Excitement and nerves swirled together inside me. Tomorrow might just change my life and finally bring me love.

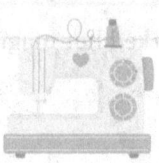

44

'If it's drinks rather than a meal, I wouldn't go too dressy,' Saffy said the following evening.

I'd given Milly an update yesterday and had rung Paulette in the evening. With my permission, she'd told Saffy I had a date which immediately led to an offer from Saffy to help me get ready. She had a great eye for style and she always looked effortlessly beautiful so I'd been happy to accept.

Saffy removed a pair of stylish jeans from my wardrobe. 'Ooh! These still have the label on.'

'I've never worn them,' I admitted. 'One of the Cake & Crafters had a pair on and I thought they looked fabulous on her so I ordered some but haven't had the guts to wear them. I usually wear leggings and I thought those might be a bit trendy for me.'

Saffy grinned at me while shaking her head. 'Tonight's the night and don't start on the age thing again. You don't look your age and, even if you did, sixty's the new forty and something to be proud of.' She placed the jeans on my bed and turned to the railing, riffling through the tops. 'We have a winner!'

I hadn't worn the top either. I made most of my own clothes

and favoured plain colours or dainty patterns but this particular one had caught my eye on a mannequin in a Keswick shop window and I'd impulse purchased it. White with a giant turquoise flower, it had a chiffon overlay, floaty sleeves and a tied waist.

'You don't think it makes too much of a statement?'

Saffy led me to the mirror and held the top up against me. 'It *does* make a statement and that's *I'm a beautiful, confident woman and you definitely want to see me again!* Can't you hear it?'

I had to laugh. Saffy was so good to be around and I felt recently as though I was seeing the real strong, confident, capable woman that she was rather than a scared young girl putting on a brave face.

She wanted to do my make-up and then my hair before I dressed. As she wound tresses of my hair around a styling wand she'd brought with her, I asked her how it was going with Felix and her eyes lit up.

'He's amazing. Perfection, no notes.'

'Perfection, no notes? What does that mean?'

'That I don't have any notes to give him – you know, feedback on things to improve. He's a ten out of ten. Twelve out of ten! He's gorgeous, obvs, but he doesn't know it. He's funny, witty, clever and such a nice person.' She released a spiral of hair and wound another tress around the wand. 'I thought Kyle was the one but we got to uni and he turned into a bad boy which 100 per cent confirmed to me that bad boys are *not* my vibe.'

She continued to curl my hair while she told me more about Felix – how good he was with the staff and customers, how he never lorded it over anyone else that his parents owned the place, how passionate he was about cooking and how he loved being able to cook and bake simpler dishes for the café but get more adventurous for the evening bistro.

'You seem so happy and settled here in Willowdale,' I said.

'I am. Waitressing isn't my dream career but The White Willow's such a great place to work so it's ideal for me while I explore my art and maybe go down an interior design route.'

'Perfection, no notes?' I asked, making her laugh.

'Perfection, but with just one note.' Her smile slipped and her expression became wistful. 'I wish I could be here with my parents' blessing.'

'How are things going with them?' Paulette hadn't said anything the last few times we'd worked together so I'd assumed there was no change.

'Dad visited yesterday.' The monotone words and lack of smile suggested it hadn't been a roaring success.

'But not your mum?'

'No. She's still hurting apparently. I can't even...' She shook her head, sighing. 'Grandma made me show Dad the footage of Kyle being drunk and some of the messages he'd sent me, proving he was the one who'd gone off the rails and that he'd lied about it. Dad wanted to know why I hadn't shared it all earlier so I told him I wanted my own parents to believe me without me having to produce evidence. I also told him that I was really pissed off with them that they hadn't. I felt bad saying that but he needed to know. I don't understand why they'd automatically think the worst of me.'

'I'm sorry you weren't believed before. Now that your dad knows the truth, I presume he'll tell your mum.'

'Yeah. He was pretty gutted about the whole thing. I thought he was gonna cry but he gave me this huge hug instead – nearly broke my ribs. He wanted me to send him the videos so he could show Mum but I told him that, if she doesn't believe him without seeing them for herself, there's no way forward for her and me. Even if she does believe him, our relationship will never be the same again. It can't be. The way Mum's treated me and Grandma is bang out of order and it's not like either of us did anything wrong. The damage is done and she needs to take responsibility for that. I know it sounds harsh, but...'

I nodded when she tailed off. 'You've been treated unfairly and it's bound to leave scars.'

Saffy picked up a wide-tooth comb and ran it through my hair, loosening the spirals.

'I told Dad I want to come home to clear my room out and I don't want Mum there. He tried to talk me out of it saying it's my home but Mum made me feel like it wasn't and that can't be undone. I'll never move back in, even if she does get her act together and apologises to me and Grandma for everything she's done. Willowdale's my home now. I've got everything here that I've ever wanted so why would I leave it? In fact, I change my verdict. Willowdale is also perfection, no notes. I don't need Mum's validation to be happy here.'

She put the comb down and fluffed up my hair before instructing me to close my eyes while she gave a mist of hairspray. 'I'll chat to Trevor while you're getting dressed. Don't mess up your hair.'

'Yes, Mum!'

Saffy did make me laugh and I loved what a bundle of positive energy she was, but the situation with her parents made me so sad. I totally understood why she hadn't wanted to show them the evidence of Kyle's lies but I was glad Paulette had made her show her dad because hopefully it would help move things forward.

Once I was dressed, I had to concede that Saffy was right about the outfit. It was bolder than anything I usually wore but it did look good.

'You look amazing!' Saffy said, beaming at me. 'How do you feel?'

'Surprisingly good, actually. I really wasn't sure about it.'

'Get rid of all your doubts. You sparkle tonight. So, who's the lucky man? Grandma said he's someone you knew years ago.'

'He is. His name's Will and he came into the shop, which was very unexpected. He bought one of the pictures you made from my old sheet music. It's probably more of a catch-up than a date but here's hoping.'

'Remember what I said when you were doing your journal? You're never too old for love. I'm sure you'll have an awesome time.'

'Thank you, and thanks for being my stylist. I really appreciate this.'

* * *

Much as I'd have loved a drink or two to settle my nerves, I'd decided to drive and forfeit alcohol as I wanted to keep a clear head for what could be a difficult conversation.

The Olde Oak was a pub in central Keswick with a bar at the front and a restaurant at the back. It was a good choice because the bar area was a higgledy-piggledy mixture of small rooms and tables tucked behind pillars giving us privacy to talk. My heart was beating so fast as I approached the pub that I had to pause outside for a moment to catch my breath.

Inside, I spotted Will waiting by the bar. He turned round and smiled at me, melting my heart. A smile was a great start.

'Perfect timing,' he said. 'I've just ordered a pint but they're changing the barrel. What would you like to drink?'

'A soda water and lime, please.'

After paying, Will led me to a small round table with a wrap-around seat by the furthest window.

'Thank you for being patient with me,' he said once we sat

down. 'I really appreciate it but, as you might have gathered, Fen gave me a kick up the backside.'

'I thought so, but I didn't ask her to.'

'I know. She told me it was all her. She also told me she'd blabbed about some of what's been going on. She's prone to over-sharing with people she likes.'

'She likes me?'

'Of course! Who wouldn't?'

'You'd have every reason not to.'

'Believe me, that's never going to happen. We both know that we had something special between us. That wasn't me imagining things, was it?'

'Definitely not. Everything you were feeling, I was feeling too. I couldn't wait for you to come back and for us to spend the afternoon together. Talking about a future with a man I'd only just met should probably have scared me but it didn't. It felt right. But then I picked up a voicemail from the hospital...'

He'd already had the headlines when I chased him down the street, but I gave him the full details about how I'd panicked and sped to the hospital without even thinking about leaving a note or a message behind, terrified at the thought of losing Cliff. I shared how devastated I'd been when I realised that Will would have turned up and found me gone but that it was too late at that point to do anything about it.

'I'm so sorry,' I said. 'It broke my heart imagining you waiting in the lobby for me and what you must have been thinking when you realised I wasn't coming.'

'I was absolutely gutted. I waited for maybe ten minutes before I asked at reception and, when they said you'd already checked out, I waited a bit longer hoping you were moving your car or that one of us had got the time wrong.'

'How long did you wait?'

He hesitated, perhaps debating whether to tell me the truth. 'Three hours.'

'No! Oh, Will!'

'Don't feel bad. In your shoes, I'd have done exactly the same thing. I'd have needed to get to the hospital and it wouldn't have entered my mind to leave a note either.'

His hand was on the table and I instinctively placed mine over it as I thanked him for being so understanding. His fingers entwined with mine, sending electricity zipping up my arm and round my body, my heart pounding as he held my gaze.

'I asked them for your number but, of course, they couldn't give me it.'

'I tried to find you later but I couldn't find any music and drama teachers called Will. But, of course, there wouldn't be... James.'

He grimaced. 'I can't believe you tried to find me.'

'I had to. I had to tell you what had happened. I couldn't let you think you meant nothing to me.'

'I wish you had found me.'

'Me too.'

The intensity of Will's eyes on mine was almost too much to take. I wanted to sweep the drinks aside, pull him towards me and kiss him as though there was no tomorrow. Was he thinking the same?

'Did you tell Cliff about me?'

'No.'

He looked down at our entwined hands. 'I have to ask...' He paused and looked up. 'What would you have done if you had found me?'

It was a fair question and it deserved an honest answer. 'I told a friend about us recently. I'd kept it secret for all this time and it was eating away at me so I needed to let someone in. She asked me that same question and I told her what I'm going to tell you. I don't know. All I can tell you for sure is that, that night in the hotel and the morning after, I was ready and willing to end my marriage.'

Will still had hold of my hand, which surely had to be a good sign but, as I thought that, he let go and picked up his drink. My hands slipped onto my lap.

'Any other questions?' I asked. 'Anything you want to know more about?'

'Probably, but I think I've interrogated you enough for now. I know that can't have been easy to share and I appreciate your honesty – then and now.'

I wasn't sure whether that was the end of our evening together but I didn't want it to be. Even though I'd told him I'd chosen him before the phone call, it felt as though my inability to confirm that I'd have chosen him after the accident was casting a dark shadow over us. That couldn't be our final conversation.

'Why don't you tell me more what's going on with you? I'm a good listener, remember.'

'I know. I remember everything about you,' he said, the intensity returning to his gaze, the atmosphere between us crackling once more. 'And everything about that night.'

'So do I. And I've relived it over and over and over.'

My hand was on the seat beside me now and he shuffled a little closer. His fingers brushed against mine and he kept them there. It was the loosest connection but it was enough for me for now.

'Okay, here goes,' he said. 'Fen's already told you a few things so I'll come back to them in a bit but I know she didn't expand on the work situation so I'll start there. As you know, I taught music and drama when we met. I still do that although I'm a department head now, which is why I live in Keswick – moved here for the promotion and to be closer to my family who, as you've discovered, live here. Outside of work, I'm also the co-director of a music school owned by my best mate, Aaron. He's the nicest, soundest bloke you could ever hope to meet. I've been friends with him since primary school and we've always had each other's backs but someone accused him of something really bad.'

He took a sip of his drink and I noticed his hand shaking as he put the glass down.

'I still can't believe this happened. I teach piano at the music school and Aaron teaches guitar and drums. One of his guitar students boasted to her best friend that Aaron was having sex with her during her one-to-one lessons which, of course, was a blatant lie. The friend told her mum, the mum reported it to the police and, quite rightly, they had to investigate. It became a huge thing. Except the girl had made it all up and we could prove it because all lessons are recorded for safeguarding reasons for the teachers and the students. All parents know this up front and sign a document to give their consent and all students should know this too but I guess the girl never thought it would go further than her friend. As soon as the police mentioned video footage, she admitted she'd lied and that Aaron had never once said or done anything inappropriate.'

'Why would she do that?' I asked, shocked that somebody could make up something so dangerous.

'She said she and her friend were talking about attractive older men and she mentioned that her guitar teacher was hot. Next moment, she'd made up a whole lie to impress the friend. So Aaron has been through hell and, even though the police know there's no case to answer to, mud sticks. The accusation spread like wildfire and parents started pulling their kids out of the music school – even from lessons which Aaron doesn't teach – which has left Aaron facing financial ruin. With so few students left, income has plummeted to the point where he can't pay the mortgage on the school and he's struggling with his house too. That's why I was selling mine. I was going to downsize and give him the difference to tide him over but it's fallen through so I can't even do that.'

'That's horrendous. I'm so sorry for your friend and for you.'

'It's mainly about Aaron. I've got no financial investment in the music school and there were never any accusations about me, although losing a stack of my students doesn't look good. The head at our school knows all about what's happening and the authorities know too, just in case anything creeps out of the woodwork down the line. It hasn't been a pleasant experience for me but it's been nothing compared to what Aaron has been and still is going through.'

'Is there anything he can do legally?'

'The girl was stupid and naïve but she didn't do it maliciously. Aaron doesn't want to destroy her life too and, even if he did pursue a civil case and won it, what good would it do? He'd still have lost his reputation and possibly his home and business.'

'Does he have a wife and kids?'

'A husband, which makes the accusation even more ludicrous. They've got two adopted kids, both in their late teens, who are showing amazing resilience in dealing with it. They think it's funny that anyone thinks their dad's *hot.*'

'It's good that they can find the humour in a dire situation. What a horrible thing to go through.'

'I just wish there was a way to make it all better. I know the money from my house sale wouldn't have had a massive impact but it would at least have bought them time.'

'That's such a generous thing to do.'

Will shrugged. 'He's my best mate. He's always been there for me and this was me trying to be there for him.'

We were near the end of our drinks so Will got another round in, suggesting we move onto a lighter topic of conversation when he returned. He wanted to know more about Created With Love so I told him how my love of crafts had led me to Cake & Craft Club last September. We talked about music, his teaching, his children, Trevor. The conversation flowed easily and, while neither of us were overtly flirty, there were sparks flying between us. Every so often, he'd move a little closer to me around the seat and I'd do the same until our legs were touching, our fingers entwined once more.

The landlord called for last orders and, all too soon, glasses were being cleared away and we were the only customers left. When some of the lights went off in the bar, we took the hint and left the pub. Will told me he was walking distance away and pointed up the town, but he insisted on walking me back to the car park, even though it was in the other direction.

'Tonight's been good,' he said as we stood by my car.

'It has. Thanks for listening.'

'Thanks for explaining.'

We stood there for a moment, smiling at each other.

'Would it be too much to...' He put his arms out to either side and he didn't even need to finish the sentence. I eagerly stepped into his hug and, as he wrapped his arms around me and pulled me close to him, I felt overwhelmed by how much love I felt for him and wondered what he was thinking.

'Can I see you again?' he asked when we stepped apart – reluctantly in my case.

'I'd love that.'

'I would too. This week's tricky for me, though – a couple of school events on evenings – but I'm free on Saturday if you fancy a walk. Unless you're working.'

'I am, but I'm sure someone will swap with me. I'll text you when I've confirmed it.'

He held my gaze once again. 'You have no idea how much willpower it's taking not to kiss you right now,' he said, his voice husky.

'I think I do because I feel the same.'

'I don't want to rush things.'

'I know. Me neither. Goodnight, Will.'

'Goodnight, Yvonne.'

And he leaned forward and gave me a gentle kiss on the cheek which made my innards feel like jelly. I could still remember how his lips felt against mine, feel his hands in my hair, his breath on my neck and I longed for a repeat of that incredible night together, but it was right for both of us that we took the time to talk and get to know each other again because it would lay the foundations for a positive future together. It was exactly as I'd written on the cover of my journal – *tomorrow starts today*.

45

On Saturday morning, Will met me on the bench beneath the giant willow tree on the village green ready for our walk round Derwent Water. I'd have suggested meeting at the shop but I knew Paulette would be dying for an introduction and I didn't want him to feel any pressure from my friends at this early stage in whatever it was that was happening between us.

Rather than walk all the way round the lake, Will suggested we walk halfway, have a late lunch in a hotel just beyond the southern tip of the lake and catch the boat back to the jetty near Willowdale Hall.

The weather was ideal – a fair few fluffy clouds to reduce the heat but with no threat of rain. The conversation on Tuesday had been stop and start at times but today it flowed, just as it had done all those years ago, while we caught up on the past two decades. I asked about other relationships and Will admitted to a bit of dating and a few short-term girlfriends but nothing serious because nobody compared to me.

'I didn't think I'd ever see you again,' he said, 'but I couldn't get you out of my mind. Nobody else stood a chance.'

I shared that I'd never dated either, for the same reason. We laughed a lot, we held hands and we hugged and, even though we didn't kiss, there was no mistaking the chemistry between us.

We had our lunch on a wooden terrace with stunning views over the lake and fells, watching swans and geese and other waterfowl gliding through the water.

'What are you thinking?' Will asked me, as I gazed into the distance.

'How great this day's been and how I don't want it to end.'

'Me neither. It doesn't have to. I don't think I could manage another meal but we could go out for a drink tonight if you like.'

I smiled at him. 'I'd like that very much.'

Spotting the boat leaving the previous jetty in the distance, we completed the short walk to the jetty near the hotel. When it arrived, we sat on the back seat where Will put his arm round me and I cuddled against his chest as we cruised round the lake.

A little later, as we approached the jetty closest to Willowdale Hall, my phone rang.

'It's my estate agent,' I said, connecting the call. 'Hi, Lorna, how are you?'

'Really good. Just checking you haven't found anywhere to live yet.'

'No. I've been keeping an eye online and nothing's appealed so far.'

'I might have your ideal property. We'd sold a house in Willowdale months ago and the buyer has been dragging his heels with it. We've just heard that it's fallen through and the owners are desperate to find a new buyer quickly so they don't lose the house they're buying. It's bigger than we've been discussing – three bed rather than two – but the overall square footage is similar to Mallard Close...'

With the boat secured to the jetty, it was time to get off. Will held his hand out to help me down while Lorna continued talking.

'...and it's modern, which I know you like. It's a little over budget but that's because the location's stunning. You should see the view, Yvonne. I know you really want Willowdale so I do think you should take a look.'

'It sounds great. I can probably stretch the budget a bit.'

'Fabulous! Is there any chance you can view it this afternoon or tomorrow? I can give you an exclusive on it this weekend but I'll need to put it online tonight which means potential viewings next week.'

'That could be tricky. I'm working tomorrow and I'm out at the moment.'

I made an appointment for Monday but, when I disconnected the call and explained the situation to Will, he said there was no point me missing out on having exclusivity and he'd be delighted to accompany me today, so I called Lorna back and arranged to meet her at the house in forty-five minutes.

* * *

My love for Gosling's Rest was instant. It was the last house in the village at the Willowdale Hall end and set back quite far from the road in an elevated position behind a couple of rows of trees.

'It's an upside-down house,' Lorna said, handing over a copy of the sales particulars after meeting us on the drive. 'Does that bother you?'

'Not at all.' Presumably it had been built that way to take advantage of the views from the living space. 'When you said modern, I assumed you meant the inside, but the whole building looks pretty new.'

'It is. The house that was here before was a wreck and the

current owner – a property developer – managed to get permission to start over as long as the design was sympathetic to the style in the village.'

The developer had done a brilliant job as Gosling's Rest didn't look out of place at all with slate roof tiles and a combination of slate stone and whitewashed rendering. There was a lot of glass and a slate balcony running the whole length of the house.

Lorna gave us a tour of the downstairs first, saying she wanted to save the views for last. We looked in the family bathroom and two double bedrooms, the one at the front of the house being ideal for my craft room due to an abundance of light, before finishing with the en suite master bedroom which enjoyed a view over the front garden. It was a spacious room with sumptuous furnishings and the most enormous bed. Will was standing so close to me that I could hear him breathing. His hand brushed against mine and I flushed from head to toe as I imagined tumbling onto that bed with him and finally reliving our Manchester experience.

'Upstairs?' I suggested to Lorna.

'Absolutely. The upstairs is open plan and there's plenty of scope to use the space differently.'

We followed her up the oak staircase and straight to the front of the property to breathe in the most beautiful view across Derwent Water and the fells on the east side. I already knew I wanted Gosling's Rest but this fully confirmed it.

'That's impressive,' Will said.

'The doors onto the balcony open up fully,' Lorna said, pulling on a handle and sliding the doors back to show us. 'Oh! That's my phone. I'll leave you to have a wander round up here on your own and meet you outside when you're done. Take your time and feel free to go downstairs again.'

'What are you thinking?' Will asked when she'd gone.

'That she's just found me my new home.'

'I can see you here.'

I could also see him here with me but it was way too soon to voice that. 'Better explore the rest.'

I turned, intending to head into the kitchen but something at the opposite end caught my eye and I grabbed Will's arm. 'Look!'

The owners were evidently musical as there was a cello on a stand at the end of the room and a baby grand piano positioned so the pianist could look out over the view as they played.

'I don't suppose I can tempt you?' I asked, but Will was already on his way over to it. He pulled out the wide stool and we sat down beside each other and, without a word, began the same first duet we'd played in Pianos of Distinction – 'Fly Me to the Moon'. Will's playing was exquisite and note-perfect. Mine was a little clumsy without the music but it somehow worked. Just like us. We played 'Clair de Lune' followed by 'Piano Man' again and it was like the years had melted away and we were back in Manchester, although the electricity between us was even stronger than it had been back then.

'I loved that,' I said a little breathlessly as we came to the end of 'Piano Man'. 'I'm sorry I couldn't remember all the notes.'

'I'm impressed you could remember any of them after all this time.'

'I might not have played them on the keys but I've played them in my mind so many times.'

We were so close and the air was fizzing. I longed to kiss him but I didn't want to make the first move. I was in a brilliant place in my life right now and so ready for this but I wasn't the one who'd been hurt. Will was going through a tough time and he'd only just found out why I left. He needed time to process that.

'How is it that we've spent so little time together yet I feel like I've known you for my whole lifetime?' he said.

'Because I think that, on some level, we have.'

He gave me such a tender smile. 'I wrote a melody for you.'

My heart leapt. 'You did? Will you play it?'

I'd never heard anything quite so beautiful and couldn't speak when he finished. He hadn't told me he loved me but that piece of music just had. I gazed at him, tears pooling in my eyes and I don't know who made the move but, next moment, we were locked in a passionate embrace. His tongue teased mine, his fingers ran through my hair and down my back and I clung to him, my body yearning for so much more than kisses. As we tumbled against the piano keys, eliciting an uncomfortable clash of notes, we pulled apart breathlessly, laughing.

'That was beautiful,' I whispered.

'The music or the kiss?'

'Both.'

He kissed me once more, a little slower this time, but we had to reluctantly break apart to finish our tour and find Lorna.

'What did you think?' she asked.

'I think you've found me my new house.'

'Really? Yes! I was certain it would be the perfect match for you.'

I glanced at Will before answering. 'Definitely the perfect match.'

Lorna reminded me of the asking price but said the owner had accepted an offer and was happy for Lorna to accept the same offer from me. It sounded reasonable so we had a deal. She went inside to switch off the lights and lock up.

'You've just bought a house,' Will said, smiling at me.

'I can't believe it! I usually take way longer than that to think about things but I've been making all sorts of spontaneous decisions lately.'

He took my hand in his. 'I think we all know when something's right.'

'I think we do.'

'I know we said we'd go out for a drink tonight, but I'm thinking we should go for a celebratory one right now.'

I nodded. 'Definitely.'

As we walked through the village towards The Hardy Herdwick, I felt as though I was encased in a bubble of happiness. I had wonderful friends, an exciting new business, a new home and the man of my dreams back in my life with whom I'd just shared the most incredible kisses. A man who had written a melody just for me. A man who made my heart sing.

My phone rang and I took it out my pocket, assuming it would be Lorna checking something, but I didn't recognise the number.

'Hello?' I said.

'Is that Yvonne?'

'It is.'

'Hi, it's Amelia. I live next door to Marianne...'

And in one phone call, that bubble of happiness burst.

46

'Have you spoken to your sister recently?' Amelia asked.

I stopped walking, a feeling of dread in my stomach. 'Not for a while.' I didn't add that the last time had been in March. 'Why?'

'It's probably nothing but I haven't seen her in a while and I'm getting worried. I'm outside her cottage and I've been knocking on the door but there's no answer.'

'Did she give you a spare key?' I asked. Amelia was right to worry. Marianne never left the cottage so, if she wasn't answering the door, something was wrong.

'No, and I've checked under some plant pots but I can't see one.'

'I've got one but by the time I get home and drive to you... Could you break a window? Maybe the kitchen one. I'll pay for the damage.' The windows were still single glazing so should be easy to smash.

'Okay. I'll go round the back.'

'It's my sister's neighbour,' I told Will. 'She hasn't seen her for a while and she's worried.'

I put the phone on speaker to avoid having to repeat the rest of the conversation.

'There's a key on the inside of the back door,' Amelia said. 'Give me a second.'

I winced at the sound of breaking glass.

'Just putting my hand through and... I'm in. Urgh!'

Panic stabbed at me. 'What's wrong?'

'The smell. Oh, my God! There's bin bags and rubbish everywhere.'

I sighed. 'I know. She has a hoarding problem and she wouldn't accept my help.'

'I'm going through to the lounge. Hang on. Urgh, it stinks in here too.'

'Any sign of Marianne?'

'No.'

'Try her bedroom or the bathroom – first two doors at the top of the stairs. Careful on the stairs, though.'

'It's such a mess! Is this why you asked me if I'd ever been inside?'

'I wondered if she'd opened up to you about it.'

'I had no idea. Bathroom's empty and so's her bedroom. I'll try the others.'

'It's our parents' room next, then what was mine.'

'Nothing in your parents' room,' Amelia said. 'Just pushing open your door and... oh, God! I'm so sorry, Yvonne.'

I clutched onto Will's arm, tears pooling in my eyes. 'Is she...?'

'She's long gone.'

'A fall?' I asked.

'She's lying on the bed on top of the covers holding a doll in a red dress.'

Scarlett Skye. Tears burned my eyes and my throat tightened. When I spoke, my voice sounded distant. 'Can you call an ambulance? Or would it be the police? I don't know what you do when... Do you mind? Is that—'

'Don't worry. I'll make the call. I know what to do.'

'I'll be there as soon as I can.'

'I'll drive,' Will said as I hung up.

'I can't expect you to—'

'You've had a shock and I want to.'

I nodded, tears spilling down my cheeks. Will drew me to his chest and held me.

'I don't know why I'm crying. We weren't close. She hated me.'

Will knew how difficult things had been between us. I'd told him a little about Marianne the weekend we met but I'd told him a lot more during our walk earlier, including my difficult decision to stop contacting her.

Will tightened his hold. 'She was still your sister, though, and you cared about her even if she didn't act as though she cared about you.'

'I should have pushed her more. I knew she had to be ill but I backed off.'

'Because she wanted you to back off. You can't keep pushing against a closed door. You did more than most people in your position would do.'

He was right, but it didn't stop me feeling guilty.

* * *

There was a police car outside 4 Hayscroft Lane but Amelia had clearly been watching out for me as she came rushing out of her cottage.

'The police are with me,' she said. 'There was nowhere to sit next door. I'm so sorry, Yvonne.'

'I'm sorry you had to find her. That must have been difficult.'

'It's okay. I'm a nurse so it's not the first time.'

The next couple of hours passed in a blur as I gathered information and made arrangements. Marianne's death was not unexpected. A doctor confirmed she'd had stage four bowel cancer but had signed an advance decision document refusing treatment, carers, hospital or a hospice, adamant that she wanted to die on her own terms at home. It was heartbreaking to think that she'd died alone and presumably in pain, but she'd spent her whole life choosing to be alone so it made sense that she wouldn't want people around her in her final days.

I rang Paulette to see if she had any recommendations for funeral directors in the area and she gave me the details of a company she highly recommended so I arranged for them to attend. She'd swapped her Sunday shift with me to give me today off and kindly offered to work tomorrow too but I told her I'd be fine and would appreciate the distraction of the shop.

Will cleared all the bags from the stairs so that the funeral directors could remove Marianne's body safely. In the meantime, Amelia's husband had arrived home from work and boarded up the broken window so at least the building was secure until I could sort out a glazer.

With the police and funeral directors gone, Amelia asked if there was anything else we needed and I thanked her profusely for being so helpful today and for being a friend to my sister.

Returning to my former bedroom with Will, I picked up Scarlett Skye.

'I'm so confused,' I said. 'Why was Marianne in *my* bedroom holding *my* doll?'

'Probably because she *did* care about you after all.'

I shrugged. 'Maybe. I guess I'll never know now.'

It was surreal being back here and difficult to compute that

Marianne was gone. I didn't feel sad, didn't feel relieved. If anything, I felt numb.

'Do you know what your sister's last wishes were?' Will asked after a while.

'Not a clue. We never spoke about anything like that. We barely spoke at all. I didn't know her, Will. I didn't even know she was ill. I asked her repeatedly and she fobbed me off. Stage four cancer. I can't...' I shook my head. 'I'm guessing cremation – most people go for that these days, don't they?'

'Could she have left a letter in her own bedroom or somewhere else you'd find it?'

'Oh! Christmas Day! She invited me round and I was only here for ten minutes. All she wanted to do was show me...'

I dashed into our parents' room with Will following, folded back the rug, lifted the floorboards and removed the contents – two bundles of documents and a shoebox. The first bundle related to the cottage and included the deeds, and the second was for Dad's smallholding.

'Looks like Marianne sold it back to Hayscroft Farm after Dad died,' I said. 'That's news to me. I assumed she had someone in managing it.'

There was a bank book attached to the sale confirmation and I opened it out, gasping at the substantial sum of money in it, presumably from the land sale.

'That's a lot of pennies,' Will said when I showed him.

'Whether the money's still there is another matter, although I can't imagine what she'd have spent it on if it isn't. She's never done anything with the cottage and she never went out.'

I moved the documents aside and lifted the lid on the shoebox. Resting on top of a pile of photographs was an envelope with my name on it.

'Final wishes?' Will suggested as I lifted it out.

There were two pieces of paper inside – a letter and an official-looking document, which I unfolded first.

'It's my full birth certificate,' I said, clocking my name at the top. I had the short version at home – the one with my name, sex, date and place of birth – and had never thought to ask whether they had the long-form version. I scanned down the additional details and my breath caught. That couldn't be right.

'What's up?' Will asked.

I stared at the document, my stomach churning. How the hell had they all kept that from me?

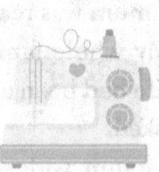

47

It made no sense. It was definitely my birth certificate – Yvonne Jacqueline Lambert with the correct date and place of birth – but Polly Winifred Lambert should have been listed as my mother and Bryan Edgar Lambert as my father. Instead, the father's name was blank and the mother was listed as Marianne Charlotte Lambert.

'Marianne was your mother?' Will said, his tone conveying the same shock I felt.

'According to this, she was. I don't get it. Why didn't anyone tell me?'

With shaking hands, I opened out the letter, hoping it would shed some light but it was only one paragraph.

Dear Yvonne

The end is near and there's much to explain. I wanted to write it all down but my hands hurt and my writing is scrawly so I've decided to record it instead. You'll find my tape recorder in my bedroom. I'm tired so I'll be doing it in parts. I hope I manage to finish it but apologies if I don't quite get there.

    Marianne

I wanted answers but I couldn't seem to move. What was going on? This couldn't be true. If my sister was really my mother, that meant my wonderful mum was really my grandma. I couldn't get my head around it. My whole family had lied to me for my entire life and my entire life had been a lie. Who was I?

'Are you okay?' Will asked.

But I could only stare at him, wide-eyed, and shrug.

'Do you want me to try and find the tapes?'

I nodded.

He scrambled to his feet and returned a few minutes later with a cassette tape player and a lead. I remembered Marianne listening to tapes on it when I was young.

'There's a tape inside,' he said. 'Do you want to listen to it now or back at your flat?'

'Now,' I whispered. I hoped Marianne had managed to record all the parts because I desperately needed answers.

Will plugged it in, rewound the cassette then pressed play before settling down on the floor beside me. It was strange hearing Marianne's voice in the room, knowing she was no longer with us. The first part was a repeat of what she'd written in the letter.

'I'm aiming to cover a different subject in each sitting,' she added. 'It'll be a lot for you to take in all at once so you might want to listen to one part at a time. You might also want a friend with you.'

I glanced at Will and he took my hand and squeezed it.

'Firstly, if you're listening to this, I'm dead. That sounds like a line from a whodunnit, but it's true. I'm terminally ill and I don't want treatment. Why would I try to prolong a life when I already think I've been far too long in a world I get nothing from and don't contribute anything to? I felt ready to go long ago, way before the cancer. You've asked on several occasions if I'm all right but I batted your questions away. You mustn't feel even a tiny fraction of guilt for not supporting me through my final days because I didn't want you to. I didn't want you to know and I didn't want you here and that's nothing about you. It's all about me. I wanted to do this alone.'

There were a few clicks, suggesting that this had been the end of her first session. Her words were slow, the sentences punctuated by coughs and wheezing. No wonder she'd recorded it in parts when a few minutes of talking so clearly took their toll on her.

'Do you want to continue?' Will asked.

'I need to know why they lied to me.'

Another click and Marianne's husky voice returned. 'The second thing I need to talk about is the mess. When they told me it was terminal, I assumed I didn't have long and that's when the build-up started. I thought there was no point clearing up as I'd be gone in a few weeks. I know that might sound lazy but...' She broke off for a coughing fit. 'But the weeks stretched into months which stretched into years and it was all too overwhelming. I'm so sorry I've left it all for you to deal with. I really was going to sort it out but, lately, I haven't had the strength to do anything. Even this is exhausting.' She had another coughing fit which cut off suddenly.

Will leaned over and stopped the tape. 'Are you sure you want to do this now?'

I wasn't sure of anything anymore. 'One more.'

He pressed play.

'Thirdly but probably the most important section for you. If you've looked at your birth certificate already, you'll know I wasn't really your big sister. I don't even know where to start explaining this one. I can imagine how shocked and confused you are and probably really hurt too. To understand why it was a secret, I need to tell you about your real father. Remember how you found it hard to make friends because you couldn't see anyone outside of school? It was the same for me but it never bothered me. I much preferred my own company. I'd walk for miles, happy by myself. Most of my walks took me across Hayscroft Farm and I kept bumping into Eli Farrow's son, Richard, and we had this instant connection. Dad was working at the farm at the time and he told me not to bother Richard so we started meeting in an old shepherd's hut. It was just as friends at first, especially as he was eighteen and I was fourteen, but you can't control who you fall in love with and we gave up fighting our feelings. We talked about a future together, running the farm, having kids. I never thought I'd want all of that but, with Richard, it seemed right.

'When I told him I might be pregnant, he went white as a sheet. I thought he was going to leave me but he said it wasn't that – it was that he'd be in big trouble because I was underage. I was so young and naïve. I thought it wouldn't matter if we loved each other so I told my parents, foolishly thinking they'd be happy. Of course they weren't! Dad hit the roof and stormed to the farm to confront Eli and Richard. He was gone for hours and Mum was scared he might have hurt them but he came back looking surprisingly calm. He'd made a deal with Eli Farrow. Dad wouldn't call the police on Richard, my parents would pretend my baby was theirs, and Eli would gift Dad a smallholding and financial support while he got it established. Can you believe that? This was my baby – mine and Richard's – but the deal was made without ever once asking us what we wanted.

'Eli banished Richard, sending him to some relatives in

Northumberland but his out of sight, out of mind strategy didn't work. Richard found his way back to me, saying he'd stand by me and we could get married. Dad called the police and I finally realised how serious it was so I told him to go, that I didn't love him, that I wasn't even sure the baby was his. I must have been convincing because he left before the police arrived. Fortunately, Dad hadn't told the police why he'd called them – he'd claimed a suspected robbery on the farm and, when they arrived, he and Eli said it was a false alarm, so there was never any suspicion of Richard doing anything wrong. As for me, without Richard in my life, there didn't seem any point going against the deal. There didn't seem any point going for walks when I knew I wouldn't bump into Richard. There didn't seem any point in anything.'

Even though her voice was weak from her illness, there was no mistaking the pain as she'd relived her story. She'd lost the love of her life and had needed to lie to protect him, push him away, make him think she didn't care and it had been too much for her. She'd given up. She'd been broken.

I leaned over and pressed the stop button. 'I've heard enough for now. Will you take me home, please?'

Will helped me to my feet and wrapped his arms around me. I clung onto him, needing his warmth on what had just become a very cold day.

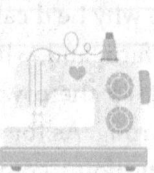

48

Will drove me back to Willowdale in silence, evidently sensing that I needed some time to try and process what I'd discovered. Back in the flat, he filled the kettle and made me a mug of strong tea.

'I keep thinking of all these aspects of my childhood that make so much more sense now,' I said as Will settled onto the sofa beside me. 'How did I miss it all?'

'Because you weren't looking for it. Who would be?'

'My poor mum. She tried so hard to get me to have a relationship with Marianne and she...' I bit my lip. 'But she wasn't my mum, was she? She was my grandma! I can't call her that.'

'Then don't. Call her what you've always called her.'

I stared down into my mug. 'I don't think this is going to be strong enough but I don't have any alcohol in the flat.'

'Do you want to go to the pub?'

A few drinks in The Hardy Herdwick slipped down way too easily, taking the edge off the shock, numbing the pain. Will could not have been more supportive, letting me witter on endlessly with whatever came into my head. The conversation flitted from childhood memories to observations about the weather to worries about what I was going to do with the cottage. It was all over the place but that's how I felt right now.

As we left the pub and the fresh air hit me, it struck me that I was more inebriated than I'd ever been.

'I've drunk too much,' I slurred as I struggled to stay in a straight line.

Will slipped his arm round my waist to prevent me from stumbling into the road and kept me upright and moving forward all the way back to the flat.

'Today took a few unexpected turns,' I said, sinking onto one of the dining chairs while Will filled me a glass with tap water. 'Some fantastic and others...' I shrugged.

'Do you need anything else?' Will asked. 'Some toast maybe?'

'Just you. Will you stay? It's okay if you need to go or you want to go. I'll be fine.'

'I'll stay. Why don't you get yourself ready for bed and I'll cover Trevor and put the lights out in here?'

I went into the bathroom to brush my teeth then into the bedroom to remove my clothes, although stepping out of my jeans was a bit of a challenge in my addled state. I pulled on a nightie before climbing under the duvet.

Will knocked lightly on the door. 'Are you in bed?'

'Yes.'

He opened the door. 'Do you have any spare bedding?'

'No.' I peeled back the duvet. 'There's a spare toothbrush in the bathroom and you can...' But my eyes were heavy and forming any more words was such an effort.

* * *

'Thought you might need this.'

I could smell coffee and I blinked in the dim light. My head hurt.

'What time is it?'

'Eight, so still quite early, but I thought you might want some time to listen to more of the tape before you open the shop.'

I nodded slowly. 'I'm sorry about last night.'

'Don't be. I'd have done the same. There's some paracetamol and a fresh glass of water by the bed.'

'Thank you.'

Will left the room and I gratefully downed the tablets and the whole glass of water, feeling completely dehydrated. The coffee was too hot so I had a shower while it was cooling and, by the time I joined Will and Trevor, I felt a lot more human but I still couldn't get my head around what had happened yesterday. Marianne's death had been difficult enough but the discovery that she was my mother... I didn't know what to do with that. It didn't feel real.

'Thank you for staying,' I said as I settled onto the sofa beside Will. 'I didn't want to be alone last night.'

'I didn't want you to be alone.'

'But you're going through so much already. I can't believe I've just added to your burdens.'

Will took my hand in his. 'Nothing about you is a burden. I want to be here. I want to help. How are you feeling?'

'Apart from the fuzzy head and the mouth like a desert? Still confused. It feels like a bad dream.'

'You could always listen to the rest of the tape after work.'

'If I wait, I'll only spend all day thinking about it. You don't have to stay if you have plans.'

'I'm seeing my mum this afternoon but I'm free this morning. Should I plug it in?'

'Fourth part,' Marianne said once Will set the tape playing

once more. 'Or I think it is... Yes, it is. I was fifteen when you were born. It was a home birth. Eli Farrow paid a midwife who wouldn't ask questions. Mum doted on you but Dad couldn't bring himself to look at you. He used to be warm and friendly but he turned into an angry, bitter man. Mum and Dad argued all the time. She liked Richard and still believed the three of us could be a family but Dad told her to get her head out the clouds. Me falling pregnant destroyed their marriage. Mum went on the happy pills and floated around in a daze, oblivious to how crap everything was. Those Friday-night school reports were so hard for me, pretending to be your sister and not a proud parent. It was easier to push you away than risk getting close and having the truth come out. And it was easier to stay away from you instead of look at you every day and see Richard's eyes. I know I was awful to you and I wish I could change every part of it but I can't. None of this was your fault. If Richard and I had been allowed to be together, you'd have been the daughter of my dreams, but we weren't and I couldn't cope with it. I'm sorry.'

'More things suddenly making sense,' I said to Will when Marianne paused.

'I'm back and I need to talk to you about the cottage and the smallholding. You already know that the cottage was left to both of us when my dad died so now it's completely yours. As for the smallholding, if you've looked through the documents, you'll know that I sold it. Shortly after my dad died, Eli Farrow did too and Richard returned to take over the farm. He was married with children and I could hardly blame him for that. It was easy to avoid him. If I went out, I didn't cross the farm and he was hardly going to call on me. I had no interest in the smallholding so I'd had someone in managing it but they stepped down and I couldn't face searching for a replacement. I waited until I saw Richard's wife go out with the kids one weekend and I marched down to the farm and told Richard he needed to buy the land back. Obviously he didn't want to but I had nothing to lose and said I'd tell his wife the truth if he didn't. He said I'd told him I didn't know if he was the father so I told him I'd said that for his own protection and he had to have known that deep down and, even if he didn't believe me, the fact remained that he'd been eighteen and I'd been a minor. I hated threatening him like that – made me no better than my dad or his – but it worked and he bought the land back. I never spent a penny of it so, as well as the cottage, all that money and the interest it's earned is yours. I'm sorry there's nothing much inside that can be salvaged. You'll need to spend some money doing it up before you sell it as I can't imagine you'll want to live here. I hope you don't. Even after the work, you'll still walk away a rich woman.'

My head was spinning. Was all that money really mine? It felt a bit weird – like I'd been awarded compensation for a bad childhood. I didn't care about the money. I cared about the truth and wished with all my heart that I wasn't just finding out about it now.

The tape clicked and Marianne cleared her throat. 'This is my final recording. I have no right to play the mother card and offer you some pearls of wisdom but I'm going to anyway. Dad used to go on and on about Cliff being a homosexual. I barely knew him so I can't comment. If he was and you married him just to escape this hellhole, I'm glad he made you happy but happiness isn't the same as true love. I hope you do find someone you love who loves you in return because it's a special thing when it happens. If you do, my advice is to love them unreservedly and never let them go. I should have fought for Richard and he should have fought for me because we were meant to be together. We spoke a few times after he bought the land. We made our peace and we both regretted that we'd wasted our lives. I said pearls plural but it's just the one. It's a good one, though. I need to go now, Yvonne. I'm so very tired and everything hurts. I'm not afraid of dying but I was afraid of living. I don't want you to be. Richard died a few years ago and I believe he's waiting for me. Scatter my ashes where the shepherd's hut was. He's there. Please be happy and, even though I know I ask the impossible, please try to find a way to forgive me. I know I never showed it, but I did love you so very much and I've always been incredibly proud of you. I should have told you that but... As I say, lots of regrets. One final thing. I hope you still use Mum's sewing machine. I couldn't save the piano but at least I could save that for you.'

The tape clicked and then there was static. It really was the end.

'She's the one who dropped the sewing machine off,' I said, tears pooling in my eyes. 'We thought Dad must have had a change of heart but it was Marianne who did it. She hated going out. That must have been so hard for her.'

'But she loved you so she did it for you.'

I could barely catch my breath as the tears poured down my cheeks, punctuated by loud cries. Will gathered me to his side and stroked my hair as years of pent-up frustration and feelings of rejection finally had their release.

* * *

I was too churned up to work in the shop after all but, when I tried ringing Paulette to ask if I could take her up on her offer to do her usual Sunday shift after all, I couldn't get the words out and burst into tears once more. Will took the phone from me and told her that the grief had hit me today and I was worried about breaking down in front of customers.

'She'll be here shortly,' Will said after he ended the call.

'Thanks for keeping it vague. I will tell her the full story, but it's too much for now. When I was in the shower, I was wondering whether I'd want to meet Richard. I can't believe he's dead too.'

'Does it upset you?'

I shrugged. 'I'm struggling so much with the idea that my parents weren't really my parents, I can't even begin to get upset about the death of a biological dad I didn't know existed.'

We sat in silence for several minutes.

'I should have fought for you,' Will said.

'How?'

'By tracking you down. Yvonne's not that common a name and I knew you lived in the Lakes. I probably could have found you.'

'What stopped you?'

'My own stupid self-doubt. I thought that, after I'd gone, you came to your senses and chose Cliff. I suppose I was too scared to find you and have you confirm that.'

'It never happened.'

'I know that now. I know something else too. I asked you whether you'd have left Cliff if you'd found me and you said you weren't sure.'

'I'm not.'

Will's fingers crept into his hair and he began circling it. My stomach clenched. Why was he nervous? Surely he wasn't going to tell me he couldn't do this right now or, even worse, ever.

'What's going on?' I asked. 'You're worrying me.'

'When we met and you told me how loyal you felt towards Cliff for everything he'd done for you, I thought I understood but I didn't. Not really. I do now. I've seen what you were fleeing from, I've heard it in Marianne's voice, and I've felt it pouring from you. I think that, after we met, you were ready to leave him and I genuinely believe it would have happened if he hadn't been in that car crash. But after he was hurt, even if we had found each other, I'm convinced that your choice would have been different. You'd have picked him.'

'Will, I...' My heart was pounding. I couldn't deny it. Deep down, I knew he spoke the truth, but what did that mean for us? Was this goodbye?

'Don't look so worried,' he said, taking my hands in his. 'I'm not angry or disappointed or anything like that. You have such a kind heart, Yvonne. I knew that from the moment I met you and it's why I fell for you. You love deeply and you're fiercely loyal to the people you care about. That's why you stayed. That's why you never told him about us.'

The tears slipped down my cheeks as I marvelled at how he knew me better than I knew myself.

'He would have let me go. I only had to say the word, but I couldn't do it to him. I owed him my sanity... my life.'

'I realise that now. I understand completely and I think you did the right thing.'

'You do?'

He nodded. 'I don't think you could have lived with the guilt if you'd said goodbye to him.'

'I'm sorry I hurt you in the process.'

'You don't need to apologise. I know it was never intentional because that's not who you are. But you do realise that, now that destiny has finally reunited us, I'm not letting you go again?'

'Good, because I don't want you to.'

For the next couple of hours, we curled up together on the sofa and held each other and I knew that this was it. We'd finally found each other, we were free to be together, and neither of us were going to let go.

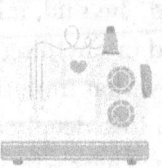

49

Will left around mid-afternoon on the Sunday. He didn't want to leave me but I refused to let him cancel his plans to see his mum. Returning on the evening wasn't an option as he had some marking to do ahead of the fresh school week.

His absence gave me the time and space to listen to Marianne's tape several times and think about all the aspects of my childhood that made so much more sense now. I'd always wondered why my dad hated me so much and now I knew. It had been about his negative reaction to Marianne's pregnancy and the impact his deal with Eli Farrow had on our family, driving a wedge between them all. I'd always believed I must have said or done something to turn him against me and it was strangely comforting finally knowing that I hadn't.

I didn't need to work on Monday as Milly was working the full day but I went downstairs when I heard her arrive and she enveloped me in a hug. I'd told Paulette everything and had asked her to update the others.

'How are you doing?' Milly asked.

'I lost it yesterday, but I'm okay today. How's your workload?'

'Not too heavy today so I'm all yours if you'd like to talk between customers.'

Paulette joined us shortly after opening time and we sat by the counter with mugs of tea discussing what I'd shared with them both.

'I can't even begin to imagine what it must feel like to discover your sister was really your mum and your parents were your grandparents,' Milly said. 'Your head must be mashed.'

'It is. Things they said at various times keep coming back to me and I understand them in a new light. There were clues but I can only see them now that I know the truth.'

'And this Richard's dead too?' Paulette asked.

'Yes. I wondered if she might have just said that to stop me going to the farm, but I found his obituary online.'

'Might you still go to the farm, though? If he got married and had kids, they're your half-siblings.'

'Half-siblings?' I stared at Paulette, wide-eyed. 'That never even entered my head.'

'How do you feel about that?' Milly asked.

'I'm not sure. I thought I was the last one standing – the end of the branch – but I'm not, am I? Oh, my God! What do I do? Do I contact them? Do I want to?'

Paulette and Milly gave me reassuring smiles.

'There's no need to rush into anything,' Paulette said. 'You've had plenty of shocks already. Take some time to let the dust settle and see how you feel then.'

Over the next few days, I went through the photos in the shoebox and smiled when I came across one of me as a little girl licking cake batter off a wooden spoon. That conversation at

Cake & Craft Club with Veronica seemed like a lifetime ago now.

I recognised Mum's neat handwriting on the back of most of the photos, listing names, dates and locations. There was a well-worn photograph of a man and I gasped, not needing to turn it over to know who it was. No wonder Marianne had found it hard to look at me. It wasn't just the eyes. I was the image of my father. Sure enough, when I turned it over, I recognised the same scrawl from Marianne's final note:

Yvonne, this is your dad, Richard Farrow, age 18.

I'd gone back and forth as to whether I wanted to visit the farm and introduce myself. Having always felt as though I'd missed out by not having any grandparents, aunts, uncles or cousins, I loved the idea of having a big family out there but, from what Marianne had said on the tape, they knew nothing about me and I didn't want to cause them any pain. No matter how much I longed to connect with them, it felt kinder to them to let sleeping dogs lie.

'You know what you could do?' Will said. 'You could ask for permission to scatter Marianne's ashes on their land. You don't have to say why but at least it'd give you a plausible reason to meet them. You can gauge then whether it's best to walk away or tell them the truth. Bear in mind that you're assuming that discovering they've got a half-sister would be bad news but that's not necessarily the case. It wasn't for your friends Emma and Oliver.'

He raised a good point. It had been brilliant news for them and the half-siblings were exceptionally close. I wasn't sure what to do for the best, but scattering Marianne's ashes where the shepherd's hut had been was her final wish and I did want to respect that. So that's how I found myself driving up the track to Hayscroft Farm a fortnight after Amelia found Marianne dead.

'I'm right here with you,' Will said, taking my hand as we exited the car and headed towards the front door.

He'd been my rock this past fortnight. Most of the time, I'd felt pretty steady but, every so often, a wave of grief or anger crashed over me. Will had let me rant and held me as I cried but I made sure it wasn't me doing all the taking. He still had a lot going on and I was there for him as much as he was for me. I'd already told him that, as soon as the legalities were sorted around Marianne's estate, I'd be giving him the money from the sale of the smallholding to pass onto Aaron. He'd refused, of course, so I'd told him to consider it a loan until his house sale went through if that made it easier to accept. It was obvious how great a weight that had lifted from him, knowing he could finally do something to help his friend.

'Ready?' Will asked as we reached the farmhouse door.

I nodded and Will knocked. A little girl – maybe aged eight or nine – answered the door, which threw me.

'Hi, erm... I'm looking for...' I realised too late that I didn't actually know the name of Richard's wife.

'Nanna!' the girl shouted. 'There's some people at the door.'

'What have I told you about answering the door to strangers?' a woman called, appearing in the porch and shooing the girl into the room she'd emerged from.

She looked up and I placed her in her mid-seventies so hopefully this was the right person.

'Are you Richard Farrow's wife?' I asked.

'Yes. Who's asking?'

'My name's Yvonne. I used to live at number four...' I pointed in the direction of the lane, 'and I was...'

I tailed off as her eyes widened and she clapped her hand to her chest. 'Oh, my goodness, you look just like him.'

'You know who I am?' I asked, shocked by her reaction.

She nodded. 'Richard's daughter. I heard that Marianne had passed and I wondered if you'd visit. Come in.'

'You're sure?' I'd never in a million years have predicted a reaction like this.

She gave me a warm smile. 'It's what Richard would have wanted.'

May had been full of unexpected moments and my visit to Hayscroft Farm was yet another of them. Richard's wife, Rosalind, had known about me for years. She maintained the farm's accounts so there was no way Richard could have bought the smallholding without her noticing. Therefore, when Marianne presented him with the ultimatum, he decided to come clean himself. She'd always known he was harbouring an enormous secret and figured he'd let her in on it one day. It was Rosalind who'd suggested a payment over and above what the land was worth as some sort of recompense for what had happened.

Rosalind wasn't a jealous woman. She trusted her husband implicitly and knew he loved her in his own way, even if Marianne was the one who'd always held his heart. She was aware that Marianne and Richard had talked occasionally and that the feelings were still there along with a lot of regret, but she'd known that nothing would come of it. Their time had passed.

Richard and Rosalind's three children – a girl and two boys – didn't know anything about me but, with my agreement, Rosalind wanted to tell them and let them decide whether they wanted to meet me or not. I hadn't thought beyond half-siblings so another surprise was discovering that Richard and Rosalind had seven grandchildren aged twenty-four down to five and that the eldest of those had a two-year-old daughter. My brain hurt working out their relationship to me – half-nephews, half-nieces and a great-half-niece? I gave Rosalind permission to tell them all when she was ready and assured her I wouldn't try to force a relationship if they didn't want one. I'd had plenty of practice at that!

Before Will and I left, Rosalind gave us permission to scatter Marianne's ashes where the shepherd's hut had been and confirmed that Richard's had been scattered there. I came away in awe of what a strong woman she was, understanding and accepting that her husband's heart belonged to another but the love he had for her was enough to make their marriage work.

A few days later, on a beautiful May Tuesday, Marianne was cremated. We'd considered closing Created With Love for the day so that Milly, Paulette and Christian could attend the service but, with it being the half-term holiday, trade was busy so closing wasn't ideal. Kelly adjusted the rota at The White Willow so that Saffy could work in the shop and Autumn kindly offered to help her. Veronica and Laughlin were now in Germany and fully aware of the situation. They'd offered to fly back but I wouldn't hear of it. I knew they were thinking of me and that was enough. Will was by my side, of course, and so was Fen who I adored. Marianne's neighbour Amelia came with her family and I noticed Rosalind slipping into the back of the room and slipping out again before the service ended.

Will and I collected Marianne's ashes on the Thursday to scatter on Hayscroft Farm. Rosalind had given me directions to the correct field, just in case I couldn't remember the way, and had told me she'd leave a flag where the hut had been, which I really appreciated because, without the shepherd's hut, it looked like any other field to me. Standing beside the flag, I didn't know what to say. I had no speech prepared and to make something up felt hypocritical. Through repeated listens to the tape, I felt like I understood Marianne better but I still didn't know her. She'd never given me that chance.

I lifted the lid from the box. 'Hope you're finally reunited with Richard,' I said as I emptied the contents.

I turned to Will, feeling panicky. 'I don't know what else to say.'

'Then don't say anything.'

'But I feel like I've let her down.'

He put his arm around me, drew me to his side and kissed the top of my head. 'All she wanted was for you to scatter her ashes here and that's what you've done. You don't need to do anything else.'

Feeling reassured, I looked up at the clouds. Wherever Marianne was, I hope she'd found peace, love and happiness at last. I wished things had been different between us and it was comforting to know from the tape that she'd wished the same.

Will pointed to a cloud. 'That looks like a lily pad.'

And it did. I smiled as 'Clair de Lune' played in my head. 'If Marianne's up there, I think Mum's with her too.'

50

TWO MONTHS LATER

'What are you reading?' Will slipped his arms round my waist from behind and softly kissed my neck.

'One final flick through my journal before I pack it,' I said, closing it and placing it into the packing box ready for the move into Gosling's Rest next week. 'I can't believe that, after only six months, I can put a tick against every entry in here. This journal has been pure magic.'

'I thought there was still one entry unticked.'

'Okay, there is, but we'll get to Venice one day.'

'How about October?' he asked, handing me a piece of paper.

I glanced down at the ticket confirmation for four nights in Venice during the October half-term holiday. 'You've booked it! Oh, my God! Will! I can't believe it!'

'I want you to have everything you've ever dreamed of.'

I placed my arms round his waist and lightly kissed him. 'I've already got that now that I've got you. I love you.'

'I love you too.'

'But Venice is a nice little addition. Fingers crossed we get to experience the *acqua alta*.'

'Whether we do or don't, it'll be incredible.'

Just like my life was with Will. So much had changed for me this year and at quite an astonishing pace since Will had walked into my shop and back into my life. I'd thought a lot about Marianne and Richard's story and how they'd never got their happy ending together and about Marianne's parting advice to me to find someone I loved who loved me back and to *love them unreservedly and never let them go*. Will and I weren't getting any younger and we had many lost years to make up for so I'd asked him to move in with me at Gosling's Rest. We loved each other so what was the point in him looking for a place of his own when his house in Keswick sold? The purchase of Gosling's Rest was set for completion next week and I couldn't wait for us to move in together and for a very special delivery to arrive for us both.

The money had come through from Marianne's estate and I hadn't changed my mind about Aaron having it but things had moved on for him. He'd had plenty of time to think about the future and, at the age of fifty-eight, had decided he wasn't interested in having to start over or in having to repeatedly fight the rumours. He'd sold the building to a property developer who was going to convert it into flats and Aaron had stepped away from teaching to take on some consultancy work instead. That left me with a large sum of money so I'd taken Will to Celestial Sounds and we'd splashed out on a baby grand piano as neither of us could imagine the space in Gosling's Rest being used for anything other than a music room. I'd asked Mervyn to deliver the upright piano he'd been storing for me to Willowdale Village Hall instead – my donation to the place where my life had finally begun when I joined Cake & Craft Club.

My childhood home had now been cleared. There wasn't anything I wanted to salvage. It was time for a clean break and a fresh start. I'd had the glass in the kitchen door replaced and had been debating whether to put the cottage on the market as it was or do it up and sell it. The latter would take time but the former could take even longer as life in a remote hamlet wasn't for everyone and a dilapidated cottage in said hamlet held even less appeal. In the end, it was resolved quickly and easily because Amelia's sister and her partner loved Hayscroft Lane, couldn't stretch to a full-price property there, but could afford to take on a project. The sale to them was currently progressing and it was such a relief to be letting go of the place that held so many painful memories.

Created With Love had developed into a successful business. The shop itself was prone to quiet days and possibly not a viable enough business on its own but Saffy seemed to have the magic touch with sponsored adverts on social media and had built us a strong online sales platform. As a result, The Crafty Crew had been unanimous in our decision to extend our lease with Ava until the end of the year and we were already busily creating our autumnal and Christmas stock. We'd decide from there whether to keep going with the physical premises or move purely online. Of course, if Ava did want the shop back after her mum finished chemotherapy as originally planned, that choice would be made for us.

As for my friends, Veronica and Laughlin had returned to the UK at the start of June. Veronica's relationship with Felicity and Rebecca was back on track and, although her daughters hadn't fully made peace with each other, Veronica did say that there'd been a thaw and she was hopeful that time would eventually heal the rift. Veronica and Laughlin had taken a trip to Austria before flying home. While in Vienna, Laughlin had evidently decided to take his own advice about not putting things off because Veronica had returned sporting a stunning engagement ring and the most enormous smile. They were currently debating whether to go for a winter wedding this year or a spring wedding next year. I couldn't have been happier for them.

Milly was totally loved up with Adam and Coral had apparently found it hilarious that her mum was dating her former teacher but, as Mr Sawdon had always been her favourite, she wholeheartedly approved. Milly had told me that she'd wanted love to come along when she least expected it and it certainly had.

Nothing much had changed for Christian. He'd been too busy balancing time in the shop with helping Emma and Killian finish their barn conversion to seek out love but I hoped he'd find it soon. He was a lovely man and deserved to have someone special to share his life with. Speaking of Emma, I'd finally been walking with her alpacas and, my goodness, had it been worth the wait. She'd generously offered to do an after-hours walk for The Crafty Crew a few weeks ago because an evening was the only time we could all be together. She'd more than doubled the size of her original herd and now had sixteen alpacas, all of whom had stolen my heart and soothed my soul. I'd since walked them twice with Will, who was also smitten, and we'd be booking another walk as soon as we were unpacked and settled into Gosling's Rest.

Saffy was still living with Paulette, although they didn't see a lot of each other between Saffy's shifts at The White Willow and dates with Felix but Paulette had told me it gave her the best of both worlds – some company but also some time to herself. She didn't seem to be bothered about meeting a new man now, although I couldn't help hoping it would happen naturally for her like it had with Milly. Saffy would be dropping down to part-time hours at The White Willow soon. Mel had loved her response to the interior design tasks she'd set her after they met and, although it had taken a while for anything to come of it, Mel was now working on the restoration and conversion of a manor house into a hotel and leisure complex and had asked Saffy to come on board as her junior interior designer. If that went well, there was potential for future projects.

There'd been some movement in Saffy's relationship with her mum. Joanne had visited Willowdale and apologised to Saffy for not supporting her decision to leave university and for believing Kyle's lies over Saffy's truth. There'd been no explanation as to why Joanne had behaved in such an extreme way. From a few things Andrew had let slip, Paulette thought she might have had a mental breakdown but she wasn't going to ask questions and be accused of interfering again. Paulette was back on good terms with Andrew but things remained strained with Joanne who hadn't apologised to Paulette for what she'd said to her. It was a crying shame because Paulette was such a wonderful person that I couldn't imagine anyone not wanting to be close to her.

* * *

The following Saturday, Will and I sat down together on our new double piano stool by our new baby grand piano in our new home and played our special duets. When we'd finished, he challenged me to a contest, seeing who could play scales the quickest. Will started on the bass keys and I started in the middle and we raced each other up the keys, laughing at the speed of our fingers, but as I reached the highest treble keys, the sound wasn't right.

'There's something wrong with the piano,' I said, frowning.

'Try it again.'

I pressed a couple of keys but there was a dull 'thunk' instead of a beautiful note.

'You'll have to check under the lid,' Will said.

I lifted the lid off the prop and gasped. What looked like a ring box was sitting on the strings. Heart pounding, I reached for it.

'Open it,' Will said when I turned to him.

I flicked the lid open but there was nothing inside.

'I might have removed it already,' he said as he lowered one knee to the floor, holding out an exquisite diamond ring in front of him. 'I fell in love with you twenty years ago after only one day and night together and, over the past three months, that love has deepened every day. I think we've waited long enough and I don't want to miss another minute of my life with you. Would you do me the tremendous honour of becoming my wife?'

'Yes!' I cried. 'Yes!'

I thrust my hand out and he slipped the ring onto my finger before kissing me tenderly.

'I thought you might propose in Venice,' I said, gazing down at the ring with tears in my eyes.

'I thought you might think that so I wanted to surprise you. It is, after all, the year of surprises.'

It certainly was and most of them truly lovely ones. Will took my hand and led me into the kitchen where he took some champagne from the fridge and filled a couple of flutes to toast our engagement.

Trevor was admiring himself in the mirror perched outside his cage.

'We're engaged!' I cried, thrusting out my hand towards him, the sunlight catching the diamond.

Trevor gave a loud wolf whistle followed by a squawk of, 'Pretty!'

'I think he approves of your ring choice,' I said to Will as he handed me a champagne flute.

'Glad to hear it,' Will said, stroking Trevor's feathers. 'I have a confession to make. I did ask for Trevor's permission before I asked.'

'Did you really? What did he say?'

'He said—'

'Pretty Vonnie! Pretty Will!' Trevor cawed, making my heart leap.

Will put his arm round my shoulders. 'That's exactly what he said so I took that as his approval.'

'I think it was Cliff's approval too.'

We clinked our glasses together and shared a kiss.

'Should we take these onto the balcony and enjoy the sunset?' Will asked.

'Sounds perfect.'

I returned Trevor to his cage temporarily – couldn't risk him flying out of the open doors.

As we made our way out to the balcony, I paused. We'd only moved into Gosling's Rest two days ago and had barely done any unpacking but there were a few special items displayed on an otherwise empty bookshelf – the additional memory bear Fen had asked me to make for Will, the picture of 'Clair de Lune' he'd spotted in the window of Created With Love, a framed picture of the advert I'd responded to for Cake & Craft Club which I'd asked Trudy Eccles – the chair of the village halls committee – to print off for me, and my *Tomorrow Starts Today* journal. Those four items represented our journey back to each other.

I looked at them all and raised my glass in thanks. I'd joined Cake & Craft Club when I felt all alone and out of place and it had been the best thing I could ever have done. My final entry in my journal about what I wanted to feel this year had been *part of something*. I'd never felt more as though I was, but I'd realised something about belonging. It didn't necessarily come from the place where I lived – it came from the people I lived my life with.

Veronica, Laughlin, Milly, Paulette, Christian, Saffy, Will and I
were an eclectic mix of people who, on paper, wouldn't necessarily be obvious friends but one of my life's passions was taking
seemingly mismatched pieces of fabric and joining them together
to make a beautiful patchwork quilt. The people I loved were
those pieces of fabric and, together, we made something whole
and beautiful. Something Created With Love.

* * *

MORE FROM JESSICA REDLAND

Another book from Jessica Redland, *Hopes and Dreams at the
Chocolate Pot Café*, is available to order now here:
https://mybook.to/HopesDreamsChocPotCafe

ACKNOWLEDGEMENTS

When the first book in the Escape to the Lakes series was released in July 2023, I had no idea how readers would feel about a new series in a completely different setting. Thankfully, you've taken Willowdale into your hearts and I hope you've enjoyed the fifth book in the series. The plan is to release four more books over the next couple of years, concluding the series at that point, so there are plenty more stories to come from this part of the Lake District for now.

I've loved telling Yvonne's story, watching her step out of the shadows of the past and embrace a new life full of friendship, love and adventure. It was lovely giving her the gift of music. I learned how to play the piano when I was young and had the most wonderful, patient teacher – Mrs Waters of Great Ayton, North Yorkshire – to whom I've dedicated this book. She took me through my first four grades but needed to stop teaching for personal reasons. She found all her pupils new teachers but I sadly never gelled with mine and lost interest before taking my grade five exam. I've always regretted never sticking with the piano because, although I passed my exams with high results, I hadn't quite mastered it. In my forties, I returned to lessons and was surprised at how quickly my (fairly limited) skill came back. I therefore knew from firsthand experience that it would be possible for an extremely gifted pianist like Yvonne to have retained her abilities despite years without playing. Brain and muscle memory are quite incredible!

You might have noticed that I've mainly mentioned well-known piano pieces in this book and, where the pieces have different names, have stuck to the common name. For example, 'Moonlight Sonata' is really 'Piano Sonata No. 14 in C-sharp minor, Op. 27, No. 2' but that's way too intense! I didn't want to put off non-musicians.

Sticking with the piano thread, thank you to two of the members of my Facebook Group, Redland's Readers, for the fabulous names for the piano showrooms. Karen Jackson came up with Pianos of Distinction and Kay Hamilton suggested Celestial Sounds which were both perfect for the very different types of establishment.

Also from Redland's Readers, I wanted a name for the farmer at Hayscroft Farm, and the group came up trumps with some amazing suggestions. I chose Eli Farrow, Eli being suggested by Kate Connolly, Tracy Buttel and Jody Rippon with Farrow suggested by Claire Woolf and Esther Peacock. Further reader group inspiration came for the name of Laughlin's dog. Thank you to Alexis Scaife for the name Lancelot and some inspiration around personality from Maria Gill.

Whenever my characters have a job or hobby of which I don't have personal experience, I always do lots of research to ensure I can portray it as authentically as possible. Where hands-on experience is an option, I try to do this. There's a gorgeous village between Scarborough and Pickering called Ebberston, which is home to the wonderful Ebberston Studios where they teach various creative skills. I contacted Michelle Russell, manager and sewing expert, to see whether I could attend one of her general sewing workshops for some tutoring in how to make a patchwork quilt. A quilt itself would be an enormous undertaking but Michelle patiently guided me through the terminology and techniques needed to produce a patchwork quilted square. I hadn't touched a sewing machine for twenty years so I was pretty proud of myself! A huge thank you to Michelle and to the workshop attendees including Claire Larkin and Kath Watkinson for their warm welcome, their advice and encouragement. You can find out more about Ebberston Studios here: https://ebberstonstudios. co.uk

Still with patchwork quilting, thank you to one of my lovely readers based in the Netherlands, Inge Slaats-Peekel, who loves making patchwork quilts and whose beautiful creations I've long admired on Facebook. Inge gave me some really helpful information on the approach she takes and some of the technical terms. I usually only incorporate a very small part of my research as I never want the technical details to detract from the main story, but I do like to have the full picture myself.

A huge thank you to my fellow Boldwood author and friend, Sarah Bennett, for some insider information on life as a military officer's wife, helping shape Veronica's character and background. If you haven't already discovered Sarah's writing, do check out her books as they're gorgeous.

I often thank my husband, Mark, and our daughter, Ashleigh, for putting up with me and the long hours I work (especially as deadlines approach) and this book is no different so a huge thank you to both of them. However, this time I also need to thank Ashleigh for some direct help. She's the same age as Saffy and in her first year at university so I've been pinging messages to her with Saffy's dialogue asking her to change it to current teen-speak! Some of her feedback did make me giggle – *Seriously, Mum! No one my age would ever say that! It's from the dark ages!*

Thank you to the powerhouse that is the team at Boldwood Books starting with my amazing editor, Emily Ruston, who helped me delve deeper into Yvonne's emotions at her various crossroads moments and make that first encounter with Will so much more memorable. Thank you to copy editor Cecily Blench and proofreader Susan Sugden for working their magic on smoothing out any continuity issues and finding those sneaky typos, and to cover designer Lizzie Gardiner for another absolute beauty. Thank you to Claire Fenby and team for all the marketing, all the reviewers involved in the book tour, and the amazing voice acting talent of Rebecca Norfolk for narrating the audiobook. Thank you to the wonderful Nia Beynon who has returned from maternity leave and, although she's not resuming her role as my editor, she's back on top form as publishing, sales and marketing director extraordinaire. Wonderful to have you back, Nia. Enormous thanks to Wendy Neale for the sales and marketing support in Nia's absence.

And last, but by no means least, thank YOU! This is my twenty-eighth novel and, without your support in buying or borrowing this book from legitimate sources, I couldn't have ever got this far, nor could I continue. I'm so grateful to you for all the love you give to my characters and settings and hope I can continue to bring you great stories in return.

Big hugs, Jessica xx